DATE DUE

Contend with Horses

Other novels by Grace Irwin

Least of All Saints

Andrew Connington

In Little Place

*If thou hast run with the footmen
and they have wearied thee
then how canst thou contend with horses?*
Jeremiah 12:5

4

Contend
with Horses

by

GRACE IRWIN

WILLIAM B. EERDMANS PUBLISHING COMPANY
GRAND RAPIDS, MICHIGAN

Printed in the United States of America

To Laura

Preface

"A thing I never know, when I'm starting out to tell a story about a chap I've told a story about before," says Bertie Wooster, "is how much explanation to bung in at the outset."

And there, in P. G. Wodehouse's inimitable nutshell, is the problem of every writer of a sequel — in this case a sequel to a sequel.

Ever since the second instalment of Andrew Connington's career was published, readers have asked me (at least five or six have) to write more about him. "You're not going to leave him there," they have said. "We want to know what happens to him." So, having found out, I have written this book.

But, painful though it is to admit, there are people who have not read the first two books. These may not find a résumé of the twenty-four years which have elapsed between part two and part three of absorbing interest. I beg them to bear patiently with the necessary flashbacks in chapters two and three in anticipation of the speedy pickup in chapter four.

GRACE IRWIN

Toronto, 1968

Prologue

"IF THE REVEREND ANDREW CONNINGTON is in the audience, will he please go at once to the Emergency Ward, St. Joseph's Hospital."

His name and .... Emergency .... no one he knew likely to be in St. Joseph's .... why the urgency? .... usually such interruptive announcements — and such announcements were not usual — contained a summons to the telephone, a discreet reference to a message. Scraps of thought, rather than his body, seemed to carry Andrew from his seat, through the shocked, curious hush in Victoria College Chapel, past the dais where the distinguished deliverer of the Renfrew Lectures waited to resume his discourse, and out into the familiar hall.

The solicitous caretaker who had brought the message could add no information. Not till he had cleared the great stairs at a pace seldom equalled in his student days, impelled by anxiety which was — surely it was! — quite impersonal, not until he reached the east door, did he remember that he had no car, either on Charles Street or in the St. Mary's Street parking lot. Of course, John had dropped him off at the Library and gone on to drive Cecily to her speaking engagement in Cooksville, had begged and insisted, glorying in his newly acquired licence.

Turning back to telephone for a taxi, Andrew now felt the stab of personal localized fear. Could none of his acquaintance in that earnest academic group have offered to drive him? Why should they? It would never occur to them that this time of all times such an offer would be welcome. The message came from one of his parishioners undoubtedly; someone else, perhaps even a stranger, who had recalled his name in extremis and asked for

7

him. Someone had phoned home and been told his whereabouts. But there was nobody at home tonight.

Well, he would know soon. For the first time he blessed the mad, unregarding speed of taxi drivers. There must be some easy explanation, some obvious, trivial — no not trivial; how could he regard anyone's accident, anyone's sorrow, anyone's crisis as trivial? St. Joseph's was in the general direction of Cooksville. But it was not one of his own — not, surely not —?

It was. And he had known somehow, fighting frantically against the knowledge, that it was. He had been in Emergency before. He was acquainted with the inevitable formalities, the impersonal routine, the long-drawn delay, the imperturbable efficiency which assessed, and postponed, and duly attended to casualties each clamouring individually for precedence. Because of this very knowledge his heart was chilled at the speed with which, when he gave his name, he was directed, then escorted, to a private room off the operating theatre. The young doctor who had been waiting briefed him as they raced to the door. Either he was moved beyond coherent speech or only phrases penetrated Andrew's consciousness.

"The nature of the injuries.... nothing we can do, I'm afraid.... repeatedly refused all but the lightest sedatives.... said she must be able to speak when you came.... insisted on your being called.... gave clear instructions.... only determination has kept her alive.... it's a miracle...."

But not for long. Cecily, her head and forehead turbaned with bandages, lay there on the high narrow bed waging a visible conflict with death. What of mangled horror was hidden by the curious flatness under a thin, loosely drawn sheet he did not know — but within the lacerated head and battered body (her left arm was free and its perfection pitifully beautiful) her spirit was chalking up the last of its many triumphs over the flesh. Measuring each long-drawn breath, upper lip scored by the desperate pressure of teeth, eyes, dry of their facile tears, deep sunken like blue-black lamps under their winglike brows, she was suddenly aware of his presence. For a moment the agonizing tension crumpled in relief. Then the small visible

8

triangle of face — by what extension of miracle had it escaped? — lighted with unearthly radiance.

"Thank God. He's let me wait, darling! I had to see you again."

Andrew said nothing. Her hand reached for his and folded itself inside his clasp in a familiar gesture.

"There are things I want to say." She was speaking, faintly but deliberately, as if to waste no precious energy on words. "First, Andrew, don't let John blame himself." (Andrew had forgotten about John.) "He loves you terribly and this will nearly kill him. You won't, will you?"

He shook his head dumbly. The tears she could not shed were pressing unbearably behind his eyes and in the anguish of his throat. She saw and gave a little cry of pity.

"My poor darling, that's the second thing. *Don't* ask why — don't, Andrew. Our God knows best. You preach it. We believe it. This isn't what I'd have chosen. But He allowed it and He will work it for good. I'm grateful — think what we've had — what others never have."

She was silent, marshalling her strength.

Then — "Isn't this funny? like those deathbed scenes in novels we used to think couldn't happen. But you think fast when you know there isn't much time. Always wondered if and how people knew they were dying. I'm glad I know. So that I can tell you. Andrew, it's all right with me. I'm not suffering, not since you came and I knew I could let go. I hate leaving you, but for me — I'm not here. I feel as if I'm seeing Christ — already. Remember Kingsley? 'How beautiful God is.' *And* good."

Even the hand folded in his began to relax. She fought her way back to recall something.

"The child. Tell her Mother sent her love. She'll be all right with you, Andrew. Dear, kiss me."

As he stooped, the face so near his own, so strange in its attenuated dedication, broke into a last flicker of her irrepressible smile. He knew why. Often in the ecstasy of their love she had murmured that it would be a good way to die. She died now trying to say it.

9

1

A BBA, ABBA, are you home?"
The penetrating call just preceded a slam of the heavy front door. It had to be slammed, the children stated in apology, or it didn't click. After all it was an old door, in a house almost fifty years old. John was going to put on a new lock someday.

"Up here."

Evadne was home. In imitation of her mother she had always called a greeting, but now it was primarily for him. "Abba" had been her salutation of especial affection ever since the Sunday morning when her father's exposition in the eighth of Romans had been far beyond the comprehension of a six-year-old. But his identification of the Aramaic "Abba" with the colloquial "Daddy" had caught her childish attention. Cecily had discouraged the habit, saying that it sounded sacrilegious. So Evadne had compromised by reserving it for great occasions. But it had become her almost invariable address of later years. Andrew knew why and was grateful.

"What's your news?"

"What's yours?" she retorted when, with the lightning speed at which he now marvelled, she appeared in his second-story study, kissed him, dropped an assortment of Eaton's and Simpson's parcels together with her capacious handbag on his desk, went through quite unnecessary motions of straightening his sermon notes, and took up position behind the chair in which his "patients," as the family called them, usually sat. Evadne herself seldom sat, except in company. She perched, or crouched, or lay with her head cupped in her hands.

"You're uncanny, Abba. How did you guess I had news?"

"You know my methods, Watson. Apply them. You have been out of the house all of four hours. You call me before you slam — shut — the door——."

"I *always* call you before I close the door."

"But you don't always clear the stairs in a leap, pass your own room where you might have deposited your — is it Christmas shopping already? — and arrive looking like a cat bursting with an undigested canary, and with an obviously uninterested question about my news. My news forsooth!"

"I still think you're clever."

"I know. You've really never been 'young,' Evadne. I don't believe you have at any time — except secretly and fleetingly — thought that I, or your mother, was a back-number, a square, a — Now, out with it. Tomorrow is Sunday and that beastly wedding tonight wrecks my evening. I hereby give notice. If you select Saturday at seven-thirty for your nuptial vows, your fond father will refuse to perform the ceremony."

"Can you perform the ceremony and come up the aisle with me too?"

"I don't know. I've never had occasion. Is it worrying you?"

"Academically, yes. Because I don't want anyone else to give me away and I won't feel married unless you officiate. Couldn't you ask yourself, 'Who giveth this woman . . . .' and answer 'I do' and just go ahead?"

"As for the matther of that——" began Andrew in a rusty imitation of broad Yorkshire.

—"It'll be time eneaf to think aboot neaming of it when it cooms," completed his daughter. It was a favourite quote. "But do keep it in mind. And how did weddings get into this conversation? Because that is my news. Ready? Get set. Julie Logan was married in Chicago on Tuesday."

She was prepared for the incredulous relief of her father's face, for the quick confirming glance of his eyes before he closed them. That brief moment of prayer, so unstudied as to be almost

11

automatic, she had seen countless times in crises — for patience, for guidance, for strength, for wisdom, but most often in gratitude.

"'God moves in a mysterious way.'" The quotation was not trite, merely a recognition that Cowper had anticipated his sentiments. Then his face sobered. "Poor John. This will be tough on him. Does he know? And how did you hear?"

"Morna Logan was ahead of us in the line-up at the Clipper Ship, just bursting with it. I don't know if she thought I'd break down with grief. I nearly broke down all right and told her what I'd thought of her sister for years. But my upbringing hampered me. So I said the right things where I could — non-committal, honest remarks: really? how exciting! Isn't that just *like* Julie? And finally, though I'm a bit stricken about this one: Julie always *knew* what she wanted. Heidi was a great help. She asked the questions I couldn't. So I got the complete lowdown. And for all Morna's chortling, her sister *didn't* get what she wanted, which was my brother, and little Pollyanna is glad, glad, glad!"

"Nice child," said Andrew affectionately, and meant it. She grew more like Cecily every day, though in his eyes she would never be as charming. To others she resembled him rather than her mother, with her deep-set hazel eyes and uncompromising gravity of expression in repose. In height — or lack of it, she would have said — she was like Cecily, and in the brown hair which she repeatedly determined to grow long and then cut again in despair of making the ponytail into a Greek knot. It had now reached her father's favourite stage, almost shoulder length, loosely waving back from a forehead that was his, though the winglike brows were Cecily's. But after a childhood in which she had unconsciously imitated his every gesture, she was now — how deliberately he could not tell — recalling in pose and movement and turn of phrase the mother whose loss she was feeling more keenly at twenty than she had at fourteen. Then, shock and circumstances and the concerted efforts put forth for her diversion had kept grief in impatient abeyance. She wrinkled her nose now in Cecily's expression of fastidious disgust, and came to sit on the corner of his desk.

"I can't feel un-nice, nor un-Christian, about disliking Julie Logan. John shuts up like a clam about her, of course, but Morna said today, laughing as if it were a great joke, that this man, Jed Somebody, was a fast worker and Julie hadn't had to propose to him as she had to John. And Julie herself sounded off one day I met her in the library — it was just after we thought she and John had a particular fight, you remember — and let me have it about Puritanical hypocrisy and religious repressions. I thought she was trying to shock me and I didn't tell you because — well I was afraid John might marry her. But the gist was that he was too inhibited to be a — what was her word? — 'expert' lover and would probably make a rotten husband because he wouldn't have an affair before marriage. I took her at her word and thought she was through with him, but not she! Were there girls like that around when you were our ages?"

And — *autres temps, autres moeurs* — in every age, thought Andrew, but in no age so emancipated in every walk of life. Julie was a post War Two Sonya but without the comparative daring, the need of rebellion, the veneer of originality. At least Sonya's parents had had the sanction of society; Julie's parents, while they would have borne the blame if their daughter had become involved in notorious difficulties, had been conditioned to believe that their views on life, their standards if any, were on no account to be imposed upon their offspring, that their hard-won attainments were of no value in enabling them to counsel or guide. Sonya had been iconoclastic and ruthless in advocating the freedom of youth from the boring company of age; Julie's parents, from the time the children had reached their teens, had accepted their position as tolerated providers and absented themselves dutifully not only from the presence of those children's guests, but from their own house when parties were held. There had been employment from which Sonya would have been dismissed, had her views and behaviour in the matter of sex been known. Now such naïve fear of abnormalcy, such dread of repressions in matters sexual, obsessed the half-educated that

13

even in the teaching profession a Julie of unrestricted habits was considered in some circles more fit to instruct the young than a bachelor or spinster, whose very celibacy was suspect; and, provided the scandal was not too obtrusive, tangible evidence of pre-marital experience was no longer a barrier to advancement among the enlightened.

No, thinking of Sonya with the retrospective indulgence which few decent men deny a woman who has flung herself, however uninvited, at their heads, Andrew decided that he preferred her to Julie.

"Yes. Oh yes," he said reminiscently to a daughter whose expression was growing quizzical. "There were girls like Julie."

"But you, Daddy, you didn't like them, did you? I mean, what do men see, what does an intelligent boy like John see, in a person like that? She's so — to me she's so phoney! And she takes herself so seriously with her science and her sex and her complete contempt for all the people — all the decent people — who don't agree with her. And for all the past. Nothing that happened before 1930 matters, except of course the Russian revolution. She makes me sick. But what makes me sicker is that she wants to bother with my brother. There are plenty of men like her. Why isn't she satisfied with them?"

"Apparently she has been."

"Oh, I forget!" Her face lightened. "What's that verse, 'This is a day of good tidings'? I'll keep my beefs till later."

"Do you think John knows?"

"I doubt it. We should have noticed. I don't think she would be considerate enough to write him. On the other hand she'd probably get a certain mean satisfaction out of it. I'm sorry if I'm judging — facing facts, I call it! And of course expressing them to you isn't uncharitable because you know the essential fairness and sweetness of my nature! Do you think there's a chance —?"

"Of what?"

"That perhaps John won't feel terrible? I've wondered if Julie hadn't become a — well, hardly a habit but a bit of an obligation. You know they've gone steady since Second Year

14

and he may feel a sense of duty; but surely he can't love her."

"No idea. And I shouldn't call it love. But I doubted if, short of a miracle, he would have taken the initiative to break it off."

"So we have a miracle. And to think I felt resentful when Julie won that fellowship! It made people, especially John, feel that she's really clever when —"

"Julie is clever, child. Give the devil his due. And don't mistake cleverness for wisdom."

"I don't often. Your influence, reverend father. And if anything was needed to keep me from worshiping the Sacred Cow, acquaintance with Julie Logan as a tyro research physicist has been it. But why oh why is John so impressed by that sort of thing? You are his father too —," she broke off, aghast at her tactless lapse. "I just mean —," she essayed lamely.

"We both know what you just mean." Andrew forced a grin to restore her equanimity, but he did not pursue the question to which he had for six years given an inordinate amount of thought. Loyalty to his son, the persistent baffled hope of reaching a satisfying rapprochement there, made him reluctant to discuss him like a case history, though his daughter was now his closest confidante. Evadne had matured beyond her years even for her sex, but she was, after all, two generations removed. A spasm of intense longing for Cecily shook him and left him gaunt and weak as with physical hunger.

Evadne did not ask why he shivered or if he was not well, as she would have done over-solicitously a year ago. She gathered up her parcels, came round to his chair, put her free arm around his neck with a quick uncomfortable squeeze, and was at the door before he could return the gesture.

"Mustn't keep you from your sermon any longer. There's Aunt Alex stirring. I'll go and relieve her fears."

And Mrs. Mansell *would* be relieved, thought Andrew. John's infatuation with Julie had produced reactions in his adoring great-aunt reminiscent of her long-distant disapproval of Sonya, and with much greater reason.

Dinner was early that evening to accommodate Andrew and

his marriage ceremony. John had come in late, gone directly to his room, and replied with a non-committal shout to Evadne's bell and summons. So the others, seated at the table in Mansell's walnut-panelled dining room, were kept waiting for his arrival. Andrew, determined against prevalent usage to keep the meal a social occasion, always refused to say Grace until all were present, though there had been times, especially with his son, when he felt rather less than gracious or social by the time that end was achieved. Tonight, however, the atmosphere was such a mixture of carefully repressed pity, uncertainty, and half-guilty relief that the sound of feet on the stairs threw them off guard and each covered a searching glance with a characteristic greeting.

"The late Mr. Connington —" Evadne.

"Well met, Son and Heir —" Andrew.

"We are earlier than usual —" Aunt Alexandra, reversing the need for apology. The three inanities chimed so like the result of "together" directions in a well-rehearsed amateur play that Andrew and Evadne broke off in some embarrassment.

The object of their solicitude was apparently unaware of it. He received his father's attempt at persiflage with awkward punctiliousness, grunted in a brotherly fashion across the table at his sister, and reserved his smile and "Sorry if I'm late" for Mrs. Mansell, who continued to deprecate the idea until Andrew bowed his head for the blessing.

"And it's not as if we were having soufflé this time," she closed in on his "Amen" with an air of finality. John groaned.

"I'll never live that one down. At least I didn't sit at the table while the bally thing fell!"

Evadne whooped and gladly pounced on the cue for conversation.

"No. That soufflé disaster was really your fault, Daddy. You should always say Grace yourself, especially when there's soufflé or Yorkshire pudding."

"It was not my fault," Andrew caught the ball neatly. "A mere mistaken gesture of courtesy. As by this time you ought to know, there are two schools of thought — among those who think

16

of it at all — regarding Grace before meals: the set and formal vs. the impromptu and informal. You have been brought up on the former, the longest example of which is the official Grace at Corpus Christi, and in my days there it was occasionally recited at a speed to break the sound barrier. How was I to know that Brother Waltham not only belonged to the latter school, but to the straitest sect thereof — those who regard the pro-meal blessing as the occasion to mortify the flesh and to combine the General Confession with the General Thanksgiving and intercession for all sorts and conditions of men? And as I have often remarked, the conduct of my offspring on that occasion was a deep humiliation to me."

"I like that!" said John. "I remember you told Mother that she set us a very bad example."

"One of your mother's unregenerate gifts," said Andrew, who always welcomed a chance to talk about her and seldom had an opening from his son, "was the ability to keep an absolutely straight face, while suggesting to those who knew her an uncontrollable and unfortunately infectious hilarity. For the one not so endowed — usually me — the combination of the joke itself and her grave, courteously attentive face with that indefinable undertow of mirth was frequently too much." He broke off. The image evoked by his description was suddenly too much for him.

"I know. It was"— Evadne plunged in to save the topic from foundering — "like a bubble . . . . no, like making fudge just before the surface breaks and it boils up to the top. Only that wasn't the trouble this time. It——"

"This was an occasion I missed. What exactly happened?" Aunt Alexandra rang for Nancy and indicated the removal of the soup dishes. Nancy, whom she had trained forty years ago just after World War I, and a soup course with dinner (she regarded fruit or vegetable juices as faddish innovations) were two fetishes which Mrs. Mansell found comforting, in a world where she did not consider every change necessarily an improvement. "Now let me hear it from beginning to end."

"Oh dear!" said Evadne as the task of raconteur was indicated to her. "I can't make it nearly as funny as it seemed at the time. We unexpectedly had this Mr. Waltham for Sunday supper. He had turned up at Sunday School, lived out of town, wanted to come to the evening service — something like that. We had had dinner at noon and had practically nothing in the house. So Mother rose to the occasion and whipped up a cheese soufflé and a salad and a plate of toast. And that was it. I remember she sent me down the cellar to get the last of the Christmas cake for dessert. And after we were called for supper, Mr. Waltham went upstairs to wash. The soufflé was at its highest point when he came down; so she brought everything into the tea-table in the living room. Then Father made his fatal mistake. 'Will you ask the blessing, Brother Waltham?' says he. Five minutes later, Mr. Waltham, having dealt at length with the world situation, with church affairs, with the three missions in which he was particularly interested, was coming down the home stretch——"

"Careful, Vadne," murmured Andrew, automatically.

"Right O. 'Never criticize a man's prayer. It's between him-self and his God,' " she quoted dutifully. "But it *was* malapropos and you know it. And then just at the end he gave thanks for 'this friendly board.' I sneaked a look at Mother just as she opened one eye to see her feathery soufflé down as flat as the board referred to. That was when I had a violent fit — I hoped it sounded like sneezing — and had to leave the room."

"Dear Cecily," said Aunt Alex serenely. "She made lovely soufflés — better than Nancy's, I always said."

This typically Alexandrian non sequitur gave the crowning touch where Evadne's efforts had fallen short. For a moment it looked as if she would have to leave the room again. John's aside, "That'll learn you, Vad," Andrew's allusion to Bertie Wooster, Esmond Haddock and the story about Wembley, temporarily linked the three in the uninitiatable circle of com-mon background and understanding, from which the younger man so often seemed, by choice, alienated. The rest of the meal passed briskly. Andrew led the short family worship with-out the feeling, so common to him of late, that his son was listening as a critical outsider. Then Mrs. Mansell pushed back her chair and Andrew went to give his eighty-year-old aunt quite unnecessary assistance.

Suddenly they all became aware that John had gone to the hall and returned with the evening edition of *The Telegram* in his hand. His dark head was down and they could not see his eyes.

"I see by the daily press," he said over-elaborately, "that Julie Logan and Dr. Jed Kuzarski were married in Chicago on the tenth. Chalk that up as an answer to your prayers, all of you. You must live right."

He did not wait for an answer.

2

~~~~~~

I T WAS A GOOD THING, probably, thought Andrew later in the evening, that Marsha Hedges' wedding had been scheduled as if to divert his attention from this anniversary of Cecily's death. Was it coincidence, too, that Evadne had arrived with the relief of her news just as he was dwelling on the events of that bitter night in reflection so vivid as almost to constitute reenactment? He was sure that both children had remembered the date; Evadne usually mentioned it, John never. And because of that and the soreness of its recurrence, he always tried to avoid consciously treating the day as an anniversary. In a sense every day was a memorial and every night a requiem.

Perhaps a good thing too, it was the type of wedding that caused him acute discomfort and demanded the utmost in nervous effort. The bride had grown up in his Sunday School but, though her mother had sometimes rallied to a special occasion, the father had, to the best of Andrew's knowledge, never walked up the church aisle until tonight. Except for several of the young people, the other guests were almost completely unknown to him. In spite of this lack of liaison, he learned after the ceremony — not for the first time in his experience — that he was expected not only to propose the toast to the bride, but also to direct the order of celebrations.

He had secretly hoped to offer his good wishes at the reception, make vague excuses, and disappear. But the evident anxiety of the parents to do the right thing by their daughter — they had ordered a "sit-down" supper at the newest "Plaza" restaurant — and their nervous dependence on him even in the matter of arranging the receiving line persuaded him that, as Cecily would have said, this was an immediate practical way of exercising his ministry. The father's preoccupation with his tie made Andrew suddenly aware that the prosperous, unchurched workingman, unless in a white-collar job, need not wear from one year's end to the other, or even possess, the one "good suit" that had been essential for respectability until World War II. Car, television, freezer, automatic washer — these were status symbols; but on any social occasion he could appear in an outfit once associated with a cowboy or hobo. Andrew was glad that their desire for a "big" wedding had not insisted on the congruity of formal dress for the men of the party. Her father's plain dark suit was obviously giving him enough discomfort. Clothes did not make the man and there was no connection between "pure religion and undefiled" and traditional garb. But Andrew caught himself wondering if the abrogation of this by-product of churchgoing symbolized a certain loss of dignity, even of equality, for the very people who would have been loudest in their claim to equality.

That was not his business. He checked himself sharply and set about the difficult task — his shyness had never been more apparent to him — of putting his hosts and their guests at ease in that stiffest of all functions: a wedding at which half the company is uncertain what is expected and determined to do it properly. He moved from one group to the next, passing what seemed ponderously heavy-footed pleasantries and wishing that Evadne had not been prevented by another engagement from sharing the burden with him. He found himself envying Prince Philip's inimitable gift for making the right opening remark to complete strangers effortlessly and spontaneously. He tried to "forget himself and put himself in their place" with the resultant conviction that he would dread, under those circumstances, to be addressed by an unknown clergyman and would greatly prefer to be left alone. He marshalled the bridal party for the head table with a punctiliousness which Cecily would have approved and manoeuvred the rest, who showed unaccountable reluctance to "be the first," into taking seats at the smaller tables.

When the wedding cake had been cut and passed, together with punch for drinking toasts, he quitted the role of Master of the Revels which had been wished on him and quite suddenly reverted to himself. The change was not in voice or manner. It was the change of being on sure ground, of saying what he felt to be of importance, regardless of his reception.

"All of you here," he said when the ring of silver on glass had hushed the desultory babble, "have given ample evidence of your regard for our bride and her parents. Your very presence is a tribute. The beautiful gifts of which Marsha has told me are another. So are the many shower gifts which my daughter has described and which make those of us who remember the depression realize that what we gave at weddings then, you give in many cases at a shower now" — murmurs and nods of pleased assent. This parson was on the ball. "There are two questions which you have the right to ask. The first is What am I doing here at all? — a good one, do I hear anyone mutter? That question could not have been asked in Toronto a few years ago. Only an ordained or licensed minister could perform the marriage ceremony. Now it can be done by a magistrate in the City Hall. Then why invite me?

"The answer is easy, you say. An office in the City Hall is a dreary place for a wedding. But that brings the second question. The ceremony could have been performed as fashionably in a home, at a hotel, more conveniently for all of you in the reception room of this restaurant. Why in a church?"

The silence, a bit uncomfortable now, did not disconcert him.

"Our bride knows her answer. She has attended the church since childhood, she is at home there. She would not, she told me, be married anywhere else for worlds. I do not fear"— was this true? he asked himself, and was temporarily reassured by a glance at Marsha's happy attentive gaze — "as I have feared with some brides, that I have seen her there for the last time until the next occasion when the church's services are formally required. Nor do I need to ask those of you who are part of the church, whether represented by mine or by another. But I do ask the rest — you who would do so much for friends and family and who act so generously on such occasions — to do one of two things. Forego these meaningless services altogether; treat marriage as a, civil bond of convenience, the arrival of children as an event of purely temporal significance, and death as the return of chemicals to a disintegrating element. For if the church and its services are nothing to you, this is logical conduct. Or if you shrink from this, if the church is something you like to think of as *there,* set yourselves to find out — in an age when people are ashamed to be ignorant about unimportant things and unashamedly ignorant about the all-important thing — what the church is, why she exists, and of how much of her blessing you are depriving yourselves."

That's enough, he thought. After all, it is a captive audience. And if it is? To how many trivial, inane, by no means tasteful speeches of the kind have I had to listen, with their rehash of the 'May all your troubles be little ones' type of joke. Still, to the point.

"I am honored to propose the most important toast of the evening. What I have already said indicates something of Marsha's character, her independent mind, her loyalty. From the comments I have heard all evening, I know I need not dwell on her charming appearance. I have heard, and ungallantly do not believe, that all brides are beautiful. But you will agree that Marsha is a lovely one." He was thankful that he could speak without equivocation: the fair hair shining under its coronet and veil, the flushed starry-eyed excitement, imparted real if fleeting beauty to harmonious but remarkable features. He paused to smile down at her with unaffected pleasure, wishing for a significant word to leave in her memory. It came. "You will also agree that she moved up the aisle like a little princess. That is what I should like her to remember" — he wondered whether to give credit to George Macdonald and decided against the literary touch — "and what I

23

should like her husband" — he paused for the self-conscious smile the word always produced in the groom — "to know: that his wife is in very truth a princess. For on the day when she confessed faith in Christ Jesus, she became a daughter of the King of Kings, and that is the highest honour that can be given a mortal. So" (he hoped the transition was not too abrupt) "I ask you to drink health and happiness to the bride."

He was not surprised by the number of awkward, appreciative comments made to him later in the evening. The average man called upon to speak is so tongue-tied, the quality of wedding speeches so poor, that he could usually count on temporary interest in even his least eloquent words. He was not surprised either and — had he grown cynical? — not at all affected by the repeated assurances from newly won admirers ("I've never heard anything like that toast of yours, Mr. Connington." "I don't wonder Marsha is so fond of you." "The way you took the ceremony too — it was different somehow; you made it seem so real. Some ministers rattle it off, if you know what I mean." "Such a beautiful little church. I've always meant to come.") that they could not wait to hear him preach. Such assurances, fervid, tearful, sober, wistful, he had heard at wedding after wedding, especially at funeral after funeral. All were apparently or momentarily sincere. In the early days of his ministry, particularly in the early days of his unsupported ministry, he had hoped, discounting the majority as misguided politeness, that the minority would fulfil their promise. Perhaps one per cent had done over the years. Now, quite without bitterness, he did not expect it. But why did they utter the words?

Unable even now to take his leave — Marsha had asked if he would drive home a relative who lived in a room on Balmoral Avenue — he found himself in a corner with the bride's father, wondering for the thousandth such time what common ground he could find between them on which to meet him with the Gospel. That the failure was his own Andrew was perfectly ready to concede. He had sought the cause of it, the remedy for it, in agony of soul after many meetings with

24

such people: decent, well-meaning, intelligent enough, not antagonistic, yet with no discernible concern for anything but the immediate — or more often that realizable future ("when we've got the house paid off," "when I can retire," "when we get the kids off our hands," "when the wife can stop working," "when we can buy a trailer and travel a bit," "when I can get a little place in the country and put in a garden") for which the humdrum but acceptable present ("we have it pretty good at the plant," "I don't mind night shifts; and the wife doesn't find it lonesome, now we've got T.V.") was preparation.

Mr. Hedges' particular enthusiasm, Andrew knew, was racing cars. A skilled mechanic, reticent on every other subject, he became eloquent when Andrew in desperation asked what he was driving now. He promptly expatiated on the model which he had recently acquired from its disgruntled owner, using a wealth of technical terminology which made his companion wonder why knowledge of the commonest theological phrases should be considered beyond the grasp of the average "modern" man.

"Not that I'd want you to think I did him down, you understand," continued Mr. Hedges happily. "I offered to find out what was wrong, but he was one of these impatient chaps, terribly anxious to sell. He'd had it gone over by a dozen mechanics, he said, and he was fed up. So Collins — that's the boss — offered him a decent turn-in and when he saw how keen I was — I'd fallen for it from the start; I knew the year, you see, and it was a good year for that model — he says 'Here, Jock,' he says, 'you can have it for what I gave and see what you can do with it.' Well, sir, I all but took that car apart; night after night I went over it. And d'ya know what was causing all the trouble?"

"No." Andrew had never spoken a truer word. Mr. Hedges beamed.

"A wire. One wee bit of a wire in the distributor. Most cars don't have this one there at all. It was shorting, you see, and —"

A merciful interruption deprived Andrew of the operational

details. In the presence of the still hovering best man, the enthusiast hastened to the nub.

"So now I'm ready for the next rally. Matter of fact," he reminded himself ruefully, "there's a rally in Huntsville this weekend the wife and I hated to miss. But Marsha said it was the only time the church and the restaurant were free together so we felt we'd have to pass it up. I hope Marsha's boy takes to racing. He hasn't been brought up to it but he can learn. You done any yourself?"

"No."

"Don't know what you've missed. Care to come out with us some week-end?" Suddenly conscious of what he had forgotten in his audience's rapt attention, he broke off with an embarrassed "Guess not, eh?" and gave the best man the chance for which Andrew had seen him waiting, envelope in hand.

It was the moment of any wedding which Andrew Connington found most difficult. Except in cases of special friendship and with poor families during the depression, he had schooled himself to accept the donation for a number of practical reasons. For a religious ceremony in his own congregation he disliked the idea of a ministerial fee, but two evenings spent at rehearsal and reception, the frequent assumption of his services by people who were almost strangers, the small proportion which the most generous fee bore to the total expense of the wedding: these, he told himself, were considerations to weigh with the fact that most people do not value what they get for nothing.

Now, quite suddenly, it occurred to him that this might be the chance he had sought. Under the respectful politeness of most of the unchurched and not a few professing members, he had found, lurked the age-old complaint that the church was always asking for money (It never occurred to them to question how any institution would survive on the pittance they accorded it), the conviction that "the minister has it pretty soft; he only works two hours on Sunday." Perhaps if nothing else he had done or said that evening made any impression, this would sometime, somewhere, be used to validate his words.

As if to confirm his decision, the best man made the presentation badly. No racing fan either, he had been kept waiting a little too long. He had urgent business elsewhere, directing the removal of the front seat of the groom's car and the inclusion of sundry impertinent objects under its hood. His impatience, together with the fact that he was most uneasy in his role, made him unintentionally curt.

"Here's your fee, Sir. Hope you find it in order."

Andrew's hand did not close on the envelope thrust unceremoniously upon him, and it fell to the floor. When it was recovered and offered again he shook his head, smiling pleasantly.

"I have no 'fee,' tonight. Please tell Alan and Marsha that I prefer to make a present of my services to them."

His action had done no harm at any rate. The young man's almost ludicrous amazement, the father's deprecating protest, indicated that this cavalier attitude towards money was quite foreign to their concept of the cloth. The present certainly had nothing to do, he was sure, with Marsha's warm farewell (What colour was she wearing? he had promised Evadne to describe her 'going away' suit) : "I'll never forget what you said tonight, Mr. Connington." Nor did he think it accounted for the groom's "Thank you again for the kind things you said about my wife, Sir. We'll be out to church as soon as we get back."

His words had so genuine a ring that Andrew suspended disbelief. A straightforward-looking boy, nominal member of a church in Scarborough, he had come to morning service several times lately with Marsha. He seemed very young, but then everyone under forty seemed young to him now, and this groom was older than many whom he had been called on to marry since the war. Twenty-four, the licence had said — just John's age.

Marsha's relative, slightly deaf, very tired, uncomfortable at the prospect of a tête à tête with a strange clergyman, was relieved to be spared conversation. Andrew drove in grateful silence into the city, along Eglinton, down Oriole Parkway,

27

past Upper Canada College, Forest Hill, Dunvegan, and turned south again on Warren Road. Almost as automatically as he shifted gears, his mind had returned to the point of interrupted reflection. He was back six years, numb with his first agony of grief and hearing his son shout hoarsely from the bed where they had forcibly put him to recover from shock: "She's dead, isn't she, Dad? And I killed her. You know I killed her."

He had been sustained through those days, though the memory of them still burned. There was no point in dwelling on them except to "raise an Ebenezer," or to discover in what he had failed to meet the boy's need. He had been able to comfort Evadne, to deal with Uncle George's broken question: "Why did He take that child and leave a useless husk like me?" He had been enabled to conduct Cecily's funeral, having been given a brief merciful period of exaltation when the Word that he preached — "with Christ which is very far better" — was so real to him that, like the Apostle, he scarcely knew whether he was in or out of the body.

He had been given strength — and more important, the graciousness of grace — to hear in wonderment and without bitterness how much criticism had been occasioned by this action, which had seemed to him the necessary consequence of his faith. Strange — the harsh intolerance of the well-meaning towards deviation in religious custom, compared with their charitable blanket coverage of vice and crime. "Showmanship in the worst of taste." "A most embarrassing experience to hear a man preach at his wife's funeral." "He'd make an excellent actor, I've said from the first." "One thing's certain — he can't have cared *deeply* for her." "You'd expect a man to be completely broken up, wouldn't you? — the way it happened. And for him to stand up there calmly and preach." *Calmly!* There were always people, genuinely friendly people, to relay such remarks to him with indignation ("But we thought you should know").

There had even been a woman, whom he had not seen since Shorncliffe days, who had flung her arms around Evadne before she entered the mourner's car. "I knew your mother before you were born. You are the very image of her. My heart bled for you through that service. A child like you shouldn't have been asked to go through such a lacerating experience!"

Andrew had pretended not to hear. John had stared wordlessly, and turned away. But Evadne, who had been clinging to her brother's hand, crying quietly as she watched the coffin enter the hearse, started at the implied criticism, gulped convulsively, and drew herself up.

"Nothing could have kept us away" — she had managed to keep her voice steady and proud. "How many people do you think have a father who can say and mean words like that?"

Thank God for Evadne! And for the others who had comprehended or, all uncomprehending, had been moved and awed. Not least, thank God for Uncle George, who had been such a tower of comfort in the brief period that he had survived Cecily. At least the funeral sermon had the effect of making him confess publicly his late-won faith and join his nephew's church. That, after eighteen years of belief without assurance, conscious unworthiness and habitual cynicism decrying the evident work of grace within him, was a hard-won trophy.

But for John the fatality and its sequence had produced only distress, although most fathers, having nothing more than he to deplore, would think themselves fortunate. It was as if a plant that had been growing straight toward the sun now suddenly and continuously bent away. He had been anything but a difficult child to manage, quick-tempered yet with his mother's sunny disposition. Until his birth Andrew Connington had not been keenly aware of parental yearning. It was Cecily whose longing for children he had wanted to see satisfied. Fatherhood had been a constant surprise and delight, but his wife had come so far first with him that he had never been absorbed in his son. Conscious of his own lonely childhood, he had rather hoped that John might have a brother, but Evadne's arrival almost four years afterwards had proved a satisfactory answer to the problem of loneness and John had been an interested, protective, and affectionate brother from the beginning. Most of their child-rearing difficulties, in fact, had been caused by their daughter, whose childish fits of stubborn pugnacity and moody self-absorption had given poor prognosis of her later outgoing warmth and sweet reasonableness.

Without undue prodding, his first-born had run true to parental form. An avid reader before he was five, he had at six brought the annoyance of his first-grade teacher upon his unperturbed and unconforming parents. "It is very difficult for us to have a child so far ahead of the others in one respect. We always ask parents not to teach their children to read before school age." He had managed to live down the disadvantage of acquaintance with a wide miscellany of fascinating books, while his bored contemporaries were still See-See-Seeing Fluff. He had with comparatively little effort qualified for entrance into the University of Toronto Schools as his father had done before him. There, still voluntarily, he signed himself into the small Greek class — "After all, it's one subject where they're still using the same texts, so I don't have to buy them," he had said, reasonably enough, on discovering in Mansell's basement White's First Greek book, *Easy Selections from Xenophon,* and the annotated first six books of the *Iliad.*

A man would be less than human, Connington thought defensively, not to be pleased at this evidence of similar tastes. But he had made no plans for the boy's future and concealed any disappointment he felt when John, completing Grade XIII at sixteen, had suddenly asked if he could take another year to concentrate on math and science and, before his eighteenth birthday, enrolled in the honour course in mathematics, physics and chemistry. Perhaps it had been an early effort at breaking away — the more noticeable in that math and science were strenuous going for him. "He may find out later that he doesn't really like it," Cecily had said in explanation. "I think he just wants to prove himself in something you haven't done better." Andrew, eyebrow raised, had shrugged and acquiesced. Certainly in these postwar days opportunities in science were far more rewarding than in the humanities.

But that and the few other divergencies of opinion which Cecily had unobtrusively arbitrated and which he had put down as natural to an adolescent — he was still resisting the term "teen-ager" — had been no preparation for the breach which had suddenly opened and steadily, stealthily widened between them from the night of the accident, six years ago tonight.

Andrew jammed his foot on the brake and peered back at the lone figure standing under the light at the car-stop. Occupied with his thoughts and with making a turn at Dunvegan, he had been slow to receive the impression of familiarity. Now he began to back. Muttering with annoyance as two cars swung around the corner behind him, he changed his mind and accelerated to circle the double block at Heath, gambling that he would reach the stop again before the next streetcar.

He won. The figure was still there, motionless, shoulders hunched, head down. It did not move when Andrew drew up, confirmed his recognition, and threw open the door.

"Howard, isn't it? Don Howard? Andrew Connington. Let me give you a lift."

Howard came over to the car then but made no move to get in.

"Hello." There was an awkward pause while he evidently could not decide on further address. "Thanks, but don't bother. There's a car at the next block."

"I saw it when I came round the corner. I'm giving you a lift because I want to see you. Oh come on, Howard. It's too cold a night to keep the door open."

For a moment he thought he would be told to shut the door and mind his own business. Then with a gesture of capitulation more indifferent than a shrug, Howard shouldered into the seat beside him.

"Where to?"

"Parkdale. King and Jameson roughly."

The car slid along through three green lights in silence.

"I meant what I said about wanting to see you," resumed Andrew as the burden of resumption was left to him. "I'm not apologizing, though I feel my neck about the fact that I haven't been in touch with you before. You're not easy to get in touch with, you know."

31

"I suppose not. Deliberately."

"I tried frequently when your difficulties hit the papers. No answer. Finally, 'The number you have dialed is not in service.' Then I wrote, care of your church. Did they forward?"

"Yes. Decent of you. I should have answered."

"Well, you didn't. Don't know that I blame you. But you've been in my thoughts often, and in my prayers. The old excuse. 'Other things crowded in.' "

"Of course. I understand. Anyhow, there was no reason for you to bother."

"No? I think there was. Tried to put a bit of it in my letter. I well remember an afternoon session of the U. C. Presbytery when yours was the first — almost the only — voice raised to support me. And later ——"

"Oh forget it. There was something I could do then. Nothing you could do in my case."

"Except write a letter to Conference which apparently accomplished nothing, and a letter to the Press to which they declared that the question was closed and they were printing no more correspondence on it. I don't flatter myself that it would have helped at all. But I wanted you to know that I was standing by."

The pause was less strained and shorter.

"I guess I wasn't open to help. Everything seemed to hit me at once; so I finally did a turtle act. Actually I didn't feel as alive as a turtle. More like a performing vegetable."

"A state I have never been able to achieve," said Andrew. "And I rather doubt that you did, really."

"You didn't have your wife go off" — Andrew's wince passed unnoticed — "and take your children and then, after a period of every sort of rumour, have the Powers that Be adjudicate that since I could not rule my own house I was unqualified to rule the Church of God." He laughed shortly. "In view of the Scriptures they don't bother with, I was touched to find them digging that one out — quoting from the King James too, to make it more impressive."

Andrew did not laugh or interrupt with sympathetic comment. He prayed that his concern would make itself felt, and waited. The car turned south at Dufferin before Howard spoke again.

"Don't think I'm minimizing what you've had to take. And I haven't forgotten about Mrs. Connington — Cecily. Only damn it, Connington, you've had the satisfaction of being in the right. You never played into their hands by making a fool of yourself."

"I never had your provocation."

Howard shot him a quick grateful glance. For the first time he moved in the seat so that Andrew could see more than an averted profile. It was a large-boned face, ugly with the ugliness that a woman might have found endearing. On their few encounters Andrew had hoped for the fellowship he missed so sorely in the ministry, an equality of basic attitude and purpose, some stimulus in communion. It had been briefly his, though largely by correspondence, with John Lester until a grim accident in the mine shaft had claimed that devoted life. Howard, younger than he and less talented, had brought to the friendship a single-minded adaptability which Andrew admired as lacking in himself. But their opportunity for exchange had been short before Howard was called to a charge in Winnipeg. Then the war sent him overseas as padre.

"You wouldn't have let go anyway. Decent of you to suggest it though." His utterance had lost some of its clipped monotone. "I could take it better — I tell myself I could take it better — if it weren't for that. But the house was do damned *empty*. And I felt so — so filthy somehow, and conspicuous, after the police chased all over, checking the hospitals and then finding that she had simply left the car at Malton without a word. I couldn't bring myself to go to a pub. I didn't want to meet people. So I got two quarts of Scotch and went back to the house. I've always been a teetotaller. I was starting on the second quart when the President of the Presbytery and two of my elders came to condole. It was, I gather, quite a session!"

Andrew whooped, and apologized: "Sorry — it was the pun that got in amongst me. Believe me, I didn't laugh when it made the papers."

33

"Neither did the congregation. Can't say I blame them. Some of them were decent as they come. But embarrassed. And, of course, it gave colour to Nan's leaving me. My language to the deputation was not parliamentary. I had evidently been a 'man of ungovernable temper in my family life.' No wonder my wife was driven elsewhere for solace."

His voice grew dull again to cover the note of pain. He paused, but Andrew felt that he wanted to continue.

"Have you seen her since?"

"No. He followed her over there. His firm was transferring him to the Aberdeen branch, so the thing was well-timed. He was divorced already and that was all she wanted from me. That and the children. I had thought it was only the children."

"But surely the youngsters —?" Andrew had turned south from King on Jameson and stopped at direction in front of a new high-rise apartment. Howard made no effort to leave the car.

"They were all hers. I don't suppose you can understand that, Andrew. I faded out after they came, and if there is such a thing as weaning children from their father, she did it. Any attempt I made to interfere was a signal for attack. So to keep the peace I let things go. She never liked Canada, detested the suburbs when I was called to Southport, never wanted to be a minister's wife. Yet she had her friends and sympathizers in the congregation. Let's forget about it. I certainly failed all along the line."

"Don't say that when you don't mean it."

"Well — what else can I think? I can't go around saying, 'I meant well. I was kind to my mother.' "

"You're teaching now?"

"Yes. Lucky for me they don't throw even the little ones back these days. I was out in the sticks until things blew over. Then the Toronto Board was desperate enough to hire me. Better salary than I had before, too. I'll say that for it."

Andrew thought he knew the feeling which prompted the exaggerated carelessness. He came to a swift decision.

"My Evadne is looking for someone to take our young peo-

34

ple's service — pinch hit actually — on the first Sunday of December. Loyally she says she wants me. Actually a change would be welcome. It's a short preaching service and what is called 'guided discussion' afterwards. You were — are — good at that." He changed his tense in time. Howard looked at him in silence.

"Are you asking me to take it?"

"What do you think I'm doing?"

"I can't possibly. What would your congregation say?"

"Depends on how good you are."

"How do you know I have anything to preach?"

"Just a feeling. Haven't you?"

Howard was breathing hard. "I don't know. Honestly. I don't know. I've got over the pain. Better not open it up again. Forget about it. Not that I don't appreciate it."

Andrew felt a faint relief. He had taken the risk, he had asserted his friendship, he had made the offer against his logic and better judgment — he was particular about what was preached from his pulpit. The refusal let him down easily. But the imperious, the overriding impulse which had prompted the offer, surged up again. He threw caution to the winds and spoke earnestly.

"Don, I can't force you. And if you find, on reflection, that you have nothing to say, just let me know. But I want you to preach. I want my young people to hear you. I think that this meeting of ours was no accident."

"Look, why don't you say right out that you don't need me at all? That this is a magnificent gesture of Christian charity? That ——"

"If everyone accepts a gesture of Christian charity as graciously, I don't wonder there is so little of it. I'm not sifting my motives. It may be infernal do-goodiness, it may be unenlightened selfishness. I may be a smug busybody. But as far as I am my own judge, I'm doing it under compulsion. At one time you knew what that means. Perhaps you still do. In any case I'd be mighty sure, if I were you, of my motives for refusing."

Howard stared at him thoughtfully. "That makes sense. All right I will — not accept necessarily," he added hastily, "but assess my motives. And I'll let you know. Yes, I promise. Thanks."

Full of concern, Andrew drove south by way of the lake shore and University Avenue in order to avoid traffic. From the Exhibition grounds on, however, the route was so full of memories that, by the time he turned in at his own drive, Howard and his problems had been pushed into the background of his mind. He unfolded his large frame from the front seat of his car, closed the garage doors, and stared for a moment at the familiar house — the house of the Three Returns he had called it, when on Aunt Alex's insistence they had moved back after Mansell's death. He was not sleepy, though he knew how rapidly Sunday School time would come around. Why had they ever fallen in with the trend to morning Sunday Schools? A few years ago he would have gone for a walk around the still pleasant streets — avoiding the high-rise apartments which were altering Avenue Road past recognition. Now he craved bed, even if he could not sleep, even if it made the yearning for Cecily an agony of frustration.

He lay, trying to recapture instead the wonder of her determination to survive till he came, the thoughtfulness which had sought to comfort him. How well she had known her son! And he had tried to carry out her instructions. But how keep a boy from blaming himself when he was determined to blame himself? The accident, from all that could be learned, had been nobody's fault. A dog suddenly galvanized on Highway 27 by the lights of an approaching truck; a swift swerve in answer to Cecily's cry, as it recovered and dashed to the right side of the road; the car striking an unseen obstacle on the soft shoulder and swiveling across into the truck's path with Cecily in the place of impact, John amazingly thrown sideways and clear. The boy had not been exceeding the speed limit, the sober truck driver testified. If his father suspected that he had been crowding it so that the car went needlessly out of control, he did not let himself dwell on the suspicion. Such

36

freak accidents happened to far more experienced drivers. Perhaps, however, that was behind John's agony of remorse, that and the knowledge that Cecily had wished to drive herself — "I can think over my speech on the way," she had protested, and then given in at the sight of her son's disappointment. In vain Andrew had tried to persuade him that the same accident might have occurred and his mother been alone; badly shaken and bruised, the frantic boy had done what he could until the ambulance came.

Well, it had cured John of car fever, though the cure was worse than the disease. For almost two years he could not be persuaded to take the wheel; for months after the funeral he refused to enter an automobile.

That first year of near collapse was understandable. He had refused advice and returned to school only to flunk all his Christmas tests and be so incapable of concentration that the Dean of the Faculty told him there was no point in completing his year. So, after a Christmas which Andrew preferred to blot from his memory, he consented to listen to the doctor's advice and quit for the term. Bill Woodhouse, founder of the mission which had grown into Andrew's church, after five years of service in the Navy had married an attractive Wren from Calgary, taken a course in Hotel and Resort Management, and was now manager and part owner of a ranch hotel in the foothills of the Rockies. John had known Bill from babyhood, listened raptly to his sea stories, strutted about in his cap and jacket when Bill stayed with the family on leave, and, though unenthusiastic, needed no urging to accept his invitation for an indefinite stay out West. And since a complete change of scene seemed desirable, Andrew was grateful to send him under the nominal care of someone whose influence would not be disruptive, whose views and attitudes had been largely patterned on his own.

Perhaps a little too much so: perhaps with the best of intentions Woodhouse had talked too often and too warmly of his hero. At any rate, when the boy returned in September, physically stronger, ready to resume his interrupted course, there

37

had been no lessening of the uncomfortable tension with his father. Inchoate and indescribable, the older man felt it: a state of resentment, though of what he did not know, a covert criticism, unanswerable because unvoiced. Connington believed that he could diagnose the case and could have used the correct terminology — he had not made a thorough study of depth psychology from Freud to Harry Stack Sullivan for nothing. But how meet the need when the patient refused to talk? In the early stages of the breakdown he had suggested professional treatment; suggested not because of his belief in its efficacy, but from an honest desire to set aside prejudice and what had been referred to by his critics as his "Almighty complex." John had rejected the offer furiously. And, now that he was back at college studying and living with apparent normalcy, on what basis could a father suggest that there was need? — especially when the only grounds he could adduce, dislike and rejection of himself, would be considered completely healthy by the expert, and his own reaction held suspect?

He turned wearily on his side and watched the curtain blowing in from the open window — old-fashioned sash windows — as he had done the night he knew that he loved Cecily. It was the same window in his old room, but not the same bed. This was the bed he had shared with her, and he — fetishism was the term, he was aware — had not been able to bring himself to part with it when he had given up their smaller suburban house near his church. Cecily had thought it better for his work that they should live in the district especially while the children were growing up. The argument did not hold now with new developments and fashionable subdivisions reaching far into the country. He had not been sorry to leave the place where every opening door, every sound on the stair, suggested but denied her presence. But it was on this bed that his son had been conceived. How had he lost him?

The break should have occurred sooner, some would say. Had it been unnatural that, even in religious matters, there had been no period of rebellion, of open scepticism, even of the posed indifference by which clergymen's families traditionally show discomfort at their supposed restrictions? Considering the matter with his customary logic, Andrew Connington did not think so. His own early scepticism had been the logical result of inadequate presentation of the facts in school, complete lack of training at home, and affectionate admiration of his wittily iconoclastic Uncle. Conversely, a happy family life — living with Cecily had been fun — far more diversion and social occasion involving the children and their friends than the average parents provided, his own powerful ministry about which he had neither illusions nor false modesty, the reality of faith expressing itself in weighty concerns as in trivial, free discussion and appraisal of every anti-Christian argument or attitude: surely these were bound to predispose an intelligent youngster towards, if not saving faith, at least the attitude where saving faith could be granted?

Other factors had contributed. The war years in such a family could not fail to affect sensitive children, no matter how their parents attempted to keep them from unnecessary depression. John, deeply impressed, had heard and insisted on reading for himself the newspaper accounts of Dunkirk. That summer at the lake he had been overheard giving three-year-old Evadne a graphic account, illustrated with a tiny fleet of assorted boats. He had listened to the distilled elixir of Churchill's speeches and to the grave, brave, halting broadcasts of George VI. He had repeatedly seen his father, face grey, turn away from the telephone and go out to comfort — in some cases to break the news to — some stricken family. He had come home with stories of atrocities and enemy victories and submarine warfare and Trojan horse activities, distorted and enlarged by his school friends, and demanded the truth from his parents. He had demanded too — and the answer had taxed their power of explanation — a synthesis of this horror of evil and suffering with the good and loving and all-powerful God in Whom they believed.

But their answer *had* satisfied him. And the next step came with unexpected swiftness. Their neighbour's son died in the city's autumn scourge of poliomelytis. The boys had come from school together and John had taken his friend's paper route the afternoon on which he sickened. For the next three days, kept home under observation himself, John asked for hourly bulletins. The final news, broken to him by Cecily, seemed to make personal and intense the stories of multiplied mortality which had to that time been "unhappy far-off tales." His fit of crying was natural enough and his woebegone face at the funeral — neither Andrew nor Cecily had any use for the modernity that acquaints children with the "facts of life" in stark unnecessary detail, while screening them over-protectively from the great inescapable fact. But the solemnity outlasted his first grief. Less than two months later, a small but determined figure presented itself in his father's study one evening and asked to join the Church.

Andrew, turning to lie on his back again, momentarily suspended recollection, as his right foot knotted in the agonizing surprise of a cramp. That was one of the interesting — painfully interesting — things about growing old, he thought: the extension of personal experience to comprehend a multitude of frailties, fears, distresses, viewed unsympathetically in arrogant youth and vigorous maturity. This cramp, for instance — he sighed in grateful relief as the imperious muscles relaxed — he had never known what cramp was until two years ago. He had read, with unadmitted impatience, of those so badly overcome by it in the water as to lose their heads and drown, had seen with pity but without sympathy the fear on Aunt Alexandra's face as she felt its seizure. Never again! In the mental realm and the spiritual too — if he lived long enough, would he approve the Gallic epigram which he had always considered, and still did consider, in fact, an exquisitely worded excuse for weakness: *Tout savoir est tout comprendre; tout comprendre est tout pardonner* etc.? Perhaps not. But how wise was the Scriptural warning: "Be not many of you teachers, knowing that you will receive heavier judgment."

In his most rigorous attempts to assess their treatment of John, though — his mind picked up the interrupted train of thought — he did not see that they could have acted otherwise

40

on that occasion. Both by temperament and by conviction he disapproved of efforts to produce "conversions" or "professions of faith" with deliberate emotional appeal or mass pressure. In the case of children he considered it scripturally and psychologically indefensible, and nothing that he had seen of the results of such techniques had altered his opinion. So, while treating John's confidence seriously and discussing the issues as with an equal — he found it impossible to talk down to children, remembering his own childhood too clearly — he had tried to prevent him from taking, under unusual emotional stress, a step of which he might not realize the implications.

His efforts had been met with a determination equal to his own and a logic as consistent.

"You mean you don't think I believe on the Lord Jesus Christ, on Jesus Christ as Lord?" The boy's quick correction was evidence of his close attention to a recent sermon.

"I do, John. Really I do. But ——"

"Doesn't it say, if you believe you will be saved?"

"Yes."

"But you don't think I'm saved? Then how old do you have to be before you can believe the Bible?" He saw his advantage and pressed it as Cecily would have done. His head was down, but every now and again he raised his dark-blue eyes to meet his father's and their earnestness was irresistibly compelling. "When you heard me swearing last summer you quoted the Bible at me. Why do I have to pay attention to that part and not the other? Is it more important not to swear than to be saved?"

"It isn't a question of being saved —" The words were out before Andrew realized their weakness.

"But you can't join the church if you're saved? I thought you said that was what the Church *was*. And that there was nothing we could do ourselves. What else do grown-ups have to do, Dad? Prove that they are good enough, some way?"

Andrew caught himself on the point of saying that he did not want him to take a step that he would regret later and realized that he was in no condition to argue further.

41

"I'll think it over" (talk it over with your mother, he had nearly said). "Now let us both pray about it."

The basic sincerity of the boy's prayer almost made him give in immediately. So did John's parting shot as he turned back from the door on his way to bed.

"You think I'm just doing this because Fred died. You wanted me to take him to Sunday School when he moved here and I did. But if he had asked to join the church and you hadn't let him, you'd be sorry now, wouldn't you?"

Cecily had been no help in dissuasion.

"I see all your arguments but I don't think we have a leg to stand on if we refuse him. You know people who became Christians at ten years and even younger."

"But ——"

"Are you sure it isn't lack of faith?" she asked disconcertingly. "Aren't you afraid it may not be real and that people will think we put pressure on him and brought him up in an unhealthy religious atmosphere — and all that sort of rot?"

"Touché. Right as usual, Mind-reader. Maddening too, because I really didn't know what I was thinking until you said it."

"Darling, if I think your thoughts before you it's because that's exactly what I'm afraid of. And we should be ashamed of ourselves. Here we've prayed for this since he was born —"

"If not sooner."

"I didn't. I was afraid by that time even to believe that he would *be*. But now the prayer is granted and we don't believe it."

" 'O ye of little faith.' "

"Let's wait and see if he brings it up again. The little mortal is pulling his weight in other fields. He is class convener of the school's paper collection tomorrow and Saturday. No one can say he is unnaturally pious. If this is a passing fancy he may forget all about it by then."

"But you don't think so."

"No I don't. And I do hope he won't. If he's responsible enough to think of salvation, he is responsible to God and we'd better not interfere."

42

On Sunday night after church, John, apparently considering that his parents had been granted sufficient time, appeared for his answer. In the meantime he had behaved normally enough: he had led a well-organized canvass of the neighbourhood, collecting paper in a fleet of express carts, baby carriages, wagons, and bicycle-carriers; he had directed its sorting into piles (newspaper, brown paper, tinfoil) ; and he had, somewhat regretfully, of course, taken second place in quantity to a rival class ("they had more kids in the room though, and the paper wasn't sorted as well") . He had passed the usual family Sunday, varied by dinner at the Mansells' with their two distantly related war guests.

His father was never to be disturbed unnecessarily on Sunday. Cecily enforced the rule so unobtrusively that Andrew was scarcely aware of it. After church was after hours, however, and when his mother and father saw the small, pyjama-clad figure in the living room doorway they knew that there was no change of purpose on his part, no evading of the issue on theirs.

It had been a quaintly solemn occasion, the morning of the next Communion service. John, the only new communicant, answered the few questions put to him by his father, recited the Apostles' Creed with a ring of personal conviction in his young, nervous voice, and was duly received into membership of the Catholic and Apostolic Church. He had never since decried his action or denied his belief or its responsibilities. To this comfort Andrew had clung through the years of nebulous estrangement, through all the actions and attitudes which he found exasperating and inconsistent.

Clinging to it now, he presently, in an awful exhaustion of sleeplessness, fell asleep.

Howard did not call Sunday or Monday. On Tuesday Andrew, realizing that his private number was not listed, telephoned him at his school and left a message. The call came through within half an hour.

"Sorry to interrupt you at work," said Andrew tentatively,

43

"but I don't want this inspection of motives overdone. And I do want a definite word. Young Evadne had Spencer Cornet lined up for the service months ago. He has had a change of position and leaves for Taiwan this week. You will have more than the usual gratitude if you pinch-hit at this short notice. But I'd like to reassure her."

"I'm no substitute for Cornet. He's a draw and at least ten years younger."

"Will you come?"

"Look, Andrew, I didn't mention it the other night because the question didn't come up. But it might make a difference to you. I married again a year ago."

"Well?"

"Doesn't it affect your invitation? Would you have given it if you had known? Oh come on, Andrew. I'm not going to be hurt."

"Do you feel guilty on the subject? I asked if you had something to say? Has your marriage altered that?"

The line was silent for a full minute.

"No. I'm not pretending that I came to terms with the question before. I have since. But you've always taken the orthodox position —"

"Which is? I'm afraid I think that the seventh chapter of First Corinthians is infinitely more flexible and closer to the mind of God than canon law has been. Also that most people read our Lord's words in Matthew nineteen from a completely false premise."

"I'd like to talk that out with you sometime." Howard's voice was almost eager. Then it changed. "But I don't want to put anything over. I didn't marry this time in any exaltation of conviction or love. I'd had that. And God knows I could have continued as I was — I wasn't a youngster when I married the first time. This just seemed a sensible thing to do. I'd known Jean at school. She turned out to be on the staff here when I came. We were both lonely."

"Is she a Christian?"

"Who am I to say? Not your sort. Church background. She

44

goes with me on Sunday. We shop around, usually at places where I'm not likely to meet anyone I know."

There was a pause for Andrew to break.

"Back to my original request. Are you coming to preach for me?"

"You're sure you still want me?"

"I'm not sure of anything," said Andrew frankly. "I know that I met you, that I have been convinced that our meeting and this unexpected need of a preacher is no mere coincidence. I have asked you to come and I want you to come if you have anything to say. And you know quite well what I mean by that — not a nice challenging address on current events or the Peace Corps or the New Morality. Cut it to the essentials. If the Risen Christ is no longer your Lord, if you no longer have dealings with Him, don't come. Now what about it?"

There was a long expulsion of breath, as if it had been held, tense.

"I think I'll come."

Andrew broke the news to his family at dinner. He had expected some reserve, if not disappointment, from his puritanical Evadne, and guarded support from John, who had taken to making random remarks about flinty moralism and lack of charity among evangelicals. Aunt Alex, he took for granted, would remain aloof, if not completely in the dark on the issue.

On the contrary, Mrs. Mansell recalled the whole affair with remarkable accuracy and tended to confuse the issue by adding, contrary to her custom, details gleaned from sources which in any other woman Andrew would have considered gossip.

"It's a load off my mind to get it settled," was Evadne's first remark after listening, frowning slightly with concentration, to her father's brief account. "I'm sure you know what you're doing, Dad."

John's disapproval surprised him.

"Well I hope you do — that is," he added hastily, "I hope

45

he doesn't let you down. It's all right to do a friend a good turn, Dad, but what about the effect on the kids?"

"What effect?"

"Oh Dad, you know what I mean. You're not keen on this 'anything goes' attitude in the church. If you have in your pulpit a divorced, remarried man who goes on binges, what standards are they supposed to keep?"

"That wife of his," said Aunt Alex severely, "left him no choice. Some men would have refused her a divorce and made it impossible for her to re-marry. I consider that Mr. Howard acted very well."

Somewhat dazed by this unexpected support, Andrew turned to his son.

"We" — the pronoun was deliberately chosen — "should be careful in this matter of judging. Don Howard does not 'go on binges.' By the record and his own statement he got drunk — roaring drunk on what many men can take, because of habit, without much effect — once in his life and under extreme provocation."

"Even granting that," persisted John (Is his objection genuine or simply a desire to oppose me? Andrew wondered), "I've heard you often enough on the childish attitude of people in movies and T.V. shows where the only reaction to any bad news is to go out and get stoned. And he was a minister at the time."

Andrew reached a long arm for the Bible lying ready on the buffet.

" 'Brethren,' " he read, " 'if a man is overtaken in any trespass, you who are spiritual should restore him in a spirit of gentleness. Look to yourself, lest you also be tempted. Bear one another's burdens and ——' "

"That's all right," interrupted John, "but there are other things about the character of ministers, above reproach or something like that. I'm not saying this guy didn't have provocation. I'm just saying that I don't think he's any example to put up before us. And Vad has gone to a lot of trouble about this service," he added with inconsequential generosity.

46

"If you wanted to give him a chance to preach, you could have asked him for a regular service."

Andrew went white. Mrs. Mansell was obviously torn between her adored nephew and her special favorite. Evadne began a disclaimer and broke off, feeling its inadequacy. John, quite aware of the sting of his criticism, was uncomfortable but stubborn. Finally his father spoke.

"I can do that — I should do it even now, except that any change in the arrangements would let Mr. Howard know that there were objections and put him off entirely. But, you must take it from me, Evadne, I believe that he will come through with what your service needs. John, this is no matter of maudlin sympathy with me. There is no more lonely man in the world — humanly speaking — than a minister in Don Howard's position. And for the reasons you have listed he is often left alone. Other men may be reinstated in their profession. The one thing he is kept from is the one thing he needs if he is really a minister: to continue his ministry. I've known several who, because of one public slip, were deprived of their office. And however kind their associates are to other delinquents, it seems as if they dare not restore their own brethren in Christ. I'm talking of those who are 'overtaken' as the Scripture says, and who, no matter how deeply they repent, have the door closed to them. I'm not talking here of the incongruity of what is allowed to continue in good standing in the pulpit. When it comes to Don Howard," he went on, "I refuse to regard him as delinquent. I don't condone the drunk episode. I do know that twice in my life I've had the same urge; once I gave way to it ——"

"No, Dad! You mean you ever were blotto?"

"Not completely. But enough not to care what I did," said Andrew briefly; "The second time I had more control. And both occasions were before I was a Christian. But there is no difference in God's sight between a spectacular lapse like Don's and indulgence of other sorts — pride, harsh criticism, ingratitude. Or rather I believe that in God's eyes — though who am I to speak for Him? — there is a great difference. A lapse like

47

Don's is much less blameworthy. However, if your conscience keeps you from attending the service, you'll just have to obey it. That's what I've had to do with mine in this matter."

"Oh I'll be there," John's concession was less than gracious, "if only out of curiosity. And I hope he doesn't let Vad down."

3

$\approx\approx\approx\approx\approx\approx\approx\approx\approx\approx\approx\approx\approx\approx$

"VAD, CAN YOU GET SOMEONE ELSE to do Philip in First Corinthians?"

Evadne looked at her brother in consternation.

"John! You can't wiggle out! You said you'd take it. I'm counting on you."

"I know." John's discomfort gave his voice an edge of irritability. "But the Chief asked me today if I'd go along on the field trip to the Maritimes. It's the biggest area test so far for this serum we're developing and I'm pretty keen on the chance."

"But John ——"

"All right, all right. I'll tell him I can't go because I have to be in a Young People's Dramatic Production! He'll give the job to Solly. I expected he would in the first place."

Evadne's voice was small.

"How long will you be gone? Could we fill in for rehearsals?"

"We leave a week Saturday for two weeks. At best, even if I flew home, I could only make it for the second performance. And there's always a chance it may take longer. But I promised you and I'll go through with it. I told Mathers I'd let him know tomorrow."

The edge in his voice was sharpened, Andrew knew, by his awareness of her disappointment, for both men were sure of the outcome. It was typical of John to consider his promise binding while he employed irresistible means to win release from it. If he did not win release, Andrew knew and Evadne

49

knew what life at home and at rehearsals would be like with his resentful nobility obtruding in every action. And in this case with justification, his father thought. Most young men would not think twice about setting aside a private obligation — a church obligation at that — for a possible advancement in their careers. But he was aware that this was more than an ordinary disappointment to his daughter and he could not bear to look at her crestfallen face.

She made a final attempt.

"Perhaps we could postpone the play for two weeks."

"Vad! Have you forgotten that we're half through February already, that Easter comes in March, that your timetable will be up around the first of April, to say nothing of the work I have to do yet before I can start my thesis? I don't see how you can spare the time for this confounded Young People's effort as it is. But postpone it? No. I'll just turn the chance down. Let's forget it."

Evadne gave in.

"Don't be silly. You can't turn a chance like this down. I'll get someone else." Her voice was flatter because of its assumed carelessness. And Andrew, from long but never inuring experience of specially designed plans going awry, was momentarily inundated by the wave of her frustration.

It broke on him again after dinner when John, covering his discomfort by a faint air of injury, had telephoned Dr. Mathers and been summoned to his home for a conference. Evadne saw him out with a bright, fast-frozen smile, then followed her father to his study, flung herself into his comforting arms and in her own words "howled like a banshee."

"Why does it happen like this every time?" she demanded later when she had released herself to fumble around in her pocketless jumper for a handkerchief which she finally located up her sleeve. Like her mother again, thought Andrew fondly, she is one of the fortunate women who look appealing in tears. Even a small nose polished by stormy blowing adds to the charm.

The weeping of some women is an almost intolerable irritation. He roused himself to answer.

"Not every time surely?"

"Well, every time I try to do something for somebody's good! My time-table yet! Don't I know it? With three essays coming up, I don't exactly *need* the job of directing a play. But the kids were keen and with John at loose ends after Julie, I thought it was a chance to kill two — no three — birds with one well-directed stone."

Andrew nodded. One of her intentions was to retain enthusiasm among the young people of his church. Evadne had never allowed even her college activities to interfere with loyalty to him and his work. In her third year at the University she might well have begged off the Sunday School class of girls six years her junior, who had been left without a teacher the year before. The Victoria College Dramatic Society was sufficient outlet for her inherited talent as an actress. And she was determined to keep the first-class honours which she had attained on her last exams. Scholastic achievement with her had always been less easy, more variable and spotty than with John. But she was sensitive to her father's difficulties and felt responsible — too responsible, he feared — to take her mother's place in the work of the church.

"I suppose you know what the extra bird was?"

"Marjorie Simmons? Yes, my young matchmaker."

"Well," she said defensively, "I know she likes John, though she's far too nice to talk about it, and he was completely in Julie's clutches before he met her. She'll be a perfect Melissa, and I thought it was a good chance to throw them together. He used to be keen on the thought of acting, but that wretched course of his — and Julie — never gave him a chance. And when I put it up to him to help me out he seemed quite interested. There are always so many men needed in a play, and most boys can't act for trees, compared with the girls who want to try. He was reading Philip's part beautifully. It can be a rather prissy part if it isn't acted by somebody definitely masculine. And Mr. Howard is being terrifically helpful with the staging.

51

I'm so glad he got interested in the idea the night you had him preach. And he says Jean — Mrs. Howard — has done costumes for the school plays and thinks there are ones we can borrow. Everything was going smoothly. And then this — I nearly swore that time, Dad — this field trip comes along. I don't understand. It isn't as if I hadn't prayed about the whole thing."

Andrew made no reply. He might have been quizzical at the idea of an amateur dramatic production meriting the preventing grace of the Creator of the expanding universe; but he was not. His theology did not merely include the possibility, but presupposed it.

"I wouldn't be found dead putting on the average 'religious' play," she went on. "But Rubinstein's *First Corinthians* is powerfully good drama and Scriptural — you said it was yourself in spite of the rather weak ending. And it seemed to be getting John in contact with our group again, almost for the first time since — I've tried so often before and got nowhere."

He did not utter a pat comment on the fallacy of making one's own plans and asking God to ratify them. If the child had done just that, so had he often and with as deadly and dedicated sincerity. By what infallible touchstone could one differentiate between the idea that merely seemed so right, so God-sent, and the actual Hand of God at work? And did the thwarting of one's scheme necessarily prove that one had been wrong? Was facile success the only sign of inspiration? Then surely history, even and especially the history of the Church — in the short-term view at least — was an unending contradiction.

"My thoughts are not your thoughts, neither are your ways My ways," he murmured and was prepared for Evadne's look of puzzled reproach. "I'm not giving that as a comment, pet. Merely resting my heart on it as I've often had to do. I know what you feel about this. Sometimes the perversity seems ironically intentional. Many times I've been tremendously concerned over a situation or an individual. Very often I've been asked to help in a question of sorrow or doubt or terrible mental stress. Or I have been desperately aware of need in connection with what I felt to be God's work. Often, after hours and days, the right idea has come, the timely illustration, the penetrating word, the cogent plan: and the person or persons concerned are, contrary to all reasonable expectation, absent; the plan cannot be put into action. Why? I expect to be kept interested for eternity in finding out."

"But it doesn't work that way with some people," protested Evadne. "Look at all the stories — you've told some of them yourself — of inexplicable occurrences in answer to prayer, of genuine miracles ... physical and material, I mean. The way some Christians talk and write, things work out like the solution of a detective story, and much faster."

"I know. We both pray right now, for example, and John comes back at ten-thirty announcing that the field trip has been postponed until the day after the final performance of *First Corinthians*. Whereupon you write it up in story form and sent it to the 'Look and See' Sunday School syndicate — circulation 185,000," said Andrew dryly.

"You're not kidding!" agreed Evadne warmly. "By the same token, the young men whose advances I have spurned should all by rights (two of them at least) have been back next day, having realized that a sweet, pure girl like me was really what they wanted, asked if they could come to church, been converted —"

"Oh come now, you couldn't live happily with two of them ever after!" objected Andrew.

"No. The one I didn't want would have a call to a particularly dangerous mission field where white women could not endure the climate. And I should be left to the one I really loved. Only fortunately — and to reassure you, Abba, in case you wonder — I haven't met him yet. Perhaps I never shall. Probably I have a psychological Thing about you which will unfit me for normal marriage — whatever that is these days," she rattled on. Was her lightness a trifle overdone? "But to return. Why does so much of that sort of thing happen to some people? They write as if it was a must if you are 'living the victorious life.' I'd be willing to accept the dictum that I'm not. But when it comes to you — it just doesn't hold."

"No aspersions must be cast. 'We stand on guard for thee.'

53

Bless you, my loyal fighting minority. Well, to reassure *you*, a great number of such things have happened to me in answer to prayer, but not the return of an embarrassment of regenerate females, I'm thankful to say. I think most Christians who trust in God at all times could tell of such things. Yes, even of those answers which in this age impress us most: the arrival of needed money, or the cure of a hopeless ailment — as if the material and physical is harder for our God to manipulate than the spiritual. It would be sheer ingratitude for me to put them down to coincidence. But it would also be sheer dishonesty to pretend that prayer works on the slot-machine principle, or not to admit that many times I can't see it working at all ... when the heavens are as brass." His voice dropped on the last words. He was no longer speaking to her.

Evadne leaned against his chair looking down at him. Her eyes went from him to the double photograph holder which he kept on his desk. What a magnificent-looking man he had been, she thought, with hair as dark and thick as John's, and direct hazel eyes in a strong, unlined face. Had been! She caught herself indignantly. He still was, although the great head habitually settled forward on his broad shoulders and the hair, increasingly gray, was thinning on top. It was a fine face, with more kindness now than arrogance in the determined set of the jaw, the eyes in their deeper sockets more patient and understanding, the handsome features refined to beauty by suffering and meditation. It was a face any woman would find attractive, she thought, wishing that some would not make it obvious that they were attracted and give her a succession of bad moments. That was selfish, she told herself not for the first time. Her father was lonely, he was still young enough; if he wanted to marry again, she ought to be perfectly willing. But she wasn't. She kissed the top of his head and shifted her weight from the chair to the desk so that she faced him.

"When you feel like that, does it — it doesn't ever shake your faith?"

Andrew laughed and she found the note of genuine mirth **inexpressibly** comforting.

54

"Evadne, lamb, faith is not a thermometer that responds to variable temperatures. And it isn't an opinion based on the calculation of probabilities either. Still less, thank Heaven, is it what so many equate it with these days when they talk about faith in your fellow men, faith in electricity, faith in the aeroplane which takes you from one continent to another. 'Faith is the assurance of things hoped for, the conviction of things not seen.' Feelings, opinions — what they called 'frames' in the eighteenth century — these rise and fall and are shaken."

"Go on," she said breathlessly as he paused, "because I've had some pretty low 'frames' of late. Only, though I couldn't explain it, I *knew* that my faith hadn't gone."

"Faith — let me be personal — *my* faith is a fact. It is something that was given to me — that happened to me, if you like, about thirty years ago. It, the intellectual part of it, was based on other facts, historical facts: the life and death and resurrection of the Jew, Jesus, at a given point in time, on a given place on this planet. . . ."

"Oh come now, Daddy, don't be old-hat," said Evadne. "You *know* it's crude to believe in the *physical* resurrection. What really happened — only the Oriental imagination puts these Great Truths in story form and the simple account of the disciples passed through the mythologizing process — was simply that the friends of Jesus were strangely convinced that their dear Friend could not really be dead. He was *with* them just — I read a prominent clergyman's explanation in the paper last Easter — just as said clergyman knows that his departed mother is not dead — is still with him."

"God help him. Yes, I know," said Andrew wearily. "One of the points I've never heard these chaps explain is why, in that case, the apostles and Luke and Paul related clearly that the disciples saw and touched and ate with Him off and on for forty days, but after that made no such claim. Why the clear-cut differentiation — the absolute disappearance after the ascension when the benighted liars said that He was 'taken up' — just how else His departure could have convinced them I don't know — presumably He could have whizzed off horizontally! What gullible fools we moderns think the early Church was composed of."

"I'm sorry. I was rude and interrupted."

"Exactly. It's the modern attitude. People prefer a discussion period to the lecture method."

"I don't. Not when you're the lecturer. Please go on."

"The fine thread of my discourse has been snapped," said Andrew severely. "Let this be a lesson to you."

"You were just saying — Oh help! Shall I answer for you?"

Andrew's hand had already closed on the telephone receiver. "Hello. Yes, Mr. — Brother Mordan. Yes. Tonight, if you like. In the vestry. No, it's no trouble. I left a book up there that I need for reference. In half an hour then. Oh well, the traffic is all downtown at this time. Good-bye. I always have trouble with that Brother business," he added, as he put the receiver down; "lack of early association tells, though my atavistic Methodism should come to my aid."

"You don't have to drive away up to the church. Why couldn't he come here? What does he want?"

"To have a few words with me. He mentioned it on Sunday. Yes, I could have asked him to come here, but I prefer to meet him at the church."

"Any particular reason?" Evadne was beginning to scent reserves in him as Cecily had done.

"No. But now that I'm not a working man — that is, don't report at Connington Glass at nine a.m. — I should be easily available. Besides I feel that Mr. Mordan, with the best of intentions, would be inclined to consider Aunt Alexandra's ménage too affluent."

"I like that. Have you seen his split-level? With patio and terrace?"

"Ah but I mean affluent for a minister. And it is not his affair that we live more cheaply here than we did in Black Burn. No, dear, I don't know what he wants to talk about. Face the fact that it may be a private confession, in which case you'll never know."

But I doubt it, he thought, as he made the trip, so familiar now that the car seemed to find the route itself, in fact had

56

taken him halfway up on several occasions when his destination lay downtown. Mr. Mordan was a man of about his own age, a recently appointed executive of the insurance company in which he had spent his life. Since his arrival from Winnipeg a year before, he had attended Connington's church and been received into membership and lately elected to the Board. Apart from the occasional Sunday evening when he absented himself to go to a special service elsewhere, and a recent, lengthy visit to an equally successful son in Minneapolis, he was a regular attendant. Andrew was pleased though not elated to have him in the congregation — stable, theologically knowledgeable. With the death of his uncle, the Eastons, and several others who had been with him from the beginning, he realized the need for middle-aged and elderly men.

"There is something that has worried me a bit, Pastor." Mr. Mordan did not keep him long in suspense after the exchange of trivialities. "I don't need to tell you how I've enjoyed your preaching."

Andrew inclined his head slightly with what he trusted was not sham deprecation.

"But there is one element I've missed. I was asking Ella before Christmas if she'd ever heard you preach on it and she said no she hadn't. Then the holiday put it out — well, crowded it into the background for awhile; but while I was south of the border, I went to my son's church — that's an unworldly church for you: non-denominational, started up in a little store, now has a new plant that cost half a million. All voluntary giving too — like here," he conceded. "But with a radio program beamed to the Mid-Western States and the Prairie Provinces and a missionary commitment that would stagger you. Young people on fire — simply on fire — out distributing tracts and going after the lost — completely unworldly too, no makeup, no theatres, no dances." Mr. Mordan paused glowing. He was a burly individual with the bluff, expressionless face and keen eyes of a man long accustomed to the consideration of finance. Andrew knew that his tithe was paid — not all to Eucharist Church; several home and foreign mission projects shared it — with mathematical exactness; more, that his income was tithed before income tax deductions, a step which many tithers consider, not unjustly, beyond the call of duty. He had never seen him alight with enthusiasm before. It was short-lived.

"Well, the element I'm talking about — and you heard it almost every sermon, every talk there at Bethesda Temple — is judgment. Fact, the minister — the senior minister; they have a couple of assistants — gave his testimony one night at a Missionary Conference and said that when his call came as a young man, he knew he was called to preach judgment. And I said to myself, and to Ella, 'That's what I've been missing. That's what gets results.' So I thought I'd talk to you about it, ask you if you might do it oftener, see where you stood."

Andrew knew what was meant. He did not immediately meet the question head-on. He said quietly, "I don't keep a file of my sermons. In fact, I seldom write out more than notes nowadays. But I think, unless memory fails me, that I have preached several sermons on judgment in your hearing. One I recall: 'Now is the judgment of this world. Now is the Prince of this world cast out.' And another: 'Since you thrust it from you and judge yourselves as unworthy of eternal life, behold we turn to the Gentiles.' And 'though Moses and Samuel stood before me, yet my heart would not turn toward this people . . . . let them go.' "

Mr. Mordan nodded.

"Yes, I remember. Excellent sermons, expositions rather. You are the finest expositor of the Word I've ever listened to. I told my son as much. Their man is a preacher, doesn't pretend to be a teacher. But that is hardly what I mean. It may be called old-fashioned and hot Gospel. You and I know how unpopular it is in these modernist theological colleges. But it's basic to the faith. What do you preach about hell?"

"I try," replied Andrew gravely, "to preach what Scripture teaches, no less, and certainly no more."

"Well, that's the point. That's what makes them listen to the Gospel. That's what drives young people to the mission field — the thought of the lake of fire, an eternity of torment waiting for those poor heathen."

58

Andrew could not hedge. His voice was not crisp, but ragged with controlled feeling.

"But, Brother Mordan, that is what I do not believe."

"You don't believe that those who reject Christ are damned to all eternity?"

"I did not say that. You were talking just now, not of those who deliberately reject Christ, but of those who have never heard of Him. You were talking not of damnation — which simply means judgment — but, unless I mistake, of a state of eternal conscious torment. Physical?"

"You believe in a physical resurrection. I didn't expect you to quibble, Pastor."

"Believe me" — not because of the personal issue, where he was all too frequently inclined to throw discretion to the wind for the sake of principle, but from a genuine desire to preserve unity, Andrew exerted himself to be conciliatory — "believe me, Brother Mordan, I would not insult you by quibbling on so grave a question. The judgment of God — 'His strange work' as Isaiah puts it — is very real and very terrible to me. But I cannot be 'wise above what is written.' I cannot preach a doctrine which contradicts many passages of Scripture and the justice, to say nothing of the love, of God; which formed no part of the great basic creeds, and which I believe to be the result of the infiltration of Greek philosophy into a corrupted church."

"I don't follow you. What Greek philosophy?"

"The doctrine which finds no place in either Old or New Testament, of the immortality of the soul."

Mordan looked his incredulous horror.

"You don't believe man has an immortal soul?"

Andrew, to counteract the hopeless, sinking feeling in his stomach, tried to summon up what Cecily had assured him was a very winning smile. He managed to overcome his natural undemonstrativeness enough to lay a persuasive hand briefly on his elder's impassive arm.

"I believe that you *are* an immortal soul, and so by the grace of God am I," he said. Then the smile faded from his voice. "No,

Brother Mordan, 'The wages of sin is death. The gift of God is eternal life, through Jesus Christ our Lord.' 'Who' — God — 'only hath immortality.' In the ultimate day God shall 'be all and in all.' Where in those verses is there room for the existence of millions of His creatures, palpably suffering, God-hating, God-defying, but with the inherent power to continue as long as He continues?"

"But —" The Scripture silenced Mordan temporarily. Then his dread of being unorthodox came to the fore. "We must beware of private interpretation." An amazing statement that, thought Andrew, from one whose heritage was based on the right and privilege of private interpretation. Not the first time those words of Peter had been twisted — "there are some pretty difficult Scriptures which can be wrested" — Mordan was on surer ground now — "to our destruction. And, Mr. Connington, hell is definitely taught in Scripture: '. . . rather than, having two hands and two feet, to be cast into hell.' 'They shall be cast into outer darkness; there shall be weeping and gnashing of teeth.' "

"I admit and have often expounded both Scriptures in their context."

"But you don't think hell goes on for ever and ever. Are you an Annihilationist then? Not a Universalist surely?"

"No, not the latter at any rate. The doctrine has obvious attractions, but Scripture and human nature keep me from accepting it. Must one be labelled anything but Christian?"

Mr. Mordan had recovered his grip and his memory.

" 'These shall go into everlasting punishment. But the right-eous into everlasting' — and I understand from authorities that the Greek word is the same in both cases — 'life.' What about that verse? Or this, 'And the smoke of their torment goeth up for ever and ever'?"

Andrew forgot himself momentarily in the pleasure of discussion.

"You're right. The word 'aionion' is the same, and it makes little difference in the context that no one knows exactly what it means. Eternal is a better translation than everlasting and in either case could indicate the finality, the irrevocableness, of the judgment. Your other quotation presents more difficulty. The phrase 'for ever and ever' or 'unto the ages of the ages' recurs frequently in the book of Revelation. It refers equally, if I remember, to the eternal duration and reign of God and to the destruction of the lake of fire. I do not pretend to decide what it means. I do know that I cannot take these isolated references to the lake of fire (not hell or Hades, if you will not think I'm quibbling) to contradict the plain teaching of Scripture elsewhere, and the very nature of God and the Gospel. Especially when they occur only in a book which is stated to be a book of signs and which contains many figures which contradict themselves if taken literally, as in that same portion: 'before whose face heaven and earth fled away and there was found no room for them.' "

"I did not expect," said Mr. Mordan heavily, and Andrew suddenly pitied him in his stubborn but righteous disappointment, "to hear modernist views from you, views which lessen the heinousness of sin and therefore make light of the sacrifice of Christ."

"Oh no!" said Andrew swiftly. "On the contrary, Mr. Mordan. Whether my belief is true is not affected by my opinion that it makes sin far more dreadful — any more than the present success of the preaching to which you refer indicates its truth. You and I have lived long enough to wonder at the great success — numerical and financial and apparently moral — enjoyed by many movements which we consider heretical and even ridiculous. But to go back: There were two issues at stake in our original discussion: the first, the eternal conscious torment of the damned; the second, the inclusion among those damned of millions who have never heard of Christ and millions more who have never had the Gospel presented to them. We shall not know until eternity how many earnest individuals have been driven from our God — at least from our fellowship in Christ — by the second teaching. As for the first, you apparently think that a man will not come to Christ unless he believes that he will otherwise suffer untold physical agonies through eternity. Frankly I think we give a false and undeserved dignity to unregenerate

61

man by that concept: there is a Miltonic grandeur to the notion that a personality persists forever in awful suffering. I know one man at least — my Uncle George — who had been sustained in a defiant boast of atheism all his adult life by what he considered — I quote him — 'the loathsome, unjust inconsistency of calling a God like that a God of love.' He was conscious enough of his own sin and helplessness — most men are, I think, when the Holy Spirit convicts them, unless we make them resentful by rubbing their noses in it. And when he saw God as the independent Creator who died for 'a sin-reduced, unlovely beggar' like himself — I quote again — to share His own life with him: that did it," he concluded abruptly. The memory of Mansell's taciturn, bewildered gratitude always moved him.

"Well, as you say, that proves nothing," said Mordan stiffening. "But such preaching is dangerous. People need to be warned that they're hell bound — look at immorality and crime today — the war has taught them nothing — and church-members living like the world. And if the heathen can be saved without hearing about Christ, why give our money to send missionaries to them?"

"Mr. Mordan," said Andrew suddenly, "is that all the salvation of Christ means to you? That you escape never-ending torment in the lake of fire?"

Mordan hesitated.

"No. No, of course not. But you can't get away from the justice, the offended righteousness of a Holy God."

"I'm not trying to. Or rather yes I have tried — and succeeded, 'I thank God, through Jesus Christ my Lord.' " In the silence, either shocked or uncomprehending, Andrew wondered why at this moment of all moments he had not resisted the obvious zeugma. He hurried on. "Brother Mordan, this is far too big a question to play textual tennis with. I have not come to my conclusions without long and careful consideration of all the Scriptures involved — very many, such as those in the second chapter of Romans concerning the heathen, or the statement in Revelation that the final judgment is according to the works of those not in Christ, or the tremendous 'Saviour of all men, especially of those who believe' which so-called Fundamentalism uncomfortably overlooks and so-called Modernism seldom knows Scripture well enough to consider. No man believes more firmly than I that there is only one Mediator, that 'no man comes to the Father, but by Him,' that 'there is no other Name under heaven given among men by which we must be saved.' Let us consider your Scriptures together; if you like, I shall preach a series of sermons on them, or give my interpretation for discussion at board meetings. It will be for you to decide. Then, if we do not agree, let us each 'hold fast to that which we have attained' and wait for the Holy Spirit to convince the other."

Mordan's face was impassive, but hesitation betrayed itself in his silence. Then he shook his head and pushed his chair back from the desk.

"You are a very fine expositor, as I've said, Mr. Connington." The changed mode of address struck Andrew coldly. "And I don't profess to be able to argue with you. But there are some things we've got to cling to. Too many people are whittling away at the Faith these days. Mine is pretty simple but it's based on the Word. I remember when I was a boy hearing somebody say, 'A religion without hell isn't worth a damn,' and since we're talking man to man that's my view. And you haven't given an answer to some Scriptures I quoted — especially that one about 'the smoke of their torment goeth up for ever and ever' . . . something about being 'tormented day and night in the presence of the Lamb.' What's the meaning of that?"

But I've said that I believe in all that Scripture lets us know about hell, Andrew had been about to interrupt, but Mordan's manner told him it would be useless. The final challenge roused him. His elder had risen and he rose to face him, praying for the right words.

"Brother Mordan, I've heard you speak with great admiration of John Wesley. He, you remember, was accused by double predestinationists of being a child of the Devil and preaching the Devil's doctrine. When challenged to give the meaning of certain Scriptures he answered in his great sermon on free Grace. 'If I say I know not, you have nothing; for there are many Scriptures the true sense whereof neither you nor I shall know till death is swallowed up in victory. But this I know: it cannot mean that the God of Truth is a liar; let it mean what it will it cannot mean that the Judge of all the earth is unjust.' "

It was no use, he thought in great depression of spirit, when Mordan, after a perfunctory expression of thanks, had taken an evasive leave. Once away from his — Andrew had to admit — compelling presence, Mordan would talk over these heretical views with his wife and their friends who belonged to a strict separatist sect. He would write or telephone to their son, who on a recent visit to his parents had listened to their new minister with the sphinx-like face of a proofreader watching for errata, and given guarded, if not grudging approval, and he would harden in his resolve. When or how it would come — his resignation from the Board, his withdrawal from membership — Andrew did not care to guess. That it would come he was sure. And he was very very tired.

It was a restless tiredness. He did not want to read. He did not want to go home until he was reasonably certain that Evadne would not be up to welcome and question him. Time enough for her to hear, as she certainly would — in a fairly small church every arrival or withdrawal was noticed and he doubted if Mordan would take pains to make his departure inconspicuous. The child would be pained, and loyally furious as Cecily would have been. But Cecily was part of himself. He had been able to keep nothing finally from her except confidences, and she would not have endured it if he had. A daughter was not a wife and it was not fair to let her share his burdens. He was not afraid of meeting John, he thought ruefully. No question of a tête à tête there!

He slipped on his overcoat and passed into the short communicating corridor. After the warmth and glow of his vestry the church, kept at an economical sixty degrees when not in use, was cold and dark; but its dark stillness was welcome. Even without the faint light from street lamps, he could find his way ungroping to his pulpit chair and then, restlessly moving, down to the communion table. There he slumped to his knees and remained, head bowed on his arms, as if he were praying.

"But God only knows if this is prayer," he said aloud after many moments of racing, incoherent, dejected thought, in which again and again he began a petition only to find his mind far away in protest, conversation, argument, reminiscence. Recently, while reading the letters of John Newton, he had been relieved and comforted at that most honest saint's disarming admission of his own frequent inability to concentrate in prayer. Odd, Andrew thought, that such inability increased with age. How sure he had been in the first, astonished flush of conversion, when the sudden wonder had made prayer gratefully effortless, that ability and strength and satisfaction in prayer would grow with experience. As to a point they had. It was perhaps another unforeseen phase of growing old. He had been struck, turning the pages of the hymn book the previous week in search of an elusive verse, to find how many hymn writers, who had seemed ancients in his early days of singing hymns, had died before they reached his present age. Newton himself, Watts, the two Wesleys, were among the great exceptions; Michael Bruce, Toplady, Bishop Heber, Cennick, Herbert, Anstice, Frances Ridley Havergal, Addison, had never faced the passing of middle life and the decline of their powers.

I'm feeling like a commercial for Geritol — have you the Gray Sickness? — he told himself shortly. God forgive me. I'm sorry for myself. I know it. I'm ashamed. Self-pity is despicable, especially in one who has so much to be thankful for. But I'm full of it, wallowing in it. And I don't even know that I want to pull myself out of it or be pulled out of it.

The very statement set his mind at work to find a cause for thankfulness. His knees were making him more conscious of them than of his prayer by this time. So he judged it lawful and expedient to relieve them and ascended the shallow steps to his pulpit again, staring down the shadowed, familiar aisle. The church building surely — if ever a loving people with 'a mind to the work' had built a long-awaited church, his had been that people. Too poor in the depression to do more than patch up the old hall and fit the basement for Sunday School rooms — during the war the young people scattered, and building materials on priority for Wartime Housing — they had immediately after the war contributed magnificently of their share in the general prosperity.

Even this building — his eyes took in its graceful proportions lovingly — had been beyond expectation. Its design and specifications had been the gift of a wealthy architect, one of his uncle's friends, in gratitude for the help Andrew had been able to give his younger son, invalided home from the R.C.A.F. in a desperate state of nerves.

Andrew had preached joyfully in the old, dismal, rudimentary structure; some of his happiest memories were there. But these clean, neo-Classical lines, this artful simplicity of proportion, were a joy to him, and the name which he had suggested when a name was needed for the congregation, and which still caused raised eyebrows among strong Non-Conformists until it was translated, seemed especially appropriate to the new building. He gave thanks for it now.

Far too small — that had been the only disparaging remark audible at its opening. Mr. Connington would need a much larger church than that with the city beginning to creep up around them in the postwar boom. But a seating capacity of three hundred called for more than their property and funds could provide and the present size had proved adequate — almost adequate for their most successful services and far more than sufficient recently for Sunday evenings and for the summer months.

Andrew, in the humility of his evening's disappointment, subjected himself — by no means for the first time — to a merciless review of his failing, in an endeavour to explain the paradox of his career. His Shorncliffe experience had taught him much; but with the response and devotion of a new congregation he had been encouraged to hope for great things — that is, great things in spiritual conquest, great opportunities to exercise his powers of preaching and teaching, which he knew to be

66

mature and remarkable, if not unparalleled, among his contemporaries. Because of the shortage of ministers during the war he had on occasion been asked to preach in other churches of his own and other denominations, and had received calls to several independent congregations. But his own people had needed him. There had been no question in his mind where his duty lay, even though the church was not able to support him, and he had continued to work in Connington Glass, taking over more and more responsibility as men were called into service.

After the war all the contributions of the congregation were put into their new church; so he waived the question of an increase to the pittance they were paying him and, refusing to exist on Mansell's charity, continued to work for him — half-time according to arrangement but in fact almost full-time as orders poured in. It had been arduous, for he refused to deviate from the church program which he considered essential: Sunday morning and evening services, a midweek prayer meeting. He had taught a Bible school class too and had acted as school superintendent after Bill Woodhouse joined the navy. But they had been good years — and he had had Cecily. His work had been her work. The fact that her husband's work was time-consuming did not make her feel neglected; she was far too intimately involved with him in that work. She took on any task he could not perform — any class that needed teaching, any visiting for which he had no time. Her happy gift of seeming at home with every sort of person had gone far to bridge the gulf which might otherwise have existed in his oddly assorted congregation. It had been — still was to a greater extent than most churches — what a Christian church should be: those who had been on the dole and those who lived in comparative affluence, the uneducated and University graduates mingling together in projects and fellowship, as well as in formal worship.

Well — ideally! There were times when all Cecily's tact and all his powerful, pointed expositions from the pulpit could not avoid a rift; and, perhaps inevitably, the hurt feelings or insolence of the poor, rather than the arrogance of the rich, was the more frequent *casus belli*. But she had seen the funny side on occasions when he was sure that his ministry was useless if such stupid controversies could arise in spite of it. With her, nothing had ever been as bad as it sometimes seemed to him. The fire through which she had passed during their estrangement had prevented lesser flames from scorching. They licked lambent around her and irradiated.

But she was not with him now. What *fools* they are, he thought savagely, reverting to his conversation with Evadne, who liken the living Presence of Christ with His own to the mixture of vivid recollection, yearning, and self-projection which they call the 'presence' with them of their beloved dead.

"Dear Lord," he said aloud, "if Thy Presence were no more real to me than my Cecily's — and I know by Thy grace I shall be with her again — I should be of all men most miserable. Thanks for not removing the sense of Thy Presence from me. I am grateful, Thou knowest. But, O my Lord, sometimes I miss her so."

Self-pity again, he rebuked himself. The number of men, the vast majority he sometimes pessimistically thought, who had never known even the shadow of which Cecily and he had enjoyed the substance! It was not the clean wound of her taking, not the constant sense of loss nor 'the pain that was almost a pleasure' of yearning recollection. For these as for his other needs, the tired, frantic urges of his body, the desperate dearth of mental energy, the apparently insoluble problems of others, he had proved Christ sufficient. What was depressing him now, with a depression which came with increasing, vitality-sapping frequency, was his sense of personal failure and the consequent unsparing self-examination, the effort to shred off all self-justification and see: not why things happened as they did — his diagnosis was pitilessly clear — but how and where he could have acted differently, to what extent he had been at fault.

Lack of success in the sense of a numerically large and influential ministry was not personally distressing. His ambition had been surrendered to his Lord's will many years before. If that Lord mysteriously willed him to comparative obscurity, he was not rebellious. In his more elated moments he could rejoice at being in high company — for his reading of source history showed him the essential loneliness and discouragement and unpopularity, the long periods of apparent failure, of most of the spiritual giants, and he was wryly amused by the easy success stories into which their lives are turned by modern biographers, who try to inspire, but rather drive to near despair those who would emulate such heroes.

Yet the paradox remained — a puzzle to his friends, a deterrent to many admirers. Large churches all over the city and its suburbs boasted congregations of two thousand and more. These churches were glad to call to their pulpits ministers whose sermons their most loyal adherents found indifferent. Popular preachers who drew crowds like those he had once attracted to Shorncliffe were too few to be numbered on the fingers of one hand. And none of them had to the same degree his gift of welding intellectual content and Scriptural exegesis with passionate personal conviction, of making the Bible vivid, as one erstwhile sceptical University student had told him, so that characters in Old and New Testament were "like a group of statues suddenly infused with life and the power of communication."

More and more newspapers and magazines flaunted articles about the failure of the Church to appeal to the intellectual. Ad nauseam the cry went up against "obsolete theological concepts which could not be made acceptable to the Man of the Future." Andrew detested that phrase, suggesting as it did a strange, putative mixture of robot and artificially produced genitals, as popular in journalism as the Loch Ness monster and far less probable. Anxious church leaders held endless workshops and retreats, produced religious curricula to meet the new questions young people were asking about the Bible. New, snorted Andrew! Most of them know too little of the Bible even to ask the old; and for unreasoning gullibility, avid to quote any crackpot without checking the information and unwilling to do any honest research on the matter of his "intellectual doubts," give me the modern young sceptic — that goes for the older generation of sceptic as well.

And here he was, at the height of his powers as preacher and teacher — Dr. Dick Williams home from India on a rare furlough, Bill Woodhouse visiting Toronto the previous year, were unanimous that his ministry had greatly increased in depth and breadth and warmth since their first experience of it — yet here he was, passed over now even as a guest preacher, continuing for almost a quarter of a century with a congregation which held its own numerically, but scarcely more, and for whose basic loyalty, since without it he had no prospect of another, he found himself whimsically and humbly grateful.

It was his own fault he supposed. But how could one correct a fault so based in one's own integrity that correction would be betrayal? As in tonight's dispute! He had tried to be conciliatory. He could not lie about his beliefs, could not use double-talk to conceal them, even if anything less than a public avowal of Mordan's cherished doctrine would have satisfied him. Odd, how unwilling he and his kind were to learn that Scripture was greater than their school of theology. Andrew recalled the unspeakable soaring of his spirit when he realized that the tepid phrase "the immortality of the soul" had no basis in Christian theology and when, in consequence, the whole teaching of Scripture on sin and its consequence, just, awful, absolute, fell into place with the infinite, cosmic miracle of Redemption.

Still there it was! Why was he the inevitable square peg, doomed to fit no hole except the small precarious one of his own boring? That his so-called 'Fundamentalism' made him obnoxious to the so-called Liberals — whom he had found a little less than liberal to any thinking but their own current views — he could realize. It had been more of a shock to find that he was equally suspect among Fundamentalists. And with the latter there had been a succession of shocks. Liberalism was an amorphous, eclectic system united only, it sometimes appeared, in its scornful incredulity at the thought of a literal great fish swallowing a literal Jonah; but each branch of Fundamentalism had its special taboo, its special fetish, and, agree with it in essentials though he might, disagreement on the taboo ranked him as heretic.

The unfair — no there was self-pity again — the *humorous* feature of his isolation was that he was suspect in all quarters as a speckled bird — Newton's pet phrase had been a comfort to him; amazing how, in the communion of saints, one clasped hands with another across time and space — whereas he aimed at union and, to the best of his ability, practised it. Not the least evidence of grace at work within him had been this gradual breaking down of prejudice, a growing willingness, the result of deliberate willing, to concede liberty of opinion on questions which were unquestionably decided in his own mind. The Absolute Deity of Christ he believed to be the minimum of Christian faith; yet he refused to condemn any man who called Jesus Lord and claimed His power at work within him. He exposed inconsistencies and proclaimed the faith with stringent logic from the pulpit, but refused to be drawn into divisive controversy in private.

And with what result? he asked himself moodily as the chilled air roused him from the pulpit chair and drove him into the clean, biting cold of the February night. For a few moments the ominous sluggishness of the motor kept the question repeating itself in crazy rhythm. Then with a reassuring roar the car started up and the endless interrogation varied. Why was his deviation alone intolerable when all other deviations were allowed? What was his singular aptitude for attacking the sacrosanct cow? To judge by the quoted comments of prominent clergy and laymen, to judge by journalistic column, novels, and essays, St. Paul could be stripped of every vestige of sanity, intelligence and the misnamed charity of which his description was the apogee; the man after God's own heart could be reduced to an upstart brigand, his adultery the only adultery decried by an increasingly adulterous society; any great man or woman of history could be gleefully muckraked; Jesus Christ himself could be accused of childish rage, limited insight, psychopathic egotism and — all Andrew's familiarity with the suggestion could not suppress a shiver of horror whenever it recurred — homosexuality; and these views met a wide, smiling complaisance, a head-nodding consideration. But let anyone

71

suggest that Albert Schweitzer was not a cross between a reincarnation of Messiah and Einstein, and the religious world — not only the Liberal religious world — joined in shocked vituperation. Andrew had found this out when, as one member of a panel at a college forum, he had answered a specific question by expressing some doubt that the publicized doctor's "reverence for life" was the greatest concept of the century. In reply to further questioning he had stated his reasoned conviction that Schweitzer, judged by his own published statements, was not, in the historic sense of the word, a Christian. Schweitzer's later identification with Unitarianism had amply justified the comment, but the press, which had for years ignored Andrew's existence, gave disproportionate publicity to these remarks. In the ensuing conflict of reports and letters to the paper, his early career and the Shorncliffe controversy were reviewed and distorted, apparently with the object of showing the evidences of former depravity predictive of this nadir. Andrew had resisted his natural prompting and his friend's urging to reply. Several letters had been written in his defence and the matter had died down.

One result there had been. For the first time John, then sixteen, had become conscious of his father as a controversial figure. Cecily, whom he questioned, had explained Andrew's departure from Shorncliffe Church, championing him as ardently as though she had never opposed him. But he wondered if the boy had really been satisfied or simply silenced by the adult assumption, in which Uncle George and Aunt Alex had joined, that his father must be right. It had not been easy for a schoolboy to see in print, and know that his fellows were seeing, his father's name tossed about from heavy jest to virtuous opprobrium.

Well, I seem to ask for it, he sighed, roused by an indignant horn behind him to the realization that the light ahead had turned green. And yet I never do ask. Always it seems to be wished on me. As if by an ironic — he caught back the phrase unfinished. Nice statement for a man who quoted,

"My times are in Thy hand;
My God, I wish them there."

But my conclusion regarding baptism for instance. How completely undesigned and unwanted — and how far-reaching in consequence.

It had come about towards the end of the war. He was teaching the combined Young Men's and Young Women's classes — designations now out-of-date in the postwar reduction of adult Sunday School attendance — and one of the girls had lingered after the hour to speak to him. She had never asked any question before and her request surprised him.

"Mr. Connington, will you teach us a lesson next Sunday on baptism?"

She had been working in an office, he discovered, with several earnest Baptists and had found herself unable to meet their arguments. Andrew, generally acquainted with the history of the vexed question, had been so constantly occupied since his conversion with matters which seemed to him more pressing, both in theology and practice, that he had never considered deviation from the Church of his forbears and of his adoption. Whenever the Scriptures had seemed to bear out the claims of the immersionists, he had been offended by their divisiveness, their overemphasis, he felt, on the physical element of the ordinance. He had noted the inconsistency of their praise for Luther, Calvin, Wesley, Whitefield, and Newton, when a considerable section would bar from the Lord's Table these very saints whose hymns they sang and whose sermons they quoted. And though there had been no conscious struggle, his unworded decision had been that he preferred to be "wrong with Plato than right with Aristotle."

Now faced with the need to justify his position, he had flung himself, wholeheartedly as usual, into an effort at unbiased appraisal. All the pertinent Scriptures, the accounts of early Church practice, the evidence of the large baptistries in primitive church buildings, the polemics and apologies from paedo-baptists and adult-immersionists — all came under his close, objective consideration. To his astonishment he discovered that few, if any, modern scholars from Oscar Cullmann to Karl Barth disputed the fact that immersion was the practice of the primitive Church. Still more to his astonishment, he found himself unable to identify with infant sprinkling, the Biblical teaching on baptism; unable to avoid the conclusion that the christening ceremony was a combination of the Hebrew presentation of children with the pagan Roman lustratio — and its practice among Protestants a survival of *ex opere operato* superstition.

"So what do I do now?" he had asked Cecily plaintively, when his research had stretched the requested lesson into a series of lessons, and the class, fascinated and a bit dazed, had been left in no doubt concerning his conclusions.

"Is that a question?" Cecily had inquired resignedly.

"No. No, I suppose it isn't. I can't believe as I do and not let the congregation know, Cecily. Even if the class did not know already."

"*You* can't. I quite agree."

"And approve? You haven't disagreed with any of my arguments, darling."

"I've tried," she said ruefully, "but, Andrew, is it so awfully important? I mean, think of the smug spiritual ignoramuses we have met — no, I'm not referring to Baptists at large! — but to the individuals who, by virtue of the one act of immersion, call people like you — all right, *and* John Wesley — disobedient believers. Think of the great men and women who haven't . . . ."

"I do. And the thought of it has kept me from considering the question seriously before. And I believe has kept untold numbers from undergoing baptism. I'm amazed at the uneasy conscience that exists on the subject. But I cannot excuse myself from continuing in what I believe to be non-Scriptural practice . . . or from telling my people where I stand."

So he had told them, as she had known he would do. Simply and more winningly than she had ever heard him speak, he had told of his quest, the occasion for it, his effort to lay aside all prejudices, and his final conviction.

"If I required additional proof that this is according to

Scripture," he had admitted frankly, "I should find it in the repugnance with which I have viewed the rite, the fierceness of opposition which I found in my heart and mind against it, even while I was being inexorably convinced. Hardly any other question has so divided sincere Christians — and the faults have often been on the side which I now consider theologically correct."

He was not, he had told them, willing to join in this divisiveness. Quoting John Bunyan, he refused to allow "water baptism" to be a bar to the Communion of believers. He would not wish to baptize any who were not convinced by the Holy Spirit that it was God's will for them. Nor would he be a party to any attitude of superiority, or of regarding as unspiritual Christians those who, with minds open on the question, were not so convinced. Infant sprinkling, he now realized, he had long regarded as a dedication ceremony, and he challenged them to ask themselves whether they regarded it as more than that. Did they actually believe that the unconscious baby was saved by the act? Or lost if it was not performed? Or made a member of the Church in later life by it, apart from personal conversion? He would continue to dedicate children without sprinkling, on the clear understanding that it did not signify baptism. If the parents, knowing his mind, wished for water, he would, while making his position clear to the congregation, comply with their request (Cecily had been inordinately amused by this proviso which had never been tested). If the church disapproved of his stand — the practice of immersing the adult or at least the responsible and requesting believer, the acceptance into membership of other Christians whatever their mode of baptism — then he would willingly resign his ministry.

The congregation, which was essentially united by that• ministry, had proved open to the new teaching. After discussing the question and some of its implications at several meetings, they had been moved, both by his reasoning and by his refusal to make it a matter of controversy, and had, without audible opposition, declared in its favour. Some, silently disapproving, had drifted elsewhere; some, reared in Baptist circles and drawn by his ministry, had taken their place. When the new church was built, a cruciform baptistry, copied from that of a third-century church in Rhodes, had been incorporated into the classical design of the chancel. And there, to their distress and disapproval, the visiting officials of the United Church had discovered it.

Andrew Connington's ejection from one of the large and fashionable churches of Toronto had been regarded by the conference as a private — and deplorable — squabble between himself and his session. The circumstances which had led to that end, duly embroidered and distorted, had not inclined the session of any other city church to offer him its pastorate. When, in the heart of the depression, he began a struggling work in an impoverished outlying suburb, there had been no interest shown in it and no money available to establish it as a mission church. Yet the Conningtons, though denomination meant nothing to Andrew, thought of themselves as United Church members. When hymn books were needed, they had been United Church hymn books and the order of service had varied little from simple United Church procedure.

Cecily, particularly, had hoped that their church would ultimately be recognized by the parent body. They both realized the disadvantages of complete isolation; and no other church with which they could seek alliance had fewer positive divergences; if the theological basis of the United Church was diluted, it was at least capable of sound interpretation. If the Apostles' Creed, found in the Book of Common Order and in the hymn book alike, was believed in its entirety by a minority of the laymen and a smaller minority of the clergy, it was still there: primitive, Scriptural, splendid, pregnant. Reform from within, rather than schism, thought Andrew, not blind to the fate — and the subsequent charge of schism — of many reformers so minded.

So when the postwar building boom sent fingers of housing development west, north, and east of Toronto's broad palm, and when large denominations and smaller scattered sects began to stake their claims for church property, it did not

escape the notice of the United Church that a small but distinguished-looking building was already established in a rapidly
expanding district under one of their own clergy. The advantages were equally apparent to Andrew; but negotiations,
proceeding pleasantly, were suddenly brought up short when
his practice regarding baptism was disclosed.

It was then that Andrew learned the relative importance
to the officials of an organized denomination, of ritual and
belief.

He could apparently have believed and preached any doctrine from Karma to Mariolatry. He could have denied — it was
fashionable to deny — the inspiration of Scripture, the depravity
of man, the virgin birth, miracles, atonement, and resurrection
of Christ, the need of forgiveness for sin, the resurrection of
the body, and the life (at least the individual, personal life)
everlasting. In such case he would have been excused or praised
for the honesty of his views, the fearlessness of his speech, his
unwillingness to be bound by outmoded concepts. But to practise the form of baptism which the United Church's own committee on the subject had recently admitted to be Scriptural:
this was intolerable. He pointed out that, according to the United
Church rubric, baptism could be administered by sprinkling,
pouring, or immersion. He referred to the protests of many
colleagues required to "do" the babies of completely indifferent,
non-church-going parents, as a half-social, half-magical routine.
In vain. A desirable site was presently purchased some two
blocks north of Eucharist Church and a retired minister, with
the reputation of being a good organizer, was appointed to
visit and gather together the United Church families in the
district.

Well, that had been that. The nucleus of his own congregation had been unaffected, but the pull of denominational
loyalty and respectability had drawn most of the new families
who otherwise might have joined him. Presbyterians, Anglicans,
Baptists had already provided for their adherents. The disadvantages of an independent church became more apparent as

77

opportunities of employment took many of his most dependable members from the district and from the city.

Again he was at fault — the square peg, he told himself as he inserted his key in the front-door lock and gave just the right extra pressure and pull necessary to release the catch. The action was so automatic that his thoughts flowed on without check. Some men built an enormous congregation without affiliations — the Democratic Tabernacle was one example, the Bible Church for Everyone, another. But he could not use their methods. He was temperamentally incapable even if he had approved them. To preach the Gospel so that lives exemplifying it were built on the teaching of Scripture: that was his calling. These churches went from planned Revival (foretold on large banners, though how one could announce a revival and set dates for its duration was a mystery to him) to Mammoth Missionary Campaigns. Their services were introduced and interspersed by singspirations, where sentimental lyrics, often untrue and set to cheap music, were sung, hummed, whistled, and variegated under prancing leaders, who might be consecrated in their gyrations but who would certainly have astounded St. Paul and brought severe strictures from John Wesley. Instrumental music rather than the preached Word was the chief feature, if one could judge by newspaper advertisements of musical sawyers, electric guitarists, trumpet trios, and saxophonists, pictured with happy grins and sombreros or six-gallon hats. The pastors of such churches preached in them comparatively seldom. Every Sunday some "internationally famous" visitor, usually from the United States, some missionary to a foreign country, some youthful convert from the stage or television ("Hap Day of 'Happy Time Breakfast Hour,' now Happy in the Lord") witnessed and challenged. The Signs of the Times and the Imminent Second Coming of Christ were favorite topics. Andrew knew the long history of antichrists — in modern times from Napoleon to Mussolini — all numerically satisfying the required 666, each one quietly yielding place to the next. He wondered equally at the courage with which men publicly predicted the date of the Coming and at the conveniently

78

short memories of their hearers, once the deadline was passed. But that Coming Disaster loomed large as an attraction he knew. "I'm saved, so I don't need the Bible," one of Evadne's college classmates, member of an extreme premillenarian school, had told her. "I like to hear the terrific things that are going to happen in the near future." During the week, the Young People were kept busy with films, witness meetings, chorus singing, and an opportunity to work off youthful social energies in unworldly surroundings. Numbers were important. Keen rivalry existed, Andrew knew, between the two largest groups, and bitter was the cup of the official Youth Activity leader who found his group thinning to the rival's expansion.

Andrew Connington had examined his attitude on every feature of this religious extravaganza to decide if his revulsion was due to natural, unsanctified pride. Rather, he was convinced that such methods dishonoured God, although they were used by many sincere and devoted Christians. He knew that it had occasioned criticism among new members with an evangelistic background, that he did not give the "Altar Call" after his services. Apart from the misnomer of "Altar Call" in churches which deliberately had no altar, Andrew found no basis in Scripture for the mingling of cajolery, threatening, pleading, and often despairing compromise — "No one is looking. If you wish us to pray for you, hold up your hand"; becoming finally: "All who wish to rededicate yourselves hold up your hands" — into which this conventional appeal usually degenerated. To him it constituted a denial of faith in the work of the Holy Spirit. Only a few times in his entire ministry, believing himself especially impelled by that Spirit, had he employed it.

And not on every one of those occasions did You show me the reason, Lord. I had to take it on faith. He realized that he had been staring at the twelfth chapter of Hebrews without reading a word. He gave it up and switched off the bed lamp. Even as I have to take tonight's fiasco on faith, and hope, if Mordan is wrong, that You will show him, as I failed to do.

79

4

ANDREW HAD COMPLETED his Scripture reading and given out the second hymn. The fine electric organ, which had been Mansell's gift, swelled through the church — it does sound like a pipe organ; that ad doesn't lie, he said to himself, and noticed that an usher was showing a late comer into a pew halfway up the aisle. She was a stranger, he thought at first, and was pleased that his congregation did not betray by a turned head or a craning neck their awareness of her arrival. Not that strangers were unusual at his services; but the single, very late entrance of as striking a stranger as this would in the early days have diverted attention from any part of the service. Was she a stranger though? The early April sun slanted across his face in the pulpit as he rose to sing, but not before he had solved the puzzle of her vague familiarity. Then the service claimed him, and the small, pleasurable feeling of recognition gave way to a total involvement in his work. If it were not for this — this "transport all divine" which seldom failed to possess him in prayer and in preaching — he would have given up long before.

"I'm terribly ashamed of coming so disgracefully late." Beth Harris-Kemp greeted him at the door. She had remained quietly in the pew until the church was almost empty and they were free to talk. "I thought I knew your church, but a half dozen others have gone up since I went away and by the time I walked two blocks from my car and found the wrong building — well, at any rate you see that I wanted to hear you again."

"It has been some time," agreed Andrew. "Did you get my letter?"

"Your letter?"

He frowned in an effort at recollection.

"Surely I wrote. I had every intention of writing. Don't tell me I'm senile enough to take the intention for the deed. I can remember wondering about your address and intending to send it care of Easton's firm. He was your lawyer too, wasn't he? Well, apparently I didn't."

"I'm glad you had the thought anyhow." She made a gesture towards the front of the church and pulled her furs closer around her shoulders. "This April air can be dashed chilly after the Mediterranean. Are you rushing somewhere? I'd like to talk for a bit."

"Excuse me while I tell John to drive the others home. That is, if I may trouble you for a lift?"

She accompanied him to the vestry and wandered casually around it while he removed and hung up his gown. Her unneeded furs dropped until they fell carelessly on either side of one arm to the floor like draperies on the Praxiteles' *Hermes*. Russian sables and a fantastic price — Evadne had pointed some out with a sigh of mock yearning one evening at the symphony. He was again glad that the women in church had not allowed their attention to be distracted. The haute couture lines of her beige woollen dress revealed a figure still girlish. She had looked older than he when they last met. Since then, time seemd to have spared her its devastation and she would now pass as the younger. She smiled directly at him and her brown eyes were soft with recollection.

"This reminds me. Do you remember the first time — no, the only other time — I visited a vestry of yours?"

"It isn't the sort of thing one forgets."

"*You* might. I couldn't. After all, my whole life was altered from that day."

"If experiences of that sort were common enough to be forgettable, I'd be a happier man — an even happier man," he corrected. "Len spoke of you constantly. I think you restored

81

his faith in mankind — or rather, and more to the point, in God."

"If not in Uncle Ben! You were the one who might have lost faith. But you've never let yourself get calloused, have you? Oh I've heard a good deal by the grapevine. Yet, you know, I was almost afraid to come today for fear you might have — how shall I put it — professionalized?"

"Don't," he pleaded. "That sounds so 'finalized.' "

She laughed and he relaxed comfortably, conscious that he could relax with few people as easily.

"Look, I mustn't keep you from your family. Sunday is your busy day. Or should I say your busiest? But I wanted to ask you — may I join your church?"

Andrew paused in the act of pulling on his coat and turned to stare.

"I know. It must come as a bit of a shock. After all these years. I was going to wait until I had come a bit oftener. But I really have waited a long time. Life's too short to put things off. So may I? Unless there is a probation period?"

"Not that. But I think you should wait until you know a bit more about us. We are not a fashionable church."

"Andrew Connington, do you think that after our family's connection with Shorncliffe, I could imagine you building a fashionable church? Do give me credit for a little intelligence."

"Sorry." He held open the door of her low-slung Mercedes Benz and let himself cautiously in beside her. "I'm not used to these rush tactics. Candidates usually take some time to decide and more don't go through with it than do."

"Do you mean baptism? Yes, I heard about that. My spies are everywhere."

"They must be. No. Baptism must be a question of personal conviction. And your spies will have told you that it is not a condition of membership. Not, I think, in any of our churches."

"You have some affiliation then?"

"Yes. Not easy to come by under the circumstances."

"Do tell me."

"It's a genuine ecumenical venture. A small group exists, simply designated as Scripture Churches — I did not choose the title — independent congregations from various denominational backgrounds. They allow considerable latitude of constitution but have a basic orthodox creed."

"How does it work with your church — practically, I mean?"

"Satisfactorily, I think. It cuts down our sense of exclusiveness, and the diversity broadens our Christian charity. I was suspect for awhile when they discovered that I use the Revised Standard Version."

"Is that why your Scripture reading is always so striking? I remember from away back."

"Away back would be the American Revised. I think I have convinced them by now that adherence to the King James translation is not an article of the Creed. But you were asking —?"

"How to join your church."

"Naturally I expect a confession of faith. But I think we covered that years ago and I'm sure you would tell me if you had changed. It's just —"

"Just that I've lived in Toronto both while you were at Shorncliffe and since you began this work, and never showed any interest in membership before."

"I couldn't have put it more concisely," said Andrew.

She glanced swiftly at him, then, to his relief for the Sunday traffic was thickening, back at the road.

"Look, you'll have to take my word for it. I would have joined years ago. You could have done with some help and encouragement in the early days. And I feel like a piker — wasn't it Chesterfield who decided to patronize Johnson after the *Dictionary* was a success?"

"I doubt if my church is such a *fait accompli* even now."

"Then I may not be too late to be of some use. But let's be frank. I'd have had to join alone. Roger would go with me to Merridale though he didn't seem to get much out of it. But he was a Presbyterian and, if he gave the matter any thought, he took for granted that God was too. He came with me a few times to hear you at Shorncliffe but ——"

"He didn't like me?"

"No — No. I wouldn't say that."

"I should," said Andrew smiling. "Why, Beth? I've often wondered, and wondered where the fault lay. I'm not flattering myself, but I don't think that my preaching is effeminate."

"To say the least."

"Yet, although I have a decent number of men in the congregation and some youngsters bring their University friends so that we have a fair proportion of students, women are by far my most stable supporters. Can you shed any light on it?"

"Not without sounding fulsome! I think I can, in Roger's case at least. For some reason you make men uncomfortable — unless they let themselves go completely. I suppose *you'd* say unless the Holy Spirit thoroughly converts them. They don't mind a minister being competent in his own line. They rather like to patronize him as an unworldly dependent. Or they like to be pally with him, initiate him into their lodge, give him a tip on investments. You don't fall into any such category. You know your way around. You're a splendid preacher — they admit that — but your preaching has always been pretty hard to take and stay put. And — we have to face it — men are the great conformists today. Women are bad enough, but ask any school teacher who tries to interest youngsters in a new idea. Girls will come out on their own. Boys won't be found dead at a club unless at least six others are found dead too. Or haven't you found that out with your own youngsters?"

"Enlightening," said Andrew, avoiding a discussion of his offspring.

"Well, I digress. You know about Roger. The doctors said that change and a better climate might prolong his life. So we had two years, drifting from the Pacific Islands and the West Indies to Spain and through the Mediterranean. He died in Italy thirteen months ago. By that time I was caught up in some work for the Save the Children Fund and it seemed a good idea to go on with it. But there is a lot of detail to be settled here and for the time being I was tired of travelling. So I arrived in Toronto Wednesday and here I am."

She waited for comment.

"Look," she began again, the childish injunction at odds

84

with her worldly-wise assurance, "I've thought this over well. I don't want the ordinary church with its round of bazaars and women's meetings and fund-raising projects. I've had enough social life for twenty in my time. A good deal of it was involved with Roger and the business and the family. I felt I was being a good wife. But that's over now. The youngsters don't need me. I'm a grandmother five times over, yet! I need your preaching — and teaching too. I've had far too little of it or of preaching like it. Social welfare work is all right but I need food for the soul. And my best intentions to get it from the Bible myself can do with some prodding. I taught a class years ago. I'd be glad, if you think I'm capable, to teach one here or do any other work that offers. But it's no charity offer. I need your church. I need what I heard and felt and saw this morning. Will you let me in?"

She swung the car into the Mansell drive and spoke again.

"Don't say now. I shall be out tonight. That's another point. Merridale has given up its evening service. Not that I wonder. We hardly ever attended it ourselves except when Roger was officiating as usher. I think the session voted it out so their nonattendance wouldn't be on their conscience. I remember you on one-service-a-day Christians. Will your conscience take the strain of forcing me to become one?"

"I don't suppose you asked her where she bought her dress. Rome, I suspect," ventured Evadne, when he had satisfied his family's reasonable curosity. "Or how much those sables cost. Sitting in the choir has one advantage. I can take in something like that without disgracing my father." She jumped up and touched him on the shoulder as she went to the sideboard. "Don't take me seriously, Daddy. I heard every word and it was very good. But what a text: 'the lust of the flesh, the lust of the eyes, and the pride of life'! She must have found it a dilly. Which category do sables come under?"

"I imagine they were a gift from her husband." Andrew felt he should give Beth the benefit of the doubt.

"She's married, is she? I thought you said . . . ." It was John's first question.

"Her late husband. He died a few months ago. And, Vad, I have enough trouble putting my own worldliness into proper categories without acting as guardian for others."

"How old did you say she was, Dad?"

"I don't think I said. She was at college about my time. My age — a year or two either way."

"Cripes! She certainly doesn't look it."

"How tactful can you get, John?" said Evadne rebukingly. "He just meant for a *woman*, Daddy. Well-preserved is the term. Is her hair natural?"

"Our conversation lacked an opening for that question," returned Andrew. "You are the family judge in such matters."

"I'd say yes, though I'd need a closer look. Dark hair looks so hard when it's touched up. But I couldn't see *any* gray. Maybe they have a better method in Europe."

"Why not ask her? You believe in direct speech."

"Are we likely to see her again?" — quickly from John.

"She said she'd be out tonight. But people have very often said that and not appeared for months if ever. Ask her too, Vad, if she felt any warmth about the ears from" — he glanced at his watch — "one-thirty on. No, I'm off coffee at lunch. You going, John?"

"Yes, Sir. I'll probably miss supper. But I'll see you at church." There was a touch of unnecessary defiance in John's voice. "Thanks for the car, Aunt Alex."

"Unless I am much mistaken," said Mrs. Mansell with one of her surprising incursions into the contemporary scene, as if a conservative turtle popped its head out to make an observation on current events, "our John is interested in another young lady." Aunt Alex had despised the expression "girl friend" for thirty years and refused to use it now, although she would have been the first to admit that the term lady was seldom applicable. "Do you know who she is, Evadne?"

Andrew at the dining room door waited for her answer.

"No. I wish I did. This shift of the research lab to the

sticks has moved him from my watchful eye. Heidi saw them on Bloor one evening but she was dashing for the subway and didn't get a good look. I think it must be someone he works with because he never calls her in the evening and it's been on since he came back from the field trip."

"Marvellous, Mr. Holmes," said Andrew with a lightness that he assumed to hide his deep concern in whatever involved John. "I hope you are going to work along with the Yard in this."

"My poor abilities are at your disposal," said Evadne joining him on the stairs. "It's a man's world though, isn't it? Fat chance I'd have of hiding any new attachment. I have to bring them home for your inspection, have them call for me ——"

"I hope so. The day any daughter of mine meets a man on the corner for a date to save the blighter the trouble of calling for her ——"

"Right, right. You went away up to North Toronto every time you took Mother out in the evening. But where the Ridouts lived is practically mid-town now. By the time a comparative stranger comes in from Port Credit to our place to take me to The Royal —"

"He could stay down and work in the Library till it was time to pick you up," said Andrew. "Darling, do you think I'm unreasonable? I just feel that you are worth a bit of effort. But I'd hate you to feel that I'm cramping your style."

"You are rather — in more ways than one." Evadne gave him a swift hug. "And it isn't reasonable in a way — at least as things go now. Only somehow I think you're *right*. So if the young man — to quote Aunt Alex — is put off, I'll just know he isn't worthy of me! But about John. If I know the signs, he's involved again all right. Only he doesn't seem happy about it. I wonder why. And why does he go to her place — if he does — on Sunday and not bring her to church? I hope she isn't another Julie."

"If you care to hear the comment of Christian experience" — Evadne wished that other people, including herself, referred to Christian experience with such unembarrassed naturalness, such assumption of its supreme and everyday relevance — "let me go

87

on record as saying that in things good, fulfilment always exceeds anticipation (and you seldom hear that from the 'natural man') and that in things bad, it usually falls very far short. So take my advice and don't worry." And, he thought wryly, I'll try to take it myself.

His words were proving true in the matter of Henry Mordan's departure from the Board and congregation. With his recollection of the unpleasantness fomented by Dr. Williams' exit from Shorncliffe, he had been unduly apprehensive. This situation differed in two respects. Apart from honest horror at his pastor's heresy, Mr. Mordan was not eager to have him ousted from the pastorate and be obliged to remain in the church himself. Andrew's preaching had been the main attraction to Eucharist Church and now that he knew the city, there were other congregations in which he felt more at home.

The other factor, on which Andrew had been afraid to rely, was the loyalty of his board and of the church as a whole. Mordan's decision to "come out and be separate" did not free him from the duty of making his reasons known in private to his fellow members in the church, particularly to special friends. This he had done with suitable reluctance but so thoroughly that by the time his official letter was read before the board — its regular meeting had been postponed until April because of Passion Week services — it had no shock value. The ten men and two women sitting around the long table were silent briefly after the secretary finished his reading, but the silence was one of discomfort for their pastor rather than of disapproval. Then the chairman, the boy whom he had saved from drowning at the first Sunday School picnic, now a dentist, looked down the table at him and smiled.

"I guess it's no secret, Pastor, that we've heard all this before tonight. And we're unanimous in a vote of confidence — if that's the way to put it. As to whether you want to say anything on the matter, so that we will have it first hand if we are asked any questions — that's entirely up to you. We doubt," he added with jocularity which fell flat because of the earnestness behind it, "if after what we've heard from you all these years, we'll be damned by listening to you, now."

Andrew began to speak and found that he could not. His British reserve, which could remain outwardly unmoved by any amount of opposition, always crumbled under kindness.

"Thank you," he said after a moment. "Thank you. As I promised our ex-member when he came to discuss with me the point at issue, I purpose presenting the Scriptures involved to the congregation in a series of Sunday morning sermons. There is nothing that I have deliberately concealed from you. I do not assert that our brother is wrong and that I am right. But I cannot claim to be 'wise above what is written.' I dare not, against my conscience, make declarations which I find incompatible with the God of the Bible, the God and Father of our Lord Jesus Christ. You have all heard me decry the popular presentation of God as a weakling to be outraged with impunity, and of man as sickly, wistful, without responsibility for his choices and decisions. You have heard me preach of the God of love who is also the God of holiness and justice — of the impossibility of sinners' dwelling with the everlasting burnings. That there is judgment I believe. That the judgment is awful as the Scriptures proclaim it, I know. Only through Christ is there freedom from judgment and only in Christ is there knowledge of that freedom. But the duration, the mode, the recipients, the conditions of that judgment are not revealed to me. I will not preach Dante's *Inferno* as inspired revelation and, as George Macdonald puts it, 'speak unworthily of God.' "

He sat down. He could not remember rising. Then Jack Dillon, the secretary, cleared his throat. He was a young man, married but unemployed when the church began. Andrew had driven him twice a week to night school to complete his matriculation, and he had obtained an elementary teacher's certificate after the war.

"I don't think any of us feels competent to argue with you, Pastor. And if Henry Mordan did, he would be here. But that isn't the point. You don't want us to accept anything on your say-so — you've told us that dozens of times. And I've got into

89

the habit — you shamed me once by asking me if I did — of going home and checking over the portion that you've been preaching from, to see if what you said agreed. And I've never caught you out — to say nothing of what I never would have got from the passage on my own. But I'll say one thing. I haven't heard many preachers besides you, but when I was in the services I heard one or two of these chaps who seem to gloat over what they call judgment. And I always came away mad clear through. It's your sermons on the forgiveness and love of God that knock all the props from under me. One on Hosea I particularly recall". — his voice changed suddenly — "so what do you say, Mr. Chairman? Shall we proceed to other business?"

It was the longest speech Andrew had ever heard him make and he was touched by it — particularly by the reference to Hosea. Rene Dillon, a pretty girl in her teens when he first knew her, had gone into canteen work during her husband's absence overseas and for the first time had money to spend on clothes and gaiety. The result, an affair with a Norwegian airman, had left her to face Jack's return with a fifteen-months-old baby in addition to their two children. She had returned to the church penitent and afraid. Since she would not write, Andrew had been willing, if reluctant, to shoulder the painful task of breaking the news; but she had begged him not to do it until Jack came home. Dillon had come unexpectedly while Andrew was out of town. Cecily, who accompanied the frightened young mother to the station, had given him an account of the meeting.

"Why she insisted on taking all the children I'll never know, Andrew, but she did. Perhaps she was afraid to tell him in private. Anyhow, as soon as he saw her in the crowd at the barriers, he came dashing over. He kissed her, and picked up Bonnie and Jackie and hugged them. Then he went off around the barrier with his bag and met us again. He noticed me, asked about you, and went back to the family. Then for the first time he saw Meryl. You know what a fair little thing she is. She stood there holding Bonnie's hand, staring up at him and he looked over his shoulder at Rene and asked who it was. Talk about drama! I never want to go through another moment like that.

Rene looked as if she could die but managed to whisper, 'It's our daughter, Jack' — which was, to say the least, a euphemism. O Andrew, there must have been joy in heaven over Jack today. He looked at Rene — you know how crazy he always was about her and what a miserable time he felt she had when he was out of work — and just got it — like that! Then he got down on one knee and held out his arms. "Come to Daddy, Baby," he said. That was where I left." Cecily was crying by this time, Andrew remembered, and he had not blamed her. Another Ebenezer.

5

VERONICA LYNCH, whose acquaintance they did not make until two months later at the graduation ceremony at which John received his M. A., could scarcely have been less like Julie Logan. Julie had been dominant and assertive; this girl was almost colorless in self-effacement. Julie had been blonde and tall; Veronica was a small, softly curved redhead, with no indication of the pyrrhic temperament. Julie had aired her scholastic prowess; Veronica — Evadne had been right in her guess — was doing subordinate work in the lab and taking courses at night for a pass degree. Julie had been publicly possessive, alternately teasing and criticizing; Veronica, irreproachably ladylike, listened quietly to conversation in which she took no voluntary part, responding, when John looked at her, only with a faintly secretive smile which made Evadne, who took an instant and illogical dislike to her, want to stamp on her very small and pretty foot.

"She has a fishy handshake," she said firmly, when John and Veronica had gone off to procure refreshments. "I never trust people with fishy handshakes."

"Look here, Vad, you cannot automatically dislike every girl John looks at — except the one of your choosing."

"Apparently I can. Do you like her, Daddy?"

"I don't know her at all. And I long ago gave up any egotistical illusion that my first impressions were final. I reserve decision, even sometimes until the third meeting!"

There was a reserve in his reservation, though he did not

admit it to the women of his family. The girl seemed a nice little thing. Alone with John, she probably revealed more personality than when first subjected to the critical eyes of his family. In any case, some men found such plastic femininity strengthening to their ego. He could see that she might find it an ordeal to meet John's father; still, he wished that the slate-grey eyes had met his directly, that he was not conscious of a certain guarded watchfulness. And for all her gentle demeanour, there was plenty of will power behind that ordinary face with small freckles sprinkling the fair, fine skin. He suspected — he feared he knew — why John had not brought her out to church.

If Evadne read his thoughts, she was not afraid to use direct methods to find out. Amused and by no means detached, her father presently followed the apparently casual conversation.

"Johnnie, you like chocolate ice cream, don't you?"

"I can take it or leave it."

"Well, trade mine for your strawberry. What a mob! It's worse every year. Didn't you tell me, Daddy, that when you got your degree they had only one convocation? And one garden party?"

"Yes. And no more crowded than today's either."

"At this rate, by the time I graduate they'll cut refreshments out altogether. And only that prospect sustained me through the heat in Convocation Hall."

"Pig," from John.

"I suppose I am." She passed the plate of small cakes to Veronica. "You wouldn't think from my conversation that I hear and inwardly digest two deeply spiritual sermons every Sunday, would you? By the way you've heard my — don't protest, Daddy — father preach, haven't you?"

"I'm afraid not."

"Aunt Alex," interrupted John, "would you care for another cup of tea?"

"Then you don't know what you're missing," said Evadne stoutly, disregarding the obvious red herring. "What church *do* you go to, Veronica?"

"The Immaculate Heart of Mary."

93

Andrew thought it time to interpose, though he did not doubt his daughter's ability to deal with the declaration for which she had so openly probed.

"Isn't that the new building with the Byzantine dome?"

"Yes."

"I wasn't certain if I had the right one in mind. I saw some fine reproductions of it in a recent article on new church architecture. And I think — wasn't a man named MacTavish connected there recently?"

"Father MacTavish was our parish priest. He is studying in Italy now."

"Yes. I had some correspondence with him a year or so ago. He has written an excellent brochure on St. Jerome which I found very helpful."

Veronica was not able or willing to rise to the topic of Jerome, but the difficult corner had been turned and she looked more at ease. Evadne's cherished movie camera and the conversation alternately took random unremarkable shots, until the thinning of the crowd gave an opportunity for which all, except perhaps Aunt Alexandra, had been waiting. Andrew, recalling the garden party at which the Shorncliffe charge had hung in the balance, was roused from brief abstraction. He saw that John and his girl were on the point of departure and heard Evadne say with happy guilelessness which did not fool father or brother for an instant, "Good-bye, Veronica. I've wanted so much to meet you. Now remember. You must come soon to hear Daddy preach."

"Aren't you afraid of being struck on the head with a blunt instrument?" inquired Andrew, as they fell in on either side to support Mrs. Mansell to their car.

"No, I'm not," she said almost belligerently; "I was quite deliberate —"

"We were all perfectly well aware of that."

"And I meant every word of it. Why should we always act hush-hush whenever Roman Catholics are present? Why should-

94

n't she come to our church? What is she going with John for, if she isn't willing to hear his father preach?"

"My dear, I thoroughly agree with you but——"

"But you couldn't say it. Well I could, and did. But — Abba, he can't possibly marry her, can he?"

"Why not?"

"Why not? Daddy, she doesn't believe — she believes — John and she are poles apart in what they believe. What do you mean, Why not?"

"I just wanted to be sure of the ground of your objection: the fact that you didn't take to her, the fishy handshake, the very name Roman Catholic. Which is it?"

Evadne, shaken, settled briefly back in the car to collect her thoughts, then sat forward on the edge of the seat to continue the conversation. Aunt Alex, unlike many elderly women, never obtruded herself. She heard, the family declared, what she wanted to hear, and was conveniently deaf on occasion. Sitting erect beside her nephew, she observed the pedestrians, the green lawns, the great old red-stone-and-brick houses, and the incongruous new blocks of apartments on St. George Street with impartial attention, through eyes which still required glasses only for reading. Perhaps weeks later by an unexpected remark or question they would know how much she had absorbed. And the remark would never be made to the wrong person.

"It really isn't because I didn't take to her, I think. I'd naturally prefer to like John's wife. Then I could feel like a sister and he wouldn't get so far away from me. But if this girl really loves John, I'd try to like her. I usually like people better after I've known them awhile —"

The credit is not entirely due to the other people, thought Andrew.

"As for the fishy handshake, I suppose I'm silly. I just can't see why people let their hands drip down in yours like that. Perhaps it isn't her usual handshake. She may just be reserved about being hearty with new acquaintances."

"George used to say," observed Mrs. Mansell unexpectedly, "that some people still regard a handshake as a pledge of good faith: like Easterners not killing a man who has eaten their salt; something to that effect at any rate."

With this observation, she turned to look with regal disapproval at a generously built woman in tight shorts and a striped halter waiting with her baby carriage for the light to change. Her "Tch!" was eloquent and, after a moment's courteous silence, the others realized that her contribution had been made and no comment was expected.

"As for the name 'Roman Catholic,' I don't know. You always taught us to distinguish people's views from the people themselves. Remember little Rita von Zuben I used to play with? I did want her to come to Sunday School with me and I tried hard to convert her — John and I between us — when I was seven! And you are keen on G. K. Chesterton, and Maritain and Gilson. About Roman Catholicism I'm biassed — not prejudiced." Andrew smiled to hear himself quoted. "I feel that not to be Protestant is to betray our heritage. 'Be of good cheer, Master Ridley,' said Latimer when he was dying, 'We shall this day by God's grace light such a candle in England as I trust shall never be put out.' Or that poor man in the time of Bloody Mary — the one who refused to state his belief in Transubstantiation but was afraid to die and kept saying on the way to Smithfield: 'I can't burn. I can't burn.' I'll never forget your telling that story — and that when God suddenly gave him assurance he cried, 'Now I can burn!'" She stopped with tears in her voice. The past was very real to Evadne.

"Thomas — Father — Campion did not die a very pleasant death," he reminded her tentatively.

"I know. But that was political. You know it was. If priests took part in plots against the government, they obviously faced the death sentence for traitors when they were caught. After all it was the sentence that William Wallace received — and Sir Walter Raleigh originally." It had been going on between them for years, this testing of her logic by suggestion and question thrown out to see how much of his teaching she had absorbed. "At least I haven't read of a case where a Roman Catholic was executed merely for his belief; where he was asked to recant

96

or abjure and he'd be spared. The whole situation was different. Drinkwater says — I read his biography of Cromwell just last week — that the Puritans did not care — in the sense of wanting to exercise compulsion — what the Roman Catholics believed; it was the compulsion *they* exercised on others when in power that made them intolerable. Glory, when I think of the popular picture of Cromwell as a killjoy and a spoilsport."

"To say nothing," her father agreed, "of the fact that all through England ravages are blamed on Oliver which were really perpetrated by Richard at the time of the Dissolution of the Monasteries."

"Yes. Julie used to be strong on that. She didn't believe anything really and did not want to, but she was full of cracks about joyless Protestants and our repressive Puritan heritage."

"Julie didn't believe anything," said Andrew. They had arrived home, Aunt Alex had gone in to rest, and Evadne and he had wandered out to deck chairs in the garden. "Yet you thought John might marry her."

"And we both felt sick about it. This is different. Logically we should say. 'It's better for her to believe even if we think she's wrong.' But is it, Dad? Is it?"

Andrew leaned back in his chair closing his eyes against the strong June sun. Evadne squirmed around in hers to watch him as he framed his slow answer.

"What a person really believes in his heart whether we agree with it or not, is to be respected. But some people — you called Julie phoney and I agree with you — say that they can't believe because they do not want to, because they refuse to examine the evidence and face the implications. And some 'believe' because they have been brought up in the framework of certain teaching and will not submit their beliefs to scrutiny or listen to anything on the other side. I cannot call that genuine belief because it is afraid. We do not know which it is in Veronica's case."

"I'll bet you have your opinion."

Andrew opened his eyes, smiled, and closed them again.

"One can have no secrets from so discerning a daughter," he murmured.

"Well, we can certainly find out by whether she comes out to Church or not. I suppose there's nothing we can do till then."

There was no answer. "Is there nothing we can do?" She glanced at her father's profile, unsmiling now and drawn. She thought suddenly how helpless and vulnerable he looked with his eyes closed. "You are going to tell me to pray, and I will. Will I ever! But Daddy, aren't you going to fight?"

The challenge, the voice, even to the queer little anguished note which denoted intensity — over a quarter-century Andrew could hear her mother saying almost the same words. And again he had to disappoint.

"Perhaps — to paraphrase — *orare est pugnare*. I hope your Latin is equal to that." Then more slowly, "John is doing the fighting at the moment, Vad. Don't fool yourself. It is inevitable, with the background he has had. But he already feels that he is fighting me. We must do nothing to intensify that feeling. You've been closer to him for years now than I have. Don't make him think we are taking sides against him."

"But I can't act as if I approve, when I don't."

"You've done it once or twice, though, haven't you? Or at least kept your disapproval from becoming offensive?"

"That was with strangers. And about things that were really none of my business. This is."

Andrew did not contradict her. The determined set of her usually generous mouth contrasted sharply with her unhappy, puzzled eyes. He stretched out his hand and waited until it closed around hers in a comforting, companionable clasp.

"I know. You see a clear-cut issue. So can I, believe me, dear, so can I. On the one side, the Roman Hierarchy, the Inquisition, Spain and the Armada, the I.R.A., the Index, Papal Infallibility, claims regarding mixed marriages and the children of such marriages; on the other, Wyclif, Huss, the Lollards, the Glorious Reformation, the Protestant martyrs, gallant little England, the Evangelical Revival, the English Bible, and our family and your childhood and everything it stands for. . . ."

Evadne's face was alight now and passionate.

"That's it. On the one side, confessionals, the Mass, those

ghastly Sacred Heart pictures and cheap statues, the dreadful coldness of their funerals, their silence when you try to talk religion; and on the other side our hymn-sings around the piano, our family prayers, people like — like Dr. Williams and Mr. Easton and Mr. Woodhouse speaking so naturally of Christ and His power — and, of course, you!"

"You realize that from her point of view," said Andrew, "the pictures are quite different. Especially if her background is Irish. On the one hand, the State Church, identified with the hated usurpers — the fact that it hasn't existed in Veronica's day doesn't matter — or over here a confusing assortment of often ugly, prosperous buildings attended by loud-singing, prosperous, covertly suspicious aliens (I use the term classically); on the other hand, until now, soaring, stained-glass interiors, dear, familiar ritual, comforting family uniformity, prescribed devotions, midnight mass on Christmas Eve — and from Britain a lingering sense of martyrdom because of past discriminatory laws, a sense of belonging to the Old Religion ——"

"But they don't! The Reformation corrected abuses. They are beginning to admit it themselves now."

"I'm just trying to show you the view from Veronica's side. Perhaps, depending on her mentality and interests, the sweep is larger: all the evils of nationalism, the capitalist system, the ugliness and heartlessness of the industrial revolution, over against a peaceful, romanticized Mediaeval Europe with one benign Church mothering all art and aspiration, setting a just price ——"

"Oh rot! Have you read Coulton lately or ——"

"Yes. Also Hilaire Belloc! You don't need to convince me, Vad. But remember that sentimental pictures, no matter how true to fact, are primarily subjective. The sort of revulsion that John seems to have experienced may have altered his completely."

"Dad, are you trying to scare me?"

"No. Trying to think honestly about my own reaction. Honouring you, young one, by thinking out loud. And with us there is another element," he went on, "an element of fear. The well-advertised conversions from G. K. Chesterton to Claire Booth-Luce to H. V. Morton, which we rationalize by considering their background, the apostasy and division of Protestantism, the pull of aestheticism ... but if John —"

"Brought up under your ministry and having every opportunity to know the Truth," continued Evadne. The dialogue was reminiscent of the Gryphon and the Mock Turtle, her father thought in the midst of his gravity. He interrupted deliberately.

"Can even consider selling out, or in other words, marrying into the Other Camp —" he paused to let her have the last word. She caught his intonation and her tone was less desperate than her words.

"Then what can we expect of other people?"

"Exactly!" said her father. "Well, if not succinctly stated. That's the way we both see it; therefore the only logical way to see it. And we both know what we would have God do about it."

"So — ?"

Andrew released her hand. He clicked the spring so that his chair dropped to horizontal position and lay with his arms clasped behind his head. There was no lightness now in his voice.

"There is one thing more important in this matter than our will."

"John's happiness?" said Evadne, incredulous.

"No. John's good. I was going to say God's will but it is the same thing. Perhaps, too, it might not be an inordinate stretch of Christian love to consider Veronica."

"Oh, her! All right, I know we must consider everyone but why her particularly? We considered Julie but we were mighty glad when she went out of John's life. As far as I'm concerned, Veronica is a run-of-the-mill little creature who has caught my brother on the rebound. She's completely unsuitable for John and she knows quite well what she is doing."

"Nevertheless," said Andrew earnestly, "she may become the mother of your nephews and nieces," — and of my grandchildren, God forbid, he thought involuntarily — "and we have no right to dismiss her feelings for John summarily. More than that she is a soul for whom Christ died and, whether we like it or not, she has been thrown into our path. We can't think of her as an obstacle, an inanimate object."

"I wish I could. You can do things with inanimate objects."

"Such as? No, don't tell me. It's as well these comments are not being recorded. They might sound a bit at variance with the 'pure religion and undefiled' of which we are the undisputed representatives."

Evadne leaned over and shook him.

"You know I'm saying what you are thinking."

"You are. But things that I must keep from thinking. Pray to be kept from. And keep praying."

"Right," said his daughter, sobered. "Sorry I interrupted, Abba, really. Tell me what I — we — must do. And I'll try."

Lord, who am I to tell anyone, with this sense of futility upon me, thought Andrew, with a sudden plunge into the bleakness, the horror of great darkness which he on rare occasions experienced in the loneliness of night. He struggled to free himself from it, but his speech was laboured.

"Don't classify Veronica. Don't think of her as 'a Roman Catholic.' She may be unsuited to John. She may be incapable of making him happy. We think so and we may be right. But here is the all-important matter: Is her religion the closed, watertight compartment that it is with many people — by no means all Roman Catholics? Or is it a real and transforming experience of the power of Christ — a personal relationship with Him? If not, is she open to such a revelation? If not, it will not be a good marriage because it will be against John's deepest convictions. Fight as he may, he is spoiled for anything less. And anything less will either make him miserable or make him callous to avoid the misery. Now, see if dinner is ready, dear. I have to visit at Sunnybrook tonight."

101

6

NDREW? Is this an auspicious day to ask if you feel like sacrificing yourself for the good of the cause?"

"What cause?" Mrs. Beth Harris-Kemp's tone did not suggest any painful prospect.

"I suppose I could say the cause of Canadian culture. But it's more selfish than that. Will you come to the Stratford opening with me tonight?"

"Tonight?" He hesitated, reaching across the desk for his date-pad though the gesture was unnecessary. He knew that it was empty. The voice on the other end of the telephone continued on a rather hurried and apologetic note quite unlike its usual matter-of-fact assurance.

"I know it's late. And you're probably busy. But I do wish you'd come. Otherwise I'll have to go alone and I dread it. I'd sooner pass it up altogether. Roger was a patron, you know. So we always attended opening nights. Jim — Roger's younger brother — was here on business from Vancouver and was going with me. But he had to fly to Montreal unexpectedly last night. You'd be doing me a terrific favour. And *King John* is supposed to be their tour de force this year. Or have you tickets for it already?"

"No, Evadne and I have been talking but we've made no plans so far." It was hardly decent to hesitate longer. "Thanks for asking me, Beth. I'll be glad to come. When shall I call for you?"

"You won't. That is, if. you'll trust me to be chauffeur —

chauffeuse? I heard you say once that you weren't keen on driving and I love it. If you can get away by four o'clock we'll have dinner at the Queen's. I've booked a table there so that we can be leisurely instead of going to the dinner jam at the theatre. This whole thing is my party. Oh thank you, Andrew. You've saved my evening."

Would that all philanthropy were as easy, thought Andrew, as the rich undulating countryside around Baden and New Hamburg flowed past Beth's smoothly handled Cadillac. She was using the larger and closed car, he gathered, for some reason vaguely connected with her hair and dress. And she had, quite unnecessarily and with an awkwardness foreign to her, mentioned several woman friends who might have accompanied her but who were otherwise engaged. Andrew was content that they had been. The late afternoon was Canadian June at its best, pleasantly warm with a light cloud-lifting breeze. The sun was still high enough to make the tinted glass of the windshield unnecessary though they were driving due west. The dinner jacket which he had feared might be a bit tight for him — he had not worn it for over a year — allowed him to relax without discomfort. It was all very restful.

"I should reproach myself for letting you do the work," he murmured, "but I'm glad of it."

Her responsive smile was dazzling.

"I'm glad you're glad. This is fun. And you need the change."

Probably true, thought Andrew. This was the first excursion, the first recreation for which he had not had the planning or responsibility, since — he did not exert himself to remember how long. Always, since Cecily's death, he was the father arranging and arbitrating, the nephew solicitous, the host considering, the pastor deploying, concerned, usually expected to speak, to make decisions. Now he was just himself, the entertainment laid on — and being thanked for it into the bargain! He need not even talk, at least not to initiate conversation. He sighed with the sheer luxury.

She glanced at him but did not break the silence. Beth's advent at the church, Andrew, after two months of cautious

103

appraisal, was inclined to consider a cause for unqualified thanksgiving. His doubts on that first Sunday morning had proved to be without foundation. She had returned the same evening and to all services since, even appearing occasionally at prayer meeting. She had joined the church at the May Communion service, joined, by her own request, on profession of faith, as she did not consider a letter of transfer — this statement had endeared her to several of his elders to whom her wealth made her slightly suspect — of sufficient validity. Andrew received her into fellowship, suppressing a wish that she had a husband with her, for the addition of a couple into membership was a rarer occurrence than that of an unattached woman and, he felt without proof, gave a lift to the morale of the congregation out of all numerical proportion. To her regular and large financial contribution he was sincerely indifferent. Of much greater importance was her willingness to help, her participation in women's activities and in the Sunday School, where she offered her services as a substitute teacher — a most thankless position.

But of supreme value in his eyes was the unobtrusiveness of her interest, so that no criticism had reached him of hurt feelings or resentment. There was no doubt about it. Her previous social activities might have schooled her in diplomacy, but the grace of God rather than diplomacy was required in such a situation and that grace was evidently at work within her. Andrew, scrupulously fair, gave thanks for this evidence that grace was also at work in the women of his congregation. It had been his and Cecily's continual prayer for the church: that its members be bound together in love and that no bitterness take root among them. So far, in spite of disappointment and discouragement from outside, the prayer had been granted — granted, Andrew admitted, by the quiet departure of those who did not feel or share the love, but granted nevertheless. So — he caught himself in the act of qualifying the thought with a "thus far" — he could "raise an Ebenezer" for Beth.

The humour of the phrase struck him suddenly an hour later, as he faced her across the arrayed silver and white linen of their table in the old-fashioned elegance of the Queen's Hotel dining room. She was evidently well-known there from previous visits and had booked not only a dinner table but a room for her convenience. Going to meet her as she descended the wide staircase, Andrew suddenly realized that she was a beautiful woman, a term he would have hesitated to apply to her twenty years before. The décolletage of her full-length gown was decent, he noted with pleasure, having seen during his wait half a dozen plunging necklines which vied in outstripping all others. Beth's evenly tanned shoulders and arms and back, set off by a turquoise shantung, retained much of the firmness and patina of youth and even the inescapable stringing under the chin was scarcely noticeable beneath a face which positively glowed at him. She stopped on the second step as if to evoke his approval. He said nothing for a moment and she was about to finish the descent when, as though plucking up her courage, she lifted her head and posed with one hand out, in a dramatic gesture.

" 'You see the picture,' " — they had been quoting scraps of Shakespeare idly during the drive — " 'Is it not well done?' "

" 'Excellently done.' " He was glad to have Shakespeare take the burden of response. " 'If God did all.' "

She laughed unaffectedly then and took his arm as they turned to the dining room.

"Now, you have me. No, I can't say it's in grain, though the ads claim it will endure wind and weather. Certainly water doesn't take it off, worse luck! How do you like the bouffant hairdo?"

"It's new, isn't it? From the Continent? I haven't seen anything like it here before."

"A guarded compliment if I've ever heard one. No, nothing to drink, thank you — you still don't, Andrew? Yes, it is the coming thing, was hitting Rome when I left. My hairdresser is just back from Europe so, feeling reckless, I had him experiment in honour of the occasion. What are you smiling at? Not trying to keep from laughing outright, I trust."

Andrew laughed outright.

"Not at the hairdo — which is most striking and becoming, though it will take a bit of getting used to. Just that I had been

105

thinking of you as an Ebenezer and I wondered if the term had ever been used before in such a context."

"Ebenezer. Isn't that just an old-fashioned name? And I thought it was a man's name at that."

"O come, Beth. Surely you know what an Ebenezer is? 'Here I raise my Ebenezer,' or 'Each sweet Ebenezer I have in review.' "

"Of course. I don't remember the second. The first is in a hymn. What hymn? I've sung it, but I'm ashamed to say I never wondered or asked what raising an Ebenezer meant. Will you excommunicate me?"

"The churches would be depleted if *that* were made a ground for excommunication," said Andrew and told her.

She sobered instantly.

"Thank you for thinking that of me. And you can't feel it more inappropriate than I do. It's you who have been ——"

She was interrupted by a couple pausing to greet her on the way to their table. Andrew, rising for the third or fourth time to acknowledge introductions, realized that to act as Beth's escort was no way to visit the Festival incognito. It was brought home to him how completely the social life of Toronto had left him behind. In the University — universities he would presently have to say — in the churches, he still had a considerable acquaintance. He seldom went anywhere in the city without meeting people he knew, more often people who made themselves known to him. But of the parties fortifying themselves around the nearby tables, those in the know, who would shortly be caught by newspaper photographers sweeping from car to foyer, to be seen tomorrow under the caption "Among those present" or "Lovely gowns mark Stratford opening," he did not recognize a single one. A few faces were familiar when Beth attached names: captains of industry whose pictures often accompanied items in the daily press on their philanthropic or cultural or sporting interests, politicians both provincial and federal; women prominent for their patronage of arts and letters. They all seemed to know one another and Beth, whom they greeted with high-pitched enthusiasm.

"So *good* to have you back. I heard you'd come and have been

106

meaning and meaning to phone. But then we flew to Hawaii. And I was on the committee for tonight. See you at Tom's, Mr. Connington. So glad to have met you. I know I've seen you before, but my memory for names is shot — simply shot."

As the evening passed, there was more than a flicker of interest in him as Beth's escort, though Andrew was slow to become aware of it. Some sixth sense spotted the photographer whose sixth sense had informed him that the mature, dark-haired woman who sauntered up from the parking lot as casually as if she were not wearing a Givenchy original and an avant-garde coiffure was more newsworthy than half-a-dozen lovely young things for whom his camera remained silent. The photographer swore silently when her distinguished-looking escort turned his back on the camera at the very moment of take, as if he had just become conscious of the placid Avon below them. But in the foyer where known and unknown, those who came to see and those who came to be seen, were filtered slowly through the ticket doors and began their quest for their particular section, they were interrupted repeatedly for introduction and chat; and when seated by the aisle in the third row centre ("I hope these seats aren't too close for you, Andrew?") there was conversation with the party immediately in front, and presently a couple (the President of the Hamilton Board of Trade) crossed the aisle to chat, until the third trumpet sent them back to their places.

If his vanity had been piqued, it could have found solace in the fact that several evinced knowledge of him either from his face or from hearing his name. One even said, "Oh, of course, Mr. Connington has become a legend in Toronto. He always has something interesting and controversial to say." (Legend, forsooth! Symbol he had already been called. In the gobbledy-gook of the times he would be a myth next.) And a man asked if he was still preaching, having heard that he had given it up for business. Then in the anticipatory lull before the cannon saluted the new season, he had evidence that his hearing was not failing as badly as he sometimes feared; it caught quite clearly from two rows behind: "Harris-Kemp. *The* Harrises, you know.

107

Husband simply rolling in it since the war. Died a few months ago. Do you know who's with her?"

The cannon, the Queen, the calculated, eye-catching, bustling surprise of a novel opening; if Beth had heard, the diversion was complete. Andrew, realizing that he had never witnessed a performance of *King John,* settled down to enjoy it without the bother of haunting comparisons.

Before long, pleasure drove out all other reaction. The seats were just right, for if most Festival actors had a fault — mentioned by the purists and the hard of hearing with monotonous regularity every year — it was their tendency to sacrifice Shakespeare's words to action, his lines to speed, gesture, and even, on occasion, to gimmick. From where he sat this damage was negligible, and he revelled in the many-faceted glory of the language. He was always susceptible to drama. Aristotle's "purgation through pity and fear" was an experiential not an academic truth to him. And in addition, he usually found himself murmuring at some point "There but for the grace of God go I." Still, though his mind was caught up in the intricacy of words and the interplay of character, though his excitement mounted and his heart felt constricted over the anguish of Constance and the fearful innocence of Arthur, yet in the ambivalence of consciousness this enjoyment was heightened by his situation. The delicate assault upon his senses of exotic perfume, whether the woman at his side stirred or whether the scent suddenly isolated itself from the scents around him, sharpened his consciousness of the fact that there was a woman at his side: for the first time in many years a woman in a woman-to-man relationship, warm, personable, herself pleased, eager to please with her presence.

A long, tingling sensation, almost pain in its delight, began at the back of Andrew's neck and ran through him. Even the toes in their polished shoes came alive with it. It was the relaxing sensation of a hot bath, the more than fleshly comfort of a woodfire to a tired, cold body, the happy nostalgia of a gay long-unheard tune, the near-agonizing relief of cold water down a parched throat — all this plus a deeper satisfaction, a renewed sense of youth and importance. He was happy.

When, in 1919, he had been discharged from the Canadian Army in England, he had spent his first night in a Devonshire cottage and wakened to the sun aslant patchwork quilts, a breeze wafting the sea-smell through his window, a tendril of honeysuckle waving over the sill — and the realization that he need not get up for hours. He did not think of this now; but as he had lain still and contented then, so now he sat unmoving, expansive with the pleasure of full sensation. The play, his attention to the play, was unchanged; he would have said it had the supreme claim on his attention, was the chief source of his pleasure. But his attention was more concentrated, he was capable of larger pleasure, as mind and senses were at once sharpened and soothed by the long-missed, tangible thrill of a woman's presence beside him, belonging.

In a scene of almost unbearable tension, Arthur turned Hubert from his purpose. There was a moment's tribute of silence, then a long spontaneous thunder of applause. Still in the double exultation of his well-being, Andrew turned to communicate it, turned with a smile of admiration at the performance and of shared enjoyment, turned naturally, expectantly, as he had often done to Cecily.

But it was not Cecily.

He had not thought it was. He had not been for the fraction of a second so carried away that he was not perfectly aware of his situation. His mind was not given to rejecting sensory evidence. He had, for instance, envied but could not emulate those who were transported in prayer so that they forgot time and space. Even in his greatest spiritual experience he would have been able to give a full account of his actual surroundings. So his recent happiness had not been based on any illusion that Cecily was with him, any identification of Beth's person, attractive and compelling in its own right, with his wife's. Yet with the familiar gesture a complete sense of emptiness engulfed him. There was response but not *the* response. Unfairly, illogically, he was swept by resentment, a wordless feeling of waste: that he should be there, alive, yearning, incomplete. The crowning insult was not that Cecily was gone, but that a woman was there who was useless to him. Longing cut him like a knife.

Beth had anticipated his gesture and look so that she saw both the smile and the almost simultaneous revulsion. The sequence startled and puzzled her. She had been prepared for the smile, for no woman as conscious of Andrew Connington's person as she had come to be could fail to notice the relaxing of his tension, the communicative physical harmony which had gradually overcome him. The expression which erased the smile she would in another man have interpreted as passion. But Beth Harris-Kemp was too shrewd a judge of men, even where she would willingly have believed, to think that a few hours' proximity had brought Andrew Connington from friendly indifference to such a state, or that, if it had, he would have revealed it so plainly. Then what?

Instantly reading in her questioning eyes the degree of change in his own, he controlled a face which felt suddenly limp and featureless, restored a smile which felt like a grimace, and joined belatedly in the prolonged clapping.

Shaken by the surge and counter-surge of emotion and thoroughly ashamed that the effect on him had even momentarily been evident, Andrew put forth an effort, which his cooler sense would have described as misguided, to be especially considerate to Beth, whom he felt that he had somehow treated badly. It was not her fault that she was not Cecily, not her fault that the spell was broken. Apart from a remote interest in the climax of the play, almost as though he were viewing it through the small end of field glasses, his great desire was to be alone, to be spared conversation, to go on feeling empty and maimed and not — for a few hours at any rate — to pretend to be full and whole. Yet he had so often, so regularly, concealed his feelings, carried out responsibilities in direct variance to his own preferences, that it was second nature and he did it, this time as usual, very well.

He was still doing it after more than an hour at the party given by one of the Festival patrons. But it was with unmixed relief that he seconded Beth's decision to tear herself away.

110

"Let me drive," he suggested as he took her keys to unlock the car. "You'll be exhausted and I'm quite wide awake."

"I told you I like driving. And if I'm exhausted I shall lie in till noon, or later," she said lightly, sliding in behind the wheel in one long movement. "Which I doubt if you'll do. Now relax. Go to sleep if you want. I'm never sleepy when I'm driving."

"A merciful dispensation that." Andrew got in beside her gratefully, feeling in spite of his assertion, that he might at any time take advantage of her permission. A glance at his watch showed him that it would be at least three o'clock before they reached the city. He had been glad that Evadne was off with friends to visit Upper Canada Village. Aunt Alex had greeted his announcement that he was going with a friend to Stratford by a far-away look in her old eyes and a few brief recollective comments on her attendance with Uncle George at the Tent opening in 1953. She would, if asked, repeat her information to John without addition. Not that he had to account to his children for his movements! But he was not anxious to have a casual engagement subject to speculation.

"The Dolce Vita requires more energy than I seem to possess these days. Surely most of those men have to turn out to business tomorrow?"

"I doubt if many of them — those our age — have appointments till ten at least. I think it's good for you to be seen around like this, Andrew. No, I'm not going to say you should be pastor of Shorncliffe. But you might increase the — the scope of your influence. I was furious to think that Frank Saunders didn't know you were still preaching. I want these people to come and hear you again. Heaven knows, they need it."

"Heaven," returned Andrew equably and not lightly, "knows many things the explanation of which is not granted to me. But I doubt if my attendance at a Stratford opening will draw large numbers to Eucharist. Don't mistake me, Beth. I enjoyed it thoroughly, but as a diversion, not a means to an end."

Except as I try to make everything I do a means to an end, he did not say aloud.

111

Beth was not sidetracked. In the dim light he watched her fine, decided profile with aesthetic enjoyment. Her full lips with their strong curve looked good from the side, even when she spoke — no mean test of attractiveness, he thought.

"Large numbers perhaps, no. But I've heard you say, haven't I, that one soul outweighs the entire material universe in God's eyes?"

"'A hit, a very palpable hit.' And a listener who really listens. Bless you, Beth. *That* encourages me, regardless of the world not making a pathway to my mousetrap."

"Well — if the mountain won't come to Mahomet, Mahomet must go to the mountain. Why don't you have a book of sermons published?"

Connington stared at her for a moment. He was thoroughly awake now and very glad that the conversation had swerved from the personal.

"'Not the first are you to turn and ask thus.' I don't know what has undammed this torrent of quotations in me tonight. It must be the effect of Shakespeare, who was, as the proverbial old lady said of him and the Bible, altogether too full of them. My dear Beth, have you any idea how difficult it is to get any book — much more a book of sermons — published?

"They are published, though. I've seen volumes. All the bookstores have a religious section."

"Yes, but whose? Billy Graham's, Norman Vincent Peale's — I am not classing them together. Occasionally a Toronto firm risks a slim collection from a fashionable preacher. If I had stayed at Shorncliffe I might have rated a couple by now. But the idea has been broached to several publishers." He did not say that the idea, the initial work, the scalding indignation when it was rejected, had been Cecily's.

"It could be subsidized."

"Yes. The difficulty then is that publicity for its sale costs as much as the subsidy. And without advertisement, stores won't handle it, and only my immediate and enthusiastic supporters would buy."

Beth set her chin and stepped on the accelerator to pass two enormous vans travelling in convoy.

"I'm not giving up so easily. Have you any collection ready?"

"One that I have edited. Most of my sermons are preached from bare notes these days. So we have recorded untold numbers. But typing from a recorder is no easy job and the church doesn't afford a paid full-time secretary. I —" he hesitated, then shrugged his hesitation off — "there's nothing so pathetic as a would-be author, but since you are interested, I *am* working on a book."

"Do tell me, if you don't mind talking about it. Is it a novel?"

He had not talked about it to anyone and would marvel tomorrow at this breakdown of his reticence under the influence of isolation, night, and sympathy.

"Not a novel. Nor yet autobiography. Nor essays. A series of commentaries, I should call it, on present trends and changes. Strung together by my personal reminiscence. That sounds extremely feeble. But they aren't feeble — occasionally I think I even achieve humour — and irony. They are — how shall I put it? — statements that need to be made to restore the balance of our thinking. And I feel — forgive this pomposity — that I am fairly well equipped to make them. Perhaps if it does not see the light now, it may have posthumous interest."

She heard him out, hands gripping the wheel. Then she glanced his way. He could see the flash of her dark eyes in the light of a street lamp as the almost deserted road narrowed through a small town on the route.

"Andrew, stop talking like an old man and a failure. I want to see you in print here and now. Your posthumous publications can come later."

"That figures," said Andrew meekly. She stopped to laugh but was not diverted.

"All right, all right. But you talk as if it wouldn't be *much* later. Dash it all, Andrew Connington, do you realize how young you are — don't laugh at me, I know your age. I mean how vital and alive. Some of those men you met tonight, fifteen years younger, are fossilized. They haven't had an idea in their heads

113

for years, except making money. I doubt if they've read a book since they left college — those who went to college. Don't you realize what a personality you have, what authority, what a sense of humour, what versatility? You don't go in for small talk, but don't you know how you dominate a group as soon as you begin to speak?"

She stopped, a bit breathless in her exasperated exhortation. Andrew thought her questions over for a moment.

"Yes," he said candidly.

She could not have been more shocked if he had wrenched the wheel from her. He grinned amusedly.

"Well, did you expect me to say No?" he inquired reasonably. "There is no virtue in denying the truth. You would be equally a hypocrite if you denied that you look superb — that you were one of the most strikingly attractive women there to-night and that, unlike me, you could easily pass for fifteen years younger. What you have said about me I have been told at various times by — by men and women whose integrity and sincerity I respect as I do yours. And for goodness' sake, don't think that because I don't 'do my boyish modesty stunt and go pink all over' and murmur little deprecating Oh-no's and You-don't-mean-it's and Going-on-being-me's, that I am smug or that I don't appreciate being told — bask in it, in fact. Because I understand and you understand that in these last few years when such things are said, it is to console me for the puzzling fact, which I know quite as well as I know my assets: and that is, how very little these assets make for success today unless conjoined with other qualities with which I am not endowed. Or perhaps with circumstances which are not mine to control — or, if you like, which I fail to control."

She recovered her equilibrium.

"You are an incredibly honest man. I suppose 'all the girls' have told you that too. What a 'line forms to the left' person you make me feel.

Andrew was genuinely concerned.

"I suppose it is inevitable that you should take it that way. Actually my honesty, as you call it, was a compliment. Normally

114

I shouldn't go past a noncommittal murmur. But I trusted you not to think I was taking myself too seriously. And I was — am — grateful for your trying to console me by boosting my ego."

That restored her. She became her forthright self again.

"Let us get one thing straight. I am not trying to console you. I don't think you need consolation — certainly not my consolation, because I regard you as a success in the important and genuine sense. I've always been a bit impatient with 'lame dogs.' It's one of the less pleasant Harris characteristics which I share with Uncle Ben. I joined your church for my sake, not for yours, and don't you forget it. But I am concerned with the people who are missing out on the type of ministry you have to give, and I think sometimes you are too little concerned with the type of success which would bring you into their orbit. Forgive me if I'm interfering and nosey. A managing woman can be an abomination."

Andrew felt that a strong disclaimer was only fitting.

"As far as your interference is concerned, need I remind you of Ebenezer?"

Beth laughed.

"That's right, as our American friends say. Then, let us revert to these non-posthumous publications of yours. May I have the manuscript that is ready and see what I can do about it?"

"Provided you let me know what you are doing about it."

"Independent! I want it to be published in a way to ensure the widest possible circulation. If the publishers have any sense, they'll take it gladly. But if some subsidy should be necessary — Andrew, why shouldn't I spend a bit of what I have in abundance on a phase of the Lord's work which I think very important? Let's be impersonal about this."

It was a good note to close an evening which had at one point threatened to become perilously personal to Andrew. Satisfied, or perhaps content, with the restoration of camaraderie, Beth drove the rest of the way in companionable silence. She swung the car off the 40I at Bathurst, and Andrew who had been dozing at intervals protested sleepily.

"This is all wrong, Beth. Let me take a taxi from here. Or

115

better from your place. I was brought up in another era, remember. It goes against the grain to be driven home."

She hesitated.

"If I thought you'd come in and have something to eat."

"Eat! After that party?"

"Then on no other consideration will I hear of it. This was to be my do from beginning to end. Don't worry about me. I drive straight into my garage and go right into the house. Susan will be there and probably not asleep yet. She fusses very pleasantly over me."

He made no further protest, except a warm reiteration of thanks when they reached his home. She stopped the car on the wrong side of the road for his convenience, and waited until he came around and stood beside her.

"In the words which a less-than-eloquent friend of mine uses on all occasions, 'I can only say Thank you.' I really should be able to do better than that, though I'll phone in the clear light of morning with some choice phrases."

He had to bend down to address her, steadying himself with one hand on the open window frame. She put her left hand on his in an impulsive gesture.

"You've thanked me quite adequately. And since this is Honesty Night, you are perspicacious enough to realize that at Do's like this evening's a woman has more cause to feel grateful than a man. And I do, Andrew, believe me."

"You'll be all right getting home?"

"Quite."

The hand was still on his. It was a gesture that might imply nothing but friendliness; it was a gesture that left the way open to a response of warmer intimacy. If I were a Continental, I should kiss it, thought Andrew, and that would be the perfect graceful finale. But we don't do it. I've never kissed anyone's hand — except Cecily's. I can't just shake hers off.

Before there could be any embarrassment, the problematical hand gave his a little farewell pressure and returned to the wheel. The motor purred.

"See you. 'Bye."

116

He watched her car move down the street, the signal light flick and disappear around St. Clair. The faint smile on his face was compounded of many emotions, chief among them, appraising admiration.

7

REALLY, VAD, IS IT any of your business?"
The sharpness of John's voice arrested his father
even as he was opening his mouth to indicate that
he was in the next room. Evadne's answer closed it and he
waited irresolute.

"Yes. Yes in a family like ours I think it is. You certainly
made it your business last year when——"

"I should say so. Think I'd see my sister mooning around
over a married prof old enough to be her father?"

"O.K. O.K. I *listened* to you, didn't I? And all I had was a
bad crush and I knew it was a crush and that I'd get over it.
I'd even told him and we laughed about it together. So it was
perfectly innocent and wasn't doing any harm——"

"No? What about your reputation as a Christian around
Vic? And if your Sunday School class had heard of it?"

"So you said at the time." Evadne's voice had the quiet of a
crisis past and a decision reached. "And if you remember I took
your advice. So it gives me the right to ask the same of you."

"This is an entirely different situation."

"Yes. A worse one. Because that would never have amounted
to anything. This may, if you don't stop now."

"What if I don't intend to stop? What if it does amount
to something?"

In the attic storeroom, Andrew dreaded most that some
creak of the floor, some chance movement, might betray him.
Of the two evils, discovery at this juncture was far less desirable

than the continuance of unintentional eavesdropping. Not only would Evadne know that he had learned her unsuspected secret — and he had thought she had no secrets from him! — but the potential effect of her plea would be ruined and John steeled against the talk for which he himself had been awaiting an opportunity. Desperately uncomfortable, for he could imagine the irretrievable disaster of later discovery, he prayed that the situation would be turned to good account.

It had certainly been thrust upon him. He had taken advantage of a cancelled meeting to check a quotation, which in turn had driven him to search for a copy of Thucydides. And once in the storeroom, though the Thucydides still evaded him, he had come on old bound copies of the *Strand Magazine,* one of which included a story of the Sepoy Mutiny which had held him spellbound at the age of eleven. There it was — with the remembered illustration of the doomed garrison and their ladies, impeccably garbed in dinner dress and spread out in death around the table, the sole survivor croaking to the captain of the relief force: "The caviar! For God's sake, don't touch the caviar!" At this point, Andrew, who had settled comfortably in a superannuated armchair behind a pile of books, had been made suddenly aware by dialogue, first muffled, then startlingly clear, of the approach of his offspring. The exchange which had drowned and prevented his effort to greet them had been made at the door of John's room. They had not closed it when they entered. He heard Evadne fling herself on the bed. Glancing sideways he noted that his door had swung almost to and that piles of books and boxes screened him from easy view, even if anyone glanced in. They were speaking more loudly in their intensity and his hearing was keener than his sight. He could have stuffed his ears, he supposed, but why?

"John, you don't." It was almost a wail. "You can't."

"Oh, can't I?" Was there an undertone of discomfort in the bravado? Then, as though anxious to face it out. "Why not?"

Evadne was equal to that one.

"Because she's a Roman Catholic."

119

"Doesn't that statement show the very bigotry you accuse them of?"

"John, honestly! We've been to every kind of Roman Catholic service. Look at Dad's library and the books we've been encouraged to read — not ours, theirs, by Faber, and Newman, and Fulton Sheen, and Thomas Merton, as well as all their Knights of Columbus pamphlets. Veronica came to one service the night you brought her to supper — I suppose she got special dispensation —?"

She paused but John did not contradict her.

"and sat like a frozen fish with her eyes down all through it. And since then you haven't been coming out Sunday nights. Regardless of how" — Andrew, holding his breath, was relieved that she did not bring him into her appeal — "the congregation needs support, especially in the summer. If loyalty doesn't mean anything, I'd think for the sake of your self-respect you wouldn't let her dictate to you like that."

"Nobody is dictating to me, I can tell you." John's voice was lower. Andrew marvelled that he was controlling his temper.

"Then there are probably more subtle methods of exerting influence." Evadne had obviously taken the gloves off. She tried another approach. "I — oh Johnnie, I can't bear to be disappointed in you. I've always been so proud of my brother. There's no excuse for your getting involved. My stars, a man can do the asking! A girl has to wait to be asked, and it's pretty lonely waiting sometimes. But I shouldn't consider that an excuse for me."

"Look, Vad. There's no point arguing about this. It's simply one of those things — "

"Oh no, John! Next you'll say 'this thing is bigger than either of us.' Rot. Just one question. Do you believe what the Roman Catholic Church teaches — for instance about the Mass and Transubstantiation? About Mary? About the saints and purgatory? About the power of the priest in hearing confession and granting absolution?"

"No. Of course, I don't. But — "

"Then **how can you** think what you feel is love for a girl who does? The sort of love we have seen in our family? That we've been brought up to believe in as the basis of Christian marriage?"

There was a long, baffled pause. Andrew, cold with tension, tried to gauge from the silence whether the words had made any impression. The next speech told him.

"All right, John. Go ahead with it." What on earth was the child going to say? Something bridge-burning, something irrevocable, he could tell from the rising pitch of her voice, the odd little intake of breath. "But I don't really know why you carried on so about Mother's death. I'm glad now she died when she did. This would have killed her and much more painfully."

Andrew stiffened, as if waiting to hear a blow. The interval of silence screamed.

"God damn you, Evadne." He hardly recognized his son's voice in its agony of fury. "How *dare* you say that to me?"

"Because — " But what she was saying, her voice still unflinching, was drowned in the sound of John's incontinent departure. The carpeted stairs, even the stairs below, protested the sound of his feet and the slam of the distant door came as an expected but uncompromising period.

Feeling very old, Andrew stood up slowly, his limbs stiff from the effort of keeping them motionless. It was of no importance now to conceal his presence, though he would have preferred loneliness to what he must face. At the door of John's large, pleasant room he paused. Evadne still lay across the bed, her stricken face, very small and colourless, cupped in her hands. She was not crying, but her eyes were bleak. They took him in with no sign of surprise or shock.

"You heard?"

"Pretty well everything. I was in the Armoury and you had the conversation launched before I could interrupt."

"I don't mind. I'm just as glad you did." Her voice was listless. Like himself she seemed to be drained of motive power. He went to sit beside her but she drew herself to a crouching position and swung her legs to the floor. "No. Let's get out of here. He might come back, though — though I don't think it's likely for awhile."

121

Down in his study he stood at the window waiting, while she wandered about meticulously examining one familiar object after another. Presently she came over to him.

"It's lucky that you gave John a chivalrous upbringing. I thought for a moment he was going to hit me. It might be better if he had."

"No."

"I think it would have been easier than to hear him say —. Abba" — feeling was returning to her voice now and her face twisted piteously — "how could John say that? I've hardly ever heard him say 'damn' since you told us what it meant and why we shouldn't, but even to think *that* — " Her voice dropped to tonelessness again. "I feel quite sick."

He knew. The commonplace blasphemy, the ignorant thoughtlessness of its usage, had never taken the edge off its shock to him. And in his son's mouth, in the mouth of a Christian, it had appalled him, become an ugly, deliberate curse. But he held out his hand to Evadne though he could scarcely manage a smile.

"Perhaps we should be thankful that he said it."

"Thankful!"

"He was thinking unspeakable things anyhow. And if we pray, God can make this work for good. 'He maketh the wrath of men to praise Him.' Don't forget, child. A boy like John cannot say those words — especially to you — with impunity. If he had controlled himself, he might have felt nothing but resentment and self-pity. Now he will inevitably feel guilty and remorseful."

"He — " Evadne stopped to find a handkerchief for eyes suddenly moist. The different quality of this crisis was evidenced by the fact that she had not yet burst into tears. "He had reason to be angry! It was a dreadful thing for me to say."

"Yes."

She looked up at him, earnest in her misery.

"I said it on purpose, you know. I mean, I didn't just lose my temper and blurt it out."

"I gathered that. The speech was rehearsed."

"I've been thinking out for weeks what I'd say if I got a chance to talk to him. Only I didn't say half of it because conversations never go the way you plan them. But I tried — in fact I prayed — to find one thing that would hit home if nothing else did. His really vulnerable spot. And I so hoped I wouldn't have to use it. But that was it. And I'm not sorry. And it was true. Do you think it was wrong?"

He smiled at her sudden change.

"If you thought and prayed and it was the one thing and you're not sorry and it was true, how can I say it was wrong? We've tried waiting and saying nothing! Sometimes only drastic methods work."

"I had to be drastic. Do you know she's wearing a ring?"

Andrew had not thought he could feel more gaunt.

"It's not a diamond. One of those friendship rings. But it's on her ring finger. I didn't tell you before because I didn't want to hurt you but —— "

"My little buffer state." She had put her arm around him with quite unconscious protectiveness and he returned the gesture. "So it has gone as far as that, has it? I suppose, after investing in a car, John's bank account doesn't run to a decent diamond."

"Until November."

"You're right. Until November." They were both silent as the possibilities latent in that phrase opened before them. George Mansell's will had included a generous bequest for his great-nephew and great-niece, to become theirs on their respective twenty-fifth birthdays. John would be twenty-five in November. And though he was so far continuing in research at the University in preference to a commercial position at a much higher salary, the legacy would make him financially able to enter on marriage — as we used to consider marriage, thought his father, before the days when brides supported their husbands through college and the two brought equal salaries into the household at intervals for most of their life together!

123

Evadne's voice broke the ramification of his thoughts.

"You heard about me and Professor Stanhope, then."

"I did. I'm sorry to have eavesdropped there, Vad."

"I'm glad you know. Actually I let John make more of it just now than there was, because it gave me a bit of a lever ——"

"My amazing daughter! Wise as a serpent if not harmless as a dove."

"It's true. Believe me, I was going to tell you last year, only first I thought I had probably given it away — you always used to know when I had a crush on someone, from the time I was eleven — "

"A strange assortment, I remember. Mr. — what was the name of your drama coach? — Rex Harrison, Peter Lawton, Syl Apps, Prince Philip — mercifully *not* Elvis Presley."

"No. Ug. You didn't guess then?"

"Afraid not. Either my attention was concentrated elsewhere, or you are becoming a mistress of dissimulation."

"I don't think. I felt as if it stuck out all over me. But honestly, the second reason was that I felt silly about it. And you were talking to me about important things, and I didn't want to lose your respect — not that there's anything to respect but — "

"Darling, I do respect you. And I have considerable respect for your intelligence."

"Well but that's it! How can one be so intelligent and such a seething mass of emotion at the same time? I knew perfectly well it was a crush — I can feel them coming on by now. Oh, he was the visiting professor from Cambridge and he had a beautiful accent and sense of humour — and it's always older men, Daddy. I'm sure it's the Father Image."

"I don't know. I shouldn't call Rex Harrison the Father Image."

"But he liked my essays and I found all sorts of reasons for dropping into his office and we met once on Bloor when he was going into the Brooks Bond place for a 'tolerable cup of tea' and he asked me in. Oh yes. Then he told us in class about a Greek movie at that reconditioned place on Yonge Street and — more or less accidentally — I met him there one afternoon and we

124

sat together. But I had mentioned the movie to John, and blest if he and Julie weren't sitting behind us. So he gave me what for in no uncertain terms that night. But all the time I knew he was married — quite contentedly — and I was very critical of some of his views. Besides he wasn't a Christian. But none of that prevented me from thinking about him and dreaming of him, and saying over and over to myself a few nice things he said to me, and going hot and cold when I spotted him on the Vic staircase with the width of the hall between us. How can we women be such fools, Daddy? I could laugh at myself and see exactly what I was doing. I even told him what a crush I had because he would see it anyhow and I felt less ashamed if he knew that I knew. And if he touched me — casually, don't worry. He was very nice and I've always been *Noli me tangere* on principle even when I'm dying to be touched, but at any rate I'm glad you know now. And you don't despise me, do you?"

"Silly. As for women being fools, I wish all of them, and more men, could view themselves, their motives and reactions, as objectively as you do."

"You mean John, particularly?"

He did mean John particularly. Evadne's reminder of the coming birthday brought back with startling clarity the gray November day twenty-five years before, when he had first seen, held in the nimbus of Cecily's maternal radiance, the sleepy pondering face of his son. What an irrelevance the calculation of time was! A quarter of a century that seemed like yesterday; seven years that seemed like an eternity. And always — what youth could never understand or learn except by going through and to it — the immediacy, the unchanging "nowness" of personal experience, so that he could look back at the Andrew Connington that was then and look through him from the Andrew Connington that was now, and be, despite the knowledge and changes, the same person.

But how little one can anticipate or be forearmed against contingencies. In all his shared joy with Cecily, in all the discussion regarding their dealing with their child and children — carefree, though concerned, discussions because, as Chris-

125

tians, they did not share the heavy-footed conviction of conscientious unbelieving parents that the future depended primarily on them — the one possibility he, at least, had overlooked was the one which had become actuality. He had not foreseen divorce between himself and his son, separation so definite, though elusive, that he could talk more easily, more intimately, to the veriest stranger who came to him for advice. He could not communicate with the boy whom he knew so well that he could have interpreted the motives which drew him from his family, the resentments and discomforts and rages and decisions which ran counter to a pattern of life and thinking which his reason could not dispute.

Perhaps that was the trouble: John's uncomfortable sense of his father's comprehension, an undefined yearning for privacy, an ego-craving need to achieve a sense of independent entity. Andrew, turning over the matter in the days succeeding his talk with his daughter, tried to see how he would deal with this in the interview for which he was steeling himself — steeling myself to talk to my own son. Lord, how pitiful! And difficult to bring about, since it was obvious that John would do everything to avoid it. This trip he was now making, back from Elam Lodge in the early October sunshine of a brilliant Saturday afternoon, John had been asked to share. As the oldest pastor in their little conference, he had given the theme talk for a Young People's retreat on Friday evening and led the devotions that morning. But at Evadne's suggestion, John had been invited by the executive to help organize games and to lead a group discussion on a topic for which his work particularly fitted him. He had refused. It had been a plausible refusal, his father understood, with mingled suggestions of lab responsibilities and previous commitments; but it had plunged Evadne into deeper gloom than the frigid relationship between her brother and herself since their quarrel was making habitual; and it emphasized the improbability of reaching him by any devious channels.

"If thou hast run with the footmen and they have wearied thee how wilt thou contend with horses?" Andrew swung suddenly from Highway 48 on to a curve of the old road which stretched invitingly up a hill and through some newly grown timber. He had an urge to walk and straighten out his thoughts as he could seldom do when driving. The quotation from Jeremiah throbbed through his brain and he considered it dispassionately. "Don't let me take myself too seriously, Lord," he said aloud.

From the top of the rise, the hills rolling their flagrant panorama to the sharp blue of Lake Simcoe made him catch his breath with their beauty, and the clean, crisp air in his lungs was another sensory joy. When I consider what people — Thy people — have suffered, are suffering, I know that it's colossal gall for me even to *think* I'm contending with the cavalry. Only — as Thou knowest, and I thank Thee Thou *dost* know experientially — there are no comparisons in individual suffering. For that matter, I'd never have thought that I'd come to consider the Shorncliffe business, that desolate period, estranged from Cecily, as "running with footmen." I suppose these are the "dusty middle years" — more than middle with me — that men talk about. So many become calloused then, even Christians. Keep me from that, Lord. And keep me from injured pride or desire for my own way with John. But don't let me shirk my duty — Thou knowest the intense discomfort I feel at the prospect of facing the issue — if I can do anything to keep him from spoiling his life.

Because that, with all desire to be unprejudiced and objective in the matter, is what I'm afraid marriage with Veronica would do. Her religion, focal point though it seems to him, has little to do with my reaction to the girl herself; it could even be fortunate that it gives me definite ground for objecting to marriage, because if she belonged to my church, I should still consider her unsuitable. Evadne can't see what he sees in her. Neither can I, but considering John's last seven years and his experience with Julie, I can see that what he is in love with is merely a projection of his needs at the moment. I wonder if he really thinks it love or is deliberately settling for second best. Apparently Julie's attentions were flattering to a boy who felt young and on the fringe of the superficially worldly crowd in

127

his course. Why he should feel that way is a mystery. I never did. I don't think Vad does. Perhaps it's a general lack of confidence. If his mother had lived —. But he is, Julie herself pointed out, too 'inhibited' to approve of her morals. Her marriage was a relief, in a sense; it was also a slap in his face.

On the rebound — and quickly realizing its possibilities (Andrew erased the parenthesis from Hansard, but he believed it nevertheless) — was Veronica, familiar if hardly noticed before, working with him every day, her exceedingly feminine presence making itself gently obtrusive. John's father was quite sure that the stifled shyness, the guarded politeness, which made her so dull to him, so exasperating to Evadne, was not her aspect as revealed to his son. He had seen the type often, almost invariably as the wife of a brilliant man concerning whom people wonder what he ever saw in her. Where Julie was daring and sexy, Veronica was conservative and womanly. Where Julie drew attention to herself, Veronica's presence served to set John off. And in this her family had, perhaps not unconsciously — again Andrew tried to be scrupulously fair — abetted her.

Not that he had been able to learn very much about the family. John's chief aim seemed to be to keep their paths from crossing. But earlier in the summer, when Evadne's telephoned invitation had brought Veronica for Sunday five-o'clock dinner, it had been natural to ask random friendly questions, though each one of his or Evadne's had brought a quick, suspicious glance from John, an effort to turn the conversation before another could follow.

Aunt Alex had been the most successful, both because John adored her and because her gentle, slightly vague, *grande dame* manner precluded interruption and gave no impression that her conversation had any motive but kindly interest in the young visitor. From the pool of answers, certain facts had emerged: that Veronica was the eldest of six girls; that her father had been killed twelve years before by an explosion at the factory where he was a skilled mechanic; that her mother worked as a department supervisor in Simpson's drygoods and — this from some unascertained source of Evadne's — that one of

128

her mother's brothers was in the priesthood, while her only maternal aunt was a teaching nun of the Ursuline Order.

Well there was the picture, unmistakable and significant, thought Andrew as he reentered his car and drove it back to the highway: John, always, in spite of his father's attempts to defer to him, second in his own home, the admired, welcome, helpful male in an all-feminine household; John, used to sailing under the lee of his father's scholarship and recently overshadowed by Julie's academic brilliance, now the undisputed superior in education and position; John with the nagging consciousness of "walking afar off" spiritually, finding relief in an atmosphere of dutiful, unquestioning, almost mechanical piety. Add to this the sense of being deus ex machina — his decision to buy a station wagon instead of an MG had only one explanation, as had his choice of holiday at a different time from the rest of the family and his roundabout request to "use the cottage with some friends" when the family were in the city — and a not undeserved admiration for a hardworking family in economical straits; no, it was easy to see the coil of circumstance and sympathy which was being drawn about him. And always in the background the shadowy, problematical figures of priest and nun making any change of the family's loyalty unthinkable and possibly — depending on their personalities — exerting a powerful influence for the church they represented.

On an impulse Andrew decided to avoid the thickening traffic and turned west on Steeles, cutting his speed to suit the hilly, narrow, wooded road. It was funny, except that he could not see the situation in a humorous light, what a champion of the 'working' people John had recently become, in view of his former impatience at his father's economies, and his own extravagant tastes. Andrew had had occasion, quite recently, to quote to him Churchill's dry comment regarding the Labour Party — "they are not the only people who labour" — in answer to a lofty diatribe to Evadne to the effect that it would be well for "some people" brought up in the lap of luxury to learn how the other half — "right here in Toronto, to say nothing of India and China" — lived. It was a statement with which Andrew

129

·thoroughly concurred, but it had seemed rather malapropos, aimed at the youngster whose efforts among the poor of their own congregation and whose tenderheartedness towards all suffering and need had been much more noticeable than her mentor's. Vad was certainly having to take it these days!

Still, that was doing John no harm. Other things being equal, he would prefer for his son a wife from a family which had faced such struggle than from the parasitic wealth of the Logans or the assurance-giving social position of the families in the vicinity of the Mansell home. But other things were not equal. And neither social nor intellectual snobbery entered —

He was conscious of a man coming towards him on the roadside, conscious, oddly enough, of a king-size cigarette in the man's mouth as he drew nearer, before he recognized John. Why was he walking out towards Yonge Street? Of course, the Lab was just off Steeles down a side road. So he was smoking. Andrew had rather suspected it lately. Ridiculous to feel so hurt, as if it were a personal insult. But that, of course, was just what it was. For a man of twenty-four to begin a habit which had never attracted him beyond the usual childish experimentation, a habit which he had resisted in his teens and openly condemned — to begin it just when the advanced science journals to which he subscribed were bringing out startling information on its dangers — this argued either nervous distress or another effort to achieve independence from the parental image. Evadne had said that Veronica's fingers were nicotine-stained. Old Gimlet-eyes, he had called her.

Now the feeling uppermost, as he stopped the car beside his surprised son, was embarrassment for the embarrassment he was sure the boy would feel, and fear lest that embarrassment increase his opposition towards his father in the interview which was inevitable. For, though the pit of his stomach sank a distinct two inches at the prospect, Andrew recognized that an opportunity like this might not soon recur.

"Where on earth's your car?" he asked as John slid in beside him. He had not missed the other's uncertain gesture as if to throw away the cigarette, nor the half-defiant decision to retain it. In his right hand now, resting over the seldom-used ashtray, it was ostentatiously ignored by both.

"In a garage halfway from Finch's. Just managed to get it there before the motor conked out. Thank goodness, it's still on warranty. But they can't get a replacement till Tuesday. Thanksgiving weekend of all times."

"You're welcome to this one tonight — Thanksgiving too if you need it."

"Thanks." Andrew had hesitated to make the offer for fear of the very stiffness which unconsciously rendered the gratitude void. "But I'm sure Aunt Alex will let me have hers."

"I'm afraid Vad took a gaggle of youngsters to the retreat in it. You'd better take this."

"Oh — yes, I forgot. Well, thanks. If you're sure you don't need it."

It was not an auspicious beginning. Plato's remarks regarding the burden of gratitude were perennially true, thought the benefactor, searching for a better opening.

"You were on your way to the Lab when it happened?"

"Yes. I promised Mathers that I'd look in on the test. Most of the others are out of town till Tuesday. A chap at the garage ran me over there. Blinking bus never runs when you need it. So I was hoofing it to Yonge. And I should have been late as all-get-out getting home." He spoke with belated, if grudging, courtesy. "A good thing you came along."

It was not much better but it would have to do.

"I'm glad I did." There was no point easing into it. "I've wanted for some time to talk to you, but we never seem to have a moment."

At least, a kinder way of putting it than that you never want to talk to me, and I haven't had the courage to ask you, he thought. As it was, he could feel the atmosphere condense.

"No. It's a rat race all right." John's effort at drawing a red herring made his voice falsely genial. "It looks as if we'll be doing more night work anytime now. Mathers says the Federal Government is coming through with a grant just on the strength of our last report. And if it goes through ——"

131

"I'm very glad, but it's something else I want to talk about now." Well, that was flat enough. What had Beth said about his power to dominate as soon as he began to speak? He was going to need it! The wall of silence was so thick that if there had been any reply, even of gesture, he could not see it. He caught himself on the point of asking sharply if he had been heard, giving a pointed reminder that some comment was in order. Thank Heaven he had restrained himself! That would have predoomed the whole conversation. He forced himself to smile — good grief, he supposed it would be described as a quizzical smile — and the voice which issued from his throat was so full of humour and understanding that it brought him perilously close to nausea.

"Don't you think a remark like 'What do you want to talk about, Dad?' is in order?"

John was franker in face of the unavoidable than he.

"I guess I have a fairly good idea."

Andrew sighed with relief.

"Then I'll stop these cloying preliminaries. They're an insult to both of us. Except for one thing. I'd give a very great deal, and certainly anything of material advantage, if just this once you'd let down your barriers, talk to me, let me talk to you, as father and son instead of as strangers. If I've done anything to cause your attitude this past considerable while —hurt or disappointed or failed you inadvertently (God knows it has been unintentional) — let me know how."

There was a long pause which he waited deliberately for the other to break. Finally he broke it.

"I think you exaggerate about my attitude. From what I hear, most fathers and sons find it sticky going to be confidential. No, of course, you haven't done anything. You've been extremely good to me and I'm very grateful ——"

"Come off it, John." It might have been Mansell's embarrassed growl. What on earth was the use of this exchange? Yet he must pursue it, must manage to keep the thin edge of his own honesty as a wedge in the threatened closure of their relationship. "That's not what I'm asking and you know it. Right?

Without any help from you so far, and very well aware that any rights I have to question you in the matter are those of affection and concern and fatherhood, I am asking you to tell me how things stand between you and Veronica."

"I suppose you know she's wearing my ring."

The tone was noncommittal. Andrew's was equally noncommittal in return.

"That meant one thing in my day. Now, it may mean much or little. In your case, however, I should take it to mean —?"

Again a pause; then a guarded reply.

"That we are thinking of getting married? Yes."

An odd way for a lover to put it. Somehow it gave his father hope. He pursued the question.

"On what basis?"

"What the — ?" John was obviously taken aback. He recovered his flat, factual monotone, though the next question had a rude, sarcastic twist. "Now just what answer am I supposed to give to that?"

Andrew bit back a sharp retort. Dear Lord, he prayed silently with the swift invocation which had become habitual. I love this kid. Keep me from wanting to push his face in. Keep me remembering Your patience with me. Aloud he said reasonably, "I thought the question was clear enough. You are a Protestant. She is a Roman Catholic...."

"Dad, isn't it time all this intolerance was done away with? Haven't I heard you say from the pulpit that all who call Jesus Christ Lord are your brothers — and sisters? That you feel far closer to — to Bernard of Clairvaux or Augustine than to Karl Marx or Bertrand Russell? Shouldn't that go for Veronica who believes rather than Julie who didn't?"

"You quote me correctly. You have also heard me discuss the much-abused word 'intolerance.' Since you are making use of it, be honest enough to admit where intolerance applies in connection with my question. I asked on what basis you intended to 'get married' — your phrase, not mine — and I meant exactly that. Almost any Protestant minister would perform the ceremony or recognize it as legal and binding, whether performed

133

by Protestant or Roman Catholic. Not one of them would take the liberty of interfering at all in your future life, regardless of your religious views or customs. I do not say that this attitude on their part is right; I do say that it is 'tolerant' in your sense of the word. On the contrary what conditions does Veronica's church lay down?"

"We haven't discussed it — particularly."

Andrew had stopped the car in their driveway and now stared at his son, wordless. John did not meet his gaze. His young face remained set in rather pathetic aloofness, but there was no reason to doubt his statement. It was not a subject, his father suddenly realized, which Veronica would introduce until necessary, and John, if he was at all correct in his attempt to understand the boy's confused interplay of thought and feeling, would leave it alone as long as he could. They walked into the house together.

"I . . . I don't like to rush you, Dad, but I have to get ready for a date."

"I'll come up while you change," said Andrew equably.

He had not been in the room — virtually a small apartment — since the day of Evadne's effort. He did not know whether or not to hope that John was thinking of that occasion now. But time was going.

"Last week" — he resumed the topic from a new angle — "I talked to a self-styled atheist in his thirties, a man brought up in a Christian church which he was vigorously repudiating. I found that he had no idea of the Apostles' Creed. Said he had never heard it. Incidentally, he did not know what a 'Hail Mary' was, though he admitted that he could say the Lord's Prayer! That ignorance doesn't apply to you, John. Whether you have discussed the matter or not, you are perfectly well aware that at the present time, unless you are married by a priest, the ceremony will not be recognized by her as legal, and your children will be considered illegitimate. Moreover Veronica's priest will not marry her unless you take instruction in her church. Even that ceremony will take place only in the vestry or chapel. The way any devout Catholic wishes to be

134

married — in the Church with a full nuptial mass — is impossible unless you become a member. Believe me, if you persuade Veronica now to set this latter demand aside, it will be a constant source of reproach and conscience with her. As for not being married by a priest, even if you prevail upon her, the family will never cease their efforts to have your marriage made legitimate. I'm not blaming them. How could they do otherwise, believing as they do? But it is not your belief. And marriage — any marriage — has enough rocks to founder on without heading for a reef like that."

John turned at the bathroom door to fling his towel over the shower rail.

"Isn't it possible" — he was breathing rather quickly — "that I am the best judge of that? If marriage by a priest means so much to her, is it such a great concession for me to make?"

Standing there in his earnest, belligerent dignity and his shorts, he looked irresistibly young and comical. Andrew had a momentary urge to forget that the bare shoulders were level with his own, put an arm around them, and laugh him into their one-time camaraderie. But nothing was less suitable for the occasion than levity. So he answered seriously,

"To your first question, the answer is no. You are of age, the decision must be yours. But no, I don't think you can possibly be the best judge. You have no conception of the hell on earth of being estranged from your wife . . . of living in the same house, even sleeping in the same bed with someone who has become a stranger to you because you disagree on basic matters. I had — your mother and I had — a time of such anguish." He caught his son's questioning, half-hostile look before the blue eyes glanced quickly away. "And I can tell you — so could she — that it is an experience to make one long to die. That is, if you have known what love is."

He paused, but there was no reply. He went on more slowly.

"To your second question, yes. It is *too* great a concession. For your belief means as much to you, John, no matter how hard you are trying to minimize it. Of your own free will, you entered into covenant with Christ, at your own request you made a public confession of your faith. It was a real and personal experience to you. Whether Veronica knows anything of such experience you do not say. And your silence speaks against it —"

"Gosh, Dad, two people in love don't talk religion all the time."

"Two people who share a living faith in Christ don't need to talk religion all the time," riposted Andrew quickly. "It's the basis, the jumping-off place, for all they say and think and do. Is that your experience with Veronica?"

There was no reply. John was fumbling intently with his cuff links.

"I don't deny that people within the Roman Catholic communion have found such faith. But if they are true to the teaching of the church, they cannot admit that yours is sufficient outside it."

"What about —" John was obviously uncomfortable. He flung the query over his shoulder as he brushed his thick dark hair with unnecessary vigour. "What about Pope John? He has quite a different attitude. He is all for closer relations between them and us — separated brethren, he calls us."

Andrew suppressed a sigh of exasperation.

"From what I see and read — and there is no lack of publicity — he has a delightful personality and a heart of gold. But there is not a shred of evidence that on any doctrinal matter the Church's official attitude will alter in spite of all his statements of paternal solicitude, or that he has any conception of union with us except on the basis of our unconditional return to the bosom of what he calls Mother Church. Remember too that it is to the Shrine of Mary that he makes pilgrimage on important occasions and that his favourite prayer is to this effect: 'Hail Mary, hope of the world. In death's hours may the strong angel that watches over me, lead me where the just abide with thee. In thee may there find repose my soul everlasting.' "

"Well, that's beside the point," said John coldly. Andrew found himself wishing, with a queer sense of paternal shame, that his son would argue better. The logic which had been

136

praised in collegiate debates and which had shown to advantage in teenage arguments with Evadne seemed to have deserted him. It would be much easier to counter point with point than to have his statements blunt against this inept, unchallenging resistance. "Don't think I'm not listening, Dad, or that I don't appreciate what you say. But it's my life after all, isn't it?"

He was evidently poised for departure but Andrew did not intend him to depart yet. He crossed to the door and stood there, effectually blocking all but a forced exit.

"No, John, of course it isn't." His words were quiet but incisive. "You know better than that. 'You are not your own, you are bought with a price.' 'Your life is hid with Christ in God.' It isn't something you can dispose of at your own preference, or for your own happiness, unless you are sure that it is His will, that this marriage is in Him. More, it's a question of Veronica's life. If you love her, your concern should go far beyond what pleases her at the moment. There is no more reason — far less, I believe, but I am trying to speak with moderation — for her to influence you than for you to exert yourself to win her. Very little publicity is given to those who leave the Roman Church, especially to those who become Protestants, but their numbers — both of priests and laity — are considerable. Think of Jim Watson's wife — or of Tony Vittorio and his — or the young Hungarian whom Mary Reid brought to talk to me. And how her own faith grew when she found that she couldn't give it up for him —"

"Look, Dad, I simply must go."

"You'd better take these." Andrew handed him the car keys, but did not move from the doorway. "There's something else I must say, and it's more important even than your punctuality. We have both avoided it. I am urging you to take a stand with her now because — and this is where the imbalance arises — after marriage, although she will be allowed, even obligated, to make every effort to convert you, you will be bound by your own promise never to try to influence her, whatever her need, however great your concern may be for her salvation —"

"Dad, you're not giving me the line that Nickie won't be saved because she's an R.C.!"

"Since when has our concept of salvation been a fire insurance policy?" snapped Andrew. Then controlling himself. "Aren't you quite deliberately misconstruing? Very well. Say that you have the right to set aside your own life and Veronica's. You have no right to set aside your responsibility for the children who almost certainly will be born to you. Yet to be married by a priest — married legally in Veronica's eyes — this is the very thing you must do. By your own signed statement you will have them brought up in her faith, and never, even if she should die, talk to them about yours or attempt to exert any influence whatever over their beliefs, no matter how mistaken, how wrong, how dangerous they may appear to you. I know there is talk of the Roman Church softening these demands. The Anglican Church particularly is pressing for it. But if — and it has not happened — if the demand should be abrogated in individual cases, how does Veronica feel on the subject? Will she insist?"

There was no answer.

"Think what it means — though I doubt if you can: a divided household, religious observances in which you have no part, yourself suspect in your children's eyes with none of the give and take, the question and answer, the homely unity in which you were reared. And even if they should ask you, no matter what depth of conviction you have, to be bound in honour not to deal honestly with them — to forfeit your privilege, to say nothing of your right and duty as a father. John, whatever suffering is entailed, you dare not face your Judge with the neglect of their souls laid to your account."

He stopped. John was beside him, his set expression unmoved.

"Is that all?"

His father stood aside to let him pass. He had scarcely reached the hall when a strong conviction came over Andrew. His hand fell on his son's shoulder in so compelling a grip that he turned and the two men faced each other for the first time, tired hazel eyes level with unhappy blue ones.

"No. Not quite." On Andrew's voice, hoarse now with the

138

intensity of long pleading, there was a note of severity. "And I pray that you will be given grace — you'll need it — to consider this: is what you feel for Veronica love? Or is it a compound of reactive pride from Julie's marriage and an unacknowledged desire — which it is time you dredged up and looked at — to punish me because for some reason I make you feel guilty of your mother's death?"

A startling change of expression swept John's face. There was a long second's silence before he flung off the restraining hand and made his headlong departure down the stairs. Andrew felt the house vibrate with the slam of the front door before he himself had reached the third step in his descent. He paused, waiting. Then a thinner slam and the roar of an engine told him that his car was gone. He continued slowly down in a body that seemed to have grown heavy in the last hour. Aunt Alex would be waiting for dinner, and his Thanksgiving sermon for the next morning had still to be prepared.

All during the quiet meal, while he responded pleasantly to his aunt's desultory comments, and afterwards, as he wrestled to concentrate on the text of the hundred-and-third psalm, he kept trying to interpret the look in his son's eyes. Was it hatred? Or terror? Or sudden, unwilling realization?

At any rate he was wryly amused and very slightly comforted that John had not thrown the car keys back at him.

8

ANDREW, ARE YOU AS TIRED as you look?"

There was warm concern in Beth's voice. Unfailingly tactful, she had found something to busy her in the Bible Class room, and the church was clear of people when she met him on his way to the vestry. He paused and smiled.

"Impossible to say. How tired do I look?"

"Dreadfully. Is anything worrying you?"

Andrew hesitated. He could not lie and yet, for all her sympathy, he did not want to confide in her about John. He said.

" 'The cares of this world,' I suppose, if not particularly 'the deceitfulness of riches.' I'm quite well, Beth. Really."

"You don't look it. I worry about you. Look, could you come somewhere with me for Thanksgiving dinner tomorrow? The Guild — no, Terra Cotta. They serve a superb dinner and it's a lovely drive to the Caledon hills."

"I'm sorry. Thanksgiving is one New World custom that Aunt Alex is keen on. I know she is counting on me for the occasion, and Evadne too."

"Don't you take your family responsibilities seriously! Phyllis asked me down to Oshawa, but I was indefinite. Why not bring them along? And John, if he isn't busy. I'm sure I can still get a reservation."

"I must seem most ungrateful, Beth. It isn't only that I heard Aunt Alex discussing the menu with Nancy. But Vad is up

140

at camp with a gang, and I rather think intends to bring one or more to dinner with her. We probably won't know until she arrives tomorrow. So I'm afraid — Why don't you join us? We'd love to have you."

Beth's hesitation was momentary.

"No. I'd really have asked for that one. Mrs. Harris-Kemp will join her daughter and listen to the merry babble of her not-too-well-disciplined grandchildren. See what you've consigned me to."

"Your 'head is bloody but unbowed,' I think." Andrew said good-bye and left her, not knowing whether he was sorry or relieved.

He had no ready excuses, however, when she telephoned him on Tuesday morning.

"You must have had inside information about yesterday's weather when you said no to my invitation. A day to drive anywhere it wasn't! My windshield wipers were almost useless coming home along 40I."

"I'm sorry. And to think that I wished that trip on you."

"Think nothing of it. We women are forgiving creatures. I say" — she sounded as if an idea had suddenly occurred — "does that mean you would be inclined to make reparation?"

"What kind of reparation?"

"Caution, thy name is Connington! Have you seen what sort of day today is?"

"I've been up for hours. Of course. Beautiful."

"Then how about running up to my cottage? I want to talk about the book. And I'm having some alterations made that I should show some interest in, or I'll find when it's too late that everything has been done the wrong way. I've been intending to go up, but weekend traffic is bad. Besides the local workmen have gone citified and don't work Saturday. And it's hard to get people to go during the week. Men, I mean. And a man on the spot would carry such authority. Will you come? Please."

"If I can be of any help——"

"Wonderful. Frankly, I don't know much about building. You know what people say about art: 'I know what I *like*' but

141

I'm a bit hazy how to get it done. The last time I did anything of the sort, the doors were hung all wrong, and I didn't notice till I went up the next summer. You could be a great assistance with suggestions — and just your masculine presence."

"The lowest form of flattery. Very well, for what it's worth, you have it."

"Oh, good. Wear something old. We'll be roughing it."

"Will it be all right for you with the top down?" she asked as he came out to the car an hour later. "I like to make the most of the sun while we have it."

"I'll let you know if I can't take it." He assured her dutifully. "In passing may I say that I'm glad Evadne can't see your idea of old clothes for roughing it. Simple soul that I am, I took you at your word."

She had the grace to apologize.

"I didn't want you to rip anything good. Your outfit is just right. It's pretty primitive at the lake. These aren't new. They've seen plenty of wear really."

The latest cut in matching sportswear impeccably fitted to casual looseness, her two-toned scarlet tunic and slacks did look good. So did the gaudy Liberty triangle tied to accentuate the lacquered line of her hair; so did the pair of enormous costume rings which were set with a midnight blue stone and which called attention to the long, slim, brown hands on the wheel; and so, in completion, did the curiously laced, cork-soled boots of midnight blue suède. Andrew approved. Hearts just as true and fair could beat under such costumes as under the sedate widow's weeds of the previous century. But they did not correspond to his idea of roughing it.

Nor was primitive his adjective for the cottage which looked out on Couchiching from its own five acres of stone-walled property. He had never described the Mansells' summer home on the St. Lawrence — now sacrificed to the Seaway — as primitive; and, recalling its early condition, he no longer applied the term to the Haliburton cottage which Cecily had inherited, not certainly since electric lights and indoor plumbing had been installed. But neither place was in the same category with this spacious dwelling. The fifty-year-old original stone-and-timber house had been turned into a giant living room, flanked by modern wings carefully built to harmonize outside with the basic structure, while inside every refinement of rubbed wood, built-in cupboard, plumbing fixtures, and a separate electric heating made "getting away from city life" a question of geographical displacement only. The sashes of the early house had given place to vast picture windows, and the Mansell kitchen on Russell Hill Road needed remodelling badly, to judge by the completely fitted, well-planned unit with which Beth finished her conducted tour. "The old one was impossible, so we just ripped it apart, extended it to include the summer kitchen and began again."

"And what is the latest project?" asked Andrew, nodding towards a couple of men who were shuffling a pile of flat cut stone at the far end of the wide verandah.

"They seem to be starting on the patio. Let's see if they have finished the swimming pool. Or would you like lunch first?"

"I'm here to work, remember. And did you say swimming pool?" He indicated the lake fifty yards away.

"Quite. But you wouldn't go in there today, would you? And yet you might like a swim. The water can be too cold even in August for some people."

He conceded the point and admired the thirty-foot tiled pool. To judge by Beth's technical explanation of the heating system and the springboard, and later, when they joined the workmen, her comments and directions on the arrangement of the patio, her need for his assistance was negligible. On their return to the house he told her so.

"You need my help about as much as — as this place needs a patio."

"No, but really you have no idea how much better I feel with you along." Then hurriedly, "The patio is primarily for Phyllis and her crowd. For Tim and Anne too, when they come up. You know how keen the young are on barbecues and a barbecue without a patio isn't right according to them."

They had one themselves, though, on the little promontory

overlooking the inlet west of the house. Beth's snack luncheon included thick steaks from the freezer, salad which she had brought up from the city, substantial rolls which emerged from the electric oven by the time the food was ready. For the most part she suggested the conversation, as they shared a small portable table in cool air warmed by still, October sunlight. He realized suddenly, during a pause, how poor he was at casual chat. Theology, literature, even politics he could rise to instantly, but he could hardly introduce these topics and she did not. And to this sort of tête à tête he was necessarily unaccustomed.

"How much time do you spend here?" he essayed.

She gesticulated vaguely.

"It varies. I thought I would be here a good deal of the summer, but while Roger and I were away, the children had got used to divvying it up between them. Their youngsters are just at the age when they like a cottage. Of course, Jud — that's Tim's eldest — is going to camp now. Presently they'll all be at that stage, and later they'll find it too dull here except when they have their own crowd. So I left it to them most of the time. They wanted me to stay longer of course, but frankly after a few days I find the children wearing — particularly when I yearn to discipline them and their parents won't. So I went out to Yellowstone with Nora Evans, went on up the coast to Alaska, and visited Jim and Anne-Marie in Vancouver. And took visitors from overseas to the Festival several times. I don't want the children to feel any burden of obligation to me. Fortunately — if you like to put it that way — there are a good many women, widowed or unmarried, who are glad to go places."

He did not know if it was the occasion for levity.

" 'Fortunately' seems a harsh word in connection with the multiplicity of widows."

"Or unmarried? At the rate the young are rushing into matrimony regardless, the class will probably be extinct in another few generations. However, I just mean that *as* a widow myself I'm fortunately not unique."

Andrew felt that he should fill the pause. Unable to think of a suitable remark he said nothing.

"Do you — do widowers have the problem to the same degree?"

Andrew realized suddenly that he never thought of himself as a widower. But then he was not fond of general classifications.

"I can't speak for others. With Aunt Alex and the children still at home the problem hasn't really arisen — of companionship for every day or for holidays, that is."

"No. Of course it may any time."

"True. And for social life," he went on ignoring the lead, "I haven't any in your sense of the term. Besides, my position puts me in a different category for solo appearances — A or E depending on the point of view."

"Yes, I know." Her voice held a suggestion of impatience. "From outside, from the point of view of others. Any man for that matter has the advantage. An extra man is never supernumerary —"

"Prove *that* by the new math," said Andrew trying to divert her. He did not succeed.

"I'm not talking about your position or profession. I'm not talking about a clergyman or a father or a nephew. I'm talking about you, Andrew Connington, person in your own right and with your own rights as a person."

The phrases jarred on him. For the first time since the pleasant, mutually beneficial renewal of their acquaintance, he felt her not merely as distant, but as alien. Yet the charge of using jargon, which he would unhesitatingly have made if the words had been spoken by John or Evadne, would be an unpardonable snub. And an explanation of his feelings in deeper, more precise terms — such as he would have given to Cecily — would sound pious and pedantic. The spell of the carefree day was broken. He merely countered,

"What rights?"

If she felt the chill, the dissolution of intimacy, she was beyond caring; or perhaps cared enough to risk a temporary loss in order to gain her point.

"The right to be yourself, to think of yourself occasionally, to make provision for yourself, to express yourself, the right to

145

personal happiness, if you like. Physically and mentally you are a young man yet — at the height of your powers anyhow. Why write it off as if life were over for you?"

This is absurd, thought Andrew, with the disappointing realization that he had been regarding her as spiritually adult when she was capable of such immaturity. He wished he had not come. Quotations leaped at him and an urge to bombard her with them: 'Ye are not your own' — when had he used that one recently? 'For me to live is Christ.' 'He that loseth his life for My sake and the gospel's shall keep it.' 'Yet it is no longer I that live, but Christ liveth in me.' 'If any man would come after me, let him deny himself.' The impulse to set her right, to put her in her place, in return for her well-meaning, but not purely disinterested criticism almost gained the upper hand. With an effort he overcame it and said with deliberate lameness:

"We aren't on the same wave length this time, Beth. I'm sorry to disappoint, but you'll have to face the fact that I don't use those expressions, not for myself. I can't see them as applying to me as a Christian."

She was astute enough to recognize defeat, if not to accept it as final. There was a long silence while the warmth of October sunshine and the flamboyant spectrum of colour, softened and shaken in the almost unmoving water — together with the submissive stillness of her recumbent body in the chair beside him — exercised their soothing. Then she looked up at him until she drew and held his eyes.

"I'm the one to be sorry, Andrew. Do you realize now just how much I need your ministry?"

It was the right note and she did not hold it too long. "About *The Crowded Solitude* — did I tell you that I met Keen at the Granite Club on Sunday? He says if the printers don't strike — and he thinks they will take it to arbitration — it should be out by November first. That's pretty late, he tells me, to get it across Canada for the Christmas trade, but they are pushing it."

"It's little short of a miracle that you have got it out at all, to say nothing of before Christmas," said Andrew warmly. "You tell me you didn't subsidize it. Just what are your methods? I

146

know something of the difficulties, remember — 'Books of sermons don't sell unless they are famous name brands' — 'Canadians don't buy books except at Christmas.' "

"But this isn't a book of sermons — 'pithy and profound comment by the stormy petrel of the Canadian ministry.' I'm afraid the publicity will take that line and you'll just have to put up with it."

Andrew winced.

"I hope the end justifies the means. No, I have put the matter in your hands — with reservations on the subject of editing. And they have been very good about that — even left in my references to Schweitzer, though it was touch and go for awhile. If you need extra captions, I might make an effort in that direction. How about 'Shockers from the Study.' 'Somebody in there hates you.' 'Songs of a Sourpuss.' No? Don't say I didn't try."

"It's obviously not your line." Beth was her assured self again. She had acted promptly with Andrew's manuscript. She had exercised considerable influence and persuasiveness with her publishing connection and if her statement that the book was not subsidized was strictly true, she had, though Andrew was not told, made a gentleman's agreement to buy up unused stock, if it should not be a success. She felt that she could afford to be magnanimous; but she had too much sense to leave Andrew burdened by gratitude. "The book will sell itself once the public gets hold of it. We just want to make sure that the public does get hold. Sal Turner is wangling already from radio and T.V. interviews."

"You know what P. G. Wodehouse says about the effect on sales of an author's public appearance."

"Regardless of P. G. Wodehouse," said Beth who didn't, "any publicity is better than no publicity."

"And — Wodehouse again — the banning by one bishop is good for 5000 sales. How does your stock stand with bishops, Beth? Could you persuade one of them to ban me as dangerously orthodox or heretically theological?"

147

"You know as well as I do that they — the established churches — won't take that line."

"No. Ignoring altogether or damning with faint praise, I expect. They will probably suggest that I haven't thought my position through in the light of modern scholarship. Query: What scholarship? In any event I shall always be in your debt for this."

"Don't squeal when I come upon you for payment. Now are you equal to exercise? Janice — Phyllis's eldest, in case you don't know — asked me if I'd bring her some small cones. Her art class is going to make Christmas decorations. There should be plenty under the spruce and balsams down there."

A casual ramble in woods long since cleared of underbrush, an inspection of the patio which grew under their eyes ("The longer we stay, the longer they work," observed Beth shrewdly), a round-about drive to show the farmhouse where her paternal grandmother had been born, a chat about the early days of railways, and a pleasant meal in an excellent little roadhouse off the highway ("You may be all spirit, but I'm simply starving after so much fresh air") : by the time they reached Russell Hill Road at ten-thirty, rapport was completely restored. Perhaps Andrew's awareness that he had been ungraciously annoyed and Beth's unconditional surrender had strengthened her position.

He was ready for bed when Evadne announced herself at his door.

"Did I waken you?" he asked. "I thought it was early for your light to be out, but I tried to be quiet coming upstairs."

"No. I turned out the light because my eyes were tired and I couldn't study any more. But I was waiting for you." He got into bed and she squatted cross-legged at the foot.

"Sure you're warm enough? Pull this over you."

"I'm fine." The flat band which held her brown hair back from her forehead matched the yellow, viyella flannel housecoat he had given at request for her birthday ("Frederick's annual sale — half-price and a perfect dream"). "I'm just wondering if it's too late for you to call Ursula Pethwick or if you should wait till morning."

"Wait till morning, if you are asking me. And who is Ursula Pethwick?"

"You remember her, Daddy. She came to Young People's last spring and gave a terrific survey of Hindooism and its outworking in the present setup in India."

"Of course. *That* Ursula Pethwick. A very keen mind — and not at all hard to listen to. But why should I call her — and at eleven p.m.? Is there a crisis in Indian affairs that won't wait till morning?"

"If I said that, you'd call it ill-timed levity," said his daughter rebukingly. "Can't you see I'm serious?"

"Sorry, pet. If there had been an accident or bereavement you would have told me right away. What is the trouble? And why should Ursula Pethwick come to me?"

"Because I told her to. I met her on the subway today and she looked simply awful. So awful that I felt I could mention it. I thought she'd been ill. I hate people commenting when you just look worse than usual for no particular reason."

"And has she been ill?" asked Andrew patiently. Any conversation with this child of his was welcome, but there were topics of deeper interest than the personal appearance of the almost unknown Miss Pethwick."

"That's just it. She said Not exactly. And then she burst out — she has always been so reserved — very helpful but quite offish — it was as if she had to say it to someone."

"Say what?"

"She's dreadfully worried about something or somebody. Said it was a personal crisis and she didn't know what to do or how to meet it. So I suggested she talk to you. Said you were good at helping people, and that even if you couldn't help, she would feel better for talking it out with you. She demurred at first." Evadne paused and raised one eyebrow in unconscious imitation of him. "I like that word. Don't think I ever used it before. Why are we dropping so many good words? There isn't really another to express just what that does. 'Object'? no, too strong; so is 'refused.' 'Hesitated'? Too weak."

149

Andrew smiled and put his arms behind his head. This was a youngster after his own heart.

"To make room for 'empathy'; also 'finalize,' 'alphabetize,' and all the circumlocutions of 'spell out' 'frame of reference' 'in terms of.' "

"Oh, did I tell you about the Syrian actor who lectured to the Drama group at Vic about his experiences producing Shakespeare in Cairo — and quoted his own paraphrase of Hamlet: 'Lay not that flattering *alibi* to your soul'? I suppose presently we shall be asked to prove our 'unction' for the night of the murder."

"At least a foreigner has some excuse — 'laying an unction' isn't a metaphor he meets every day," said Andrew. "But there is no excuse for my 'degreed' clerical friend who is paid — sour grapes, I know — for contributing in his column a gem like the one which appeared this last Saturday night, one, if a prize one, among many. Did I read it to you, Vad? No, you weren't home. 'Positions which may have had value twenty years ago can hang like an albatross over our heads today.' "

"Oh dear. And the appalling thing is that probably nobody else notices. Daddy, you *must* do something. Which reminds me about Ursula Pethwick."

"Ah yes. Whose demurring produced this semantic digression."

"She said you would be too busy and that she isn't a member of the church although she has heard you and enjoyed your sermons very much. But when I asked if she had gone to her own minister, she didn't feel that he would be much help. She doesn't know him, and his chief interest is in young people — you know, the coffeehouse approach. And then she said something that astounded me. She said that she didn't think anything but prayer would help and that she didn't think he believed in prayer. Wondered if you would pray. So I urged her to come."

"Did she come?"

"She phoned, several times. I couldn't tell her where you were because I don't know —" Her eyes met his and glanced quickly away — "but I promised I'd tell you when you came in. She

150

said it didn't matter how late. She hasn't been sleeping anyhow."

"Well, we've wasted half an hour."

"I know. But I wanted to explain. Anyhow, I've hardly seen you for days. I'm Vad. Remember me?"

She swung forward on the bed to kiss him. He gave her an affectionate hug, then pushed her off, rolled on his side, and pulled the telephone towards him.

"I suppose you have the number?"

The call was answered on the first ring.

"Are you there?" That gives her background away, thought Andrew. People of only one background in the English-speaking world say, "Are you there?"

"O Mr. Connington. How kind of you. No, I wasn't asleep. You really mean it? I have no fixed hours just now. I'll gladly come at ten. You're quite sure it's not too much trouble. No, I can't explain further over the phone. Thank you so much. Yes, I'll try to sleep now. Good-night."

Andrew returned the receiver to its cradle.

"Is John in?"

"He missed dinner. Phoned that he had to work late at the lab. He came in just before you. I didn't see him. I thought perhaps," — her eyes met his with the understanding of a common concern — "it was better for him not to get the impression that we are checking up."

"The instinctive wisdom of woman — too seldom, I fear, put into practice," said Andrew approvingly. "It's time you turned in too, Pet. Unless you want to talk."

"Some other time, I'll unburden my soul. Why should strangers have all the privileges? I'm glad you got Miss Pethwick though. Whatever has happened, it's pretty serious to her."

151

9

U RSULA PETHWICK'S APPEARANCE as she took the "patient's chair" which he held for her promptly at ten o'clock the next morning confirmed both his previous impression of her and Evadne's summary of her present state. About my age, he thought. Marked English accent. Emotional but controlled, and nobody's fool. She had a pale, close-textured skin, straight, high-bridged nose, a mouth that had learned to laugh rather sardonically, and fine brown eyes, showing the strain of close reading, behind strong glasses. There was not a thread of grey in the straight, brown hair which was cropped unfashionably short. It was her hat, her gloves, the lines at eyes and throat, which suggested her years. Eyes and mouth and manner spoke of recent strain.

He leaned back in his own chair.

"Shall we omit the preliminaries? I mean the irrelevant ones about taking my time and not knowing exactly why you are here and so on? Just try to tell me what is distressing you. I don't need — perhaps I do need — to assure you that nothing you say will be repeated, without your permission."

Quite evidently she was willing to talk. But she could not decide how to begin. After a full minute of false starts, her opening words surprised him.

"Mr. Connington, can a sane person be committed to a mental institution?"

Merciful Heavens, he thought, is she afraid that ——?

"I'm not talking about myself," she went on, smiling faintly,

152

"though I must say I've wondered if you would think me unhinged when I told you. But I've never come up against such a thing or even thought of it before, and it seems so fantastic that I doubt my own judgment. What do you think?"

"In this particular case, whatever it is, nothing yet. But," — his face hardened momentarily — "very definitely it is possible. I have known of at least two cases."

He did not mention that in one case he had lost a church member by his interference. He had been shocked, on enquiring the reason for old Mr. Goodwin's absence from church on two successive Sundays, to hear that the man, a faithful and appreciative attendant, had been taken fifty miles from the city to a home for the incurably senile. The elderly man's pitiful, but clearheaded account of the situation had sent Andrew back to talk to his son, a teacher and guidance counsellor at the local high school. It had been a heart-sickening interview, conducted on a thin surface of polite regret and bland assurance concealing the younger Goodwin's uneasiness and his wife's resentment. It left him in no doubt that Mrs. Goodwin's determination not to have her father-in-law as a member of her household had instigated the action, which, if the victim's story was credible, had included drugs and virtual kidnapping. Andrew, thoroughly roused and finding his pleas unavailing, had begun to take action, but it was too late. After a month as an outcast, realizing his son's poor-spirited treachery, the old man had obligingly died, intestate. Gratitude for this and for the comfortable addition to their income had not assuaged the unrighteous indignation of the heirs. If their departure from the church was unobtrusive, its quietness, Andrew felt, was due to anxiety to avoid embarrassing disclosures. Just as well, he thought. It had saved him the greatest single problem of discipline that he had faced since the excommunication of Ben Harris.

"You have, really?" Ursula Pethwick's voice was eager. "It sounds dreadful to say, but it makes me feel that I'm on surer ground, that it's less likely to be just my imagination."

"Could you give me the details?"

153

"Of course. It begins about six years ago. I was classifying a rather large bequest of early Canadiana for the Royal Ontario Museum."

"I had the impression that you were a teacher."

"Not now. I specialized in history and taught for several years. Then I had a rather lengthy illness. And I was not cut out for teaching at all. So I've had a number of jobs: receptionist, researcher for authors and professors — that is how I met your very nice daughter, Mr. Connington. But this is beside the point. Have you met Mrs. Jonathan Sanders?"

Andrew shook his head.

"I could say 'The name is familiar' because I've reached the stage where most names are, but it wouldn't be honest. No."

"I thought you might have met her because the Sanders were quite prominent socially. Her husband was a cabinet member in the Provincial government and held various posts. But that is a long time ago. She was — is ninety-two now."

Unexpectedly, her voice broke. He saw, before he looked away, that tears had come into her eyes.

"I'm sorry. I don't usually get emotional. At any rate, Mrs. Sanders telephoned the Museum while I was working there and I happened to answer. She had a rare collection of Indian ivory carvings which she wanted to donate and wondered if the authorities were interested. I was sure they would be and during our conversation mentioned that I had been born in India. She had gone out to Calcutta, she told me then, as the ward of her uncle, who had been Danish attaché in London. That was a coincidence, too, because my mother was Danish. When I told her, she said that I must come to tea and see her other Indian treasures. I thought it was a polite generality; so I murmured something and more or less forgot about it. Two weeks later she telephoned again and insisted that I come. So I went."

Andrew, as she continued, became more interested in her unconscious self-revelation than in the object of her admiring description. Daughter of missionary parents, educated in England, then on scholarship in Canada, she might have overcome the double handicap of hypersensitive intelligence and relentless integrity, except for the undiagnosable ill health which had recurrently plagued her. As it was, eking out the meagre pension of her retired parents, she had found herself, after their deaths, still in precarious circumstances. She was not anti-social, he gathered, but the type that makes few friends and cares deeply about them. Expatriation, illness, variable employment, and inadequate means: he could see how these would contribute to her loneliness and increase her native tendency to withdraw, which Evadne had mentioned. Yet there was a tough resiliency about her and a concealed yearning for friendship. And this contact out of the blue had developed into friendship, giving her a new interest, a common ground for endless conversation, unexpectedly a sense of belonging, of being needed.

"It's hard to explain," she went on earnestly. "Mrs. Sanders has had such a full and fascinating life. And she has always been a bit of an autocrat — the fortune is hers, though of course her husband must have been reasonably well off. Did I say that she met him in India, at an Embassy ball? But, perhaps because she is very Danish — very much like my mother — we had that sense of — not intimacy exactly — almost of relationship."

"Yes," said Andrew, suddenly warmed by recollection of Dr. Murray. "I had it once with a man more than my father's age."

Her occasional visits on invitation had become, always at Mrs. Sanders' suggestion, regular and more frequent. Andrew guessed that, in spite of Ursula's modesty about any contribution of her own to the acquaintance, in spite of the old lady's wealth and the friends retained by wealth and position, few visitors to the mansion on Park Road could give the childless widow such intelligent companionship, such unassuming devotion, such stimulating conversation as the woman before him. Mrs. Sanders was the complete chatelaine and directed the running of her house. Her housekeeper had been with her for thirty years.

"I must be stupid, Mr. Connington," said Miss Pethwick, looking anything but stupid, although obviously sincere, "but

155

it never occurred to me that Enid might resent me. It wasn't as if I had usurped any relationship that she had had."

"Now you think she did?"

"I know it. In fact, looking back, I should have realized that, after I stayed with Mrs. Sanders while Enid went on holiday in April — she hadn't been able to shake the flu germ and Mrs. Sanders sent her for two weeks to Jamaica — she hated me. But I'm taking far too long to come to the point. Only it's such a relief to talk about it." She paused and visibly marshalled her thoughts.

"I've had a difficult research assignment recently, and Mrs. Sanders was in the hospital for two weeks in July; she contracted pleurisy and Enid couldn't look after her and the house too. But she had come home. I saw her once — no, twice. And she was recovering nicely. She never stayed in bed unless absolutely necessary. That was like my mother, too. Then I went to Ottawa to consult the archives and came back to find several telephone messages from her. I called and arranged to visit her on Tuesday — three weeks yesterday. Monday night Enid phoned and said that Mrs. Sanders had had a heart attack and was in Whitby."

"With a heart attack?"

"That's what I asked. Enid was very nice, quite pathetic. Conciliatory, I think. 'What could I do?' she asked. 'I'm not strong enough to manage her. She has gone quite out of her mind.' But Mr. Connington, surely a frail woman of ninety-two who has plenty of money to pay for care could be put in another type of hospital — even if she were insane."

"You don't think she is?"

"Mrs. Sanders is as sane as she was when I first met her," said Miss Pethwick with conviction. "From what Enid said I had no idea what to expect, but I felt that if she was rational at all, she shouldn't feel deserted. I couldn't get away until Saturday, but then I took the bus down. I had telephoned first and been told that it was quite all right to visit." She drew a deep breath. "They had moved her out of the reception wing into the ward for incurables. She was out of bed. There were twenty women in the ward — all of them I should judge quite hopeless — and just room to put a wooden chair between her bed and the next. There she sat upright, fully dressed, incredulous and heartbroken, but keeping herself icily under control. Mr. Connington, I managed to keep from breaking down then, but I cried all the way home in the bus. And with intervals ever since."

"Could she tell what had happened?"

"She knew about the heart attack. It had been a slight one she said, but the doctor had advised the hospital. They got an ambulance, drove very fast, and the next thing she knew, she was in Whitby. 'I've been kidnapped,' were her first words to me."

"Has she a lawyer?"

"Yes. Do you know Beryl Sexsmith?"

"Everyone knows of Beryl Sexsmith. Yes, I've met her. Top of her profession. Well?"

"That's just the point, Mr. Connington. Beryl Sexsmith has been not only her lawyer, but her friend for thirty-five years. When I said I should get in touch with her immediately, Mrs. Sanders was greatly cheered. She hadn't had a visitor. In fact, until last Thursday she had seen nobody except me. She asked if I would bring stockings and handkerchiefs when I came again. All the time we were talking, a woman on a bed at the end of the room was screaming at the top of her voice ... just a steady, recurrent scream. I can't tell you some of the other things that went on." She stopped, wincing at the recollection. "So I tried to get in touch with Miss Sexsmith. It just happens that our visits have never coincided and I haven't met her. She was busy — then in court, then out of town. But meanwhile I went to get the hose and handkerchiefs from the house. Enid was furious when she found I had visited Mrs. Sanders, practically accused me of interference, and told me that it was Miss Sexsmith who had her committed to Whitby."

Andrew's eyebrows indicated his amazement. Miss Pethwick continued quietly, as though afraid that emphasis would detract from the credibility of her statement.

"I wrote to Miss Sexsmith then as carefully as I could. I think

157

now that she was avoiding me. You have no idea, Mr. Conning-ton, how utterly helpless I have felt, with nothing but my own conviction to go upon. The doctors and nurses at the hospital were most kind. But I realized, as I talked about Mrs. Sanders, that many or most mental patients think nothing is wrong with them and that they are very plausible. I felt that the staff was thinking me naive. Besides she had been committed and the staff was only doing its duty. Quite possibly, after the routine tests they may adjudge her sane — but by that time it will be too late! And I have absolutely no right or claim to interfere. So I told Miss Sexsmith how Mrs. Sanders appeared to me and how cheered she had been at the thought of seeing her. I described the conditions of the ward. O my God!" she broke off and held her hands against her temples. "Three weeks cooped up there would drive a sane person mad! I'm not pleading special priv-ileges, really I'm not! I believe that the poorest person should have the best care that we can give. But realistically, Mr. Con-nington, in the interests of our economy — to reduce the argu-ment to the lowest level — if Mrs. Sanders *is* deranged why should our tax-money go to support a woman of fortune, when they say the public institutions cannot accommodate half the people who should be there?"

"A sound argument," said Andrew, "but obviously ——"

"Not the one that matters. No. I included it to show — my-self as much as anyone — that I can still think objectively in the case."

"And have you had an answer?"

"Yes. Here it is." She did not hand him the letter immedi-ately. "It arrived yesterday morning. Meanwhile I had gone to visit on the two weekends. I would have gone oftener, but the round trip by subway and bus and taxi takes five hours and I have had to work nights to keep up with my assignment. I cannot concentrate these days and find that it takes much longer to get the work done. Last Sunday I found her quite cheered. Miss Sexsmith and Enid had visited her on Thursday. I don't think Enid had a warm reception! Mrs. Sanders has used the name 'Judas' (always apologizing) more than once in that

158

connection. Did I say that she has settled an annuity on Enid so that she will have one hundred and fifty dollars a month for life whatever happens?"

"To take effect when?"

"On Enid's fiftieth birthday, last March. But to go back, or rather on. She told me about their visit, what they were wearing, how long they stayed. Nothing could have been more lucid. I have been reading Kierkegaard and she translated a passage of Danish for me from a footnote, and explained a reference to Danish custom which had puzzled me. Now read this."

The letter almost thrust upon him was bland, cautious — could it be placating? Miss Sexsmith had visited the patient and was convinced from her observation that Whitby was the best place for her. She was not sure that the visit had been a good thing but "Mrs. Sanders would probably have forgotten it in fifteen minutes. She did not even recognize Enid at first. The screaming described was going on, but it did not seem to impinge upon her consciousness." Miss Pethwick was thanked for her interest and the letter closed on a note of superb legal finality.

Andrew had begun to read with an open mind. When he finished he knew one thing: he did not like or trust Beryl Sexsmith.

Ursula Pethwick had recovered the letter and was staring at it in bewilderment.

"How *can* she say 'the best place' for her? 'Not impinge upon her consciousness.' Mrs. Sanders told me that they had to raise their voices to hear each other's. 'Fifteen minutes after.' She told me, three days later, that Enid was wearing the gloves I had given her on her birthday — 'you remember? brown kid with a white cuff.' Mr. Connington, the Sanders helped Miss Sexsmith start out in law during the depression. She met her first wealthy clients through them. How can such things happen? Why would anyone want to do such a thing to her?"

"Do you know anything of Mrs. Sanders' affairs — legal and financial?"

"Miss Sexsmith has complete power of attorney. Enid is staying on at the house by her permission. Incidentally, there was a T.V. aerial when I went to get the things — also by per-

159

mission, she said. Mrs. Sanders detested T.V. and wouldn't have it in the house. Enid used to watch it at her sister's, when I stayed for the evening. But Mr. Connington, why Whitby? Why not a rest home with three nurses a day if necessary? Isn't that what one would expect of a trusted friend — granting, as I don't, that Mrs. Sanders needs to be put anywhere?"

Andrew mused.

"You know, of course, that once a person is committed he ceases to be a legal entity. In other words she cannot make or change a will now. Has she spoken to you about a will?"

Ursula Pethwick flushed as if with shame. Her thin-veined hands clenched in her lap and her speech suggested the clenching of teeth.

"This makes me feel utterly beastly, as if I were soiled and couldn't wash. You must just take my word that I never thought of money until all this happened and until I realized that Enid was jealous of me — and afraid. Did I mention that a man came on the line when I telephoned the other night — her brother, I think, or brother-in-law — and told me to keep my nose out of the business? When I think of her entertaining her family in that lovely home and Mrs. Sanders waiting hour after hour in that hell ——"

"You were saying about the will?" prompted Andrew.

"Yes. Actually she gave me a rough idea when she changed it last spring, changed it to Miss Sexsmith's annoyance, she told me. She is leaving most of her estate to charity. She has no remaining relatives of her own. Some connections of her husband, a few friends, and Enid are to get legacies, quite modest ones. She intimated that she was leaving me something. I gathered from her tone that it was a few hundred — 'to take care of taxis' she said. She always told me I should use taxis and always asked if I had done so when I went to see her. I used to say that the subway is more dependable and that I like exercise because — well, there were more interesting things to talk about than finances."

"Quite. Now the first thing is to get your friend out."

Ursula Pethwick's eyes widened with an almost childish expression of hope.

"You mean you believe me? You don't know me at all. You take my word that she isn't — she is —"

"Not necessarily." Andrew's smile disarmed the qualification of the words. "As far as your truthfulness goes, I accept it without reservation. But you may be mistaken. I shall have to get other evidence. Regardless of her sanity, however, judging from Miss Sexsmith's own description of her state, there is no need for her to be in a public institution for the hopelessly and violently insane. That is, if she is wealthy as you imply."

Ursula shrugged her shoulders expressively.

"I have no idea about amounts. The taxes on her property alone must be fantastic — a fourteen-room house with at least one-hundred-foot frontage. She became interested in CARE last year and wrote a cheque for $10,000 dollars as I should write one for ten — well, rather more casually," she added with a rueful smile. "Yet she was a shrewd business woman; told me that she had refused to buy some stocks in which Miss Sexsmith had invested heavily and that they had gone down almost to nothing. I'm afraid I can't give details because I haven't a good head for finance. But one gets an impression."

Andrew was getting some impressions of Mrs. Sanders' lawyer, which he did not feel it necessary to share with his visitor. She continued:

"But do you think you can get her out? I watch the death column every day in fear and trembling. She just can't last much longer, though I'm amazed at her stamina. I shouldn't bother you with my problem. You haven't the slightest call to do anything for either Mrs. Sanders or me. But I'm so desperate that I'd ——"

"Use the devil himself, I suppose," said Andrew who had been trying to interrupt. "But you're wrong to apologize, Miss Pethwick. Any injustice is my business; any injustice that can be righted is the business of every Christian."

She looked at him for a long moment, and he thought she would cry again.

161

"I can be grateful though," she said huskily, "and I am. Honestly I'm not foolish. I know that she has had a long and fortunate life. I feel that I wouldn't mind — now — if she dies, as long as she can die with dignity, out of that place. Properly speaking, I should be more concerned for the other poor souls with her. But I can't be. Because — and I know how silly this must sound in a woman of my years but — I *love* Mrs. Sanders."

"I don't think it foolish. Now," he went on briskly, "this requires finesse. I have only a bowing acquaintance with Beryl Sexsmith but — to paraphrase Mike Nicholls — 'that woman is a lawyer,' and how! Also I should think her a woman who covers herself very thoroughly. Perhaps in view of her trusted position and Mrs. Sanders' lack of close connections she has felt quite secure. Amazing how few so-called friends will visit a mental hospital. That remark may be uncharitable, because very few know what to expect or if they are welcome. So I think she didn't count on your interest and pertinacity. I wonder if another letter from you ——"

"I have one sketched out," said Ursula eagerly, producing a neat sheaf of paper. "I write, or rather type, things as they come to me. I felt I had to be very careful for fear I had mis-judged her —"

"Or for fear you hadn't," murmured Andrew glancing at the typescript. "This is good: 'judging from your letter, you and I might have been visiting two quite different women.' It needs teeth in it, though, to produce results. I wonder if a letter with my signature would have any more effect. I mean," he added hastily, "just to show that someone besides yourself is concerned."

"Oh would you? Would you really? I know it would make a difference. I'm a complete nobody — I think she counted on that if she thought of me at all — but you have a name in Toronto. I really shouldn't let you stick your neck out."

"My favourite indoor sport." Andrew's eyes were still on the letter. He crossed out a sentence, inserted a caret, wrote a marginal note. "And the value of the name is nil in some quarters. But if I am to sign this, or something like it, I must

162

see for myself. Can you drive to Whitby with me now?"

"But visiting hours don't begin until ——"

"Clergymen have a few privileges," he reminded her. "And if they are not honoured there, at least we can have lunch and be ready when the bars are raised. I should like our letter to reach Miss Sexsmith tomorrow."

Miss Pethwick made no further objection. Andrew excused himself while he cancelled a luncheon engagement, postponed an appointment at Connington Glass, and asked Aunt Alex to take a special telephone message. Within fifteen minutes he was heading north on Avenue Road towards the 40I. Beside him sat Ursula Pethwick limp with relief.

"Oh, Mr. Connington" — from the almost happy sigh he estimated the intensity of her grief and anxiety — "you don't know what a load you have lifted."

"Careful. We haven't done anything yet."

"I know. And I realize that we may not succeed. But the feeling of bafflement, of frustration, of not knowing where to turn, of being alone with it —" She let her hands speak for her. "And to think that all I was going to ask you to do was pray."

Andrew's eyebrow went up.

"All! No wonder we don't have prayers answered! Well, I've prayed. In fact I'm praying. But on occasion *laborare est orare*.

She did not require a translation.

By the time they reached Whitby, Andrew had decided to wait for the regular hours so that his companion could go in to introduce him. He drove on to Oshawa, fortified her with lunch at the Genosha Hotel, and by the time they made their way through the sad, straying, or immobile figures in the outer corridors and wards, and waited entrance at the locked door, he was completely prepared to have the interview confirm Ursula's description.

It did. The bleak surroundings, the ghost-like gathering around him — like the shades crowding Ulysses at Taenara — the pitiful exhibitionism of one poor, wraith-like figure, could not

163

detract from the dignity, the iron self-possession, of the woman they had come to visit. She received him with unassumed courtesy as if they were in her own home.

"Of course I know your name, Mr. Connington. You were at Shorncliffe Church years ago, were you not? I'm afraid I lost track of you after that."

"Mr. Connington," ventured Ursula, "is hoping that we can arrange for your removal from here very soon."

"That is kind of you." Mrs. Sanders inclined her head towards him, but smiled at her with a warmth which softened the gaunt face and ratified the impression of affection between them. "But I trust it will not be necessary. My lawyer visited me last Thursday and I expect that she will straighten out this unfortunate situation. In fact, I am slightly disappointed not to have heard from her before this."

They did not dare, under those clear, searching eyes, to exchange glances. The woman down the ward had begun to scream — loud, unvarying, causeless screams which beat the air with deadly regularity. The exhibitionist came up, nudged Andrew, and repeated her performance.

"I shall not apologize for my companions, Mr. Connington." Mrs. Sanders' gesture suggested the captain of a liner deprecating a period of stormy weather. "But I certainly cannot ask you to endure this discomfort for my sake. I have thought myself allergic to noise. Believe me, I am overcoming that allergy."

Andrew hesitated. His natural reticence found in this queenly control no encouragement to offer spiritual ministration. It might be considered an impertinence, certainly an embarrassment. Then — Mrs. Sanders was admiring the tiny Japanese garden which Ursula had brought her and replanted in a plastic container, for nothing breakable was allowed in the ward — he took another glance at the wasted figure momentarily off guard, at the unconscious betrayal of her pleasure in the single beautiful object beside her. He might never see this woman alive again. The opportunity and responsibility were his.

He took his Bible from his pocket and read the twenty-seventh psalm, then after a moment's hesitation a few verses at

164

the end of the fourth chapter of Second Corinthians. The two women listened, attentive and expressionless. Then he prayed.

"Thank you, Mr. Connington." The conventional sentence might have been in return for a proffered chair. "Thank you in the name of my own minister, who has not been to see me. I doubt if he knows that I am here. May I see the translation you are using? It was not familiar to me."

Her capable old hands took the book with evident appreciation of its quality. A soft, red morocco with India paper, so slim he could carry it easily, it had been Evadne's and John's joint Christmas gift.

"A beautiful edition," she returned it to him. "I do not remember hearing that last passage before. Is it very different in the King James version?"

Andrew's letter to Miss Sexsmith, brief, urbane, lucid, just reached the post office in time to be registered. Miss Pethwick had taken it down in shorthand on their swift homeward drive and typed it in duplicate on his machine. In it he spoke of his visit, his impression of Mrs. Sanders' condition, her faith in her lawyer, and the urgent need of action. After some thought he added a postscript.

"It has occurred to us" — no need to elaborate on the pronoun, nor, he felt, to give any explanation of his connection with the matter. Much better, on the whole, for her to be set guessing — "that the Member of Parliament for Mrs. Sanders' constituency might be interested. I believe that M.P.'s have often been effective in remedying similar situations."

The next morning Andrew found himself still obsessed by Ursula Pethwick and her problem. Prayer meeting the previous evening had exercised its usual healing power on his questing mind and disturbed spirit. He had thought that a good night's rest would put the matter in proper perspective and set him free for other tasks, during the inevitable delay while they awaited the lawyer's next move. He had not neglected to pray for her privately, though with the strange, helpless feeling that he was praying to reverse an accomplished fact. But with a new day the events of yesterday lost none of their pathos and horror. He had never been able to achieve a professional disjunction when faced with the victims of mental illness. In this situation, arguing from a single case of injustice, he felt anew the burden of the numberless cases, undisclosed, unavenged, and added his voiceless cry to the age-old: "How long, O Lord?" altering it presently, as he always did, to "God be merciful to me, a sinner."

He was shocked that he had so quickly presumed Beryl Sexsmith's guilt and that of the shadowy Enid. What motive could be common to both? The lawyer could not be a legatee and, if Miss Pethwick's information was correct, Enid's legacy was not enough to keep her in the style to which, as Mrs. Sanders' housekeeper, she had become accustomed. Her position was well-paid and did not involve onerous work. Surely it was to her interest to retain it as long as possible, with her annuity already available and the inheritance a comforting expectation. And how could the continuance of normal life — a tenuous prospect at best — be anything but an advantage to a lawyer whose fees for handling investments must be a regular source of income and whose three percent of the estate was a fixed ratio, whenever death came.

Something crossed the shadowy distaste with which Andrew was reviewing these sordid considerations, a deeper shadow of question, but it was elusive and he could not capture it.

If there was some motivation of which he was ignorant, it had been compelling. For the women had not acted independently. A doctor — no *two* doctors were, in the paternal, if inadequate provision of the law, required to certify a person insane.

Perhaps they could help. Perhaps their testimony would clear his unease. Either it might prove him wrong — though in no case could a friend be excused for putting a ninety-two-year-old woman in her present surroundings — or, if it confirmed his suspicions, it would at least mitigate his feeling of guilt for entertaining them and provide incentive for strong measures. Ursula had told him the name of Mrs. Sanders' personal physi-

166

cian. He wished that he had asked at the hospital for the other signatory.

Dr. Roy Southend had a pleasant suite and a charming nurse in the Medical Arts building. Andrew was fortunate enough to catch him in the lull of a recently cancelled appointment. He found, at strange variance with his surroundings, an example, almost a caricature, of the old-fashioned general practitioner — big, bluff, gray-moustached, reassuring. Not at all on-the-make, thought Andrew, trying not to think any disparagement of the blue-eyed smile, which faded only slightly when he told his business.

"Ah yes. Sad thing that. Poor old soul! So much better if she had died in the spring."

"Just what did happen?"

"Coronary occlusion, clot affecting the brain, resulting in senile psychosis. Very common when the heart suddenly deteriorates."

"But," objected Andrew gently, "I know that Whitby is a fine hospital; a last resort surely for a woman of Mrs. Sanders' age and position, especially the ward that she is in."

"The authorities take over once a person is committed. Rest assured, Mr. Connington, they know their job. Why, there are never enough beds for those requiring admission. There isn't the remotest possibility of their confining anyone unless it is absolutely necessary."

The first remark is true. The second by no means follows, thought Andrew. Aloud he said,

"Surely nurses — for whom she can well afford to pay — could have kept her under surveillance in more pleasant surroundings?"

"My dear fellow, you couldn't get nurses to tackle an assignment like that. Enid — that's Miss Waters — loves her like a daughter, but was completely terrorized."

"By a woman of ninety-two?"

"Ninety-two or not, she's a strong woman. Always a bit of a despot. And with a temper. Clever too. A lovely old lady in her right mind," he went on, correcting the impression. "Unfortunately, in this type of illness it's the other qualities which

167

come out. I don't suppose you've ever seen the strength that a quite ordinary person achieves when insane —"

"I have. I have had to struggle with one," said Andrew. "Dr. Southend, I saw Mrs. Sanders yesterday. Whatever her condition three weeks ago, she strikes me as perfectly sane, certainly reasonable, and weak enough to be harmless now."

The doctor laughed pleasantly.

"My dear chap, if there is one thing more amusing — sadly amusing I grant you — than another to us doctors, it is the ease with which a layman can be taken in by the insane. They can always put it over. I could tell you funny stories about it by the hour. But neither of us has time."

"I had hoped," said Andrew tentatively, ignoring the hint and the amusement, "that you might visit her and review your estimate, considering your long acquaintance."

"Acquaintance? Friendship! My wife and I count Mrs. Sanders a personal friend. I tell you it was no pleasure to sign that certificate. Only we have to get used to these things in our profession. Otherwise we'd go mad ourselves, eh? Now rest assured, she is in the right place."

"That's what her lawyer says," commented Andrew deliberately. The doctor shot a swift glance at him.

"Miss Sexsmith. Yes. That should reassure you. Very fine woman. Loves her like a daughter too."

God keep me from such filial affection, thought Andrew. He pushed back his chair and thought he discerned relief in the other's polite, instant rising. There was no ostensible reason to refuse the proffered hand, though he thought that his own must feel like Veronica's in that hearty grasp. He said nothing, but Dr. Southend fed a stream of talk into the parting.

"Glad you came to me. Your concern does you credit. I like to see a minister put himself out for — Mrs. Sanders wasn't one of your parishioners?"

"No." Andrew did not enlighten him.

"Just a friend. Well, let this be a comfort to you. She isn't

168

nearly as disturbed by her surroundings as you were — or as I would be. Probably hardly notices. Good-bye to you."

Andrew turned back as though he had forgotten.

"By the way, there must be two doctors to sign, I believe. The other was —?"

He paused. For the first time an expression of annoyance crossed Dr. Southend's pleasant face. He looked as though he would refuse but evidently realized that refusal would nullify the whole effect of the interview. His laugh was a trifle dry.

"Dr. Sheridan. Charles Sheridan. But I doubt if you find him in. A busy young man with no time on *his* hands."

"Thank you," said Andrew. He did not try his luck by asking for Dr. Sheridan's address. He doubted if he would find it in the Medical Arts listing and he was right. The public telephone book in the lobby gave it and he phoned, not surprised that the line was busy. He was presently informed by answering service that the doctor was on his hospital rounds but had office hours from two to four. So before two he found himself alone in the small, basement waiting room of the doctor's modest East Toronto house.

Dr. Sheridan was neither big nor bluff, neither traditional nor reassuring. He was slim, wiry, arrogant. Andrew felt that he regarded general practice as a stopgap till he could specialize in some field. Perhaps marriage — he had heard a child's voice complaining loudly while he waited, and there was a playpen on the front verandah above — had slowed him in pursuit of his goal. Yet his manner at the beginning belied first impressions by being ingratiating. Andrew wondered a little.

"Mrs. Sanders? Mrs. Jonathan Sanders? Not a patient of mine. Oh yes, yes, yes, yes. Of course. I remember now. I was called in on the case by my friend Dr. Southend. It had slipped my mind. I've been working like a dog lately."

Andrew thought he understood. The effort at recollection was too forced. But if Southend had reached him on the telephone and given him his cue — Ludicrous. He was thinking along the lines of Sir John Appleby in a Michael Innes mystery.

Sheridan's story, though naturally with no personal over-

169

tones, corroborated the other, as if rehearsed from the same script. Only at the end when Andrew, aware of uneasiness beneath his probing and so probing persistently, with a hint of the authorities, publicity, and a test case thrown in, did his natural character reveal itself with sudden sharpness.

"You're wasting your time, I can tell you that." It was almost a snarl after the assumed purr. "Names like Roy Southend and Beryl Sexsmith swing a lot of weight in this city. You — you ministers object when we interfere in your bailiwick. My God, why every layman thinks he knows enough to shove his nose into ours!"

"Good day, Dr. Sheridan." There would have been no handshake even if Andrew had not closed the inner door on his words and, immediately after, the door of the waiting room, where two women and a child were now sitting. The open air was relief. There was relief too, though grim relief, in his feeling that war was declared, and that though the *casus belli* was undisclosed, the enemy was no phantom.

Beryl Sexsmith must be given time to act. He had requested an immediate answer to his registered letter and a friend in the post office went to considerable trouble to find that it had been delivered. A call to her from Aunt Alex, who voiced, like a veteran trooper, his carefully written and factually truthful sentences regarding the next meeting of the Women's Canadian Club, established the fact that the lawyer was at her office, though engaged. He could not possibly hear by post before Friday and he doubted that she would telephone. So he put the matter from his mind and caught up with his other work.

Friday's post brought no reply, nor did Saturday's. He had just glanced through his fairly large assortment of mail when Ursula Pethwick telephoned. Her voice was high with excitement:

"Mr. Connington, she isn't there."

"Mrs. Sanders?"

"No. I mean, yes. I phoned as usual to see if I might visit and they said" — her tone dropped to emphasize the importance

170

of the words — "that Mrs. Sanders had left the hospital, that her lawyer had taken her away on *Thursday evening.*"

Andrew could not suppress a whistle.

"Quick results! Where is she now?"

"I don't know. They thought she had gone to a rest home but were not at liberty to divulge the name. They suggested I get in touch with her lawyer."

"We will," said Andrew.

Immediate efforts to communicate with her at the office or at home were unavailing, and weekend services presently claimed his attention and energy. He did satisfy, or rather confirm, a conviction when young Dr. Jonas, one of his stewards, dropped into the vestry after counting the morning offering.

"Could you, without breaking the Hippocratic oath, tell me something, Doug?" Jonas had grown up in the church, but Andrew put the matter delicately. "Are you doctors ever asked to commit — to certify — a person about whose insanity there is a margin of doubt?"

Jonas laughed shortly.

"What do you mean, Pastor — ever? I shouldn't say it is as common as requests for abortion, at least in my experience, but it happens. Oh yes, it happens. And sometimes when I was starting up in practice, the inducement was quite tempting. If I hadn't come back to the church after my brief period of 'I'm through with all that stuff,' I might be a richer man."

"When you refuse —?"

"The general attitude is: 'If you won't, someone else will.' Mind you, I don't by any means think that doctors outside the church all do it. Or unfortunately that some inside may not. I just know that I probably would have given in, if it weren't for —."

He stopped, uncomfortably tongue-tied. Andrew took him up quickly.

"Thank God for that. And thanks for not resenting the question. One never knows where the line of professional etiquette may be drawn."

171

"Yes, I know. We doctors stick together ... and bury our mistakes," quoted Jonas. "Well, there are other loyalties."

On Monday Andrew received his answer. Miss Sexsmith recalled their meeting and thanked him for his interest in her dear friend. Mrs. Sanders had sufficiently recovered from the desperate condition which had made immediate action necessary, although of course another such seizure might occur. She had accordingly been taken to an excellent nursing home where a room had just become available. With the passing — to a marked degree — of her mental illness, her physical condition was appreciably weaker, and the doctor had ordered a period of complete quiet. Her friends could rest assured that every care was being taken — the thirty-five-dollar-a-day hospital charge indicated the best of treatment.

Andrew did not rest assured. Not only the fact that Miss Sexsmith did not divulge the new address but her statement regarding Mrs. Sanders' health struck him as suspect. A woman who had retained the strength to dress herself and remain out of bed after the three weeks she had undergone was scarcely likely to collapse when the strain was lifted. Or was she? At any rate Ursula, who in an effort to narrow down the field was using her spare time to ask the cost of accommodation in all nursing homes listed in the yellow pages and finding none which quoted such a charge, balked at the idea of forcing her presence against a physician's order.

"Consider my position, Mr. Connington," she said. "If I should insist on visiting and she died the next day, I'd feel that I was the cause and should certainly be blamed."

"Well, until we discover the name of the hospital, the question is purely academic," said Andrew reassuringly.

"But we must do that. Otherwise how do we know that Miss Sexsmith is telling the truth at all? And at least I could write her a letter."

Andrew's brief note — Miss Sexsmith was never to be reached by telephone — brought a prompt reply. Of course he could have the name of the hospital. It had been omitted in error. He would, it was hoped, respect the doctor's request that Mrs.

172

Sanders have no visitors for ten days. After that he would be welcome.

After that there may be no one to visit, thought Andrew, no longer amused at the detective-story direction of his thoughts. The susceptibility to pneumonia of the bedridden aged was common knowledge. If Mrs. Sanders was being kept in bed — and she could easily be rendered too weak to insist on rising —

No. That was going too far. But at least he could satisfy himself about her condition. He knew the rest home, a pleasant one some little distance from the city, though not as expensive as the price quoted. Possibly, though, extra nursing attention was being included in the given estimate. Ursula's telephone call confirmed the ban on visitors. But Andrew intended to exercize his special privilege and, if necessary, force an entry by the sheer commanding weight of his presence. It was already Wednesday evening. More than enough time had elapsed.

But early Thursday morning a half-expected telephone call threw his plans into disarray. Almost a month before, the ten-year-old daughter of Bill Woodhouse had been thrown from her horse while riding with a party on the ranch, and rushed to the hospital in Edmonton with severe head injuries. Andrew had been kept informed by letter of the long-drawn seesaw from despair to hope to fear. He had agreed, during the first, frantic telephone call, to go West if the child did not recover, and conduct the funeral. Now he was reminded of his promise.

"If it's asking too much, Andrew" — Bill's voice was dull with fatigue — "I'll understand. But —"

"I'll let you know my flight number as soon as I get it." Andrew had been awakened by the call. He made a reservation for a flight at two p.m., realized that one or two minor arrangements on behalf of Bill must wait until the business world was stirring, telephoned to ask Don Howard to preach for him on Sunday, and went down to break the news to the children and Aunt Alex, who, fully dressed and with her hair done, never missed breakfast.

"O Dad!" He had not heard that note in John's voice for

173

years. "I never realized — I guess I thought — she's so young, and such a sweet kid!"

Andrew, startled at the pain in his tone as he slumped in the chair beside his unfinished breakfast, remembered that of the family only John had known the child. The sorrow of the rest was primarily for Bill and to a lesser degree for Mrs. Woodhouse whom they had met infrequently. But the little girl had been two at the beginning of John's eight-month sojourn with the family. She had made a great fuss of him, Bill had told John's father. She always sent a small gift to Uncle John at Christmas while he had remembered her at Christmas and birthday ever since. And her name was Cecily.

No one else spoke. Evadne, he could see, was struggling with tears. Mrs. Mansell had the grace of silence at such times. Her feelings were sad, but remote, numbed with the merciful anodyne of old age.

"Why on earth should a thing like that happen?" John was speaking more to himself than to them, and his voice was puzzled, not bitter. "Dad, tell Bill and Leslie how I feel. And if there's anything I can do ——"

"You'll write, of course. Better, why don't you come on out with me? That would really be a help to them. Or, if you can't get away so early," he added, to leave the proposal without personal involvements, "take a later flight."

For a moment the suggestion was considered. Then his son looked up at him and away in sheer panic.

"Oh no. I couldn't. I'd be no help. What on earth would I say to them? You tell them how I feel. Besides" — he recovered himself and withdrew, almost but not quite, into his customary reserve — "I've told you what a critical time it is at the lab. I really have to be there."

Andrew did not press him. The brief interlude of spontaneous feeling and expression had been grateful. He prayed that it, and the happening which had caused it, might not be wasted in the struggle.

The next four days, for he stayed on at Bill's urgent request, were full and difficult enough without the presence of a problem

174

son. He had to calm Leslie Woodhouse's near-hysterical grief — she should never have allowed the child to ride that horse! He was escorted for walks by the eighteen- and sixteen-year-old boys, wooden in their sorrow and, after years of absence, wary of their father's hero. He met the remarks, questions, warm western outpouring of presence and provisions from neighbours — a term which took in those living within a radius of twenty miles. Conscious above all of Bill's resigned but poignant yearning, he found his only relief in the funeral sermon and in the Sunday service which the local clergyman insisted that he conduct. At these, after preliminary agonies of self-doubt and emptiness, he had the awful, the solemn, the vibrant release of inspiration and knew that the words he spoke were not his own. But power had gone out of him, and when Woodhouse drove him to the plane he hoped that no acquaintance on the flight would interrupt three hours of reconstitution.

"I don't need to say thanks, do I, Pastor?" Bill lapsed into the old address. His eyes were weary but peaceful. "I know the Lord never lets me down; but it's good to have one human being who never does either. I wish I could repay a bit of what your being here has done for me and Les and the family —."

Quod — that last — *est. demonstrandum,* thought Andrew.

"I've hardly had time to think, or to ask, about yours. How is my friend John now? Thank him for his message. Is he taking things better?"

Andrew hesitated. Then he realized that his preference for being on the giving end was false pride.

"Prayer, if you can spare it from your own concerns, will be gratefully received," he said and told him the most recent developments.

Perhaps this reminder kept the thought of his son uppermost during the homeward flight, interrupting his efforts at prayer, superimposing itself on his petitions for the Woodhouse family, for Miss Pethwick, for Mrs. Sanders, and blurring the pages of *The Divine Relativity* by Charles Hartshorn and Michael Innes's *The Secret Vanguard,* which, in despair of achieving concentration, he tried in turn to read. When he gave up the struggle and

175

settled to consider the situation, his thoughts, instead of constructive petition, resolved themselves into a forensic statement of the case he would present to John and to his unofficial fiancée. This, setting forth to Veronica the inadequacy of her claim on John's enduring interest; to John, the impoverished condition of his thinking and the probability of future remorse; to both, the Scriptures relating to Rome's dogmatic accretions and the basic tenets of the Christian faith: became so vigorous, so ramified with example and illustration, that he felt greater exhaustion than when he began the flight, as great exhaustion as though he had delivered them aloud. His whole being was fused in a solid, silent anguish of insistence:

O Lord let Thy will be done. Don't let all my influence go for nothing.

Which is it, Andrew? Not a voice, yet it spoke, clear, searching, almost amused.

He stopped aghast.

Both Lord. You know it's both.

But if they are not identical?

How can they fail to be? To what purpose fatherhood and constant concern — human, faulty, granted, but always with repentance and renewed effort? Of what value continual prayer and self-examination and the attempt to set an example without imposing a pattern? If this is not Thy will, then I am self-deceived. But if I have not deceived myself, then how can my failure be Thy will?

My Word shall not return unto Me void.

But that is the point. That is what concerns me.

Is it really? What if your apparent failure, the crossing of your hope in this particular instance, *is* My will. What if My will is to be worked out in John's heartbreak and frustration? What if in My will and purpose you are never to see in this life the result of your faithful fatherhood to John? Which, in that case, will you choose?

It's sight or faith again. And I'm demanding what I feel must be Thy will. I cannot see how John's good can be accomplished otherwise.

176

But if I see otherwise. My thoughts are not your thoughts. Are you willing?

Andrew had always disliked fishing because he could not bear to see the worm squirming on the hook. He felt like that worm now. The Hook seemed remorseless, boding as little good to him.

Yet without it I cannot catch fish.

Right, Lord. You win. "Righteous art thou, O Lord, when I complain to thee." Yet I would plead my case before thee. I still wish you'd do it my way. (Perhaps if I am completely willing, He will.) No, there can't be any strings attached, any "Seek ye first" . . . with an eye to the addition of "these things." (I'm being disarmingly honest.) Dear Lord, I want to come clean. It's like peeling one layer after another off an onion. (See, I realize what a hypocrite I am.) Oh take it — take my will for what it's worth. I give up. At least I think I do.

When the plane touched down at Malton, he was sound asleep.

He was just putting his bag down in the hall when the phone rang.

"It's probably Miss Pethwick," said Evadne, who had driven him from the airport. "I told her what flight you were coming in on."

Ursula was apologetic.

"I know you have just arrived, but I thought I should tell you. I called the hospital this afternoon since the ten days are up. A nice woman answered and told me the visiting hours. Then suddenly she asked my name and went off the line for a minute. A man came on and said that only the people on Miss Sexsmith's list could visit Mrs. Sanders. He could not tell me who was on the list, but I wasn't. He was polite but quite firm. What am I to do?"

Andrew glanced at his watch. "It's three — no, I'm still on Western time — six o'clock. Well, I shall not ask whether I am on the list or not. I'll drive out there now."

It was seven when he presented himself at the reception

177

desk of the Far Haven Rest Home and asked the number of Mrs. Sanders' room. "Twenty — " The girl at the desk, perhaps the pleasant voice of Ursula's description, seemed to recollect something and stopped in mid-sentence. "Could I have your name, Sir?"

"Andrew Connington," he said pleasantly. "What a very particular hospital! Do you always screen your visitors?"

"No. Not really." She had surreptitiously consulted a sheet of paper under the blotting pad. "I'm sorry. This is a special case." Obviously unwilling to deal with it, she excused herself for a moment and went quickly down the hall.

Andrew, his blood pressure rapidly rising, was about to go behind the desk and consult the room chart for himself when an efficient-looking middle-aged man, apparently the manager, took the girl's place.

"I'm sorry, Mr. — I didn't quite get your name? Mrs. Sanders is not allowed visitors."

"Except, I understand, those on her lawyer's list."

"A small list, approved by her doctor. Yes."

Andrew drew a card from his pocket and laid it on the desk, looking, he felt, like a Scotland Yard inspector exposing his C.I.D. badge.

The man was disconcerted.

"But — "

"Is this the only hospital which does not respect the ruling for clergymen? Or am I to be forced to conclude that Mrs. Sanders is being held incommunicado?"

The words and the polite but incisive delivery were too much for the manager.

"Of course not. What a suggestion! We are simply trying to guard Mrs. Sanders — in her precarious state of health — from the influx of well-meaning visitors who never realize how they tire a patient."

Like the crowd who visited her in Whitby, Andrew did not say aloud. "Her room number?"

"Twenty-three. I'll just step along and see if ——"

"That will not be necessary." Andrew had already located

the position of the stairs, and much experience with hospitals told him where the room would be. His long stride anticipated the other's movement and he presently found himself in a room, comparatively large and as pleasant as such rooms can be, where in the single bed he recognized the woman he had come to see.

Although her eyes were closed, she was not alone. In a large, comfortable chair beside her, just putting down the house phone receiver, was a short, prosaic-looking woman whom he recognized, from Ursula's description of sturdiness and colouring, as the incalculable Enid. She was plainly startled and rose from force of habit. There was a pause. Andrew waited for her to break it. It continued. He was quite at ease, but she was not and, having no directions to meet the emergency, finally floundered.

"I was sitting with Mrs. Sanders."

"Yes."

"I—we didn't want her to feel lonely."

"No, Miss Waters."

She looked uncertain.

"I — have I met you? I don't remember seeing you at Mrs. Sanders. Of course," she said hastily as he did not enlighten her, "there have been so many over all the years I've been with her. But I don't usually forget."

"Ah well, we all begin sometime." They had been speaking quietly but he raised his voice on the last remark, and was rewarded by seeing the old lady's eyes open. "Have you been here long?"

"I come every afternoon." The words were out before she realized that she had not intended to give information. She explained. "It's extra nursing care really. They are very busy here and, of course, I'm glad to do it. Mrs. Sanders has been like a mother to me."

She had not spoken loudly, but Andrew was sure that the words were not lost on the still figure beside her. The waxy features did not change but in some indefinable way they conveyed distaste and irony.

179

"You must be tired. There is no reason to stay on now that I'm here."

"Oh I'm in no hurry. The next bus doesn't pass until eight."

"No need for you to take it. I shall be staying only a few minutes. Then, if you don't mind waiting downstairs, I can drive you into the city."

Such a contingency was completely out of her instructions. It alarmed her.

"Oh no, I wouldn't dream of putting you out like that, Mr. Connington." So his name had reached her. By the intercommunication system, or from Miss Sexsmith? "No, maybe I'll be called for. My brother sometimes stops by and picks me up. I'd better go and see if he has."

He could have found her flustered departure amusing — she had to come back twice, once for her glasses and once for her capacious knitting bag — but the situation increasingly saddened and shocked him. He wondered if it was routine or deliberate policy that his short visit was interrupted twice more: by a nurse who took the patient's pulse, and by Mrs. Van Dieman, probably the wife of the manager, who explained that she always made the rounds last thing before bedtime, a meaningful phrase for seven-thirty.

In any case he saw no reason to prolong his visit. Mrs. Sanders, silent until Enid left, watched him as he returned to her bedside.

"So you got me out, Mr. Connington. Thank you."

"Your lawyer, surely?" said Andrew tentatively.

He could not read the expression in her eyes.

"Yes, she brought me here." Whatever had happened since he last saw her, she seemed to have lost all energy, all interest. Only her courtesy and — though muffled by veils of exhaustion — her intelligence remained. "It's kind of you to come. How is" — she knew the name but it seemed an effort to get it out — "Ursula?"

"Much distressed about you. Haven't you received a letter? Two letters, I believe she has sent. And flowers."

"I think not. Those flowers — I was under the impression

that Enid brought them. And cards. But letters." She was silent again. "I have been very tired. Surely I should remember."

Andrew telephoned the desk. Mr. Van Dieman answered.

"Is there some mail for Mrs. Sanders? Two letters, I believe."

"No. Why yes. Two letters did arrive today but she was asleep at the time and we must have forgotten to deliver them. I'll just bring them up now."

"Do that," returned Andrew.

He did not have to comment on the week-old postmark on one letter. Mr. Van Dieman explained, as he handed it over, that the postman had apologized for delivering it to the wrong address and receiving it back only on Saturday. Mrs. Sanders' eyes were closed when he read the contents — bright, concerned, affectionate — but she opened them, smiled, and held out her hand for the notes when he finished.

"Should you like — do you feel strong enough to see her?" Ursula had concluded both letters with a carefully worded request.

"I should very much like to see her." Mrs. Sanders' voice was firmer than it had been during his visit. There was emphasis on the next pronoun. *"She* has been like a daughter to me these six years."

Andrew decided that he could learn little more by remaining longer. Delicate questioning evoked only brief, vague remarks concerning the doctor's visits, pills, one injection. His untrained eyes could find no symptoms except weakness and lethargy, in marked contrast to her severe hardiness on his earlier visit. He read a passage from John's Gospel with the odd sensation that he was reading the Office for the Dying; he prayed, almost unable to control his voice in a sudden surge of strong emotion, and then he left her.

In the interval between closing her door and replying non-committally to the manager's urbane farewell, he decided not to mention Mrs. Sanders' request for a visit from Ursula Pethwick. But he lost no time in relaying it to her, and — to her delight and evident relief — offered to go with her the following evening.

The manager was at the desk, grave and concerned.

181

"Too bad, Mr. Connington, too bad that you didn't phone us. Mrs. Sanders has been taken to the hospital. With pneumonia."

Ursula gasped. Andrew looked at the man attentively and waited for more.

"Yes. She must have contracted it during the night. She seemed a bit feverish when we made our late rounds but we thought nothing of it. I put it down to excitement at — at having a visitor, that is, visitors. But it was plain by noon that we couldn't cope with it. The doctor said that she should be where they could give oxygen. So I'm afraid you've come all this way for nothing. If I had any idea I could have telephoned and spared you the trip. I know you ministers are kept busy with this sort of thing."

Why all the ingratiation? Andrew was nonplussed. He could not show disbelief by forcing his way upstairs to see for himself.

"What hospital?"

"They weren't sure. It depended on where they could get her in. Very short notice, you know."

"You aren't implying that you would send a patient in that condition unless you were certain of her reception?"

Mr. Van Dieman wiped his forehead. He looked piteous and Andrew felt almost sorry for him. Clearly whatever he had done had not been malicious, and he was beginning to be frightened.

"Mr. Connington, our patients are not committed here. In this case Mrs. Sanders' lawyer has full power for such decisions. And the doctor too. We just provide accommodation and care while they are in our charge."

"I see. Then you did not hear the directions given to the ambulance driver?"

Mr. Van Dieman's eyes flickered but his answer seemed sincere enough.

"No, I didn't hear where they were going. I know there was phoning to the General — that's Dr. Southend's hospital, isn't it? And to the East and Scarborough. I can let you know when I hear."

182

"Thank you. I shall be much obliged if you will. At what time did they leave?"

"About — I'd say about five o'clock — nearer five-thirty. It took awhile to get the doctor out from the city."

The endeavours of the next two hours were fruitless. Andrew's tenacity in the search was due partly to his desire to allay Ursula's anxiety, partly to a bulldog reluctance to loosen what tenuous grip he had on the still unidentified enemy. At none of the three hospitals could they get any information about a patient named Sanders, at none, word of the recent ambulance admission of an elderly woman. He was well enough acquainted with the under-staffed and overcrowded conditions to realize that, especially with the changeover to night staff, such information could easily be unavailable until next morning. He began to tell Ursula — and changed hastily to another anecdote — of visiting one of his congregation, only to find that the body had been lying for an hour in the hospital morgue, at the very time that he had been given the bright standard message that the patient had passed a satisfactory night and that it would be convenient for him to call. No conclusions could be reached from their failure to locate Mrs. Sanders. He told Ursula so, but with a cheerfulness that he did not feel. His sense of conflict with evil grew at every turn of events.

He was not, he reminded himself when he awoke next morning, a detective in charge of this case. It was prayer-meeting night. The annual Harvest Home dinner — a relic of the half-rural commencement of his church — was to be held the following evening. Church business had accumulated during his brief absence. Ursula Pethwick, too, was distressed at a moved-up deadline for her work and had a busy day before her. Andrew assigned Aunt Alexandra, always a willing and incurious lieutenant, the task of calling hospitals. And though he discovered at dinner that she had no information for him, he could not take time to plan further action.

Thursday morning Andrew overslept. He came down to find the children gone and Aunt Alex reading the *Globe and*

Mail, while waiting to pour his coffee. The post had already arrived.

"Letter from Bill and Leslie," he said absently. "One for John from Bill. Good of them to write so soon. Yes, Aunt Alex?"

"What was the name you asked me to phone about yesterday, dear? Was it Sanders? Would it be Ingrid Sanders?"

"Yes. What about her?"

"She seems to have died, dear. At least" — Aunt Alex never jumped to conclusions — "there is a notice to that effect in the Death Column. 'On Wednesday, at Far Haven Rest Home, Ingrid, widow of the late Jonathan Sanders —' "

10

‹‹

A NDREW, YOU MUST BE MAD. Do you want to face a libel suit? And lose?"

"You are sure I'd lose?"

"Oh, you'd lose." Across the small, conservatively appointed dining table in the Ladies' Club, Beth leaned forward, emphatic in her earnestness. She straightened as the elderly waitress approached, and helped herself to butter squash and green beans with apparent casualness. The moment the second dame had carried off the condiment tray she took up her sentence, both hands cupping the bowl of her water glass. The square-cut emerald on her ring finger repeated the colour of her delustered satin cocktail dress. "You'd lose all right. I've known Beryl Sex-smith for years. We are sorority sisters but, though I wouldn't trust her with a penny of mine, I'd hate to be on the wrong side of her in a case. Now don't set that jaw of yours. Listen to reason. Consider John and Evadne and your church if you don't care about yourself. Promise me you'll let the whole thing drop."

"Beth, I can't get that woman's face out of my mind."

"Beryl's?"

"Hers too. As it was in the chief mourner's seat at the funeral. Sleek, satisfied, even demure. But I meant Mrs. Sanders'."

"Mrs. Sanders is dead. You're alive."

Andrew winced.

"Don't. Liz Taylor said that, mutatis mutandis, a propos Mike Todd's three-month departure from this life."

"I say, thanks!"

He smiled without apology.

"I know you mean it well, but I can't see that her death alters the basic question of injustice, malpractice, cruelty, betrayal of trust. She may be dead. What about others who aren't?"

"You have no proof."

"The evidence of my own eyes and ears."

"Unbolstered by anyone else — against the word of doctors and a very capable lawyer."

"Not quite unbolstered. Ursula Pethwick saw her repeatedly in Whitby."

"Ursula Pethwick," said Beth almost petulantly, "could be a most suspect witness. Undoubtedly they would accuse her of worming her way into the affections of a perfect stranger — 'influence while of unsound mind' — to get her to change her will."

"The fact that Mrs. Sanders was removed from Whitby almost as soon as I visited — after being confined in a locked ward?"

"I know. You're convinced. And for what it's worth, you've convinced me. But then," said Beth, erasing with a suddenly remembered smile the lines of determination which had temporarily hardened her strong features and always chilled Andrew by accentuating her resemblance to Ben Harris, "you are a very convincing man as far as I am concerned. A judge or jury might not be swayed."

"Well I'm sorry for spoiling the celebration. I had no intention of opening up on the subject until you asked whose funeral I was attending when you tried to get me. And then I thought that your know-how in the legal and financial world might help me."

"It's my know-how that makes me warn you to lay off. Oh, I could tell you rumours of Miss Sexsmith's transactions. Not all

186

her clients have been completely satisfied with her handling of estates."

"Then ——"

"Then, nothing!" said Beth firmly. "You repeatedly remind us that 'the whole world lieth in the evil one,' and this is one time to quote 'Vengeance is mine, I will repay, saith the Lord.' If you don't take my word for it, ask any lawyer. Ask Rod Easton."

"I intend to. I'm just waiting until the will is probated."

Beth sighed, then changed her manner with the subject.

"Right. If you act on his advice I won't be nervous. I think I'll have the trifle. It's very English and good here. You too? Now what are you planning to say to Clark Manners tonight?"

"From my observation of his interviews, that will depend completely on him."

"Up to a point. But it's a good idea to have a few key statements lined up and make them anyway. If you ask me — Oh for heaven's sake, am I telling you! But, Andrew, I am excited. Think of all the people at their sets ready to watch you. And the book is beautiful."

The book, which had come from the publishers with commendable punctuality on the first of November, was beautifully edited and produced. Andrew, whose first sensation was rather abashed pleasure at seeing his name on the cover — "think of the thousands of chumps who have books published," he had reminded his gloating daughter — had the pleasure temporarily submerged by a wave of desolation at the realization, fresh in every contingency, that he could not share it with Cecily.

Perhaps he did not conceal the reaction instantly. At any rate John's "Good-looking book, Dad: Hope it gets a good press. Deserves to, but you never know" was surprisingly warm. Had there been a change in John lately, a new, delayed maturity, a quiet confidence in sharp contrast to the assertive independence of the last few years? Was it the approach of his birthday and the prospect (still undisclosed) of marriage? Andrew, by no means for the first time, reminded his God of the compact sealed on his homeward flight from Edmonton, and

187

read the brief review in the *Globe and Mail,* thankful that it used such terms as "pithy" and "profound."

He was aware that so prompt a review, coinciding with the advertisement of the book, was a favour, aware that a review of such a book in the secular press was by no means a foregone conclusion. Beth, whom he challenged on the subject, did not deny that she had "pulled wires" and he had not stinted his expressions of gratitude. The celebration of dinner à deux at her club had been her idea and, since his publicity interview coincided with her birthday, he could not have refused if he had wished. Her magnificent corsage of orchids was called for, he felt, to accompany a specially inscribed copy of *Crowded Solitude;* but he hoped that she would recognize the offering as conventional. He had deliberately chosen to send orchids. Cecily had not cared for them.

The T.V. appearance went, if not brilliantly, at least without mishap. "You looked magnificent," chortled Evadne, meeting them at his door. She looked charming herself, he thought fondly, in a shift of creamy wool that took lissom shape from her young figure. Her shining brown hair swung softly from its confining band. She had some of the eternal springtime quality of her mother, never more evident than beside the full, lingering summer of Beth's developed beauty. Andrew, in the undisturbed duality of thought, caught at the contrast: with Cecily — Evadne had it too — there had always been a suggestion of something more, a mystery, a question; with Beth the immediate was complete. The phrase "all the goods on the counter" expressed it. There was no disparagement in the thinking; it crystallized two distinct impressions.

"And," his daughter continued happily, when she had taken Beth's evening coat and followed her into the living room, "did you ever put that young man in his place when he tried to be high hat about 'The New Thought.' Your quotes from Origen, the Arians, and the French Enlightenment were perfect, weren't they, Mrs. — sorry! — Beth?"

Mrs. Harris-Kemp had protested the formal address for some time, but Evadne had reserves about familiarity. She managed it now with a smile so wide and winning that her father felt she was stretching her face unduly.

"They certainly set him back on his heels. Sure you didn't have them on your cuff, Andrew?"

"Up my sleeve. Good girl, Vad. I see some of your special punch. Guaranteed nonalcoholic, Beth, but with a deceptive kick. Let's drink."

"Right. Sit down, all of you, and I'll pour. But are there going to be repercussions on that Auschwitz bit!"

"I'm afraid there are," said Beth. "I wish it hadn't come up."

"Why," asked Mrs. Mansell, making her only contribution of the evening, "should anyone dislike Andrew's remarks about Auschwitz? I thought them very sensible."

Andrew hooted. Drink in hand he went over to his aunt's chair and clinked his glass with hers. Alexandra Mansell had been treating him on an adult and equal footing since he was ten. Probably for that reason he felt younger with her than with anyone else.

"To a discerning and unbiassed listener! Just so, Aunt Alex: *because* they were sensible. If there is one thing this mad world cannot stand, it is a sensible remark."

"That's all very well," said Beth, managing an amused smile to soften the criticism. Evadne watched her silently. "But it's in this mad world that your book must sell."

"Not to add to its madness. No," said Andrew with a sudden burst of indignation, "I have no regrets about my comments there at all. Without protesting too much, I can say that I deplored, opposed, spoke openly, when it was not fashionable to speak openly, against the attitudes and régime which led to Auschwitz. I was accused more than once of warmongering. And I'm not impersonal about that ghastly place. I had the grim task of telling a little Austrian refugee, a protegée of Cecily, that her mother had been sent to those gas chambers. But when people, ministers of the Gospel, take up the emotion-engendered cry of Martin Buber, whom as a rule I admire, that God was eclipsed at Auschwitz; go him one better and say that God died there; that no one can believe in a prayer-answering

189

God after Auschwitz — all I can ask is what sort of logic are they applying?" He stopped and finished his glass. He looked ten years younger, Evadne thought, when he was carried away in argument.

"Go to it, Dad." She quietly refilled his glass and he went on almost to himself.

"Have they read no history? Why should God be alive while his saints were tortured by Nero and Domitian, or methodically hounded by Marcus Aurelius and Diocletian? Alive for that matter when Attila swept through the Empire. Alive while — not in historical sequence! — five thousand Veneti had their hands cut off and two hundred thousand Helvetians, men, women and children, were killed by that otherwise clement man, Julius Caesar? While unspeakable things were done by Torquemada? While Bréboeuf and Lalement were subjected to the calculated mockery of their torment — or for that matter when Etienne Brulé was taken apart by the original Canadians, who took each other apart on occasion with equal lack of racial discrimination? While the Lollards were hung in chains over slow fires? Or lonely pioneer missionaries were imprisoned in Burma or eaten by cannibals elsewhere? For that matter while a million, if not millions, of Russian peasants were liquidated by Stalin? And negroes burned to death with blow torches in the South? And good men hanged or drawn and quartered by process of law? To say nothing of the appalling ravages of plague and famine, the toll of starvation in India and China alone?"

"But the scale and the cold-blooded deliberation," ventured Beth.

"I may be obtuse but I fail to see that as affecting the issue, except to prove the Scripture that the heart of man is desperately wicked. Also that the science which these God-obliteraters worship and permit to experiment with human personality, can make its worshippers diabolical. What difference whether God — apparently — disregards the prayer of one or one thousand, of six or six million? Is the extermination of six million in ratio to the present world population more devastating than the quartering of the population of ancient Athens,

190

to the world population of that time? Yet the latter could, if you like, be catalogued as 'Act of God' while the former was the act of men who had repudiated our God and set up an idol — race, nation, Hitler, self — in His place. I'm not trying to prove God's existence or His goodness or His love. I'm just indicating that to believe — or rather to concede belief possible — in spite of all these other circumstances but *not* after Auschwitz is as ridiculous as to say that man, when he learns that there are one hundred million stars in the Milky Way, can believe in a Creator, but cannot believe when he is told that there may be one hundred million Milky Ways. Here," said Andrew abruptly with a deprecatory grin which did nothing to lessen the forcefulness of his words, "endeth the lesson. The offering will now be received. I thank my captive audience for its kind attention. Vad, is that mocha cake that I see before me? Beth, this is Vad's specialty. You mustn't refuse."

"You certainly mustn't. It's partly for the book, partly because Dad told me it was your birthday. Will you have coffee? Or tea?"

Evadne's noble effort to be warm and friendly and receptive was not lost on her father, whom it moved to vague unease. John came in while they were eating, and shared the food with keen appreciation. He had watched the interview at Professor Mathers', he said, and thought it went well. Andrew deduced, from the fact that Mathers' family and several of John's colleagues had been watching also, that he had not been ashamed of his father's performance. It was the highlight of his evening.

Not greatly to Andrew's surprise, the secular press, in the smaller centers where it took notice of the book, was kinder than the larger church papers. Two of these, with unerring judgment, had given it for review to men whose general views, as expressed in occasional or regular newspaper columns, the book skilfully and satirically dissected. Granting that Mr. Connington was "adept at polemics" and possessed a "vocabulary sophisticated and extensive (although little in touch with the needs of modern man)," they deplored the "pains taken to bolster outmoded concepts," "preoccupation with abstruse theology," "egocentric experiential emphasis" in a day which called for "world vision and the outreach of interpersonal relationships." One of them decried Mr. Connington's heresy-hunting when "the only heresy is refusal of involvement — that basic denial of universal brotherly love." The other questioned jocularly the publisher's discernment in putting on the market a book which contained only a "thinly if skilfully camouflaged re-statement of nineteenth-century dogma."

Andrew withstood the urge to reply that the critic was sixteen to eighteen centuries late with his date, to ask how abstruse theology could be egocentrically experiential, to point out his radical, Scripture-based suggestions for Christian personal and social behaviour, which had been either unread or ignored. His wit too had eluded or exasperated. One accused him of levity in dealing with "the man the latchet of whose shoes he was not worthy to unloose" — and the reference was to Schweitzer not to Jesus. Another gravely challenged as serious, statements the irony of which could not, he had thought, escape a child's intelligence.

On the whole, however, they made their point that *Crowded Solitude* was not worth perusing. He had not hoped for much from those sources and was not — not really he told himself, wryly hurt in spite of preparedness — disappointed.

There were compensations. The next issue of one paper contained a letter from his nonagenarian friend Dr. Wren, praising the book for its constructive survey of the effects of a materially affluent society, its unequivocal attack on covetousness, its reductio ad absurdum of current shallowness masquerading as scholarship. It was largely ignored by the ultra-Fundamentalist press, but the scholarly editors of *Eternity* and *Christianity Today*, while taking regretful exception to his denial of the unconditional immortality of the soul, gave high praise to its relevance and vigour.

Christmas shopping was under way and the sales were reported as bright; that is, the pile of ten copies on the religious tables in Eaton's and Simpson's diminished slowly between weekly visits and the few local bookstores always had one on the counter and one on the shelf. Every Sunday members of his congregation loyally brought him their personal or gift-intended copy to autograph, and an American religious publisher arranged for an edition the following spring.

John's birthday, always observed, but big this year with omen, fell in the last week of November and on one of the nights of the Vic Dramatic Society's production in which Evadne was taking part. In one of their fleeting moments together during the hectic weeks of rehearsal, she had suggested to Andrew that Aunt Alex be deputed to ask how John wished to celebrate the occasion. They had thought themselves prepared for anything, but his actual proposal took them by surprise.

"I told Aunt Alex last night," he remarked casually at breakfast one morning, "that in view of all the dough I'm coming into, I feel it's up to me to take her out to dinner. I don't think I ever have. Will you come along too, Dad? I'll pay for yours. And if you can make it, Vad, leave early perhaps, I'll stretch a point and include you. Then we can all go on to Hart House and see your act."

Evadne gulped hastily.

"That'd be wonderful. I'll put my makeup on beforehand. In the first act I'm in evening dress anyhow; so I'll wear it."

"Heck," said John, "let's go to Ports of Call. They have a dark dining room there."

Meeting in the hall a few minutes later, Andrew and Evadne exchanged the questioning shrug and raising of eyebrows which they had rigidly suppressed at the table. Both were too fearful to exaggerate the importance of the invitation.

"He may be bringing Veronica along. Or it may be a sort of farewell party," she suggested darkly.

He nodded.

"Let's enjoy it anyhow."

"We can, can't we? Enjoy being with Johnnie again. I'm not counting on its meaning anything. But don't you feel it, the difference?"

193

"Yes. Thank God for that, whatever happens. There he is."

Andrew did not know whether it was Divine or human design that brought Bill Woodhouse's letter on the morning of John's birthday. It was a fat missive and he took it to the den to read after glancing through his other mail. He read it once quickly, more slowly a second time as though to memorize its phrases; then he sat quietly with the pages in his hand, his mind too blurred with relief for thought.

"I came clean with John about your telling me," it ran, "after praying about it considerably. I didn't see that it could make the situation any worse. What I said doesn't matter much. I felt that it was completely futile, wouldn't do any good. You must often have felt that way. But I wrote because I had to and I meant every word. Well, I thanked him for his affection for little Cecily. Said how fond she always was of him — all of us for that matter. Told him how it had seemed to knock the props from under me; then how I found they weren't gone at all, in fact were stronger than before. Something — not too much — about your help to us, what the funeral sermon did, how it meant more to me because I'd heard you when the loss was personal and I knew it wasn't just words. Then I tried to tell him about Leslie and me — that this had brought us even closer together because we prayed about it and always have on any problems. Asked if it would be that way with him and Veronica. More on the same line. Too much I felt, after I'd sent it.

"His answer — well, here is the gist. It's all off with the girl. He isn't by any means proud of his part in the business and doesn't feel that he deserves any credit. If there is any, it goes to her. I gather that he was fairly uneasy all the way through — something seemed to drive him. Never thought the term mixed-up was applicable to him but guess that was about it. I get the feeling that he wasn't really in love, but there's no doubt the attraction was pretty strong. He refers to some shock that pulled him up and made him take a good look at himself" — Andrew, numbly grateful, thought he knew what had caused the shock — "but by that time he was too far committed to back out. Only thing was that he had made no promises about the church. So he dug his heels in there; refused to take instruction or be married in her church unless she would have another ceremony — get a load of this — in yours, with you officiating. He also was flat-footed about signing over the children. 'And while on that point,' he says, 'I told her I was damned if I'd take the alternative of having a dozen children or figuring out by computer when we could — I used the word — cohabit.' Well, I thought you'd enjoy it.

"The result was stalemate. I think her family closed in strongly at that point. They argued — some clerical relatives? — a blue streak, made him feel like a heel for not stating the stipulations earlier. Johnnie felt pretty wretched about the girl but he had his back up. Said that she had never stated any either and repeated his agreement to marry her on what he called a fifty-fifty basis. In my opinion they all realized by that time that with his upbringing and background — if a bit late in showing — there would be difficulty later, even if he gave in now. He finishes up in the following way, in case you are wondering if you should have read this:

'So here I am — a bit groggy but ready for the third bout. Only I'm in no hurry to get involved again. It's a relief to have got it off my chest to you. If you want to tell Dad, go ahead. He has a right to know, but I can't talk to him — not yet at any rate.' "

So the anniversary that Andrew had been dreading was a glad celebration. Such was his calm elation of spirit that it suffered no depression when John substituted a totally unexpected announcement for the one they had all dreaded. He looked very well and very handsome in dinner jacket — he had insisted that they "go formal" to live up to Evadne's histrionic splendour — and there was a buoyancy about his manner which made his relatives feel that they had been living with his doppelganger and had just recovered the genuine John.

" 'The time has come, the walrus said' " — his words followed Evadne's assurance to Aunt Alex that she could wait for dessert, especially when Johnnie was paying — " 'to talk of many things.' Particularly to ask my family if they can endure life without me for two years?"

His very blue eyes met his father's directly before passing on to to be quizzical with Evadne and fond with Aunt Alex. When they waited wordless, he went on, "I applied to W. H. O. They want someone to work with the Indian Government on the line we've been following at the lab. So I'm on loan for two years. The appointment came through today."

"O Johnnie," Vad's voice had its little note of high-pitched excitement. This time it was almost a squeal. "Are you happy about it?"

"Wouldn't have applied if I hadn't wanted to go," was the noncommittal answer.

"Then — I'll miss you like Billy-O, but I'm glad for you. Very glad. And excited. I don't think I can eat my dessert."

"You will so eat your dessert. Pêche Melba, A la Carte and not the cheapest choice on the menu, as I noticed when you made it. Who do you think I am? E. P. Taylor?"

Evadne meekly picked up her spoon and John turned, rather diffidently, to his father.

"Good idea, don't you think, Dad?"

Andrew, who had been wondering what to say, seized the cue. "Very good idea." He did not want to give the impression of relief or of indifference. "It will take some getting used to, I'll admit, the distance and the duration. But it's a good work and I'm glad — "

Glad that he was not marrying Veronica, glad that he was taking a position which gave service rather than taking the inviting offer from Causworth's in Cleveland. He did not finish the sentence. "Is there a definite time?"

"Early next year as I can make it. The appointment was filled by a chap with a Ph.D. from Harvard. Then there was a snag. His wife backed down or something of the sort, and he reneged. So I put my name in. That's probably the only reason I got it."

"Oh, don't be so modest. You know they're lucky to get

you," said Evadne, intent on spooning the last of her Pêche Melba from its glass.

"You aren't saying a word, Aunt Alex. You know I can't leave without your permission."

They all looked at Mrs. Mansell, whose face seemed to have shrunk suddenly. She will feel his absence more than any of us, her nephew thought. But she rose gallantly to the occasion.

"I should be very very selfish not to rejoice with you. I left my dear father and came out to Canada at twenty." Sixty years passed over the quiet eyes. "So what a fortunate woman I am to have had you all with me as long as I have."

Evadne's flurry of departure — John went out and put her in a taxi — made an opportune break at this point. When he returned, Aunt Alex resumed her role of listener to the masculine conversation. But her stricken face struggling for composure reminded Andrew of another proud old face, gallant in alien surroundings. His mind began work again on the mystery surrounding her incarceration and death. The long-drawn, unhappy uncertainty about John was miraculously in abeyance. He scarcely dared, in the littleness of his faith, to believe it at an end. But he gave thanks. There would be time for the implications of his son's departure to sink in. Meanwhile he must discover if Ursula Pethwick's cry for help was just another of many interruptions in "the daily round, the common task" or if there was greater significance, if he had been "called to the Kingdom for such a time as this."

11

M RS. INGRID SANDERS' WILL, duly probated and published a few days later in the daily papers, indicated the former alternative. Its details tallied with Ursula's vague account. Of the near half-million dollars, the residual bulk was divided between two charities. Ursula had thought there were three, and on consulting her he discovered that the third, of which Dr. Southend had been a director, was missing. The childless old lady had not intended her death to cause individuals to rejoice. Except for her church, which came in for a modest bequest, there were only eight other beneficiaries. Six of these received three and the others, Enid and Ursula Pethwick, five thousand dollars apiece.

"It's much more than I expected, Mr. Connington," she said earnestly. "In the hospital, she said again and again that if she got out she would change the will to leave me far more. But are you sure you don't think I should refuse this?"

"To benefit her estate? To what purpose?"

"No. Just to prove that my interest" — again the rare, dark flush surprised her pale skin — "wasn't mercenary, that I loved her for herself."

"I'm quite sure Mrs. Sanders knew that. And I see little point in making a gesture to impress Miss Sexsmith or Enid."

"There's one thing — besides the omission of the Cancer Fund. I was quite sure that Dr. Southend was a legatee, and that Enid was to get six thousand."

"Was that before or after the change?"

Ursula's face cleared. She leaned back in the comfortable chair out of the immediate light from his desk-lamp under which they had been examining the provisions of the will.

"Before, of course. All she told me after was that Miss Sexsmith had disapproved of some changes; 'and I had to remind her that it was my money, not hers.' "

That would not endear her to her lawyer, thought Andrew, seeking a pattern in the ravel of facts; but it scarcely accounts for such treatment; especially as she is the one person who couldn't lose, in fact, who stood to benefit by her client's continued life. Unless — The tangle of suggestion needed straightening. He said to Ursula:

"Not only Miss Sexsmith would have disapproved. Have you any idea why she would lessen her bequest to Enid, or, for that matter, leave out the doctor?"

Ursula smiled reminiscently.

"I told you I loved Mrs. Sanders, but that doesn't mean I think she was an angel, or the soft, sweet old lady of sentimental songs. Well, you saw for yourself. She was a bit of an autocrat and used to attention. From some things she said to me, I gathered that she thought the doctor was what she called 'presuming' on their long acquaintance. She didn't like being treated familiarly and jollied along. And to do her justice, she never called him in unless there was something definitely wrong. Besides — I remember now — she asked him to go to her cleaning woman (you see, she is a beneficiary, Mrs. McTavish) who had broken her arm. She had fallen from a ladder in her own house and was badly shaken. Dr. Southend told her to get a taxi and come to his office — kept her waiting an hour and a half in the reception room. Mrs. Sanders was furious when she heard."

"That thread is untangled," said Andrew, more to himself than to her, "And Enid?"

"I feel very sorry about Enid — or should if she hadn't — " Ursula's face hardened again at the thought of what had happened. "I do know that in recent years she had been 'getting above herself,' as Mrs. Sanders put it, having fits of temper and sulking when she didn't get her own way. And I realize now that my arrival, when she thought of herself as a close companion, must have been difficult. But she never was a companion in any real sense. They had nothing in common. And she had drawn a good salary, although not excellent according to present standards — Mrs. Sanders was still in the Twenties in her attitude towards such things. But she lived on the fat of the land, went everywhere in taxis. And the annuity was beginning to come in. At all events, when she went into a bad tantrum — last February it was — Mrs. Sanders told her to find another place, insisted on getting another woman in, and gave her a few days off to look around. Enid went to her sister's in Peterborough and promptly had a heart attack."

"A genuine heart attack?"

"So she said. She came back very white and shaky and penitent. So Mrs. Sanders just kept her on — even sent her to Jamaica to get over the flu, as I told you."

But with that threat hanging over her and her legacy already reduced — if Miss Sexsmith had informed her — she would be easily influenced. If someone needed to influence her? Another thread in place.

He could not leave the matter unsolved. Even his sermons that Sunday on "The love of money is a root of all evil" and "The prince and the judge ask for a bribe, and the great man utters the evil desire of his soul; thus they weave it together" reflected his obsession so clearly to the initiate that Beth Harris-Kemp, though agreeing uncomfortably with his deductions, sat through them looking like a well-rounded feminine impersonator of her Uncle Ben.

Monday morning found him in his lawyer's office. R. Smith Easton, nephew to Andrew's old friend, was the sole representative of the firm still bearing the name. Ten years younger than the minister of the "church I stay away from," he was officially attached to no congregation. His wife and family were casual Anglicans, but although he had wryly and successfully resisted his late uncle's attempts to bring him under the Connington ministry, he regarded Andrew with considerable respect and called upon him on the infrequent occasions when he required the benefit of clergy. Andrew had officiated at the funerals of his parents, offered a startingly unconventional prayer of dedication at the opening of a war-memorial youth centre financed by Easton's Service Club, married several of his friends. He hoped, though the hope was still without a hint of foundation, that the Word which he tried to proclaim at each opportunity would bear ultimate fruit. Meanwhile the two had such friendship as can flourish with mutual liking, plain speech, and a diametrically opposed view of what matters in life.

"My God, Andrew! Sorry, force of habit." Smith Easton had listened, his face a judicious mask, throughout the clear résumé of Mrs. Sanders' case. Now he glanced across at his friend, with sardonic admiration in his rather small brown eyes. "You do like to live dangerously. Don't suffer from boredom that way, I suppose."

Andrew waited. His mouth responded faintly to the other's amusement but his eyes held out steadily for a serious answer. After a moment their gaze broke down Easton's guard. He rose abruptly, tossing aside the tortoise-shell paper knife with which he had apparently measured the facts as they were stated, and went to the window. The sight of cranes and steel girders piling up a new skyscraper between two sedate old buildings on Adelaide Street seemed to engross him. He spoke without looking around.

"If I were you I'd forget the whole thing."

"Why ask the impossible?"

"You know what I mean. Wash it up. The old lady has gone. Nothing can change that."

"There are other old ladies. And men. Also younger people. And there is justice."

"Granted. But it's a wicked world, as I don't need to tell a theologian, at least this theologian. And you can't right every instance of injustice."

"I'm not trying to. Just the occasional one which falls — which is thrust unavoidably — in my way."

"Look at it this way," said Easton persuasively. "There's nothing to be gained. If you could prove your suspicions to the

201

hilt, there is no other will that we know of. Your little friend has got her money — more, she says, than she expected. Who has the grouch? No one that I can see but the housekeeper."

Andrew repressed an invocation.

"It's not a question of money. It's treachery, perjury, cruelty, betrayal of trust, disregard of an individual's rights."

"But according to you that has all happened. It's over and done."

"In the name of British law," said Andrew staring, "what can a lawyer be disbarred for? Or is one never disbarred?"

"Oh yes. And far more than you suppose or hear of. But it's usually a public scandal, something involving big finance or politics. And the evidence must be irrefutable. This is a small — a private affair."

"Which I intend to bring into the open. Miss Sexsmith counted on its privacy."

"I thought you disapproved of Christians' taking legal action?"

"Of taking legal action against Christians for their own gain. Yes, I believe that is forbidden in Scripture. In this case, if nothing is done, how many more poor creatures may be cheated by the very system designed to protect them? *Quis,* to coin a phrase, *custodiet ipsos custodes?*"

His lapse into quotation did not disguise the passion of his earnestness. Smith Easton sighed.

"You can't have been listening to me, Andrew. Granted for the sake of argument that everything you suspect is true. You have no way of proving it."

"What is a good lawyer for? I'm not asking for charity, Rod. I'm prepared to finance an enquiry. An autopsy first, to determine the exact cause of death. You can obtain an order to exhume, can't you? Fortunately Mrs. Sanders made no secret of her horror of cremation. A statement from the hospital where they say she died as to the time of her re-entry and her condition then. Information regarding her whereabouts in the interval. An examination of the report given by the resident doctor at Whitby to see if it tallies with Southend's diagnosis. Evidence that she was legally committed there in the first place, and, if so, why she was so speedily removed after my letter reached her lawyer. This is the sort of thing I can't find out on my own. Will you act for me?"

Easton turned to the window again.

"No." The refusal was flat enough. It lay on the silence between them, and he picked it up and worried it almost petulantly. "And I'll bet my late revered Uncle is making his grave reverberate with *Amens*. You've had enough of this Don Quixote publicity, Andrew. I'm not getting you into another scrape where you'll look wrong and your motives will be impugned, no matter how right and pure they are."

He came back to sit down at the desk, and began again defensively in answer to Connington's silent, unconvinced gaze.

"All right, I'm not only concerned about you. Never can get away with that altruistic line! But I mean it, every word of it. Now, from my point of view, it's not good business. I'd be taking your money — far more than you can afford — without a chance of delivering satisfaction. I'd get the firm in wrong, as I said, have a libel suit on my hands, if I couldn't get every 'i' dotted and every 't' crossed. I know the situation. The woman is as slippery as an eel. She has political connections and a tie-in with half-a-dozen firms and combines. There've been several instances where she was suspected of shady practice and each time her tracks were so carefully covered that everybody backed away. You've got to face the fact, whether you like it or not, that you're no match for her in her own line. Leave her to Heaven."

Andrew did not join in his short laugh. He fell back without comment from Position One.

"Will you do something else for me then? Strictly as business."

"Anything I sensibly can. I'd do this too, Andrew, but ——"

"Find out — at Surrogate Court, you can, can't you? — roughly what the Sexsmith's takings are. Also anything about her financial position or involvements."

"But what good ——?"

"What sort of friend do you call yourself?" snapped Andrew.

203

"At least give me the satisfaction of knowing if there was a motive. I'll find out somehow. But I hoped you could make sufficiently discreet inquiries."

Smith Easton conceded the point. Whether to show that he acted in the name of friendship, or to keep his firm dissociated from any commitment, he insisted on having Andrew to lunch at the University Club a fortnight later. In spite of determination to play down his client's suspicions, he evidently relished the results of his investigation.

"It isn't what we call big money," he said at the celery-and-olives interlude. "Three percent of $489,673 would bring her just under fifteen thousand. That could be her fee. There are always adjustable expenses in connection with searching for deeds et cetera. And she has the sale of the house — a decent commission there. To say nothing of disposing of Mrs. Sanders' antiques for which, I understand, several galleries are clamouring. I'd say with careful management she could gross twenty thousand."

"Not much incentive for a wealthy woman, surely?"

"Depending." Andrew was amused to see that the lawyer in Easton had unconsciously assumed the burden of proof. "Miss Sexsmith has always lived it up. Never been a saver. Quite a gambler too. According to current rumour several of her investments went sour a few months back. Fact, she had to sell her house in Don Mills to cover her losses. Her present ménage — a place she had a second mortgage on, I understand — isn't at all the style to which she had become accustomed."

Ursula Pethwick had mentioned some shares which had failed to win Mrs. Sanders' approval. Connington found Easton's sudden preoccupation with steak annoying, until he noticed that the table beside them was now occupied and that the lawyer had become cautiously casual. Not until they were served coffee in the empty lounge, did he make his final contribution.

"I said that the person with a legitimate grouch was the housekeeper. Apparently she feels so, too. Strongly enough to file suit against the will."

"On what grounds? After all an annuity of a hundred a month plus five thousand ——"

"Won't go very far for a woman used to her standard of living. The grounds cited are these: thirty years in service at insufficient salary; broken health due to the difficulty of the situation; induced expectations of being adequately provided for."

"Will it stand up in court?"

"Won't have to. It has been withdrawn."

"Then —"

"Nobody knows. Presumably Miss Sexsmith has seen fit to settle out of court."

"At her own expense?"

Smith Easton laughed the laugh of a man with few illusions.

"Perhaps. It would be cheaper than having a will which she drew up herself contested in court. My guess is that one or two of the beneficiary charities will find that the actual legacy falls a bit short of the proposed amount. There are always such accidents as a falling market, an unpaid tax. And a charity wouldn't run the risk of suit."

" 'The law is the true embodiment
Of everything that's excellent.' "

quoted Andrew without his usual enjoyment of Gilbert's quip.

"Okay," said Easton, who was also a Savoyard, "but don't think that Miss Sexsmith embodies the law. For every one like her there are a hundred — well, dozens — of honest hardworking blokes, like me, who do the best they can."

Apart from sticking their necks out, thought Andrew. He also thought that he must be growing in grace — or was it just in diplomacy? — that he did not think it out loud. He merely said:

"So it boils down to this: An ornament to the profession, in temporary need of funds, decides to advance by six months or several years, the death of a benefactor, friend, and trusting client, in order to come into a sure thing a bit sooner. And with the connivance of an unscrupulous doctor and a disgruntled servant, she gets away with it in cold blood, broad daylight, with a wealthy, prominent, but unfortunately aged woman. And

205

there is no process of justice to bring her to trial or even to expose her?"

"That's the way it stands. Yes. The system is only human and so are its administrators. You just have to learn to live with it, Andrew."

It's not living with it, thought Andrew in the ensuing days. It's living with myself if I don't do something about it. Rod Easton's conscience is his own affair. And I'm not blaming him, or even judging him and the others. I'm sure he's right when he says nobody else will touch it. I could try Stanislaus Kowalsky, but that would put him on the spot because I helped him while he was qualifying for practice here. And after what he went through before he came over, it wouldn't be fair. Cam Denbigh has the root of the matter in him, enough to take the risk, but he is just a junior in the Carter firm, and they'd never let him do it. No. It's my personal responsibility, not theirs. Leave her to Heaven? That's easy. I'd like to. But has Heaven any assignment for me in the matter? *"C'est moi, C'est moi.* The angels have chose to fight their battles below." Come off it. You'll be saying, "Me and Gott" presently.

The decision to laugh at himself, to rationalize his retreat, submerge his unease in preparation for Christmas and for John's departure, resulted in a state of nervous tension, of inability to plan or concentrate, which no determined efforts at prayer could dispel. The very avenue of prayer seemed blocked and, after wandering in bypaths of forensic debate, recapitulation of evidence, speeches and letters to Miss Sexsmith, he found himself settling for such sentences as "All right, Lord, I've tried." "Take the will for the deed, this time." "You know I want to pray." — sentences so juvenile and finally so belligerent that he was reduced to a new low in self-esteem and a new loneliness in being.

Ursula Pethwick had begun a fairly regular attendance on his evening ministry. The outpouring of emotion and energy on her friend's behalf had exhausted her powers of resistance and she had acquiesced, though regretfully, in the decision that legal action was impossible.

Something of her earlier fire flared up, however, when she stayed to speak to him on the Sunday before Christmas.

"Beryl Sexsmith was at church this morning, Mr. Connington — for the first time since the Sunday after the funeral," she said without preliminary.

"Oh?" Andrew wished that she had not brought the matter up. He had come to feel her presence as a rebuke — quite illogically for he knew that Ursula thought he had gone far beyond the call of duty. "She attends on high days and holy days, I take it."

"If she came oftener, I'd have left before this. I don't really know why I stay on. Sentiment, I suppose. But there was a special reason for her presence this morning. Do you mind looking at this?"

She handed him, with a dramatic gesture which oddly typified the drama into which her most unhistrionic, reserved personality had been thrust, a church calendar. Her running commentary almost anticipated his perusal of the page to which she pointed.

" 'To the Glory of God and in loving and reverent memory —' it is, would have been, Mrs. Sanders' ninety-third birthday. That's really why I went this morning. I should have preferred your service. Mrs. Sanders had a poor opinion of Mr. Binscombe. She was very fond of Dr. Smale who died last year. And ever since Mr. Binscombe drooled at the funeral over the 'tender, loving, sacrificial care which she had received throughout her illness,' I've hardly been able to listen to him. But see this: '... choice piece selected from her own collection and presented by her grateful friend, Beryl Sexsmith.' It was filled with white roses — an antique silver bowl she was very fond of. Miss Sexsmith's name has been inscribed on it. Oh well. It really doesn't matter now. I just thought you'd be interested."

"I am." Nothing else occurred to him to say.

"I hear she's going away soon, to the West Indies, for her health. Well — I'm glad I heard you tonight, Mr. Connington. It restores my perspective. Evil —" she hesitated before completing the sentence — "Evil, hasn't always won. Even though it usually seems to these days."

Probably because its agents put forth considerably more effort, thought Andrew, on whom these farewell words, intended to encourage, had the opposite effect. The graceful public gesture, the sanction of the church: everything was so plausible. Could he be wrong? Had the lawyer acted — he recalled Mrs. Sanders' sad, clear eyes, the inimitable recollective sanity of word and gesture — mistakenly but in good faith? Was the chain of evidence merely of his own forging and his reading of character completely wrong? He caught at the possibility and knew why he was catching at it — in a frantic effort to avoid doing what he must do.

He must? He had not faced it before — the embarrassing, the ugly, the probably fruitless obligation. He fought resentfully in near panic, against the massy weight of conviction. Was the conviction from God or did he suffer from the Almighty complex, of which he had been accused — Don Quixote hallucinations, as Smith Easton had more kindly put it? He had been willing to take legal action and had been frustrated. True, Beryl Sexsmith was a human being; more (worse, he had almost thought) a fellow member of the church. But not his church. And therefore not his spiritual responsibility. If she had done nothing wrong, his interference was unpardonably rude. If she had — had sinned grievously, cruelly, covetously — God was her Judge. He could speak to her directly as He — exactly! As He was doing to him now: "Son of man, I have made you a watchman for the house of Israel; whenever you hear a word from my mouth, you shall give them warning from me. If I say to the wicked, 'You shall surely die,' and you give him no warning, nor speak to warn the wicked from his wicked way, in order to save his life . . . his blood I will require at your hand."

But was there nobody else? His underlying shyness, his reticence, made the sheer awkwardness of manoeuvring an interview to bring forward his remonstrance an appalling prospect. He had never faced anything in such grim anguish since his dealing with Ben Harris.

Even that had been different. His duty there had been plain. Harris was an elder and White a member of his own church. The injustice was provable, vouched for. And Harris had been a man.

When, on December twenty-nine, Andrew gave up struggling and — an easy feat by comparison — virtually shouldered his way past a polite but deprecating secretary into Beryl Sexsmith's surprised presence, he found, to his very slight relief, that her womanhood was less of a drawback to plain dealing than he had anticipated. Rather pretty features and a dimpled chin, a figure which determined dieting (according to Ursula) had cut down to becomingly matronly proportions — these were, he knew, reassuring and used to disarm clients and susceptible juries. But beneath the air of demure puzzlement, then of flattering recognition which replaced her first annoyance, underlying the softness of her plump little mouth, and unable to hide when the opaque blue eyes glanced directly, there was something that made him think of Lewis's most dreadful creation, Miss Hardcastle, the Fairy of *That Hideous Strength*. Once this resemblance came home to him, he had no further doubt of the justice, only of the result, of his mission.

"I was interested," he drew the church calendar from his pocket, "in your memorial for our friend, Mrs. Sanders." He had intended to say that it was a suitable gesture or a gracious act. Suddenly he decided to use no subterfuge.

"I shall not insult your intelligence by sparring for an opening, Miss Sexsmith," he said, and the pit of his stomach which had been wavering sickly for what seemed an interminable period, rose and settled firmly with the words. "It is Mrs. Sanders and her death that I want to discuss with you."

There was no answering show of frankness. Miss Sexsmith remained at a loss.

"Of course, Mr. Connington. That does show though, doesn't it, how sadly her mind had been slipping even before her last dreadful collapse? Do you know, she never mentioned you to me? I had no idea even that she knew you."

He could either fall into the trap or elude it by some reference to Mrs. Sanders' ability to keep her own counsel. He did neither.

"By her collapse you mean the senile psychosis?"

"Yes. You can't imagine — perhaps you can with your wide experience in dealing with people — the shock of finding someone you had regarded as more mother than friend, gone raging mad, not recognizing those nearest to her, and possessed of strength which I still shudder to think of. Poor little Enid — that is Miss Waters — was terrified. I was called actually out of bed. Ah well, it's better not to think of it. Thank God, the poor soul is at rest now!"

Amen, thought Andrew. Aloud he said,

"I find it difficult to understand why she should have been taken to Whitby."

Miss Sexsmith controlled her impatience with obvious effort.

"My dear man, where else? The ordinary hospital will not take violent patients."

He spoke incredulously.

"A 'violent' patient of ninety-three, Miss Sexsmith? One who could easily afford nurses, orderlies even, in her own home? I do not disparage our mental hospitals. They do excellent work in almost impossible conditions. But for Mrs. Sanders?"

Anger leaped over self-control.

"I don't know your angle, Mr. Connington. But it is becoming increasingly obvious that it is not Whitby but a wealthy woman in Whitby that arouses your righteous indignation."

Andrew could match that one.

"Would this particular woman have been put in Whitby, if she had not been wealthy?"

At last he had drawn blood. The prototype of Miss Hardcastle sat before him in the flesh; stood rather.

"Mr. Connington, I find your conduct insufferable. You come here without appointment, trespass on my valuable time, make insinuations too absurd and insulting to require answer. Will you please go?"

There was a pause. Andrew had risen courteously and his silence drove her to unintended self-justification.

210

"Whatever your concern for Mrs. Sanders, it cannot approach mine. After thirty years of close friendship and absolute confidence, do you think I found it easy? But I acted on doctor's advice and in her best interests. She — when she was in her right mind — would say the same. Now" — she had regained her poise and a modicum of appealing pathos — "I'm sorry my nerves got the better of me. Actually the whole sad affair has been such a drain that I have been ordered away for a rest. It distresses me to be reminded of it. But I am expecting a client. Will you please ——"

"No," said Andrew so gently that she started with surprise. "But —"

"It isn't good enough, Miss Sexsmith. Your story doesn't cover the facts as I see them."

She hesitated, angrily debating the means at her disposal. Andrew was glad that flunkeys or armed guards were not among them. Once again his quiet authority prevailed.

"Perhaps you will give me the facts as you see them."

"I shall. Very regretfully I am forced to believe that, taking advantage of a slight heart attack, you, with the connivance of doctors and a disgruntled and apprehensive housekeeper, kidnapped — that was Mrs. Sanders' own word — your client and had her certified as violent, both to ensure her against altering her dispositions and to hasten her death. When my letter warned you of investigation, you spirited her away, keeping her incommunicado . . . ."

"Mr. Connington" — it was the voice Beryl Sexsmith used on recalcitrant witnesses — "has it occurred to you that this conversation of ours may be recorded? There are slander laws for accusations like yours."

Andrew shook his head with weary impatience.

"On the contrary, I should welcome the publicizing of our interview. It is for your sake that I make the accusations, as you call them, in private. Now let me finish. Your motives you know better than I — and the means used at the end to make sure that Mrs. Sanders' friends would not have access to her, that other doctors would not be called in ——"

"Such absolute nonsense! Really, Mr. Connington, do you hope to establish such wild charges?"

"No." Once again the quiet negative silenced her. "I think that a good case could be made out, yes. But I also think that you are skilful and influential enough to have avoided any legal pitfalls, or even the damage to your reputation of having to face a charge."

The admission knocked the props of her sarcastic assurance from under her. She looked almost bewildered.

"Then why on earth —"

It was nearer to an admission than he had hoped. Suddenly, earnestly, he followed it up.

"Because of you, Miss Sexsmith. Because of my concern for you. Because if you have done this — and, believe me, I should be genuinely glad to be proved wrong in such suspicions — you are guilty of the sin of covetousness, which is idolatry. And that is a root of every kind of evil and eats like a gangrene. These are terms I could not use to outsiders. I use them to you because they are Scriptural and you belong to a Scripture-honouring church."

"Mr. ——"

"Forget legalities. Forget your self-esteem. I am not speaking to you as a man, but as a minister of the Word. And I am speaking, I assure you, only under compulsion. You have no reprisals to fear from me. You have everything to fear from yourself. I don't ask you to confess to me. I beg you to confess to God before it is too late —"

"Before it is too late?" Her face was expressionless, and he could not tell from her voice if she were enquiring or ironic.

"Yes. As I pray that it may not be already. Before this has such a hold on you that you cannot repent. Before the Holy Spirit ceases to strive." He had more to say but he broke off, feeling that he had said all. He noticed absently that his hands were shaking.

Suddenly, quite charmingly, Beryl Sexsmith laughed.

"I've heard of your eloquence, Mr. Connington, but the reports didn't do you justice. I'm only sorry, if rather touched, that it should be expended on the wrong object. Because honestly," she smiled to take the sting out of her words, "I'm not the monster you have so dramatically painted. I hate to disappoint you, but the facts are quite simply as I have stated. Now, will you forgive me? I really have that appointment."

She sat down at her desk and he turned to the door. The situation was ridiculous. Against the cool finality of her denial, his appeal seemed histrionic, hysterical. Every detail of the spacious office, modern, yet in excellent taste, expensive but not incriminatingly luxurious, gave his charges the garishness of cheap fiction.

Yet he knew that she was lying. Falseness lingered in the air, tainting every shade of her dealings with him, from the warm professions of affection, through harshness and anger, to the coolness, almost nonchalance of her final repudiation and dismissal. What had produced the unconcern? Was it his statement that she was safe from litigation?

There was one thing more he must say. It came to him unpremeditated, unsought, whole. Surprised by the conviction, he turned with his hand on the doorknob, turned his head only and met her eyes. "Miss Sexsmith," he said, unconscious of anything but the message he was quoting, " 'why has Satan filled your heart to lie to the Holy Spirit? . . . How is it that you have contrived this deed in your heart? You have not lied to man, but to God.' "

He had finished his task. He went past a disapproving secretary, past the waiting client, through the corridor, down the elevator, out into the downtown streets where persistently falling snow tried to whiten the brown slush on which it lighted. He was too numb with the effort, more with the sense of being used as an instrument, to assess the change of expression in her eyes. Had there been anger? or horror? In a sense he did not care. He had fulfilled his commission, but relief was slow in coming.

The previous night's snowfall had been heavy enough to make driving difficult. So he had come by subway. Elaborate decorations in Simpson's and Eaton's windows were still attracting spectators as he walked towards the Queen Street Station.

213

He looked at them with absentminded aesthetic enjoyment, remembered a request of Evadne's, and turned in to see if any half-price Christmas wrapping paper had escaped the post Boxing-Day bargain hunters.

The book department was tantalizingly near, and a table filled with the contents of a second-hand library engrossed his attention for an hour. He was about to leave with a pleasurable sense of achievement, having bought a second edition of Rutherford's *Letters,* a translation of the *Octavian* of Minucius, and an unabridged *Water Babies* for one dollar, when it occurred to him that the Shoe Repair department would replace rubber lifts while he waited.

It was then after lunch time; he had a sandwich and coffee in the basement cafeteria and arrived at Russell Hill Road about two-thirty. He had not yet recovered the power that had gone from him in his encounter, but felt his tension loosening with the invigorating five-block walk in the December cold.

"That you, Dad?" John came up from the basement, exuding a smell of ski-wax. "The police are on your trail."

His father turned from the hall cupboard, removing his scarf.

"Nonsense. I haven't had the car out. It's you they're after. Heard you're skipping the country, doubtless."

"Honest. They phoned and wanted to know where you were. Pretty suspicious when we couldn't tell them. Asked if you'd be home for lunch. We couldn't tell them that either. Suspicions obviously deepened. This man does not communicate with his nearest and dearest, I felt they were saying to themselves."

"Johnnie, you're a priceless ass," said Evadne, running downstairs, "and you've been reading Wodehouse instead of packing. But we are going to miss you. Aren't we, Abba?"

"Don't encourage him to think so," said Andrew. This heavy-footed fooling was sheer joy after the guarded courtesies of previous months. "Finished your essay, Vad? And what's all this about the police?"

"Just finished. John took the message. We were afraid you'd been in an accident."

"But no. Just wanted for questioning. Mighty suspicious, I repeat. What will I tell the gang at Summit this afternoon if anyone has seen you removed in a black paddy wagon?"

"Look out for your neck and I'll look out for mine. They're taking you for dinner afterwards, did you say?"

"Decent of them. Solly's organized everything. I hope they haven't anted in on an expensive farewell present. Cor! What did I tell you, Dad? The paddy wagon itself."

The two members of the detective division who stood at the door were evidently embarrassed.

"We were in the vicinity and thought we'd see if you were home instead of phoning again," said the elder, Detective-Sergeant McLean.

"Yes?" said Andrew enquiringly. "Will you come in?"

"The fact is," said McLean, who had not read *The Admirable Crichton,* "we'd like your help in a little investigation. If you wouldn't mind?" He glanced at John and Evadne, who remained where they were, curious with the pleasant, obvious curiosity of youngsters for whom the men of the law had no terrors. Andrew glanced at them too.

"My daughter Evadne, Mr. McLean and Mr. Shaughnessy. My son John. Anything any of us can do? We shall be glad to help." It was by no means the first investigation on which his advice had been sought. There had been young people, one-time attendants at his Sunday School, caught in a jam; parent or husband or wife in search of a missing person, giving his name.

The men acknowledged the introductions.

"Just you, if you please, Mr. Connington. We won't delay you long."

"Right." He led them past his disappointed offspring to seats in the living room, noting with amusement that McLean closed the glass doors while Shaughnessy produced a notebook. It would take more than that to foil Evadne, he thought.

"Now what is your difficulty?"

The phrase came out from force of habit — it was always others who had the difficulty — and took the men by surprise.

"It's not exactly that," said McLean after a moment. "I

215

wonder, Mr. Connington, if you would mind — this is strictly a favour, I know — telling us just where you have been today."

Andrew's mind was divided between pleasure that the Toronto police carried on the polite, law-abiding tradition of their British counterparts — he trusted that these men at least would have been as courteous in a home on River Street — and a sudden unease at the realization that he was personally involved.

"Of course, not. Though it has not been one of my more worthy days."

"Just what do you mean by that?" Shaughnessy spoke out of turn, snapping the question from force of habit. McLean looked at his junior rebukingly, but Andrew anticipated his speech.

"Just that I haven't been working. And a minister always feels apologetic when he cannot give a list of activities."

"That's all right, Sir. We don't feel that way. My daughter's married to a young curate. He works as hard as any man in an office job. But you were saying — about what you'd been doing? Just the details, in order, like."

"After breakfast, about eight-thirty I imagine," said Andrew, modelling his account on the best John Dickson Carr, "I read my mail and wrote two letters. Then I had a call to make downtown. That was about ten o'clock. I took the subway," he added to erase the memory and the mention of the call. "Then I went into Eaton's — Simpson's too, if it matters — made one or two purchases, had lunch at the basement cafeteria in Eaton's, and came home."

"You mentioned a call," said McLean casually. "Would you mind telling me where you called?"

What on earth was he driving at? Had Miss Sexsmith actually reported him for attempted slander? In any case his answer was the same.

"My call was to Miss Beryl Sexsmith, the lawyer, in her office on Bay Street."

"And how long, would you say, were you there?"

"I arrived about ten. I didn't notice the time when I left — perhaps half-an-hour or forty minutes later."

"Yes. And what was your business with Miss Sexsmith?"

"Gentlemen," said Andrew, "I am always glad to cooperate with the police. But as you have already said, I am under no obligation to answer any of these questions. And this is going much too far."

Detective Sergeant McLean looked like a bulldog, reprimanded but still a bulldog.

"I apologize, Sir. I didn't mean to be rude. But it is important to us. You won't tell us what you talked about to Miss Sexsmith?"

"I think," said Andrew, trying not to sound stiff, "that you had better go to Miss Sexsmith for that information."

McLean paused briefly.

"Ah. But you see that's what we can't do. Miss Sexsmith is dead."

The two men, watching closely, were conscious of a movement so slight that they were afterwards at a loss to describe it: "You might say he reeled," was Shaughnessy's uncertain verdict, to be amended by McLean, "I can't say that I could call it that." It was less a movement than an outward reaction to an inner blow, and that blow itself less a shock than a sense of completion, of something falling dreadfully but predictably into place. But this, with the incalculable telegraphy of sensation, was countered instantly, protestingly, by unbelief. Andrew made the trite response, half question, half denial, with no sense of its triteness.

"Dead?"

McLean said nothing. Shaughnessy, about to speak, fell silent. Andrew's incredulity passed, and his first instant comprehension returned. He asked questions, without needing to be told the answers.

"When? And how?"

"As to the first, we don't know." McLean had the gifts of a genuine detective, ability to read character and an almost uncanny feeling for undercurrents. He was satisfied that his information was shocking news to Andrew, but the quality of the

217

shock eluded him. "There's more there than meets the eye" was his dissatisfied and correct reading to his junior. He continued tentatively, "Miss Sexsmith was alive when you left, you'd say?"

"Yes." He did not feel that the monosyllable required confirmation. He must find out what had happened but it did not really matter. What mattered, mattered terribly, tremendously, was the fact.

"How would you be sure of that, Sir?"

Andrew laughed, a ragged, inappropriate laugh.

"How do I know you are alive, Mr. McLean? We were talking, face to face, up to the moment of my departure."

"And she showed no signs, of being ill or anything?"

"No." What had been the reaction to his last words, the expression in those usually expressionless eyes? "She was sitting at her desk, looking over a document — a lease or will, I should think."

Shaughnessy nodded confirmingly. McLean sent him another reproving glance. Would this young man never learn not to give things away? It was the Irish in him, he supposed.

"Now, Mr. McLean," said Andrew, and his voice was tired but commanding. "I have answered your questions. I think you owe me an explanation. What was the cause of Miss Sexsmith's death?"

"Heart attack," McLean so obviously felt this an anti-climax that he registered no objection when Shaughnessy added "Coronary thrombosis," in an effort to make it more imposing.

"I see. What I fail to see, however," said Andrew, who wished above all things to obtain the basic information and to be alone with it, "is how you justify this inquisition of me with regard to it."

"Not Inquisition," protested McLean, for whom the word existed only with a capital. "All right, Sir. You certainly have a right to know. It seems that after you left, Mrs. Temple — that's the secretary — waited for the buzzer so she could send in the next client. When it didn't ring, after about four minutes, she says, she pressed her buzzer — intercom system, you understand — and Miss Sexsmith didn't answer. So she got sort of

218

startled and went in. Miss Sexsmith was sitting at the desk, like you said —"

"Slumped," amended Shaughnessy.

"Slumped in her chair and, as we know now, dead. She tried to rouse her, then screamed for help, and the clients came in. They got a doctor between them."

"Dr. Southend?" interrupted Andrew.

"No," said McLean, momentarily surprised. "That was the name Mrs. Temple said she called first, but he was away. Anyhow, the fellow they did get from the Insurance Building down the street pronounced her dead."

"From natural causes?"

"Oh yes. No doubt of that."

"Then I fail to see," said Andrew with patient politeness, "where either you or I come into the matter. A heart attack is not usually a subject for police investigation."

"No," said McLean uncomfortably. "You're right, of course, Mr. Connington. Only the way it happened — naturally her junior came in, and the clients were there, and people from other offices. Quite a crowd before they finished, I hear. And Mrs. Temple blabbed something about you not having an appointment and forcing your way in and leaving quite sudden."

"She said they could hear you quarrelling," contributed Shaughnessy, "and that you'd been persecuting her — the lawyer — sending letters and such."

"So," finished McLean, relieved that the disagreeable part of his speech had been taken over, "we were called in. Because if she had died when you were there and you had left without saying anything, it would have looked queer, you know what I mean."

"Did you quarrel?" asked Shaughnessy, wishing to profit by the general loquaciousness. "Mrs. Temple said she could hear angry voices very plainly. And then nothing at all."

"If Mrs. Temple's hearing and reporting are accurate," said Andrew as a concession to McLean, "she would tell you that almost the last sound she could hear from Miss Sexsmith was a laugh. Her final words to me were jocular."

219

"Those were the last words of the interview, I take it? She was quite happy?"

Andrew hesitated. He was obliged to answer this no more than any other question in this very irregular interview. On the other hand, a refusal would suggest mystery. And with no good to be accomplished and every misconstruction to be feared, he wished the impression to remain of a sudden, uncaused seizure. It was common knowledge that people were taken with heart attacks under most pleasant and peaceful conditions.

"As I said, they were Miss Sexsmith's last words. She then took up her papers to prepare for her next client. And from my slight knowledge of her I should say she was quite calm and self-possessed."

The air seethed with unspoken questions. Shaughnessy would gladly have pursued the matter of the secretary's accusations. McLean had not overlooked the incomplete answer to his last query. But, instinctively courteous and knowing the law, he was grateful that they had been courteously treated and did not presume further.

The house was quiet when Connington closed the front door on his visitors. He dimly remembered hearing sounds of John's car stuck in the snow and being shovelled out. At what point of the interview he could not recall. He had thought the men would never go. Now he almost wished them back.

He turned to the stairs and found himself physically unable to face the ascent. Instead, he stumbled back into the living room and sat down heavily in the chair he had just vacated. He was trembling, but inwardly, with a cold sense of detachment from his normal self. So this was what it was like to be a messenger of God's judgment, an emissary of death.

He was not dramatizing the situation, he argued presently, as common sense brought forward its explanation of coincidence. Beryl Sexsmith might have died at the same moment, if he had been planning his Sunday sermons in the study upstairs, or if she had been interviewing her regular clients. He was not responsible for her death, any more than the Apostle Peter had been responsible at the first utterance of those fateful words;

nor had he foreseen and foretold death as Peter had done. If the quotation and its context, which a church member of her generation could scarcely fail to recognize, had caused such constriction of rage or terror that her blood had clotted in consequence, or if her deliberate rejection of the Holy Spirit's pleading through his lips had caused the sudden withdrawal of all the ministrations of that Spirit, he could not know. It was enough that he had been used as agent. And of that he was too realistic to have any doubt. The force spurring his unwillingness, the cogency overriding that very morning's reluctance, the sudden invasion of his mind by those words of pleading condemnation, the very power which had forced them into speech: these had not been his own. But the consequent sense of unworthiness, of responsibility, of having dealings with the Unapproachable, was awful. Not since he was nineteen and stood in a patch of chill mist on no-man's-land, over the body of the first man he had bayonetted — for a moment the two of them materializing out of the fog, then he alone left, shuddering so that he could scarcely crawl back to his trench — not since then had he felt so directly the cause of another's death. But then he had been' his own agent, goaded by primal instinct for survival in a situation, for him at the time, amoral. Here in an ethical case on which he had deliberately suspended judgment, he had been used — whether as prophet or instrument — to bring about judgment.

He had not heard Evadne come in. Like a person emerging from anaesthesia he became conscious that she was there, sitting in McLean's chair, deep concern in her hazel eyes. She stirred when she saw that she had come into focus.

"I hope you don't mind my being here."

"No."

"I thought you might want to be alone. But — I hope you don't mind too much, Dad. I — I — overheard."

He felt swift, unsuitable amusement.

"You mean you eavesdropped."

"Yes. I didn't think of it as being dishonourable. Honestly. I knew, of course, that you hadn't done anything wrong and I

221

was just exasperated at the careful way they went about closing the doors. Aha!, I thought — childish, I know—and when Johnnie couldn't wait, I told him I'd report, and slid through Aunt Alex's sitting room. Are you disgusted with me — or angry?"

"I'll probably get over it."

She was distressed.

"Dad, you know I wouldn't listen if you had someone for a private interview. But I thought this was a joke. And then once they began, I had to hear the rest."

"Forget it, dear. It's all right."

"Daddy, what did you say to Miss Sexsmith before you left?"

He stirred at that. She came over and knelt on the floor in front of him.

"It was all about that business of Ursula Pethwick's friend, wasn't it? Oh, I've met her various times and she has given me an idea of the trouble you've taken for her. Vowed to secrecy, of course. But you can't fool me the way you fooled those detectives. There *was* something more. Please tell me. Unless you'd much rather not."

The secret might be less intolerable shared. He told her.

Evadne's eyes widened. She swallowed convulsively.

"You said that? And she died?"

"She must have done. Almost immediately."

"Like Ananias and Sapphira?"

"Yes."

She pushed her hair back and shifted to a sitting position, cross-legged. Her eyes never left his face.

"Daddy, it's frightening."

"How do you suppose I feel?"

"Terrible, I'd think. But not that way. You only did what you had to do. By 'frightening' I mean that things don't happen like that these days. If they did, people would be dropping like flies. How do you account for it?"

"I don't." He could not have confided in her voluntarily and was grateful that she had willed the confidence upon him. Better far to talk it out than to face interminable, lonely speculation. "I don't, Vad, any more than I can account for the

222

odd case of miraculous healing, and by 'miraculous,' I mean one that baffles medical explanation. Yet such cases do occur. Remember Ralph Machell. As for this — even in the New Testament this was an isolated example. There must have been other liars and cheats. And St. Paul mentions various church members who might well have come in for such summary discipline. God's dealings never fit our mould."

"Do you think the words — would she have died if you hadn't said just those words?"

"Oh, darling, I don't know." It was almost a cry forced out by the question which was haunting him.

"Now stop blaming yourself." Evadne had never sounded more mature, more like her mother. "You didn't plan to do it. You didn't want to do it. You yourself couldn't do it. Isn't it possible that she was taken quickly before she could do more harm? Ursula told me that was one reason you weren't willing to let the matter drop. And particularly since she was a professing Christian — so that she wouldn't bring more disgrace on the name."

The explanation was as good as any he could offer. Evadne uncrossed her knees and got up. Then she took his face in her hands and laid her cheek against the forehead that had begun to ache violently.

"You're really Something, aren't you, Dad?" she said almost reproachfully. "Talk about 'The Little Sister of the Prophet'! What do you think it's like being the daughter of a man who has a direct line to the Almighty? And just what chance do you give a girl of being impressed by the feeble creeps that pass for men these days?"

223

12

THE FLIPPANT WORDS HAD an immediate effect — it did not occur to him till later to examine them for undertone — in pulling him back to the surface world above the realm where he dwelt with "the everlasting burnings." It was on the surface, spent by the power and pain of his experience, that he lived for the next days, grateful for activities which called him into human company and interrupted continued thought.

John's departure for India on New Year's night was one such. Andrew had not expected any request for a heart-to-heart talk or even a tête à tête from his son; and none was forthcoming. Some discreet information had been relayed to John by Evadne — that was evident in a deepening, quaintly respectful consideration, which made itself felt in their intercourse and which Andrew would gladly have foregone. But he was grateful for the good relationship, the restoration of family feeling, and freedom; only at the moment of departure did he realize that, from force of habit, he had been regarding that departure with some expectation of relief. Now as the boy — man, he reminded himself — left the group of friends who had eaten New Year's dinner with them, and came towards him with outstretched hand, he saw Cecily's blue eyes, Cecily's quick smile stilled to seriousness, and repressed a pang of very real pain. It dawned on him also that this farewell had been left to the last. Even Aunt Alex had been kissed and patted, and was standing beside him, determined not to cry.

They shook hands. There was an awkward pause.

"Well —"

"Well —" Evadne decided things.

"Aw, kiss him, you dope," she said, digging her new Christmas handbag into John's ribs.

There was a man's quick embrace, the first voluntary grip of John's arms for many years, and the parting was made without words. John's friends took Evadne off with them to finish the evening out, and Beth Harris-Kemp drove Andrew and Mrs. Mansell back to a memory-gathered house.

Then there was his forum at the jail. Some years earlier a woman in his congregation had asked him to visit her nephew who was serving a term for petty larceny. It had provided a long-sought opportunity, for he had often been pricked by the statement "in prison and ye visited me not" without knowing how to break through the barriers of officialdom and resentful beneficiaries. His first visits, awkward and apparently unsuccessful, but repeated because of his friend's importunity — and fortified by her prayers at his weekly prayer meeting — had led, through apparently chance encounters, to a regular and accepted visitation. The forum had been the idea of two boys serving their first term for dope peddling, and surprisingly annoyed that they could not defend their Sunday-School-imbibed beliefs against the savage iconoclasm of the current Brain and his admirers. That Brain, his thin facade of scholarship riddled by Andrew's battery of quiet questions, had not desired further encounter. In or out of jail, thought Andrew, there was little different in the attitude of the self-proclaimed Seeker after Truth; but interest had been aroused and — depending on other attractions and the clientele — he could count on attendance varying from two to a dozen at the fortnightly session.

He never tried now — at least he prayed to be kept from trying — to estimate results. He had helped several to employment and rehabilitation. He had seen others, bright, interested, apparently moved, turn up again months later serving another term. He had had several letters from various parts of Canada and one which he cherished from a grateful wife. The letters sometimes contained requests for the names of books which he left in the prison in generous quantities. But the experience was always a strain, always a new aspect of challenge. To listen, to put a tactful stop to the loquacious, to be brilliant to impress the ignorant, and plain to cut the ground of bombast from under the intelligentsia, to be unfailingly courteous but blunt in needed rebuke, to keep the difficult middle ground between not letting them feel that he had something to sell, yet not disguising the fact that he was passionately, personally concerned: this was his aim. That it was achieved, he seldom had the satisfaction of knowing. More even than his reticence, which made individual interviews difficult to guide, he had to combat his impatience — the arrogant impatience of having heard it all before — which would be fatal to his profession and particularly resented in such a group.

He fought it down in this, the first forum of the year, when the self-constituted spokesman for the evening, a dropout from a University course in philosophy and a hitherto successful careerist in small forgeries, said, with patronizing familiarity, and as though breaking new ground, "Come on now, Connington, this mystical talk was all very well for the Victorians, for people who lived in a three-storied universe. Man has come of age. Modern man has explanations, scientific and psychological, for everything that you created a deity to account for. Take myself for instance. I haven't the slightest consciousness of God, or need for his existence — much less what you evangelicals refer to as 'an experience' of God, whatever that means!"

"From my point of view, that is too bad," said Andrew equably. "Also — from my point of view — you may be more to be pitied than blamed. But why should you feel that your state of negation proves anything? Obviously my affirmation means nothing to you because presumably I don't belong to the 'come of age' group. Yet I could bring, say, a hundred individuals of your generation, equally practical, equally well-educated, to give a contrary witness. Would that convince you?"

"It would not. But there is your failure in logic. In this

case there must be universal agreement. One negation cancels a hundred affirmations."

The others looked impressed. They also looked at Andrew. "Why?"

"Well — it's self-evident."

"Not to me, I'm afraid," said Andrew unhelpfully.

The philosopher tried to keep the scorn from his voice.

"If what you believe about God is true, how can I get along perfectly well without Him, and be completely unconscious of His existence?"

"What do I believe about God to render that state impossible?"

"Well, you believe He is our Father."

"No. As a Christian I don't. Not yours certainly, except potentially. Your Creator, yes. But if I did, your rejection — or unconsciousness, if you like — of His Being, of His concern, is not without analogy. There are many human sons of good fathers — you may be one, you may be the father of one in time — who are completely indifferent to their father's concern for them, completely sure that he does not understand them, that he has done nothing for them. I'm not speaking of the retarded or defective children who are actually unconscious of a father's existence ——"

"Yes and your good god lets things like that happen!"

"Careful," said Andrew. "My 'good' God doesn't exist, according to you. If, for the purpose of blaming Him, you concede that He does exist, you are logically obliged to examine His further credentials."

"I am not *obliged,* at all. I merely show the absurdity of your claim that a God who allows such creatures and conditions is good."

"Your statement that you are not 'obliged at all' is perhaps the reason for our impasse," said Andrew dispassionately. "You begin by giving your own unawareness of God as a reason for denying His existence. You select at random ideas about this non-existing God which you accuse me, rightly or wrongly, of holding, but reject any obligation to hear why I hold them —

227

and not only I, but innumerable other people who have been deeply and desperately concerned with human misery and have given a lifetime, in many cases, of labour to do something about it.

"Let's go back to your original statement, that the existence of God is disproved by your unconsciousness of it, whereas the consciousness of others does not prove it. I have stood at the Mint in Ottawa and been invited by the guide, with a number of other people, to put my hand in a vat of boiling metal. Naturally we refused. The guide rolled up his sleeve, plunged his arm into a vat of chemical, then into that seething mass. No one, in spite of repeated invitation, followed his example — took the leap of faith, the Christian would call it. If we all had, except one, that one might still not be convinced that he could do it — or at least not deeply enough convinced to try."

"A ridiculous, a childish comparison. There was an obvious scientific reason for immunity."

"There may be an equally scientific reason for your immunity to the evidences of God. I do not know," said Andrew gently. "And I doubt if His existence can be proved, though weighty and logical attempts have been made. You are, of course, familiar with the classic arguments of Thomas Aquinas? But eventually it must be an individual matter — existential if you like — less of proof than of proving." He glanced at his watch. Time was running out. He did not wish the meeting to end in empty acrimony, and the philosopher was on the point of reply. He stood up.

"My time is almost gone and I've talked too much. Tear me to pieces at your leisure in the next two weeks, but let me cite a case in point: Here is a quotation — I'm quoting from memory — from a great thinker who predicted that belief in God would everywhere be at an end in a few years. 'The Christian religion is to my mind the most absurd, atrocious in its dogmas, the most tangled and obscure, the most flat, dreary, gloomy, puerile and unsociable in its morality, of all.'

"Now there is a statement to which any man come of age might sign his name. There were many like it. And hundreds of 'modern' young and older men caught it up as the New Thought — it wasn't; it had been stated in different ways over centuries — and modelled their thinking and consequent lives upon it, two hundred years ago in that strange, undatable period when 'people lived in a three-storied universe and everybody believed because nobody knew better.'" He paused to let this sink in.

"One young man who accepted such statements and rejected all old-hat Christian superstition could have shown some of you a thing or two about mischievousness. He lived it up, defied authority and suffered for it, on one occasion was publicly flogged almost to death, with no reaction from the society of his day except that it served him right. He planned murder, contemplated suicide, was frequently in sickness and hair-raising danger, 'no more afraid of death,' in his own words, 'than of sleep.'"

He stopped abruptly and picked up his watch from the small table beside him. There was a moment's silence while he wondered if he had miscalculated.

"Well go on. What about him?" Thank God, he hadn't. There were only two voices, but the interest of the group was behind them.

"Oh? Only that this young delinquent, without wishing or asking, became conscious that there was a God, later that Jesus Christ was the Son of God and had died for him. That experience changed his whole life, lasted for almost sixty years, and made him one of the most influential men of his age. His name was John Newton and his summation of both experiences he crystallized later in one of his well-known hymns:

'I once was lost but now am found,
Was blind but now I see.'

But, if it interests you, Mr. Hammersmith, thirty-five years ago, I — old fogey as I seem to you now — was a man come of age who could have made the same statement with which you began this discussion. I had no belief in God, no sense, no experience, no need of Him, I thought. Then one day He arrested me.

229

So look out! Guard that cherished atheism of yours. As C. S. Lewis, another ex-atheist who should know, remarks, 'God, if I may say so, is very unscrupulous.' "

On his way to the door he stopped to speak to a swarthy youngster, whose truculent interruptions had at first seemed his only purpose in attending the forum. Andrew, finding to his dismay that righteous indignation was becoming active personal dislike, had prayed and asked his people for prayer to meet a situation which threatened to disrupt the group. The answer came, as usual, in unorthodox fashion. During the next sessions de Grassi had sat sullen but silent, and Andrew learned that half-a-dozen of the others, amused at first, had threatened to beat him up "the first heckle they heard out of him."

Why he came at all, except to relieve boredom, was a mystery, but recently the sullenness had been less noticeable and one or two questions indicated that some impression was being made.

"They tell me you won't be here next meeting, Jocko," he said dropping his voice. He had a sudden impulse and set it aside from sheer repugnance. It recurred, shamed him, and conquered, all within the natural interval of speech. "I hope this isn't our last meeting though. You live up our way, don't you? How about coming to my church next Sunday?"

De Grassi was taken aback and showed it.

"Jesus Christ!" Andrew controlled his involuntary wince. "I guess I hadn't ought to say that to you, but my God, Mr. Connington, I wouldn't feel comfortable in your church."

"That's all right by me. I hope nobody feels comfortable in my church," said Andrew. "If anyone does I'm a failure. But I can assure you of a warm welcome. You and that nice girl the boys tell me you've got."

"Oh her. She ain't religious. Good kid. But she don't think about things like that."

"How do you know? Wouldn't she come to please you?"

"Look, Mr. Connington, it's all right for you, but what

would the — the — other guys and their dames think if a jailbird turned up?"

"We have at least one other jailbird in the congregation," said Andrew accepting his evaluation, "but I'll bet you'll never find out who he is. Most of the others don't know, and those who do have forgotten. O. K. I can't make you come. But don't say you weren't asked. Or that church people don't care."

13

W HAT WILL YOU DO if he does come?" asked Beth, as
usual behind the wheel of her car. Victoria University was conferring an honorary degree upon a
graduate who had achieved distinction in diplomatic circles,
and Andrew, who had known him slightly years before, was
interested in hearing his address. Beth, herself a graduate of
University College, was the current president of the Victoria
College Women's Association by virtue of her daughter's alumna
status. It was she who had reminded him of the invitation,
buried under other papers on his desk, and suggested that it
was foolish, in view of the snow-packed streets, to drive two
cars.

He smiled at her now without answering.

"No, I mean it. From what you tell me he would have
nothing in common with most of the church members, even
apart from his jail background. It's one thing to give the invitation. I'm really curious to know what you'll do if he turns
up, with or without the girl."

"Expect a miracle."

"You mean that?"

"I have to mean it. And the second miracle would be so
much easier than the first, the fact that he would come at
all, that I can trust the Lord, if He performs one, to perform
the other."

"Yes — except that an individual miracle is one thing. The
second would involve dozens of people."

"Let it. It would be good for them, Beth, good for us. It would test just how deep our faith goes — our love rather. I'm not impractical. There are some I can count on, Christians with a background not too far removed from his, who would rally round. Vad will take on any girl — bless her — though she doesn't find it easy. And if Jocko became a Christian, it would make all the difference. It's the in-between period, when he is suspicious and uncomfortable and ready to take offence, that would be difficult — and for more than actual jail-birds too; for potential jail-birds, as we all are."

" 'There but for the grace of God'?"

"Exactly."

"Well," Beth paused for the light at Dupont and swung east to Bay Street, "you're going in for miracles these days, aren't you?"

"Meaning?"

"Well, it was a remarkable coincidence about Beryl Sexsmith. Did you make a wax image and melt it? I was at the funeral. Did I tell you?"

"No," said Andrew on his guard. "Was it a good funeral?"

"Depends on what you call good. Floral tributes piled ceiling high. Important people there, in spite of the holiday. And a eulogy to end all eulogies, from her minister. I didn't recognize Beryl. How can a man shoot a line like that?"

"It may have been the way he saw her," said Andrew defending what he felt was probably indefensible. "She had recently made a presentation to the church. And doubtless others before that."

"And seldom attended. Ah well, 'she was a woman of many interests whose contribution to the life of Toronto and indeed of her beloved province will long outlast her tragically shortened life.' That reminds me, Andrew; I was approached by several with veiled questions about you and your relations with la Sexsmith."

"My relations?"

"Only in the professional sense of the word, I assure you. Your reputation otherwise is unimpeachable. It seems to have

233

got around that you were the last person to see her alive. And in view of the fact that you absented yourself from the funeral parlours and church, there is a general impression that the interview was not a friendly call. Hints were even dropped about a police enquiry. About which, of course, I knew nothing."

"No."

Beth swung the car off Charles Street and waited to be directed into line in the emergency parking lot. The pause gave her time to put her hand on his arm and smile her direct smile, teasing but warm, into the eyes that turned to hers at the gesture.

"Strong, silent man! Well, if you are interested, my chief inquisitor said that if you two had any quarrel, she would bet you were in the right. It looks as if God thought so too." She sobered suddenly. "How does it feel to be always right, Andrew? Is it wonderful?"

" 'Have you stopped beating your wife yet?' " Andrew opened his door, went around to hers, and helped her to get out, waited rather while she performed the unassistable convolution necessary. "I refuse to incriminate myself by answering that one. And your expression of humility is completely phoney. The chapel will be crowded, by the look of things," he added changing the subject. "Don't they usually have such convocations at night?"

"I believe Dr. Greatrex is going to fly to Geneva. This had to be fitted in."

The address disappointed Andrew, the more because he had come prepared to be impressed. But to judge by the enthusiastic applause and the group surrounding the speaker afterwards every time he caught sight of him in the great lower hall, the disappointment had not been general. He allowed himself to be piloted by Beth, because it was the course of least resistance, towards the old Alumni Hall, its face lifted out of recognition from the black-framed graduate-picture adornment of his college days. The food was consistent with the best Victoria tradition however, good, plentiful, and expeditiously circulated. It formed a solid punctuation to the dissolving contacts and fragmented comments which flowed around them.

"Mr. Connington." Andrew turned to greet the President with pleasure. He liked Dr. Brimley and saw no reason to doubt the fact that Dr. Brimley liked him. He was successful and popular and had an invaluable knack of remembering everyone's name and the right thing to remember about everyone; yet Andrew felt that their aim was the same, even though they were by temperament and by conviction unable to pursue it in the same way. Dr. Brimley's vote of thanks to Greatrex had been qualified, Andrew was quite sure, by the disappointment which he himself had experienced; but an amusing anecdote and a few ambiguous adjectives had made it pass critical muster.

"It's not a suitable time or place," the President was saying, where Andrew had expected only a passing word, "but I wonder if I could have a moment of your time. I've meant to telephone you but haven't had the opportunity."

Beth had been greeted with a glad cry of discovery by a group of women and was surrounded at a little distance. Dr. Brimley had been right. People coming upon him — even some upon Andrew — from all sides gave them no chance to speak. So, within a few moments he was guided across the hall and into one of the first floor offices.

"Ah that's better," said his host, closing the door. " 'Peace perfect peace with loved ones far away.' Now, Mr. Connington, it's just this business of your delightful daughter that I thought we should have a word on."

"What business?"

"I mean the scholarship."

"Scholarship?"

Dr. Brimley looked like a man whose guess has been confirmed.

"I hope I'm not rushing where angels fear to tread. But I thought that Evadne might not have told you. Scholarship isn't the word. Opportunity would describe it better. Really the things that open up for the young these days. Not in our time!

235

It makes administration more complicated than ever. But more interesting as well."

"I assure you Dr. Brimley, I am completely in the dark." Andrew did not like the admission, but it never occurred to him to equivocate.

Dr. Brimley's tact was equal to the occasion.

"Perhaps your daughter finds it as difficult to get a minute with you as my Pat does with me. The pressure of these days is incredible. But I think perhaps she had a motive. And that's why I decided to interfere. So I'll brief you — and try to make it brief. A retired schoolteacher — Vic grad — must have considerable money besides her pension. Spoke of a piece of family property just out of the city which she hung on to for sentimental reasons and has realized on phenomenally well, I gather. It seems that her dearest wish, when she graduated, was to go for a year to Cambridge. Why Cambridge, I don't know; some literary association, I believe. Well, there was no question of it. She had got through college the way you and I — the way most of us did those days. No money forthcoming and she went into teaching. Now she wants to give some Vic girl the chance that she never had. She has investigated the situation — I gather made some sort of endowment to the Women's Colleges there. Of course, scholarship is a requisite. But then she hedged it around with so many other conditions — she's dead against women smoking, for instance — that not many of our Fourth Year qualify. And the final decision rests with her.

"I've known about this for some time, but we waited till the fall term was over to decide on our available students. Then we had her to tea at Annesley with the girls we selected. Couldn't tell them, of course, except for some story about a graduate of many years back wanting to see a cross section of this year's graduates. Well — not to spin it out — your Vad is the choice. You probably don't wonder! But she has a nice way with older people."

"I doubt if Vad thinks of them as older people," murmured Andrew.

"That's it. Most of these girls don't know how to talk to

236

anyone over thirty. And a woman of seventy might as well be Methuselah! At all events Vad won her, and, of course, without trying. I heard them chatting. The child was genuinely interested in what Miss — I'm not to give the name away at this point — had to say. Compared it with what you had told her of Vic in the Twenties."

"So what happened?"

"That's the point. I had her into my office next morning and put the proposition before her. She turned it down."

"Reasons?"

"She didn't give any. Mind you, she might not be interested. It might be something she could do on her own — that is, you could do for her, and so not be the chance that it would be to some?"

He paused. Andrew thought of his commitments, the money he had lent the young Smithsons, interest free, for a down payment on a house, the note he had backed for Jim Waslow. Evadne's legacy from her uncle was not due for almost four years. Church work, Vacation Bible School, had kept her from earning the money which many college girls acquired in their holidays.

"No. If Evadne had expressed any particular longing for such a thing I should have done my best."

"Even at that," said Dr. Brimley confidentially, "the situation would hardly have been made as smooth for her as this promises to be. It is a real wish fulfilment on the part of our donor. In fact I was afraid at first that she might expect returns in the way of gratitude and ties which a young person would find irksome. But to the best of my belief, that isn't so. She has a good many interests — actually supports half-a-dozen children and is going on a round-the-world trip to visit them all."

"Surely Vad said something? It's not like her to give a flat refusal."

"No, she worded it very nicely. I could see her thinking hard as I explained the proposition. Thanked us very much but said she was afraid it wouldn't fit in with her plans. Actually suggested a friend's name — one of the other half-dozen possi-

237

bilities. At one point she mentioned you and broke off abruptly. I think she feels that you would miss her. And I'm sure you would. But Miss Simms — there I've given away the name — was greatly disappointed and urged me to ask her again. Even volunteered to talk to her. So I decided to speak to you first."

"I'm very glad you did. I'll try to get things clear with her tonight. Certainly if I am the stumbling block I will reassure her as much as I can."

"I knew you would. I knew you would." Dr. Brimley opened the door and the two men emerged into the thinning crowd. "Ah there you are, Mrs. Harris-Kemp!"

"Looking everywhere for my passenger to avoid the rush-traffic. Since it's you who absconded with him, Dr. Brimley, I'll say nothing about it this time."

"I hope you enjoyed our speaker?"

"Tolerably. I'd sooner listen to you or to Mr. Connington. Which reminds me — have you ever spoken in the chapel, Andrew?"

"In my Shorncliffe days."

"Well you should. Why don't you ask him some time, Dr. Brimley? Wait, I have an idea," and no one could have told whether or not it had occurred to her on the instant. "Have you decided on the speaker for Graduation Sunday?"

"Why — no." Dr. Brimley was also a quick thinker. "That is a very suitable suggestion, Mrs. Harris-Kemp. Mr. Connington, could we prevail upon you?"

"With Evadne graduating," cooed Beth.

"Nothing could be more appropriate," reiterated the President.

"Honestly, Beth, how were you brought up?" expostulated Andrew as they passed under North House arch on the way to her car. "I'll bet you were one of those dreadful children who asked if their friends could stay for dinner, right in front of said friends. I'm not easily embarrassed but ——"

"Nonsense. It is, as Dr. Brimley said, a most appropriate suggestion. Didn't you hear him thank me for making it?"

238

"He had to with me standing right there. Unless he had already lined up his speaker."

"Oh I knew he hadn't. I had just been talking to Dr. Quant — the new registrar. And he said they had been discussing it only yesterday and had come to no decision."

"My name, he doubtless said, was the first on the list?"

"If it had been, I shouldn't have shoved my oar in."

"Really, Beth, I ought to phone and say I've reconsidered. What else could the poor man do?"

"Nothing." Beth was quite pleased with herself. "And just you dare reconsider! You should have heard the absolutely lousy stuff that Phyl's graduating class had handed to them. And now Greatrex today on the failures of the past and the bright hopes of the unshackled future, when man at long last has been set free by science and is in complete control of his environment! You have something to give this class of Evadne's."

"Oh I grant that." Amusement was overcoming Andrew's discomfiture. "But ——"

"But nothing. Dr. Brimley likes you. If you had stayed at Shorncliffe — or if Eucharist were still within the United Church, or for that matter if you belonged to any of the larger denominations — you would have been asked before this. Well, I recently made a dashed large contribution to their new Girls' Residence. I see no reason for not getting a return on my investment. And think how pleased Vad will be."

"I know she will. Thank you." Andrew realized that he had sounded less than gracious, and became a bit awkward. "Believe me I do appreciate everything that you do on my behalf. I'm getting steadily deeper in your debt."

"Oh for Heaven's sake," she cried, throwing up both hands and catching the wheel again before the right tires hit the snow bank on Heath Street, "don't talk as if I'm a finance board. I'm Beth Harris. Remember me?"

"As a matter of fact, I don't by that name." They turned down Russell Hill and stopped at the Mansell drive to let a crowded car back out. Evadne waved from it and Andrew

239

remembered that she was off to a class sleighing party. Suddenly and unreasonably he found himself wishing that his arrival had been made a few moments later. It was not the first time that those same friends of Evadne had seen Beth with him. He concluded his speech with some abstraction. "I don't think I ever met you while you were Beth Harris. Or did I?"

Beth said nothing until she had manoeuvred the car neatly around the snowbanks at the kerb, and up the drive, stopping at the narrow path shovelled to the front door. She turned off the ignition and the sudden silence, as well as their momentary isolation between the high-piled mounds of snow, gave weight to her words.

"Andrew!" It was a laugh and a sigh. "You are a *very* difficult man to get through to. Sometimes I wonder if I ever shall. And I wonder rather enviously how Cecily managed it."

There was a different quality now in the silence. Such a silence might have followed the flinging down of a gauntlet, the challenge to a duel. Yet beneath his wordlessness, his inadequacy to meet or evade the challenge, he felt that she was not nonplussd. She let it hold unbroken, herself unmoving, gloved hands still on the wheel. Then she shook her head and turned on him a fleeting, mock-rueful smile.

"I'll just come in and say Hello to Aunt Alex. She told me how much she would miss John."

She did not stay long and refused Mrs. Mansell's perfunctory but pleasant invitation to dinner. When Andrew took her back to the car, she replied in monosyllables to his reiterated thanks, smiled enigmatically at him through the opened window, turned the key and reversed the car in almost a single movement.

Aunt Alex was still standing in the hall when he reentered it.

"Dinner in half-an-hour, dear." She was turning back towards her sitting room when she spoke again. "That Mrs. Harris-Kemp is very fond of you, I think."

The words arrested him at the staircase. With Aunt Alex it was impossible to tell if a sentence had a sequel. He waited, as much from shock as from curiosity, to see if this one had.

"And in that case" — there was no emotion in the voice, only quiet reasoning — "are you being quite fair to her, Andrew?"

It was a wasted evening, he decided several hours later, tearing up the third draft of a letter which he would normally have dashed off without a second thought. He had not been able to concentrate on reading, heavy or light. He had welcomed three telephone calls as a grateful diversion, and finally had taken a brisk walk with the new member of the family, which John, shortly before his departure, had found abandoned on the ski trail and which had foiled their intention of sending it to the Humane Society by a display of dog-strategy against which they were defenceless. Just now he was employing one of the commoner tactics, resting his Springer Spaniel muzzle on English Setter paws and regarding his new idol with unwinking, adoring gaze. Answering to no ordinary dog name, and unresponsive to Evadne's madly original guesses, he was tagged with John's suggestion of *Memento*. "To make sure you don't forget Absent Friends."

Andrew pushed his writing paper aside and drew out his cheque book. At least the paying of a few bills would not demand more concentration than, in his present state of mind, he could muster.

Aunt Alexandra's unprecedented intrusion into his personal affairs, following hard upon Beth's calculated challenge, had given him the sensation of a boxer who, staggering against the ropes for a breather after a quick right to the jaw, has been — against all rules of the ring — kicked neatly back into the fray by the referee. No further reference had been forthcoming at dinner — understandably. There was no need of elucidation. The issue had been forced upon him and reinforced, the issue which he had overlooked rather than evaded. Whatever the future, his easy, beneficial period of camaradarie with Beth was over.

How long had it lasted? Some seven months, he thought vaguely, pleasurably stirred by the recollection of her words and their implication, while at the same time on the defensive against Mrs. Mansell's insinuation of blame. Beth had taken

241

all the initiative. Every overture, every invitation, had been hers. The few times that she had been in his home, the few conventional gifts she had received, were merely returns, called forth by some arrangement suggested by her in the first place. She was a mature, sophisticated woman; and if she chose to go escorted on social occasions rather than alone, no responsibility for the choice devolved upon him.

Oh come on, how caddish can I get? I can't degrade her to the position of a socialite willing to pay for a gigolo. She's done a colossal amount for me. Think of the book. Think of her support at the church. She's an important, sought-after, attractive woman, and a good one. It can't have been easy for her to come out and practically propose. I'm a heel, really. Under the pretence of discomfort, I'm pleased that she — in Aunt Alex's words — "is very fond of me." And I've dodged her efforts to tell me so for months. Well, she has told me and I can't dodge any longer. I ought to be honoured.

And I am. Also I'm on the spot. What happens next?

It's simple, he told himself, trying to apply cold logic to a problem capable of two solutions. One solution came out clear; the other was difficult, with an embarrassing and unhappy remainder.

Not to marry her. That left the ghastly business of telling her or letting her understand, in some way that would save her self-esteem, even if the hurt went no deeper. It left him without a friendship he had been enjoying, probably without support he had come to count on. In which case also — how priggish it sounded, but it was true unless her assurances had been mere flattery — it deprived her of his ministry; perhaps would devaluate the effect of what she had already had.

To marry her: the natural conclusion of a relationship which seemed to have been sent to do him good. Presumably it would make her happy — though she might find him anything but easy to live with — and from every point of view he was surely the gainer. Aunt Alex became frailer every day. Both women were used to their own ménage, but something could surely be worked out between them. Even on the lowest plane

242

of housekeeping, the matter of shopping — once a simple business of telephoning Scott's Fine Foods or Mrs. Mansell's favourite fruit store, both now swallowed up by the chain system — was placing a heavier burden on him. Countless nagging details of household management would be taken off his hands.

Here too was the solution, in human predictability, to future loneliness. John had gone. Evadne — even while he was assuring Dr. Brimley that he would reassure her, even hoping as he did, that she would some day marry happily, he had suffered a pang of dread at the prospect of her going. And in the nature of things, the comfortable, accustomed presence of Aunt Alex would not be granted him much longer. But in the nature of the new things, which for the first time in the history of the race now made woman the stronger sex, Beth would probably outlive him.

Security, temporal comfort, convenience, deprivation to none and benefit to all, not least benefit to his career: he chalked up the advantages. The children? He had no need, if he was convinced that he was doing right, to take their prejudices into consideration. But would they not, after the first shock — and would it be a shock to them by this time? — view the situation realistically? For Evadne, especially, would it not be ultimately a relief from the sense of responsibility to him which she might even now be feeling oppressive? She had refused to accept this unheard-of offer, he was sure, for no other reason.

He had lived, in obedience to his Lord, taking no thought for the morrow. But if the Lord had been taking thought for him? If every circumstance since Roger Kemp's death had been the Lord's provision for his good?

He glanced at his watch. Evadne had said that she would be late, and he did not wait up for her although he knew he would not fall asleep until she came home. Memento rose, alert to his every movement, and accompanied him to his bedroom. He could speak to the child after breakfast. She had no nine o'clock lecture next day.

He did not love Beth. The still small word which had waited patiently until the noise of his triumphant train of

243

logic died away, was now there, requiring answer. Of course he didn't, he told himself impatiently. He had loved Cecily; he still loved Cecily. Such love did not come twice. But Beth knew that or would know it. He would tell her frankly and it would make no difference. Another kind of affection — he did not give it the same name — could grow between them, based on mutual advantage, pooled interests, his concern to satisfy her. Even physically, the intimacy of living would probably awaken in him the desire which he knew, though he had refused to admit it, he aroused in her. The revulsion of a mind dedicated for a lifetime to one passion would pass, as custom dulled its fastidiousness. No one would ever supersede Cecily in his heart. But meanwhile life had to be lived on earth — perhaps ten, twenty years of it. And the thought of new arrangements which would have to be made when Mrs. Mansell died, when Nancy deprived of Evadne's help could no longer manage the house, appalled him. He had gone dreamily on as if things would continue forever as they were. Now the prospect was black and depressing and complicated. Except for Beth.

Evadne arrived home. The muffled slam of the front door announced it. He wondered how his Aunt slept through it in her large room across the hall. That front door — another instance of the many things that never were attended to. Beth would have a carpenter or locksmith — or both — within a day.

The luminous dial of his watch read one-thirty. Yes, he would talk to Evadne in the morning. Now he wanted to sleep.

He slept, though in a confusion of dozing and dream, much of the time partly conscious of his surroundings. He seemed for an interminable period to be preparing for his marriage with Beth; searching in distress for mislaid sermon notes was an unexplained part of the preparation. When at last he gave up the search, realizing that he was late for the ceremony, Beth was at the wheel of her car, waiting to drive him to church. But when she turned her head as he opened the door, it was not Beth, but Cecily. Relief and joy and the stammering embarrassment of a compulsive urge to apologize, "But, Dearest,

244

I thought you were dead," and the endearing amusement of Cecily's face — with these he woke to reality and a renewed sense of loneliness.

He got up in the morning with relief. The pleasant shock of a shower, the prospect of a fully occupied day, partially compensated for his unrefreshing night. His morning prayer was stereotyped and a telephone call broke no sense of communion. After it, he decided to postpone prayer to a more convenient season and went down to breakfast.

Evadne was sleeping late — in fact he had to call her when there was no sound from her room after eight-thirty. She whirled, brief minutes later, into the dining room where he was reading the *Globe and Mail* while he waited.

"No time for breakfast, but I'd like coffee if there's any left. I'm dog-tired." Her father marvelled at the fresh young face which gave no evidence of such tiredness. "I can't take late hours any more. Would have skipped the seminar, but have to finish reading my essay — worse luck. Where's Auntie?"

"She gave you up and has gone into consultation with Nancy. I waited to speak to you."

"Wow, this coffee keeps hot." Evadne poured more cream to cool it. "Anything special?"

"Very special. Dr. Brimley told me yesterday about Miss Simm's offer."

She concentrated on her coffee. The toast he had made for her lay neglected.

"Didn't it appeal to you, Vad?"

"I suppose so. In a way. It was awfully decent of her. She's an interesting old dear. I liked talking to her." She stood up. "Now, I must dash. More snow last night I see. There'll be a hold up on the St. Clair cars as usual."

"Just a minute, dear. Dr. Brimley thinks — and so do I — that you would gladly accept this chance, but you don't think you ought to leave me."

"No — really? How vain can you get?" She was in the hall

245

now pulling on her snowboots. He picked up her briefcase but retained it so that she had to face him.

"Vad, dear, don't be silly. This is a wonderful opportunity. I very much want you to take it. Believe me, I'll get along splendidly."

She looked at him then, a look he had never seen before. Anger, bewilderment, pain, questioning, disillusionment — all were there.

"Thanks. That's all I wanted to know." Her voice was strained with the high breaking note he had often heard. "I'll tell Dr. Brimley this morning. It was good of them to wait. 'Bye."

She snatched her case and was gone, running down the walk and along the street. For the first time in her life she had not kissed him good-bye. And what did that look of hers mean?

Pondering in the brief period before the first business of the day — a difficult interview with a man whose wife had gone off with her golfing instructor, leaving him with three young children — Andrew decided that he had been painfully tactless. In his anxiety to set her free, like Sir Lancelot with the Lily Maid, he had overdone indifference which, unlike Sir Lancelot's, was feigned. Well, he would explain when he saw her. He had a funeral to conduct in the early afternoon. For the rest of the day he must put his own concerns out of his mind and concentrate on the real distresses of others.

It was not easy to do. Beth attended the funeral, looking superbly attractive in a new mink hat and making no attempt to speak to him, apart from a pleasant, apparently inadvertent encounter outside the funeral chapel. Whether she had made her move and was leaving the next to him, or whether she was trying another technique: in either case the impossibility of evading the crisis was again brought home. He had made up his mind. That should bring release of tension. But then why this unease, this undersurface conflict, which left him only during his moments of prayer and preaching?

Mrs. Mansell had rested all afternoon to prepare her for

one of her infrequent sorties, a Toronto Branch dinner of the Imperial Order of the Daughters of the Empire. Andrew drove her in her husband's ancient Buick, which she refused to part with, and promised to call for her later. It was Nancy's day out; and Evadne and he were alone for a meal which had been left partly prepared. The business of serving and removing, the long-playing record of Haydn's *Emperor Quartette* which Evadne had turned up so that the music came clearly across the hall, kept their conventional exchange of remarks from seeming too obviously forced. Yes, she had told Dr. Brimley. Yes, he had been pleased. Andrew, tired with the nervous strain of his day, postponed probing a situation which was new to him. Perhaps the temporary tension would wear off. He had never had more than a swiftly-passing rift with his daughter.

This did not pass. He came to dry the dishes for her, as he did on such rare occasions, but her protest was almost sharp.

"I can manage by myself. Quite easily. You're tired. No, really, I don't want you."

In anyone but Evadne, he thought, the last remark would sound like getting a bit of her own back. He shrugged and went to his study, waiting till she should finish the work. He heard her changing the record. One side of *My Fair Lady* ran its course. The dishes were surely washed by this time, but still she did not come upstairs, and the overture to *The King and I* floated up to him. Apparently he must take the initiative. As things were going he would get no work done this evening either.

He went to the head of the stairs.

"Evadne."

She answered on the third call.

"Turn off that confounded music and come up here."

She came up, on the defensive.

"I'm sorry. Why didn't you say you wanted to work? I don't often use the record player."

"I know you don't, dear. But it distracts me. And I want to talk to you."

"Oh."

247

He smiled.

"You're going to have your apology abject, I see. All right. Child, you know I didn't mean it when I said — what did I say? — that I would get along well without you. I won't, of course. I'll miss you horribly, you know that. But I couldn't have you pass up such an oppor — Vad, what's wrong?"

He broke off, startled. The face that he knew so well was distorted almost beyond recognition. Evadne, his dear, reasonable, well-balanced, compatible Evadne, glared at him, shaking with uncontrolled rage.

"Oh damn damn damn damn damn!" The frantic hoarseness of her voice emphasized the silly word, already emphatic because he had never heard her use it before. "*I* know, *I* know, *I* know! *What* do I know? I'm fed up, I'm *bloody* fed up on being expected to know everything. Vad knows! Vad will do it. Vad understands. Everybody else can come and talk. Everybody else has problems. Not Vad. She's a Christian. She can take it —"

"Dear, why ——" he began, but the torrent swept his words away.

"Of course, of course, of course," she beat her clenched fists in a paroxysm. "I must be reasonable. I must control myself. I must have a sense of humour." The mimicry was savage. "Well, I'm tired of being reasonable, and controlled and humorous. I'm tired of being different. I'm tired of fighting off wolves or freezing them before they start. I'm tired of waiting for Somebody who's dead as a dodo, or who doesn't exist. I want to let go. I want —"

She paused as though the tiredness had caught up with her. Her small body which had been stiff with her fury sagged under his gaze, and her face was recognizable now, crumpled unbearably, like her mother's when she was going to cry.

"But I don't. That's the worst of it. I can't." It was a wail of frustration. "I'm spoiled for all that. You've spoiled me. I can't bear silliness and dirty talk and stupid arguments. And it was all right. I didn't mind as long as there was something else. Something to wait for. I didn't mind waiting if there was real love. But if there isn't, what's the point? Why not make do? Why not be practical? We've got to live."

"But, darling," He took a step towards her. Instantly, as if recharged, she stiffened and backed from him. There was more control in her voice now but no relenting.

"I know. You shouldn't be disturbed. You've had a hard day. Well, so have I. But everybody else can disturb you. And everybody else has allowances made. And I'm not going to feel like a heel and I'm not going to grovel. And I don't know anyone or anything for sure any more and I just don't care!"

She was gone, shutting the door as though to avoid pursuit. He waited for the sound of her room door closing. Instead, he heard her running down the stairs, and presently the opening and familiar bang below. Crossing to the window in the upper hall he saw with relief that she did not go to the garage — she had a key to his car — but ran to the street and turned north.

Moving with almost forgotten speed, he pulled down overcoat, gloves, and hat and was outside the house within two minutes. Rubbers or overboots he had forgotten until the snow of the first crossing piled up over his low shoes; but the small figure was still in sight and he kept steadily on. To overtake her was impossible, he realized, if that had been his aim. Always a quick walker, she had a two-block start on him and was moving at a driven speed. He was content to keep her in sight, and glad, after a half-hour, that he had kept up to some extent the habit of walking. Mem, who had made himself scarce under the desk during the unprecedented noise which seemed to awaken old bad memories, had slipped down the stairs and out with him, almost unnoticed.

So for almost an hour, up Russell Hill to Kilbarry, along to Kilbarry Place, across Linsmore to Hillholme, up Russell Hill again, along side streets at random, striking Old Forest Hill Road, finally down Dunvegan, the little procession went. If Evadne was aware of their presence she gave no sign. She did not look around nor, indeed, in any direction. Under the spaced street-lamps he could see that she walked with head thrust forward, scarcely pausing at crossings to allow for mercifully

249

infrequent cars. The beauty of new-fallen snow on gabled roofs and terraced lawns and blanketed ornamental trees, the vibrant cold, the quiet of muffled city sounds, ministered, if they ministered, to a mind unconscious of them. And for once the turmoil of Andrew's mind and the effort of his body kept them from exercizing their healing upon him. He found that he had passed his favourite house on the corner of Lonsdale, its fine door and beautiful slate roof flood-lit, with an abstracted glance. Dogged as the "tail" in a detective story, he thought without mirth, but, unlike him, not stealthy, man and dog kept their quarry in view.

At Dunvegan and Heath she hesitated for the first time, and, with a prayer of gratitude made more fervent by his wet feet, her father saw her swing west. There was no corresponding pause at Russell Hill. By the time he reached the corner, the lonely little figure was turning in at the Mansell home.

When his slackened pace brought him to the house, he saw, as if in signal, her bedroom light go out. Should he go up and insist upon entrance and try to re-establish communion between them? Or wait until she had come to herself?

Then he caught sight of the Buick, realized the time, and remembered that his aunt was expecting him, was probably already wondering at the delay. He put Memento into the house as an earnest of his concern and drove down Spadina to pick her up.

Mrs. Mansell, stimulated by her excursion, was unusually chatty. Her serene, unconnected comments had never been so welcome or seemed so soothingly sane to her nephew as during the short drive home. It was still not late when he helped her up the stairs and into her bedroom. From the room down the hall there was no sound. Preferably he would let the matter rest. She would be all right by morning, surely.

The thought of Evadne lying lonely, facing a long night, perhaps wishing to apologize and be reconciled, was too much for his half-formed resolution. He tapped lightly on the door.

There was no reply. He tried the handle. It was locked.

This was absurd. No one in this house locked a door at night. He tapped again insistently.

"Vad," he called imperatively, "Vad, answer me."

There was an unwilling silence.

"Yes." The voice told nothing.

He hesitated.

"Is there anything I can do?"

"No, thank you. I'm all right. Good-night."

That was that, thought Andrew going into his study. He wished that he had not made the effort and, now that his anxiety was relieved, was aware of a rising sense of impatience and annoyance with his daughter. Evadne of all people to let him down like this! Like a petulant teen-ager. And without any justification. Particularly at this time when she should be supremely excited and happy. Chosen from all the girls of her year — crème de la crème — with enviable experience ahead of her and all hindrances cleared away — another success in dramatics behind her — every prospect of graduating with Firsts — what had got into the child?

"What is the matter with Mary Jane?
She's perfectly well and she hasn't a pain
And she won't eat her dinner — rice pudding again.
What *is* the matter with Mary Jane."

He grinned to himself as the rhyme came to mind — not irrelevantly. It had been a favourite with Evadne, who shared his dislike of rice pudding. A. A. Milne, although marked these days as rather "precious," had considerable knowledge of child psychology. But in this case there was no rice pudding.

Or was there? What had she said? "I know; Vad is supposed to understand." He could have smiled at her pathetically forced "bloody." It was hackneyed terminology, but not with Vad. She had used in it a furious effort to shock, to make him take seriously what she was saying.

He was suddenly ashamed of his impatience. What she said was true. He did expect more from her than from anyone else. But that was the price, the measure of his esteem for her. And he was available to her as he was to others. But she never

251

brought, or had not for years brought, any but objective difficulties to him. So he had presumed she had no others. Or that she was learning, as he had done, to talk them out alone with her Lord.

He shifted position uncomfortably, turning the two-hundred-and-eleventh page of the second volume of Karl Barth's *Dogmatik* from force of habit as his eye reached the bottom line, though it might have been a page of *Alice in Wonderland* for all the impression it had made on his mind. The unfair thing, the uncharacteristic thing, the hurting thing, was that she had turned on him. As if he had let her down, as if she no longer trusted and admired him.

That's what is so hard to take, he thought, laying aside the book and beginning to doodle a series of flag designs on a discarded page of sermon notes. My vanity is hurt. I suppose it was bound to come. I've been the Great White Father for so long that I thought it was a permanent appointment. And I counted on it. But I cannot see what I've done to lose out with her. She probably didn't mean it. She's upset and took it out on me because I was there. But what has upset her so deeply?

For it's stupid to tally up all her advantages and argue that she had no right to be depressed. Most of the time if one is reasonable — particularly if one is Christian — this counting of blessings will work. But I ought to know, if anyone does, that there are times when all logic and intelligence — and even faith — fails to cheer and there is an engulfing blackness. Often there is a cause, sometimes infinitesimally small. But I can usually put my finger on it. I probably could in Vad's case. What were the other things she said?

He decided abruptly that he did not want to mull over the question any longer. Evadne could talk it out with him in the morning. Meanwhile he would salvage what was left of another wasted evening. He chose to forget what had wasted the previous one. Noting with amusement that the Union Jack figured in all but two of his flags — it was, he admitted, the easiest design to draw — he tore them up, pulled the *Dogmatik* towards him and read with grim concentration until two in the morning.

In the morning there was no indication that Evadne wished to talk it out. In fact there was no indication of Evadne. It was not unusual for her to lie in on Saturday; but when shortly before lunch time, she slipped downstairs while he was at his study telephone and had gone "for the day — She says she'll be working in the library and staying down to go somewhere with Heidi tonight," as Aunt Alex unsuspiciously reported — he realized that his expectation of a soon "coming to herself" was sanguine. Evadne was not sorry for what she had said and had no intention of reasoning it out with him.

Andrew, who had been prepared to submit the matter to such reasonable examination and magnanimously shoulder an undue proportion of blame for falling short in subtlety of understanding, was taken aback. He never courted or enjoyed disapproval and opposition; but fortunately by now they sat lightly upon him. Yet disapproval and opposition from his loyal and adoring daughter, uncalled and unaccounted for, shook him badly. As the afternoon wore on without interruption, a circumstance which he would normally have seized with delight, and his planned but uncompleted sermons eluded all efforts to pull them together, he found himself seething with self-justifying annoyance.

At dinner time Aunt Alexandra's second résumé of the guest speaker's remarks the evening before, and his superintendent's lament at the number of teachers unable for various reasons to take their classes the following morning were equally exasperating.

"I wish these people had some idea of what is involved in preparing a sermon," he growled as he turned away from the telephone, growled aloud for the sheer childish relief of it. He could not face the half hour of music and conversation over coffee in the living room which was the custom if he had no engagement on Saturday. On an impulse he opened the evening paper and looked up the theatre page. Then he put his head inside the dining room door with an incoherent murmur of excuse, and walked over to the Odeon to see Hayley Mills in *Tiger Bay*.

14

HAT EXCELLENTLY ACTED AND absorbing film could not be held responsible for the flat failure of his morning sermon. Often he had been conscious of inability to express the word that had gripped him; very often he had been forced to say, "Would it were worthier." More often still he had wondered at enthusiasm for what he considered an inadequate presentation, or lack of comment when he had spoken with great freedom of spirit. But never since his first Easter sermon at Shorncliffe had such complete desolation and emptiness been upon him. And this was worse, far worse. Then he had· been able doggedly to complete a carefully written discourse. Now, the words, the illustrations, the emphases which usually came to clothe and round out the notes which lay before him: these did not come. He was driven to repetition, to clichés, clutching at often used etymologies, padding with unnecessary explanation. Worst of all, very desperation drove him to continue so that, when he sat down, his watch told him that he had spoken much longer than usual.

It was no mistaken personal impression either, he thought dully, as one after the other shook hands, either with a greeting that seemed forced or with a remark which avoided reference to the service. The rapport between him and his congregation was so warm, their expectation of receiving good from him so constant, that many seldom commented, indeed sometimes told him on other occasions how little they voiced their specific gratitude; but surely all would not be silent if the effort had

255

been less feeble than he feared. His state was so low that by the time Beth reached the door his eye was glazed and his handshake and greeting automatic. It would seem more than that to her, he realized as though across a great distance. It would seem cold, even rude, and he regretted the impression. But compared with his inner gauntness, all other regret was slight.

Dinner, with Evadne being ostentatiously solicitous to entertain Aunt Alex, was a meal to be endured. The afternoon was shortened by a request visit to an elderly member of the congregation who had fallen on the ice and was not expected to survive the shock of her fractures. He was thankful that her state of mind and their long friendship obviated the need of special effort on his part. Indeed the comfort and assurance came from her.

Coming home, he wrestled with his evening message, determined to avoid a repetition of the morning's fiasco. The sound of arrivals and youthful voices startled him into remembrance that Evadne had invited a mixed group of friends for dinner, including two theological students from Emmanuel College. If he had been less absorbed in his own thoughts at noon, the reference to a special menu at supper time would have reminded him.

Panic — panic that he thought he would never feel again in similar case — gripped him. Vainly he told himself that his worst sermon was better than the average, that he had been preaching before these fledglings were born. That was the trouble. They were prepared to find him outmoded. If he were to string together a few of the silly, unfounded, third-century heresies which were being reproclaimed as theology for the Nuclear Age, the "daring" thesis would carry its own interest. To preach the offence of the Cross, the wisdom of serpents was more effective than the harmlessness of doves. His grave but unsensational exposition of Isaiah twelve would not do, especially as the practical application which had seemed so clear earlier, would not resolve.

He would not face another disaster. The thought of pleading

ill and calling Don Howard to substitute for him crossed his mind. He put it aside with scorn. But he could not let Evadne down. More truthfully he would not let himself down with Evadne.

Going to the "Armoury" he rummaged swiftly through a filing cabinet which Cecily — bless her! — had insisted on buying and filling for him. There, discarding one after another, he found a sermon which he had delivered with telling effect during his first year at Shorncliffe. She had made him keep those sermons "as an Ebenezer." He was satisfied on cursory re-reading to find his smashing, sardonic demolition of the liberal arguments of the Twenties remarkably up-to-the-minute.

Back in his study, he made necessary changes, avoiding anachronisms, altering local references. Then, just in time, he went down to meet his guests, and exerted himself to be witty and human and in touch with the latest trends — above all not too talkative — drawing them, particularly the young men, to talk at their ease: everything, in fact, that an elderly evangelical was not expected to be.

The sermon was not a failure with the audience — he thought of it as an audience, not as a congregation. No longer able to read his closely spaced, young handwriting without his glasses, he kept them on and strove for his former freedom of glancing at the words, then at the faces before him. The photographic memory which had once rendered a manuscript almost unnecessary was fading with the eyesight, he discovered ruefully. Once, a single reading would have sufficed for almost verbally perfect repetition. The pauses while he coordinated reading and proclamation seemed awkward and halting to him; but his listeners' attention and flattering comments afterwards indicated that they were less critical.

There was in fact enough interest, if not enthusiasm, among the students, who went back to the house for an after-church sing, to make him feel pleasantly popular. One of the ministerial candidates left the group when he entered and plied him with questions about his literary references. Andrew took him to his study to lend him Chesterton's *Everlasting Man* and Comenius'

257

Labyrinth of the World, and was pleased at the young man's respectful interest in his library. Evadne's face, usually unobservable in the choir, had been a study of puzzled attention during the service. It was evident now that she was happy at the success of her party. She called on him presently to lend the support of his bass to their part-singing. One of the boys played the piano excellently; a girl had brought her guitar. It was reassuring to see a dozen of the young moderns behaving decently and enjoying themselves at the same time. Andrew recognized the fact that they were handpicked, and responding to the expectation of their strong-minded young hostess. But it was heartening nevertheless. The individual, he reflected for the thousandth time, is unchanged. Conformity to fashionable nonconformity makes him the mindless robot of popular "research."

At eleven he excused himself, realizing that the younger generation, reinforced by Evadne's excellent punch and butter tarts and shortbread and cheeses and coffee, would continue their bursts of music, interspersed by periods of desultory chat, for some time to come. The music became louder after his departure, folk songs and spirituals and some Gilbert and Sullivan taking the place of hymns. He left his door ajar and the melodies sang through his head, relaxing and precluding thought, thought which he knew would disturb his present hard-won passivity. He was asleep before the music ceased.

It had ceased in his mind when he woke in pre-dawn grayness under a sense of pressure and self-disgust which made inaction grim. He got out of bed to find that snow had been falling again. Toronto was not complaining this year about the disappearance of the old-fashioned winter! He dressed in old clothes and, securing the snow shovel, slipped quietly out the back door into the muted beauty of the white and dawn-silvered street. Physical exercise was what he craved. It might kill an incipient cold, probably the delayed result of his wet feet a few nights back. His whole depression could be purely physical. Three inches of snow had been added to the fifteen already accumulated on lawns and the thirty on piled banks hemming

258

the sidewalks. He attacked the task of removing it, in a burst of forced energy. Mem, who distrusted shovels, accompanied his slow progress from garage to street, executing a succession of backward and sideways leaps at each movement. Before the drive was half cleared, he was tired enough to return to the house, where Nancy was preparing breakfast.

"No egg for me this morning, thanks. I'm not hungry. But if the coffee is ready —"

It had not percolated long enough for strength, but the liquid heat relieved his dry throat.

"Tell them not to wait for me. I'll get anything I want later."

It was desire to avoid Evadne that drove him out again and kept him at his task, rather than any trust in the efficacy of exercise. The snow grew heavier with each shovelful, and the sudden heat of his body was no mere glow produced by physical effort. He contrived to be on the far side of the walk when she came out on her way to an early lecture. Odd that he should now be the one who evaded an encounter. She stopped uncertainly at the sidewalk.

"Well, I'm off."

"Good-bye, dear. Have a good day."

She did not go immediately. He concentrated on a patch of snow packed solidly to the concrete by the feet of early pedestrians. The flat shovel edge slid over it. He would need the ice chopper.

"Thanks for last night. The kids were impressed. Ken thinks you're awfully clever."

"Glad they know you come by it honestly." It was a poor witticism but the huskiness of his voice kept him from trying to redeem it.

"Daddy, aren't you well?" She came quickly over to him. Her face looked small and concerned, swathed in the enormous scarlet-and-gold knitted scarf, which was the latest thing for college wear. "You shouldn't be shovelling snow at your age. Don't you read the papers? Here, let me take that shovel."

"You go on to your lecture, child. I'm not straining myself."

259

She eyed him anxiously. Yesterday he would have been warmed by this return to affectionate concern, however brought about. Now he wished only that she would leave him.

"You sound awfully as if you're catching flu. I didn't think you were quite like yourself last night. Will you go in and rest and have something hot as soon as you're through? Promise?"

"I promise. You'll be late if you don't go, Vad."

He kept removing small measured quantities until she had turned the corner, then stood resting on the shovel. Her diagnosis was right. He must have caught a cold, the first in years. It was all he could do to finish clearing the sidewalk. By the time he reached the house he had a high temperature and was almost too weak to stand.

Like most healthy men, he took minor illnesses badly. The sheer bodily misery of that most wretched affliction, euphemistically named a "common cold," reduced him to a condition which his stubborn refusal at first to go to bed, his sepulchral assurances later that he was or would be all right, his shamed comparisons of his ailment with the dread diseases borne heroically by others, did nothing to disguise or alleviate. Fear of spreading contagion persuaded him finally to keep to his room. There for three days he subsisted miserably on liquids and unwillingly on aspirin, submitting to his aunt's insistence on taking his telephone calls for him and even, when on Wednesday afternoon his voice had not returned to normal and damp, forty-mile-an-hour winds came in from the east, abandoning his determination to conduct prayer meeting.

With a sigh that concealed his relief at capitulation, he telephoned Don Howard.

"It's not a service most men would think worthwhile to take, and I should feel my neck about asking you, especially on a night like this," he said in a croaking whisper when Don expressed concern at the unfamiliar voice. "Personally I often find it the best of the week. But there won't be many out ——"

"Stop apologizing. I've been there once or twice, remember. Only I feel that one of your men — Dillon for instance — could do as well as I."

"If you can't come, I'll ask him or — But it's more of a strain on them, especially with no time to prepare. Your coming will give them a lift."

"Give me one too, no doubt you're thinking. Oh I see through you, Connington. And they won't hear anything they haven't heard before and better. But I'll do it."

Was the exhaustion which sent him back against the pillows, his arm aching from the effort of holding the receiver, purely physical? He could not, he realized now, except under compulsion have dragged himself out of the house, even if he had had anything to say. The thought arrested him. He could never prepare for Sunday, unless this mental lethargy passed. Suddenly he remembered what he had announced as his topic for the morning sermon: the first in a series planned to answer several requests from his congregation, and entitled with unusual concession to the catch phrase: "Relationships Under Fire." He wished almost petulantly that he had never promised it. For the first time in many years, apart from the panic of the previous Sunday, he had no desire to preach.

A large bouquet of spring flowers arrived next day from the Women's Association. Evidently they realized that no light indisposition kept him from prayer meeting. Howard phoned a report in mid-morning, mentioning among other things the volume of special prayer which had gone up for their absent pastor. Then the postman brought cards from a few who had learned earlier of his illness. One of these, addressed in a strong, neat hand, he opened last.

It was a large square card of the new far-out genre. A right angle was formed of the same elongated masculine figure, vertical and horizontal. Nothing could been less sentimental than the verse, printed to form another right angle:

old ivory —
tower, head
in-air you
look down on
the best
of us,

but let the
flu-bug
bite and
wham!

YOU'RE FLAT OUT LIKE THE REST OF US!

and underneath, the lame sting-remover:

hope you're *UP* again soon, though!

Beth had written and underlined "Do" before the last line and added her signature without comment.

Andrew looked at it with amused appraisal. Good for Beth! It was a masterly compromise. She had made her position clear and was not going to come a step further. On the other hand, the sickness of a friend required recognition. And was there more than a suspicion of personal application in this particular cartoon? How had she learned of his condition? She certainly had not telephoned. Aunt Alex had rendered a careful account of all calls.

Well, the least he could do was to thank her. But that would reopen a situation which had reached an impasse. His initiative in reopening it could have only one conclusion. And if it had? What was the point in delay? He might as well get on with it. His current state of mental sluggishness was probably due to delayed decision.

He rolled over on his left side and dialled her number with quick, decisive strokes. The line was busy.

He waited an unreasonably reasonable time and dialled again. Still the irritating buzz repeated itself in spaced monotony. He left the receiver on the bed and proceeded to tie up the line, dialling to the last figure. After a seemingly endless interval of suspended thought, he turned the receiver over and snapped the final figure on the dial. Again the busy signal.

"Damn," said Andrew, fretfully.

Then suddenly he knew. In the interval between the effort of replacing the receiver, and his half-turn to a relaxed position on his back, it happened. The complicated mesh which had entangled his thinking and feeling unravelled. He saw clearly, with painful, stabbing clarity. He felt simply. He was again, after a long time, integral, one-willed. Symbolically and literally he drew his first free breath for days.

He could not marry Beth. Not a thought so much as a directive, it seemed ludicrously anti-climactic as the effect — or the cause? — of such spiritual purgation, such mental release. But around that relationship, he knew now, had accreted the specious arguments, the reasonable hypocrisy, which had reduced him from a man under One authority to a compromiser with expediency.

The subtlety of the temptation amazed him, seeing in close retrospect how nearly he had become its victim. For in the process of weighing possibilities, safeguarding the future, letting material considerations dictate his course of action, he had set aside, to all practical purposes forgotten, his God. The idea was so unbelievable, so humiliating to the arrogance of half a lifetime's conscious godliness, that he had ignored the possibility. He had seized upon illness as a present excuse for the fact — preceding the illness for many days — that prayer, from being an habitual attitude of mind, had ceased altogether, except in silent, jumbled phrases and public utterances which custom cast into an acceptable pattern. He was now aware, looking at himself with curious detachment, that in his concern with Evadne, in his frantic efforts to impress her friends, in his pleasure at their interest in his Shorncliffe sermon — poor thin stuff though he had known it to be — the will and glory of God had been the last thing in his mind. And, even harder to concede, he had not recognized, had refused to recognize, his defection. Now, as though asked to spread the contents of a rather shoddy pack before a discriminating buyer, he faced the verdict in undefending silence of soul.

Restless presently, as though change of mind demanded corresponding change of position, he knotted the cord of his wool dressing gown, shoved his feet into fleece-lined slippers and walked over to the window. A thaw had succeeded the stormy night and, though no sunlight rifted the gray cloud ceiling, the hard snow mounds of weeks past were dirty and visibly diminishing. Turning away to look at his flowers on the dresser, he caught sight of himself in the mirror. The harsh gray light was merciless to his unshaven, colourless face, to the lines in his forehead, the hollows under his eyes and cheek bones. Tulips and irises and daffodils reflected their living colours in cruel contrast. Either his hair had turned gray since his illness, or its untidiness emphasized the quantity of white. Automatically he picked up his hairbrush.

"If Beth saw me now, she'd change her mind," he muttered, but without conviction.

The thought seemed oddly irrelevant, but then Beth had always been irrelevant — a pleasant extra, a charming alien — to his inner being. Important, individual, helpful, good — but not his. And yet he had been prepared to make her his wife, as if he were free to marry, to take her to Cecily's place when that place had never been vacant. Strangest of all, he knew now, he had always known, that he did not want to marry her. And the reasoning which he had employed had brought about his spiritual exile. For it was the reasoning of common sense, a common sense weighted by vanity and cowardice. He had been conforming to the spirit of the age with its stress on the material and the present. He had been influenced by social behaviour which left no room for abiding loves or loyalties, which judged a course of action by physical comfort and security, which in a case like his equated I m. $-$ I f. $+$ I f. $-$ I m. with I m. $+$ I f. Not fair, of course. Beth was not any female. He might feel less culpable if she were. For her very distinctiveness, her beauty and social position and affluence had made him feel more flattered by her preference than he had been by others, whose interest had expressed itself less frankly. Even now he shrank from believing that the financial security of marriage with her had carried any weight with him. He shivered with distaste, shrugged, and left the question open. "If our heart condemn us, God is greater than our hearts and knows all things." A comforting reflection!

But cowardice had weighed heavily — still did, he told himself ruefully. The fear of loneliness, of an uncompanioned

264

age, a man's fear of difficult domestic arrangements — these were gone with his sudden restoration, gone permanently, he hoped. But the fear of disappointing Beth, of giving her pain, sheer funk at the prospect of facing her — these remained. He was wryly amused to find how large they had loomed, disguising themselves in his thinking as a touch of nobility, of self-sacrifice.

"God help me, it would still be a good deal less difficult to go through with it!" he told an indifferent sparrow on the windowsill. "I could easily — and caddishly — argue that I'm being selfish. If I were my own man, I undoubtedly should. But I'm not. Which is the point. I'm not."

15

IT WAS NOT AS HIS own man or in his own strength that he slowly mounted the steps to his pulpit the following Sunday. He had tried to evade or to postpone the sermon, but it had gripped him with the old imperiousness and he had not dared set it aside. Of the Relationships Under Fire, as the basic institutions of the ages were being "re-thought" — or more accurately, discarded — marriage, being the first on record, was the first to be considered. And what the Bible — not canon law or a state-church-dictated compromise — taught explicitly or implicitly about marriage, this, regardless of prejudice or custom or current opinion, was the sole authority for a Christian.

He paused after a slightly militant delivery of his purpose, turned back to the pulpit and, leaning on his folded arms, looked slowly and intently across and down the church as if gathering his listeners up with him in an act of discovery. It was an unusual approach, and he was not given to deliberate dramatic effects. So the expectant hush was deep and wondering. For two women the subject had especial poignancy. From different places in the church, they scrutinized him. Quite pale, he seemed to Beth's outwardly composed gaze, thinner, and rather less self-reliant. Magnificent, thought Evadne wistfully, wanting to cry because of the division not yet bridged between them, but still incurably partisan.

Then he launched into his discourse. A swift, unsparing survey of the aspects of Christian marriage which had brought it into disrepute among honest and concerned as well as hostile critics; a reductio ad absurdum of the term as applied to cases which he used as pithy illustration; a categorical denunciation of the state-church alliance or influence which in the Western world had imposed — and arbitrarily relaxed on occasion — one rigid law on believer and unbeliever: his proem sounded like the pleading of a devil's advocate.

Then, to discover if that law had sound Scriptural basis, he reviewed the passages in the Old and New Testament concerning divorce. His apposite reading from Milton's "Doctrine and Discipline of Divorce" startled some listeners with its modernity — a term always applied to any humane and logical reasoning, no matter how ancient its source. The answers of Christ to His questioners were put in their proper context of social and religious mores where divorce, at least for the man, was easier than under the most relaxed of modern laws; so that the question involving the phrase translated 'for any cause' required Jesus to give a decision on the debate between Rabbis Hillel and Shammai whether a man might divorce his wife for any — inclusively, any and every — cause. While many of the congregation were still wide-eyed at this obvious, but to them new revelation, he emphasized that the words used for divorce always signified putting away, neglect, abandonment, the wilful ruthless act of one party to a covenant. Equally surprising in its modernity was his quotation from Adam Clarke's eighteenth century commentary: "Divorce never should be permitted *but on this ground* — The parties are miserable together and they are both perfectly *willing* to be separated. Then, if everything else be proper, let them go different ways that they may not ruin themselves and their hapless offspring."

Without denying the charge that easing divorce laws causes decrease of effort to make a marriage endure, Andrew countered it by asking bluntly how much meanness, brutality, insult, indifference, lust, cruelty, on the part of both husbands and wives would have been prevented if the tie had not been indissoluble.

" '... but from the beginning it was not so,' " he quoted, and his voice dropped its polemical note, became deep and tender. "What is marriage in God's intention? What was it before, in a sin-compounding world, it became the legal transaction — cheated, broken, lust-indulging, security-offering, quarrel-and-hatred-and-ennui-producing — that it now represents to very many? How in the pristine world, when God saw all that He had made and found it very good, yet requiring one improvement for the perfecting of man, did He see marriage?"

The question hung momentarily on the air. No one else's voice can *do* that, thought Evadne. He doesn't try. He just feels what he is saying, so that here we are waiting — with him — to find out.

A dozen verses at the end of the fifth chapter of Ephesians followed, so read that they might be now for the first time spoken aloud. Andrew raised his head and smiled.

"These words, as many of you will recollect, I read every time I perform the marriage ceremony for Christians; read them sometimes wistfully, always with hope and the assurance that they might be the experience of those whom I, representing God, am making "one flesh." But it is high doctrine! Is it any wonder that Paul, whose own marriage had obviously not been of this quality — in spite of which fact he retained a regard for woman higher than that of any other New Testament writer — Paul, in an age to which fulfilment of Christian marriage was *yet* unknown — and I do not overlook many touching examples of marital happiness, both in Israel and in the pagan world — that Paul broke off in puzzlement. 'This is a great mystery and I take it to mean Christ and the Church,' he says, almost in apology for what he has been impelled to write. The prototypal relationship he could in some measure grasp, just as the prototypal Fatherhood of God, 'from whom every fatherhood in heaven and earth is named,' can become meaningful to those whose individual experience with an earthly father has fallen very far short of it. But the human counterpart?"

A possibility and an occasional experience in all races and times — Homer's lovely words about husband and wife in harmony wake a hundred echoes in secular literature — it must, he continued, be the aim of all those whose lives were being renewed in Christ by the Spirit. Because of its mutuality, of its impossibility of achievement by one party, the believer was forbidden marriage with an unbeliever. The words he had read were an injunction, not a counsel of perfection. This relationship was something to work at, to sacrifice for, to grow into, to perfect. And since it was an adumbration of the Divine, Divine help was available and essential to meet its difficulties. It was part of the required working out of their own salvation, knowing that God was at work within them. Not only individual characteristics, but every relationship of the Christian was included in that redemptive process. And if the witness of the world was again to be, "See how these Christians love one another," Divine love must be reflected in this relationship above all. And since plenty of the old Adam lingered in everyone, it would undoubtedly be not Eros, but Agape — Divine love poured out upon the undeserving — which at some time or other, either partner might feel that he was displaying! Those of his hearers — and he knew many — who were achieving such a relationship, never wondered, in Dickensian phrase, 'vether it was vorth going through so much to learn so little.' Such marriages only death could dissolve.

He was silent for a moment. A few heads moved automatically, preparing for his closing prayer. It did not come. When he spoke, he spoke slowly, as though words defied him.

"Some — some of us have been given more, or rather this relationship in perfection. I say 'given' because no one who has the experience dare say it has been of his own achievement or deserving. I refer to those who have found such ecstatic, enduring delight in the other's person and companionship, overriding all distinctiveness of personality, all minor irritations of day-by-day living, that for them, as it was in the beginning, there is only one man and one woman in the world.

"To these, whether Elizabeth Barrett, whose words:
'and if God choose
I shall but love thee better after death.'
were answered by Browning long afterwards:

'O thou soul of my soul, I shall clasp thee again,
And with God be the rest.'

or John Newton, whose tributes to his beloved Mary we can still read in notes written many years after she was taken from him, or to many lesser known and inarticulate, perhaps to you, the words 'till death us do part' mean nothing. We are convinced with a holy conviction that our union in Christ transcends the grave.

"I am being factual here, not sentimental, I am not being unorthodox or contradicting our Lord's words to the sceptical Sadducees regarding marriage in heaven. There is no resemblance between the travesty of marriage about which they spoke and what the marriage of such lovers has become; marriage in which intensity of sexual joy, initially important, more ecstatic because always secondary in importance, is symbolic of the union into which their love has grown.

"But since we have the treasure in earthen vessels, we must be careful not to regard it as we sometimes — God pity us! — regard our salvation, as something common or to be taken for granted. These are dead-levelling days, when every claim to distinction is decried, so that even those who suffer and sacrifice for others are derided as masochists or do-gooders. We Christians are being urged to forget, to deny, our unique claim and calling, a denial tantamount to denying the One who has called us out of darkness into His marvellous light. We need to wear our distinction gratefully, even gaily — to say, if necessary, you younger ones, 'Want to make something of it?'

"We need to emulate the exultation of John, the beloved, when he said, 'See what kind of love the Father has bestowed on us that we should be called children of God'; and when he cried with incredulous, breath-catching joy, 'and we *are*'!

"Even so, those of us whom God has permitted in our marriage to reflect the glorious relationship between Christ and His church — we should bear our distinction likewise with humble hilarity and keep it inviolate."

His recent illness and the expenditure of energy required to keep the delicate balance of exposition, anecdote, personal feeling, and exhortation in such a sermon left Andrew almost faint with an exhaustion far different from that of the previous Sunday. Today there was no dearth of comment. One which took him by surprise came from no other than Jocko de Grassi, seen for the first time in collar and tie and suit. His face, also for the first time, lacked its expression of sullen wariness, and he presented his fiancée with a pride which Andrew found very touching. And justified pride, Andrew thought, noting with amazement at the merciful dispensation the honest blue eyes, the strong Slavonic features, the native dignity of the girl for whom de Grassi had knifed his rival and attacker.

He congratulated the boy warmly, and his hand was gripped again.

"Cheeze, padre, thanks. Ute and me — we liked what you said. It might have been like you knew we were coming. You mean you get all that in the Bible?"

If the pair could follow that discourse, thought Andrew gratefully, it was another instance of the Spirit's interpreting language almost completely unfamiliar. They both assured him that they would come again. He found out that de Grassi had a job and decided to let further contacts wait until later. He saw that Mrs. Manfried, on whose motherly discretion he could count, recognized them as strangers and shook hands warmly with them. Others had passed during their brief conversation, and he was in the vestry putting on his overcoat before he realized that he had not spoken to Beth.

She was not present at the evening service and, though her attendance had not been invariable, the absence distressed him. He felt disappointed and told himself that he had expected too much. The combination of tiredness and disappointment made him wonder if his leading had been correct. Was the sermon — at least, the time of its delivery — tactless? He knew the answer to that one! But had he given sufficient motivation in his introduction to the series, been sufficiently impersonal in his treatment, to make general what she must feel a personal application? Well, he had tried.

He sighed and picked up "Something Fishy" from his bedside table. A little Wodehouse might relieve the tension, which would not give way to weariness.

There was a knock at the door.

"Are you asleep?" It was Evadne. He had seen little of her all day. She had been invited to luncheon with Miss Simms, had attended a tea at the College, and had remained for a group meeting after the church service. He put down his book.

"How many answers are there to that question?" he called. She came in and stood by the bed.

"Your voice is worse. Are you catching more cold?"

"Try speaking in public for approximately an hour-and-a-half yourself after a bout of laryngitis, and your voice will be worse too."

"Sure I can't get you anything?" She grinned mischievously. "I could try Flammol on you again."

"Not on your life," said Andrew firmly. "Last — what was it? — Thursday is a red-letter day in my calendar. If Dante were bringing the *Inferno* up to date, he might do worse than have an application of Flammol — 'extra forte,' *comme on dit* — for the more deserving types. Have it applied by their daughters, posing as angels of light and reading all sorts of diabolical lies from the tube."

"I couldn't help it," she protested. "How was I to know that you have exceptionally sensitive skin? I even spread on a layer of cold cream before the Flammol, which it didn't say to do in the instructions."

"And then when I felt as if I were wearing Nessus' shirt, you told me I was making a fuss about nothing."

"Well, I just read the booklet: In more stubborn cases, it said, soften the skin by applying pads dipped in hot water; then rub ——"

"I swear," interrupted Andrew with awe, "that can't be for mere man. Like Mr. Mulliner's Buck-U-Up-O it must be intended for elephants. You can laugh. Wait until you need my tender ministrations."

Evadne, who had kicked her shoes off and was hunched up at the end of the bed, stopped laughing.

272

"I've had them and I'm grateful. Do you know how good your sermons were today?"

" 'Madam, you are too late. The devil has already told me,' " quoted Andrew; then he said soberly, "No, dear. I hoped they would be right, but I was too tired to be at all sure. Thanks."

"I was talking to Dr. Brimley again this afternoon. He says that you are going to preach the sermon for the graduating class. I'm terribly thrilled. You never told me."

"No? I intended to. That was entirely Beth's — diplomacy."

"Oh." She leaned over to examine the dust cover of his book. Her brown hair, falling forward, almost hid her face. "Dad, I want to tell you. I was a bit of a pig last week."

"You mean administering the Flammol. I'm glad you admit it."

"You know I don't mean the Flammol. You know what I do mean. Before that. The things I said. And the way I acted."

"Did you say anything you didn't mean? Or that you didn't think was true?"

She considered.

"No. Actually no. At the time anyhow. But I shouldn't have spoken to you the way I did."

"Tut. This sounds like a Victorian taboo about respect for one's parent!"

"You jolly well know I always have had. Respect, I mean, not taboos. That's why I feel so awful. But I just couldn't help it. When you said —"

"Tell me, Vad?"

"I — oh, I guess people would say it was just plain jealousy. Of her. Because I didn't seem to matter to you any more. But I was wrong. I have no right to be jealous. It's your life. And I came to tell you so. And tell you about today, of course. And see how you were."

She uncurled her legs as though about to leave. Andrew put out a long arm and gave her a push which sent her back against the foot of the bed. Then he put both arms behind his head and regarded her gravely.

273

"Do I gather from your rather incoherent remarks that you are giving me your blessing? Or at least your permission?"

Hazel eyes stared into hazel eyes.

"That's a ridiculous way to put it. But, all right. Yes."

"Evadne, what do you think I was driving at in the latter part of my sermon this morning?"

The young eyes widened and lightened. She was afraid to be mistaken. But the older ones remained steady.

"You — were talking about you and Mother?"

He nodded.

"And saying that you — you personally — couldn't marry again?"

"Something like that."

"Oh, Daddy!" She flung herself at him, hugging him convulsively, half-sobbing with relief. Then suddenly, muffled against the pillow, "but, but isn't that terribly hard on her?"

"For the love of Mike," said Andrew in exasperation at this echo of Aunt Alex, "will you women make up your minds?"

She drew away hastily and sat down on the side of the bed.

"Don't get me wrong. I don't mean that I want you to marry her. But it's not just for my own sake. Please believe it. I think — I *know* it will make a difference to the people who look up to you, especially those who remember Mother. I'm sure — though I'd never have dared to say it — that they wouldn't feel the same, quite the same, if you married again. I just said that because — oh I don't know — here I've been blaming her and thinking that she has everything and has had everything, including husband and children and grandchildren, and yet couldn't be content without — without spoiling my father for everybody. But now I realize how awful it would be to be in love with you and not be able to marry you. I'm all mixed up." She shoved a foot back into a shoe and dangled it thoughtfully to and fro.

"About that," said Andrew, "I think it's time I did some apologizing. You were right, you know. I've taken a great deal for granted about you, treated you as far beyond your years in wisdom and sense of responsibility."

"And it was flattering and I was glad you did, mostly. But sometimes when I wanted to talk to you, I couldn't, just because of that. I never wanted to be anything else, but it's not easy these days being a girl."

"No. Not your sort of girl. And that's a circumstance I wouldn't change if I could. But, Vad, I'm sorry you haven't felt free to talk."

"It's just been lately. It's the Now pressure, I think. Nobody is willing to wait for anything or refuse anything. There is no future after death and there may not be much here; so we must grab while we can. On the other hand, if we believe in a life after death, we are accused of being pie-in-the-sky escapists. Yet people who talk like that have to take dope for kicks! And then some pitiful joker announces that he is having himself fast-frozen as soon as he dies, to be thawed out later when scientists have learned to overcome death. Somehow *that* is sane and desirable, but for us Christians to believe in the resurrection of the body is crude! I'm talking at random, Dad, but that's the trouble. There's no follow-through or logic. They don't even verify their quotations. Or know what we believe."

"Go on," said Andrew.

"But where? They don't seem to want answers, just to go asking. Any answer that requires thinking, especially any answer that is constructive — they will listen to any half-baked, renegade theologian, but they won't come to hear you! They'll read the latest attack on Christianity and accept it holus-bolus, but Williams, or Sayers, or Lewis, to say nothing of Barth — no, thanks! And" — her voice grew stormy with feeling — "every moral standard, any suggestion of an Absolute is out. The term 'Puritan' is all-inclusive for joy-killing, hypocritical, covert nastiness —"

"And the great objection to the original Puritans was the joy which they — unfairly in the opinion of the rigorously ascetic — found in life," reflected Andrew. "What does More say about Protestants? . . . 'dronke of the new must of lewd lightness of mind and vayne gladness of heart.' "

275

"Yes. Try to tell them that. What burns me up is that every slur upon any great person is taken and passed on without proof: Shakespeare and Michelangelo are both homosexuals now, and as for Lewis Carroll — you should have heard the foul remark Prof. Thorburn made at a study group about his joint interest in little girls and in photography!"

"Did he get away with it?"

"Oh you know me. I'm suspect, of course. Virginity is masochistic — did you know?" She gave a sudden, mischievous, amused snort. "It never occurs to the chumps that it may be a question of fastidiousness and good taste as well as moral standards! Nobody else said anything; so I asked him how he knew. He said everybody knew it. I said I didn't and asked his sources."

"Did he give them?"

"He made some vague remark about a recently republished biography, which I shall read."

"Lennon's perhaps?"

"Have you read everything?"

"No. But I picked it up a short time ago. It stresses, of course, Dodgson's 'abnormal devotion to little girls,' as Martin Gardiner puts it. But nothing of a salacious nature. Taylor's *White Knight* contends for his complete normalcy. Just perverted, wishful thinking on your man's part. And complete lack of understanding of a mind like Dodgson's."

"But, Dad, what makes people think like that? And *like* it? It seems to me that even so-called 'bad' people used to admire good and great ones. Now they can't stand to think that anyone has standards or decent motives."

Andrew cast about for suitable words. He opened his Bible at Romans.

"I don't know any better explanation than this: 'Therefore God gave them up in the lusts of their heart to impurity, to the dishonouring of their bodies among themselves, because they exchanged the truth about God for a lie and worshipped and served the creature rather than the Creator .... they not only do them but approve those who practise them.' Or here in Thessalonians: '... because they refused to love the truth and so be

276

saved; therefore God sends upon them a strong delusion to make them believe what is false, so that all may be condemned who did not believe the truth but had pleasure in unrighteousness.' And Paul speaks to Timothy about 'haters of good.'"

She looked at him thoughtfully.

"That explains it! The feeling I have that there's a dimension missing. They are like cardboard men, all front, all frantic effort to be knowing and funny, but no — no substance. And no real laughter. Oh, I'm not the only one left, not even the only virgin, though that seems to be the ultimate term of reproach. There are all sorts of kids who feel the way I do. But they can't help being affected to some degree. Because they haven't got you. Because —" she drew a deep breath and spoke quickly — "because against all these people, towering sky-high, there has always been you! More brilliant than any of them, better read, knowing all the arguments, able to laugh, and at yourself too, good, kind — don't interrupt — and believing. More than that, living what you believe: a transcendent God and His revelation, eternal life in Christ, enduring love — a wholeness, a sort of oneness."

"And then I toppled?"

"I have no right to say that. Or even to feel it. But I did. Why? There's nothing wrong with a second marriage. For most people."

"No. Nor a third. Conceivably and under some conditions, a fourth. Let's see if I can say it. In many cases the second or third marriage may be the real, the God-pleasing one. ("I'm old-hat enough to believe that God is personally interested.") But not in mine. In many cases there are circumstances, financial or domestic, which make another marriage necessary. But not in mine. So if I *had* married again you would have thought that my marriage with your mother was imperfect, or that I was finding Christ insufficient to sustain me in loneliness, or that I was settling for domestic and social comfort."

"Why — yes. How did you know?"

"Because you would have been right. In the last assumption, at any rate."

277

"But, Dad, you're not doing this just for me?"

"No. Finally I'm doing it for myself." His voice dropped almost to a whisper. The quotation came on a note of recollective surprise:

"We've only one virginity to lose
And where we lose it there our heart must be."

"Who said that? I like it."

"That unpredictable man, Rudyard Kipling. And while it is not literally true, there's a sense in which it is profound truth. For me."

Evadne sighed with relief.

"Then I won't feel guilty. Because really I like her and she's been nice to me, and if you were refusing her just for me — well, I don't deserve to have her — or you — sacrificed, just to pander my jealousy. But honestly, that isn't the point."

"I know it isn't."

He had need to remind himself of that knowledge frequently in the following days. The assurance which had clarified the issue of his relationship with Beth, the restoration of intimate relationship with his God, was still a fact, but the sharp glory of certainty had dimmed, the categorical imperative of his directive seemed, in the backwash of everyday practicality, over-demanding, even a bit preposterous. From Beth there was no word. He did not see how he could expect any, but neither could he make a move towards her. He did not hope to see her at prayer meeting. There again her attendance had been occasional, though increasingly frequent in recent months. But the silence, the absence of communication, to which normally he would not have given a thought, left him prey to depressing speculation. Had the sermon been so clear in its design that she was shamed before the congregation? Surely not. In their few engagements they had seldom, if ever, met one of his people, and if there was speculation about them, he was unaware of it. But her sensitivity might have been hurt nevertheless. Should he have explained his attitude in a private interview? Had he even done right to put an admittedly lofty concept above the happiness of a good friend? Or, if he was right, was it necessary to be so right? Did he overestimate the importance of personal example? Did his example have any bearing on his influence, his image before his people, or was Evadne rationalizing her own jealousy and youthful idealism when she said that it did?

It is moments like this, he reflected dryly, which make the great compromises of history. I never before understood Henry of Navarre's cynicism, "Paris is worth a Mass."

It was, he argued to himself later, in a week taken up with a singularly pedestrian train of postponed duties, an aftermath of a period of multiple strain. For months he had not been free of pressing problems: John's crisis and departure for the East, the publication of his book, Bill Woodcock's bereavement, his painful involvement in the affair of Ursula Pethwick and Miss Sexsmith, its stunning climax, the separate and interwoven problems of Evadne and Beth. Now there was no immediate unfinished business, no call to lift him out of the steady round. And he had a touch of arthritis! And in front of him lay Evadne's departure. And he had shown himself inadequate and incompetent — gauche even — in his dealing with Beth.

I'm not complaining, Lord, he said for the twentieth time and knew that he was lying. I know that, by contrast with the real suffering of people, past and present, I'm not enduring anything. That's it, of course. I feel that I could more easily endure some great pain or calamity, make some great sacrifice. There's nothing heroic about me. I'm not asking for painful martyrdom. But I wonder if on the whole a larger number of people can rise to that. It's the dreary business of slogging ahead with nothing to show for it that gets one down. I used to think Jeremiah's "Contending with horses" would be a more dramatic conflict than running with footmen. I wonder now. The loss of Shorncliffe was tough going, the months without Cecily were hell, her death — but there was a positive vigour called forth, to fight and face and survive them. I knew what I had to do — the principle was large enough — there was a certain glow —

At least it seems so in retrospect, he admitted ruefully. Prob-

279

ably I found it as hard then as I do now. And I know all the answers. This too will pass. And the Lord can take my hanging on for granted, without the mountain-top experience that He gives more frequently when we're younger. In a way it's like the meals and drives and walks that Cecily and I took, sometimes almost in silence — without the conscious excited delight of our first years together, because we knew each other so well and we didn't need constant reassurance. But perhaps my resistance is lower. Perhaps the down periods last longer. Perhaps it's sheer shame that I haven't grown in grace enough to be, inside, what I seem to be outside. Perhaps it's the magnitude of the need these days, and the pitifully small contribution I make to it, and a sense of the futility of what I do make, and the feeling that there should be some other way. We mortals are pitiable. God if You only knew!

But You *do* know! The realization, in its obvious simplicity, flooded the swamp of his derelict thoughts, flooded his impoverished chill with its rich glory. Not only "with strong crying and tears" but "in all points, in *every* point, tempted as we are." You knew this too! This was part of Gethsemane. Why else say "if it be possible" unless it seemed that there could be another possibility, a more obvious triumph? Even to this state — my state of unheroic, uncomprehending, blind persistence — You stooped.

"Christ leads us through no darker rooms
   Than He went through before"
— poor Richard Baxter! Suffering for years with the largest kidney stone ever known in medical history cannot have seemed very meaningful or necessary to him! And I'm complaining! Thank you, Lord. And forgive me. It is enough.

Epilogue

HE WAS ALMOST HILARIOUS in the lifting of his spirits and the surcharge of physical energy which accompanied it. For the first time he was able to transmute his enervating distress about Beth into prayer for her, and, with no more external cause for cheerfulness than before, to know again the deep inward cheer of expectancy, of waiting for some new thing to be disclosed to him, of that quiet joy in the present which was his habitual state.

On Friday afternoon the telephone rang.

"Hello, Andrew. Beth speaking. I've called to say Good-bye."

Her voice, pleasant and brisk, revealed nothing of the implication of her last words. He spoke tentatively.

"Are you off somewhere?"

She hesitated, then laughed.

"Serves me right. I'm afraid I wanted to get a rise out of you. Yes, I'm taking Phyllis to the Bahamas for a rest. It's time I remembered I'm a mother. The youngsters have been getting her down — she's had two of them in bed since before Christmas with whooping cough. So Susan is going to look after them, and we are sailing from New York tomorrow."

He said the conventional thing.

"I hope it will be a good holiday for you, too."

"Oh, I always like Nassau. And Eleuthera. We are lucky to get reservations. I've been angling for them all week — pulling wires. And they finally came through. But I forgot. You don't like that, do you?"

"What? Pulling wires?"

"Yes."

"I'd be ungrateful if I didn't like the ones you've pulled on my behalf."

"I've told you how I regard that." There was a pause, and a subtle difference in her voice. "I got my answer on Sunday." There was a brief pause. "Didn't I, Andrew?"

"Do you think I used the pulpit as a coward's castle, Beth?"

"Oh, I don't know. I was too furious to think. I was through with the church — your church — perhaps church altogether. If your ears were constantly warm for some days, it was because of the things I was calling you — smug, self-righteous, inhuman, unfair, to suggest the nicer few."

"I'm sorry." There was not much else to say.

"Well, I certainly wanted you to be sorry. I made my plans with Phyllis. And I had no intention of getting in touch with you. Not that I had reason to flatter myself it would make any difference. But I hoped it might at least embarrass you. 'Hell hath no fury.' "

"You aren't that at all and you know it, Beth."

"I do now, I think. I don't know why I'm spilling all this except that I have to be honest with you — even to my own detriment. Something about you does it to me." There was another pause and he waited, finding no suitable comment. "Tell me, Andrew. Have you been praying for me?"

"Yes."

She made a sound between a laugh and a cry.

"I knew something was at work! Because — am I boring you?"

"O Beth, come off it."

"Well, quite suddenly, I got over it. Oh not entirely. That will take a bit of time. But the anger went. And I realized that none of it was your fault, that I'd asked for it and was behaving like a spoilt child. In fact, that's just what I am. Do you know something, Andrew?"

"What?"

"It came to me like a flash that this was the first thing I'd ever wanted in my life that I wasn't able to have. Oh, I wanted Roger not to die. But once the diagnosis was given, I knew death was inevitable, and after all it does have to happen sometime. But on the positive side, I've always got everything I set

282

my heart on, even the number of my children — not as easy to manage then as it is now — and the order I had them in. I suppose I had just taken for granted that it would happen this time."

She paused. Anything Andrew could think of to say sounded lame. He told her so.

"I can tell you, 'lame' is the word for my excuses when I was pulled up short. Here I had been feeling virtuous towards most of my friends, mature in religious faith in contrast with poor Roger, and recently a valuable servant to the Most High — one He was lucky to get."

"Beth, it's decent of you to tell me this. But you needn't —"

"Let me finish. Open confession is good for the soul. Haven't I heard that somewhere? There isn't much really. I shall be away for about three weeks. You might pray that I'll be able to do something for Phyl — something that can be extended to her children. And if you'll still put up with me when I come back, I'll try to serve God, this time with no strings attached."

"That's awfully good of you, Beth." He was on the point of hooting as he realized what he had said, but was glad he had refrained when she rejoined soberly,

"It's time I faced things, my age and my responsibilities for all that I've been given. I've criticized Phyl and Tim for immaturity. . . . Andrew, do you think — this isn't a come-on, honestly — that God can make something of me yet?"

"Beth ——"

"Because there's one thing I've been to you — you told me and I've never forgotten — that I don't want to forfeit, if I haven't forfeited it. Perhaps I can earn it back."

"And that is?" he said, remembering.

"An Ebenezer."

The click of her receiver precluded answer. Had it covered a slight catch in her voice?

Andrew sat quietly for some time staring ahead of him, his mind a blurred kaleidoscope of shaken impressions. Gradually they settled into a pattern of concern and wonder and relief — relief uppermost. He drew a deep breath. The clock came into focus again. He remembered that Don and Jean Howard were coming for dinner. He thought he knew why Don had been anxious to come. A small village church a few miles out of the city had no pastor, and Don, at his recommendation, had preached there one Sunday. Now he had been invited to take the service regularly and was tremulously eager to accept. But Jean was wary about any commitment, and Andrew would be called upon, he suspected, at least to present the case favourably to her.

What was that word about rising and fighting another round?

The telephone was still in his hand. With a faint flourish, as though saluting the end of an episode, he put it back on the cradle.